James D. Houston

Bird of Another Heaven

James D. Houston is the author of seven previous novels, among them *Continental Drift*, *Love Life*, *The Last Paradise*, and *Snow Mountain Passage*. His nonfiction works include *Californians*; *In the Ring of Fire: A Pacific Basin Journey*; and *Farewell to Manzanar*, coauthored with his wife, Jeanne Wakatsuki Houston. He lives in Santa Cruz, California.

www.jamesdhouston.com

ALSO BY JAMES D. HOUSTON

Fiction:

Between Battles 1968

Gig 1969

A Native Son of the Golden West 1971

Continental Drift 1978

Gasoline 1980

Love Life 1985

The Last Paradise 1998

Snow Mountain Passage 2001

Nonfiction:

Farewell to Manzanar (with Jeanne Wakatsuki Houston) 1973

Three Songs for My Father 1974

Californians: Searching for the Golden State 1982

One Can Think About Life After the Fish Is in the Canoe 1985

The Men in My Life 1987

In the Ring of Fire: A Pacific Basin Journey 1997

Hawaiian Son: The Life and Music of Eddie Kamae 2004

Bird of Another Heaven

BIRD OF ANOTHER HEAVEN

A Novel by

James D. Houston

Anchor Books
A Division of Random House, Inc.
New York

FIRST ANCHOR BOOKS EDITION, APRIL 2008

Portions of this book appeared previously in *The Santa Monica Review* and in
West: The Sunday Magazine of the *Los Angeles Times*.

Grateful acknowledgment is made to Alfred Publishing Co., Inc. for permission to reprint an excerpt
from "How Long Has This Been Going On?," music by George Gershwin, lyrics by Ira Gershwin.
Copyright © 1927 (Renewed) by WB Music Corp. All rights reserved. Reprinted by permission of
Alfred Publishing Co., Inc.

The Library of Congress has cataloged the Knopf edition as follows:
Houston, James D.
Bird of another heaven / James D. Houston.
p. cm.
1. Kalakaua, David, King of Hawaii, 1836–1891—Fiction. 2. Hawaii—Fiction. I. Title.
PS3558.O87B57 2007
813'.54—dc22
2006048726

Anchor ISBN: 978-0-307-38808-7

Book design by Anthea Lingeman

www.anchorbooks.com

Printed in the United States of America
10 9 8 7 6 5 4 3 2 1

Once again, for Jeanne

I chant the world on my Western sea,
I chant copious the islands beyond, thick as stars in the sky,
I chant the new empire grander than any before, as in a vision it
    comes to me,
I chant America the mistress, I chant a greater supremacy,
I chant projected a thousand blooming cities yet in time on those
    groups of sea-islands,
My sail-ships and steam-ships threading the archipelagoes,
My stars and stripes fluttering in the wind . . .

       —WALT WHITMAN, "A Broadway Pageant" (1860)

PART ONE

At the Palace Hotel

Four days before he died the last king of Hawai'i spoke into a recording machine while propped up on pillows in his suite at the Palace Hotel. There are two versions of what he said that afternoon and why he said it. The official version, released to papers and soon featured in ads by the Edison General Electric Company to promote their new device, has been often quoted. I heard the unofficial version from my grandmother, who heard it from her mother, who happened to be there in the hotel at the time, a half-Hawaiian woman who in earlier years may have been the king's lover. Here again there are at least two versions of what went on between them, since the king's abundant personal life is to this day a source of mystery and wonderment and frequent debate.

During his seventeen years on the throne his detractors called him promiscuous and dissolute, a man whose addiction to the pleasures of the flesh left him incapable of ruling anything, let alone a mid-Pacific kingdom. In my view this was too harsh a judgment, given the way he'd been trained from youth. At his birth, as was the custom among highborn Hawaiians, a song was composed to celebrate his genitals, to give them a name, and to prophesy what feats they would accomplish later on. With this as your infant lullaby (and it was only the first of dozens of songs about his private parts that he would hear at parties and festive occasions throughout his life), what else could anyone expect? As a man of chiefly lineage, he had an inherited duty to display his prowess and spread his seed, and this was a duty he had not shirked. But as of January 1891, as King David Kalakaua lay in his bed above the muffled flow of trolley cars and carriage traffic along Market Street in downtown San Francisco, those feats were far behind him.

He was fifty-four, and pale, in failing health. His once-commanding eyes had lost their lustre. One attending physician said he suffered from a malarial fever. Another said it was an affliction of the kidneys. If pressed, my grandmother would have passed on what she once heard from her mother, who told her that these symptoms had come on too suddenly, that the king's health had been tampered with—a theory that may or may not hold up, depending on who you talk to. That great-grandmother of mine, I think she had a paranoid streak, which is not uncommon in the Hawaiian Islands. It made her susceptible to conspiracy theories of every type. On the other hand, she was there when these things happened.

The official version goes like this.

Sometime in the middle of January a man named Louis Glass, local manager of the Edison Company, had come to the hotel and asked the king's attendants if he might not enjoy having his voice recorded. Hearing Glass's request, the king said bring him in. His illness, whatever it was, had not dampened his keen interest in new inventions. He took pride in keeping pace with the modern world. As soon as he'd heard about the telephone, two years after it was invented, he ordered several to be shipped to Honolulu and installed in the royal household. So it was arranged that, next to his enormous bed, an intricate contrivance was set up, made of small wheels and pulleys and accoutrements of polished metal. A length of flex hose rose to a conical mouthpiece. There was an armature with a pointed stylus resting on a cylinder the size of a thick candle and made of chocolate-brown wax.

Glass explained that when the king spoke into the tube, his voice would be transmitted through the needle and impressed into the wax in a thin spiral of tiny peaks and valleys, from which the sound could then be reproduced.

"You mean my voice will be preserved?"

"That's correct, Your Majesty."

"Everything I say?"

"Every word."

"I find this amazing."

Glass pushed the phonograph a little closer to the bed and waited. The king's physicians waited too, as did his aide-de-camp, and his chamberlain, a colonel in the Hawaiian Royal Guard, there to keep the world at bay as well as to observe the monarch's every move and conversation. For his island kingdom these were perilous times. Any misstep could be costly. Before falling ill he'd been en route to meet with President Harrison, some said to make a deal that would seal the fate of his people and finally annex Hawai'i to a foreign power. Ahead of him, in Washington, D.C., influential senators were lobbying for a permanent hold on Pearl

Harbor, said to be the finest anchorage in the Pacific, while behind him, overseas American sugar growers were pressuring to maintain low tariffs that had already made them wealthy. The king, caught in the middle of these negotiations, had so far been keeping his intentions to himself.

He reached out as if to grasp the mouthpiece, then shut his eyes against a wave of fatigue. Glass waited for the eyes to open. A labored, steady breathing told him the king had dozed off.

The next day he returned, and now Kalakaua was ready to be raised, to have his body positioned so that, without moving his head, he could hold the speaking tube to his lips. The words came slowly, his voice ragged.

"*Aloha kaua,*" he said. (Warm greetings.) And then again, "*Aloha kaua . . .*"

Perhaps he was addressing his subjects back home, or perhaps the strange power of the machine itself. Or perhaps both. Speaking in Hawaiian he went on, "We will very likely hereafter go to Hawai'i, to Honolulu. There you will tell my people what you have heard me say here . . ."

He paused, as if on the verge of a larger thought. But his energy failed him. He fell back upon his pillows and closed his eyes, inhaling with great effort. Again Glass waited, again the king was silent, exhausted.

Three days later he fell into a coma, and within one more he had died in his room at the Palace Hotel, at 2:35 p.m. A U.S. Navy cruiser carried his body back to the islands. The wax cylinder followed on another ship and thereafter was played only with the consent of Kalakaua's widow. While many others heard the faint and graveled message, she was too bereaved to listen. Soon afterward the monarchy was overthrown by a coalition of island businessmen and American marines. In the ensuing turmoil the cylinder disappeared. Hawai'i moved into the twentieth century firmly joined to the United States, and the king's last and all too brief public utterance was but another lost gesture from a royal family whose moment in history had come and gone.

So goes the official version. But according to my grandmother, the king had a good deal more to say that day.

Here I have to confess that the following account comes from a composite of sources—her testimony, a diary her mother kept during those years, details I've picked up here and there in my researches, together with my own best effort to fill in certain blank spots in the record. When you're trying to re-create the story of something that happened a century ago, there's usually a bit of wiggle room. My guide in these matters is a freelance writer, a veteran of many literary campaigns. "From time to time," he told me once, "you can let yourself take liberties with the facts, so long as you don't take liberties with the truth."

The way my grandmother heard it, Glass was disappointed. He had hoped for something else. He sat there until the king opened his eyes, then asked if he would mind trying it again, a bit louder, and would he mind speaking in English this time?

Glass, it seems, had his own agenda that day. He had not hauled all this equipment up to the third floor of what claimed to be the world's largest hotel simply for the king's entertainment. Having a record of the royal voice could be a manager's dream. He could use it all up and down the West Coast. He could play it for business leaders who would love the idea of dictating letters into a machine like one that had recorded the voice of royalty. But he needed to hear the king speaking in a language his prospective customers could understand.

Kalakaua nodded, as if untroubled by this request. He waved to his physician—a tall, imposing fellow with side whiskers and military eyes—who propped him up again, while a happy Mr. Glass replaced the first wax cylinder with a fresh one.

"Now?" said the king.

"Whenever you're ready."

There was new life in Kalakaua's voice, new blood brought color to his face. "*Aloha kaua,*" he said again, and then continued, speaking with an eloquence that seemed uncanny coming from such a frail and fevered body. Between the first and second takes, something had shifted, as if that little rehearsal had cleared his mind, cleared his heart, and set his spirit free. Glass was waving a hand back and forth, signaling "No! No!" as he mouthed the word "English," shouting in silent pantomime. But the king ignored him. He was on a roll. He was almost his old self, speaking the poetic Hawaiian he'd been schooled in from youth.

Had he never ascended to the throne, Kalakaua would have been famous as a musician and composer. He'd composed dozens of songs, some of which are still performed today, songs that were also poems filled with imagery and layers of meaning. The trained Hawaiian poets were skilled in telling stories, painting word pictures that could mean three or four things at once. A song in praise of seaweed swirling at the water's edge might also refer to your girlfriend's pubic hair and at the same time mock the reputation of a rival chief.

From his sickbed the king was composing on the spot, speaking in a poetic code that would be understood by all his people back home but was entirely lost upon Mr. Glass, who hailed from Maryland. It was lost on the attending physician, a career naval officer assigned to the U.S.S. *Charleston,* then anchored in San Francisco Bay. The king's chamberlain was on this day confined to separate quarters across the hall, fighting down a fever of his own. And the chamberlain's assistant, his aide-de-camp, had heard a knocking at the door just as the king began to speak again. Having witnessed the first feeble message, he took this all to be a harmless exercise and so stepped out into the corridor.

As luck would have it, the only one present who could follow the words being etched in wax that afternoon was my great-grandmother, under the covers, waiting for him to lie back down so she could place her hands upon his chest and upon his liver.

She practiced a form of passive massage whereby the hands and arms become conduits of soothing, healing heat. In years past it had been one of the games they played, as her hands touched first the pinched shoulder or the aching neck, then slid down to deal with other aches. But on this day he craved her warmth alone, believing that the heat of her hands might counteract the heat of his fever. She believed this too. She knew every inch of his body, and her hands told her it was not too late, this sickness could still be cured. As she would record years later, "That day I did not feel death. It was not there. And yet in four days' time the king was gone."

How she came to be lying next to him in the Palace Hotel on that fateful afternoon has intrigued me for quite some time and is what now compels me to try and get this story told, and the story of her family, which is the story of my family too, I suppose, or one part of it—perhaps I should say, the part of it I choose to tell.

She was twenty-seven at the time, small and buxom, with an erect, aristocratic bearing. She had eyes blacker than obsidian, black hair that fell to cover half her legs if she wore it loose and a lifted edge to her upper lip that made the mouth a bit fuller. In the midst of her classic Polynesian features lurked a mystery that had long beguiled the king. Call it the Indian factor. Her father was from Hawai'i. Her mother was from a California tribe based north of Sacramento. Coming of age when she did, in the later years of the nineteenth century, she'd learned to speak several languages. This too appealed to the king, since he saw himself as a cultivated man, a multilingual and pan-Pacific man. Maybe that accounts for some of the distance between him and his wife, Queen Kapi'olani, who was a proud and elegant woman, also descended from a line of ruling chiefs. By choice, and as a point of honor, in an island realm increasingly controlled by outsiders, the queen spoke only Hawaiian . . . I don't know. I'm just guessing. Kalakaua claimed to be the advocate for all things Hawaiian—the language, the music, the dance, the ancient arts of healing and chanting. Yet he was drawn, in a compulsive and sometimes destructive way, to all things foreign and Western and worldly and new. My great-grandmother, Nani Keala (a.k.a. Nancy Callahan), gave him some of both. In his eyes she was Hawaiian yet foreign, familiar yet exotic. As his sometime consort and also a member of the royal entourage, she had learned to dance his favorite dances and sing his favorite songs. On her, none of his poetry was lost.

He was speaking now of seabirds and the many colors of the sea, and large canoes arriving from afar. They sail toward a wide river of orange lava pouring down a mountainside to spill into the coastal surge. The lava roars with the deep-throated voice of the fire goddess. Where it meets the water, billows of steam swell up like fog and cause the canoes to lose their way. These are large vessels with many sails and so heavily armed they are difficult to steer. One by one they founder on the reefs, while out of the cloud-white steam appear an outrigger canoe and a single paddler with arms so strong he seems to fly across the sea . . .

For two minutes the king spoke like this, seeming to gain in volume and urgency, and would have gone on but the stylus, with a scratchy warning, had reached the end of the cylinder.

Mr. Glass clasped his hands in front of his vest, trying to contain his exasperation.

"I'm deeply indebted, Your Majesty. You have been most generous with your time . . ."

"Is it finished?"

"Yes. I only brought two cylinders."

"And what happened to my voice? Is it now inside the box?"

"It is here, embedded in these grooves."

"Ah. Well, then, meet my companion, Nani Keala. We are both quite eager to hear what I sound like."

Glass adjusted the playback stylus, attached another flex hose, with ear tubes, and passed these to the king, who listened devoutly, inclining his head like a priest at prayer. He passed the tubes to my great-grandmother, who heard the distant, tinny syllables coming toward her as if from another part of the hotel—not at all the voice she'd just heard filling the room, and yet somehow it spoke the same words, made the same pictures. The faraway place it came from was not somewhere down the corridor. It was from another time. This was the Kalakaua of ten years ago, the one she'd fallen for. Her eyes glistened with impending tears.

The king said, "What's the matter, Nani?"

"Everyone should hear this."

"Yes . . . yes, this is my hope. Mr. Glass, can you make it louder?"

"One day perhaps. Alas, not yet."

"No matter. I will take the cylinder with me."

"In that case, Your Majesty will need a machine."

"Yes, of course. It goes without saying. I will want one of these delivered to Honolulu, with the ear tubes and all the rest of it."

Now Glass's frowning face rearranged itself. A royal sale might salvage and redeem this otherwise wasted expedition. His eyebrows rose in hope.

"Whenever Your Majesty is planning to return home, I can have one brought straight to the ship."

"Excellent. Excellent. Work it out with my chamberlain."

"With your permission, perhaps I can deliver the cylinders at the same time, as my personal gift to Your Majesty. You will want them well packaged for the voyage."

The king thought about this, but not for long. Once again fatigue overtook him. His nod said both "So be it," and "Good-bye."

With the slow, meticulous moves of a perfectionist, Glass packed up his machinery—which ran, by the way, on storage batteries, two unwieldy bottles half full of acid, with wires protruding from the lids. It was all portable, housed in a container made of polished walnut.

Kalakaua, still taken with the workings of this device, watched a while through lidded eyes, then turned to my great-grandmother. Trying to muster a seductive smile he murmured, "Have you forgotten where your hands warm me most?"

"Perhaps tomorrow I will remember. Today you must conserve every drop of your energy."

One hand moved across his chest. The other rested above his colon. His voice fell to a whisper. "Stay with me, Nani."

"I will."

"Whatever they try to tell you, stay right here . . ."

Then Glass was ready. With a courteous bow to the king and a nod to the physician, he took his leave. As if on cue, the aide-de-camp, returning from the hallway, opened the door and Glass eased past him, bearing the Edison phonograph, the battery bottles, and two cylinders of brown wax that contained the king's final message to the world.

The Chosen One

San Francisco, 1987

I never tire of looking out at the bay, this long blue lake, this inland sea. This morning, from my perch, I can contemplate the narrow passage they call the Golden Gate. A thousand posters and guidebooks and song sheets and old fruit-crate labels have depicted it as a sun-drenched entryway and point of glorious arrival. But today I think of all the departures the gate has witnessed, the vessels large and small leaving the safety of this nearly landlocked harbor to buck the swells of open water, heading farther west.

Almost a century ago, long before the bridge was built, the U.S.S. *Charleston* steamed between those famous headlands carrying the body of David Kalakaua home to Honolulu, its flags at half-mast, the Stars and Stripes, the red, white and blue flag of the Kingdom of Hawai'i. Offshore from the Embarcadero, flags had been lowered on every vessel. Upon the deck his coffin was displayed. After the long cortege down Market Street, it had been escorted to the ship by six Fleet Marines while minute guns had fired into the air above the city. Courts had been adjourned for the day, the Custom House and the Produce Exchange were shut down, as thousands lined the boulevard, watched from windows and from rooftops, to see the marching bands and fire brigades, sombre civic leaders, and the Society of Pioneers, and the yellow-plumed Fourth Cavalry, all saluting this final exit of the first king of any nation to set foot upon U.S. soil, and the first to die here. In our democratic land they loved him, they loved his royal excess. He brought joy and scandal and controversy and legendary appetites.

From here I can watch the fog pull back to reveal Angel Island and Alcatraz rising from blue water, and across the straits the sacred hump of Tamalpais, points so fixed in my daily view I can't imagine a world without them. They were there when I was born and first began to see. They were there a century ago, old witnesses when the *Charleston* steamed past.

I see twenty-seven-year-old Nani Keala watching from the wharf, watching the water move, the tiny whitecaps kicked up by late-afternoon breezes, and grieving for her lost companion, perhaps wishing she'd stayed a while longer with the lei-draped casket. We know her official duty was *pa'a kahili,* one who stands at ceremonial events holding upright a pole crowned with feathers. She had followed the cortege down Market Street and could have boarded the ship for yet another voyage with the king, this time to keep her vigil over the man she suspected had not been ready for death. On that winter day in 1891 she could have joined him on the deck of the U.S. Navy cruiser heading south and west toward what were still called the Sandwich Islands.

Why she remained onshore, we can only guess. The accounts vary greatly, sometimes contradict one another. Sometimes the pieces mesh, sometimes not. Only gradually has her story revealed itself. And it hasn't been easy. I started late. For most of my life I knew nothing about this great-grandmother of mine. She was one of those invisible ancestors no one talked about. You could call it forgetfulness. When people move a lot or move long distances, as so many of my relatives have done, they tend to leave their genealogies behind. I had four great-grandmothers, after all, one from northern California, one from Tennessee, one from Dublin, one whose name has already been forgotten. None of them have ever been much talked about. In this case, though, it was more than bad memory. I call it a case of white memory. I know now that in our family it was an embarrassment to have a mixed-blood relative anywhere within view.

My mother came out to the West Coast from Arkansas in the 1930s. My father, or rather the man I used to call Father, his background was Scots-Irish and German. People from other ethnic backgrounds generally made him uneasy. "People the world over will tell you the same thing," he used to say. "You're better off sticking with your own kind."

Had he known what I know now, chances are he never would have mentioned it. For him there would have been no satisfaction in learning I'd discovered a brown-skinned ancestor, a man who sailed from Honolulu into this dazzling bay back in the days when San Francisco was still a village, a dozen low buildings hugging Yerba Buena Cove.

Don't get me wrong. This fellow who raised me, Hank Brody, had a few blind spots, but in most ways he was a decent man, hardworking, hard-drinking, good at many tasks, devoted to his family and proud to be a westerner. In the 1880s his grandfather had read a book called *California: For Health, Pleasure and Profit,* financed by the Southern Pacific Company. As the author and the railroad had hoped, he caught a train in Philadelphia and rode it to the end of the line, which in those days was Oakland. I must have heard Hank say a hundred times, in his fake pioneer accent, "There ain't many of us, boys! Third generation in the land of Promise!"

He worked for the state in the Department of Weights and Measures, in the days when a job like that could still buy you a pretty good house with yards front and back and a big garage. When they passed him over for a promotion he thought he deserved, he started talking about an early retirement so he could open a sports bar somewhere, which had always been his dream. Then about fifteen years ago his heart gave out. He was spending one day a week up in Sacramento. They found him pitched forward in the front seat of his Volvo in a parking tower a block from the capitol. It was a Monday morning, said to be the most likely time for a man's life and work to catch up with him. Only later, only now, do I see how his passing cleared the way, made it possible for me to go looking in places where I wouldn't have looked before. The passing of this man I'd always called Father somehow gave me permission to seek out the invisible fathers and mothers who'd been lurking all those years in the outer branches of the family tree.

This ancestor I mentioned, the one who came from Honolulu, it took me quite a while to track him down and flesh out the details of his trans-Pacific life. He was Nani's father, Keala (Kay-ah-la), a husky lad at the time he made the crossing, a good sailor, a powerful swimmer, later on a daring horseman. For his English-speaking shipmates his name had an unfamiliar, inconvenient roll. Two days out they started calling him John Callahan, or sometimes Kanaka John, and these names stuck.

He was among the ten Hawaiians who sailed from San Francisco Bay and up the Sacramento River with a fierce and driven adventurer who called himself the Captain. The Hawaiians called him *maka lolo* (crazy eyes). He told them he'd once been a captain in the army of France. They could tell he'd never been the captain of a vessel large or small. He didn't know how to sail. He didn't know where he was going. The river took them north into the Great Central Valley, an open world teeming with herds of antelope and elk, where hundreds of villages made of huts and cooking fires and dancehouses were scattered across its long and level plain. Like Hernando de Soto heading up the Mississippi from the Gulf, he let the winds and waters carry them until they met another river coming down from the snowy mountains to the east. Here they built a fort with adobe walls, a frontier outpost, which Captain Crazy Eyes hoped would be the center of a new country ruled by him.

In time the Hawaiians saw that only his eyes were crazy. His European name was Sutter. He knew how to take command. He mounted six-pound cannons in the turrets of his fort. He befriended local village headmen, and Indians came to work for him. He planted wheat and brought in cattle by the thousands, and Kanaka John became a cowboy, learned to handle cattle, to rope and ride and brand and jerk beef for keeping through the winter.

For ten years he worked at Sutter's fort, rising to head vaquero. Then word arrived that gold had been discovered just a day's ride toward the mountains. Kanaka John joined all the others heading for the creeks and rivers that streamed through the foothills, the men from San Francisco Bay and San Diego and Sonoma and San Jose, all hoping for a strike. He devised his own way of going after nuggets, working deep stretches of river that other miners tended to stay clear of. He'd drop rocks into an empty keg, attach a rope, let the keg sink twelve or fifteen feet to the bottom. For him and the other Hawaiians, water was a second home, and the cold evidently didn't bother them much. They'd dive down with shovels and fill the kegs with sand, then haul up the kegs and dump the sand into rocking cradles. It worked fine until the Mother Lode got too crowded and white argonauts began to force them out, along with the Mexican miners, and the Chinese. That's probably why Keala a.k.a. John Callahan moved toward the rivers farther north. And maybe that's what brought him into the hill country where he first set eyes upon the woman who would become his wife.

No one is sure about the date of this meeting. Maybe the pursuit of gold had sent him there. Or maybe it was after he'd spent some years on the Sacramento as a fisherman and barge pilot. Once the Gold Rush had spent itself, there was no fort to return to. The waves of gold-hungry, land-hungry bonanza seekers who poured into California had overrun Captain Sutter and all his holdings, slaughtered his cattle, pillaged his fields, burned down his country house, and dashed whatever hopes he may have had for himself as the founder of an empire in the far west. His workers scattered, and Keala took to the river. Maybe he had finally tired of this restless life and was roaming the banks and backcountry in search of a woman he could settle down with.

She was seventeen or so, walking alone along a streambed. All she wore was a short skirt made of woven willow bark. Like a deer she picked her way, carrying behind her a cone-shaped burden basket. By this time Keala could have been in his thirties. Leading a mule, he wore jeans and boots, a homespun shirt, a kerchief, a wide-brim hat. The innocent grace of her near-nakedness made him feel foolish, sweating inside so much clothing. As he watched her pass, she wasn't offended by his gaze. She gave him a quick look and moved on, and that glance was enough.

He followed her along the streambed until she reached a compound of mud-covered domes tucked into a cove at the mouth of a narrow canyon. From out of the canyon a spring-fed creek trickled down to meet the stream. He watched her climb a wooden ladder that curved to the top of one of the domes and drop through the smoke hole. Outside the dome a man sat on the ground smoking a pipe, a man of about the right age to be her father and, as it turned out, the headman of this village. Keala walked over and hunkered next to him, and they sat there side by side in silence while an hour went by.

At last the father spoke, asking how far he'd traveled. Keala understood the question. He knew the tongue of this tribe. With so many Indians coming and going during his years at the fort, chances are he knew two or three tribal languages by that time, at least enough to get along. He had also learned the ways of courtship. Though there is no record of this one way or the other, he may have been married once or twice before. Perhaps he'd fathered children by other women from other tribes. Who knows?

Hearing Keala's answer, the father said something about the country he'd passed through, and the ranches of the white men, which seemed to grow larger day by day. Keala agreed, and in this way they began to talk, trading lore about the world, never mentioning the daughter. Though the father may have been curious about his visitor's looks, he would not have mentioned it. He listened to the melody of Keala's voice, saw his strength, the thickness of his hands. He knew a bit about Kanaka men. His uncle had a daughter who had gone with one.

After a while Keala stood up and said he would soon return.

Three days later he appeared in the village bearing a three-point buck, which he dropped onto the ground beside the dome. The father said nothing, but seemed to nod with approval.

Another three days went by, and Keala was back again. Without a word he set before the father a basket of fat and glistening trout. Again the father nodded. A good sign. If he had not found this suitor acceptable he would now be giving him a gift in return, not the deer itself, or the fish, since that would be an insult, but a gift of equal value.

A week later Keala returned carrying on his back an enormous four-point buck and threw it down at the old man's feet with an air of finality. It landed with a meaty thump. Perhaps this drew a smile. Keala wasn't sure.

He waited two more weeks. The next time, he stood before the father empty-handed. He came without a shirt, without boots, wearing only the buckskin loincloth and the headband hunters wore. After greeting the father, he stood there until the old man nodded yet again and gestured toward the wooden ladder. Keala climbed to the top of the dome and eased himself down through the smoke hole, where the daughter was waiting, standing at the edge of a column of light from the hole above. She wore the same short skirt made of woven willow bark. Next to the walls there were bunks of sapling poles, heaped with the hides of bear and deer and rabbit. She received him there, and they became husband and wife. In this way my great-great-grandfather became a member of her tribe.

He began to hunt and fish with them. He learned the ways of storing food and how to build a dome with limbs and mud. He was initiated into the men's dance society and learned the chants, much like the chants he'd known in Hawai'i, coming up from the earth and through your chest and into your throat. His young wife bore two daughters, the elder being Nani Keala, named for him, and born into the time when an ancient way of life was rapidly coming to an end.

It is miraculous that their village had lasted this long. In the years following the California Gold Rush, tribe after tribe had been uprooted, hunted down, and scattered. Why had this village been spared? Perhaps, somewhere in his travels, Keala had befriended a white man who, in turn, knew the sheriff of the nearest town. Or perhaps this tiny enclave was simply not yet worth the taking. In the year my great-grandmother was born, a civil war was being waged on the far side of the continent, but in this spring-fed canyon pocket, those distant battles weren't felt much at all. Her family's village continued to be a haven from an older era, a place where she learned to weave baskets in the time-tested way, using peeled shoots of willow, redbud and maple, and dyes from walnut husks and valley oaks, and sedge root for stitching. She learned to gather and prepare the acorns every autumn and pound them into meal. She learned her mother's tongue and her mother's songs and stories, how to read the nature signs, when to dance the dance that celebrates the blooming of the clover.

From her father she learned other things. He began to teach her English, word by word, even though some elders in the clan did not approve of this. They had tried to trust the whites, they said, but whites always broke their promises. To learn the white man's tongue, they said, is to be too much like him. But Keala had come of age in Honolulu, where he learned to read and write at a missionary school. At the fort his English words had served him well.

He told young Nani of his days there, and how they came up from the bay long ago when the wide river had no beginning and no end. He told her of his family in Hawai'i, his parents, his brothers, and how hard it was to leave. He wanted her to know these things because in his mind she was the chosen one. She was the one who most resembled his mother. From infancy Nani had a direct, unblinking gaze that took you in, seeming to say to each one who held her or looked at her, "I know you, I have known you for a long, long time."

As a child she remembered everything. He spoke to her in Hawaiian, and she spoke the words back to him, as if they already lived inside her. Over and over he spoke the names of his ancestors, unto the twentieth generation, until she could recite them from memory.

Nani was twelve when both her parents died, one right after the other, bringing to a sudden close her days in this canyon hideaway. While out gathering firewood, her mother spied a rattlesnake, stepped back too quickly, lost her footing, tumbled down a rocky embankment and cracked her forehead against a slab of granite. Her eyes never opened again. Her death left Keala despondent and inconsolable. Before long his health began to fail. He was losing strength, losing his appetite. With great effort he could walk and wash himself, but lacked the will to do much more than sit leaning against their hut.

A Hawaiian relative came to visit, a man whose name has been forgotten, a man from farther down the river valley remembered only as the Kinsman. He had heard of Keala's loss and sickness. He brought fish and meat and stayed for several days. When he left, Keala beckoned to his daughter, told her to come and sit. His voice, once resonant, was frail now, giving his words a new weight and urgency.

"Our kinsman tells me Hawai'i has another king, Nani. His name is David Kalakaua. You are a cousin of this king. Never forget that you are of a chiefly line. One day you will return to Hawai'i, and you will tell them of your father's life across the water."

She did not know where Hawai'i was, but she had a way to imagine it. Her father once told her it was a world of islands far beyond the mountains to the west, and in the middle of a wide water, wider than any lake, wider than the river at flood time, so wide you could not see from one shore to the other, nothing but water, and the islands were green domes poking up through the blue. Nani could picture it then. Long after Keala passed away, she would hold on to this picture of the land he'd come from. As she grew older she would wonder why he'd ever left such a place and why he'd never returned.

Soon Keala was too weak to leave the hut. For days he lay on his couch of rabbitskins, staring up at the smoke hole. Nothing could cure him, no chant, no poultice, no medicine pouch. The healer came with his headband of yellow feathers, his cocoon rattles and birdbone whistle. He sang and shook his rattles and filled the village with the whistle's piercing note, all to no avail. Again Keala called his daughter to him and with his hands bid her come closer.

And his hand said come closer still.

In the shadows outside the circle of light she knelt beside him. In Hawaiian he whispered, "Come closer."

When her face was nearly touching his he said, "Put your mouth next to my mouth, your nose next to my nose."

She looked into his eyes to be sure she understood. In that moment his watery gaze was strong with purpose. She leaned and brought her mouth next to her father's, tasted his breath, which was dry and acrid like the smell of wet ashes. As he exhaled, a syllable rose from his throat, a long "ha," which is the sound of breathing as well as the Hawaiian word for breath. Though Nani was close to gagging, she did not pull away. With that ragged, groaning "haaaaaaaaaaa," he passed on to her the spirit that lived within his breath.

Keala relaxed then, as if at peace. Minutes later his eyes closed. His chest was still, and he was gone.

The General and His Wife

With the passing of her father and mother something passed out of the life of the village. Over the years it had been shrinking, as elders died, as young men went off to find work at the white men's ranches. Soon it would be like other villages that once dotted these foothills, now being abandoned one by one, or burned down. How do you live by the old way when hunters must be ever more wary of whites looking to pick a quarrel? With two young ones like these Keala left behind, who can care for them now, no longer children, yet not quite old enough to fend for themselves?

They would be better off with relatives who lived down below, close to the big river. The sister of Nani's mother had married a man from another village, one the whites burned down, and they had fled to a rancheria known to be safe, where Indian families were protected. Nani had seen it once, when her mother traveled to visit the sister at the time of the harvest dance. She remembered tall trees beside rippling water and the rising call of many voices making a great voice in the night.

One day her uncle and his son came up the trail with two horses to bring Nani and her sister and their blankets down to the rancheria. They took their time, setting out in the afternoon when the sun was low. The creek trail led them past a grove of scrub oak, out onto a slope that commanded a view across the wide, flat valley. Nani gazed at the mountains beyond. Her mother once told her that long ago the whole valley had been filled with water, a vast lake between the mountains. She watched the sun drop behind dark ridges, turning the western sky pink and tinting all the air above the valley, so that far-off patches of water were eyes of pink and twilight blue.

They traveled till dark, then rose at dawn to finish the trip, a short trip of twenty miles or so, but for Nani a journey from one world to another, from one life to the next, from hill country to the big valley, from the canyon cluster of mud-covered huts to a town of shops and square white houses and white, steepled churches, where carriages clopped along and streets made crosses.

Her aunt lived in a small, unpainted wooden house in a row of identical wooden houses out beyond the main part of town. A warm, generous woman, she had their mother's smell, the same eyes and loving look. She welcomed them with hugs and food and wanted to keep them both, but couldn't, already tending three children of her own. Nani's sister would live with a family nearby, in another house like this one, which was much like the dome they'd left, a single room where furs and skins lay piled on bunks along the walls. A hole cut into the ceiling let light stream down, though here the hole was covered with a pane of glass.

Nani's uncle worked for a white man they called the General. He owned all the land around there. He owned the rancheria where they lived, and the land beneath the houses in the town. He owned the wheat fields and the orchards where her uncle labored alongside the other Indian men. The General was a hard taskmaster, they said, but a fair man, one who paid on time and treated you with respect if you worked well and caused no trouble. Few Indian men could now hold on to the lands their families had inhabited for so many centuries. The long struggle had worn them down. Here, thanks to the General, Indians could keep a dancehouse and weave their baskets, sing their songs and bury their dead in full ceremony, without fear of being attacked or burned out or losing their scalps to bounty hunters.

Each day Nani's uncle put on trousers and boots and a long-sleeve shirt and hat with a wide brim and set off for the fields. Her auntie wore a long dress most of the time, and she gave Nani a dress to wear. Much washed and faded, it hung from her shoulders to her knees. She had seen dresses before, but had never worn one. She would need it, her auntie said, to wear to the "mission school." Almost all the young people at the rancheria went there to learn sewing from the General's Wife and to learn the white man's tongue. If you do not go, Auntie said, she will scold you, and your uncle will get looks from the General.

Two of Auntie's daughters—Nani's cousins—already attended the school. They showed her small caps of soft cloth they'd learned to fashion in the sewing class. They modeled them for her, with saucy tilts of the head. If she came to school with them, they said, she would get white food to eat, pieces of meat between pieces of bread, and sweet water to drink, or sometimes cow's milk.

The General and his Wife lived in a huge house in the center of town, taller than the trees, with wide stairways and windows higher than the doors. Near the house stood a smaller building, painted white, and on the day Nani started school a white woman stood outside greeting each young Indian at the door. Nani had heard about whites all her life but had never met one, had only seen three or four at a great distance and watched them with fear and fascination, as you would watch an angry grizzly bear. You never know when they will turn on you, her mother used to say. They cannot keep their word. They talk too fast. They have a strange smell that comes from the strange food they eat.

She lagged behind her cousins, watching this woman, who was not much taller than Nani herself. Her hair was brown and tied in a big knot behind her head. She wore a green dress pulled tight at the waist. It covered her neck and arms and hung to her shoes. She smiled and nodded, "Good morning, good morning," in a voice that was high and sweet. The smell from her body was also sweet, like flowers in the springtime.

After Nani's cousins passed through the door, there was no one else ahead of her. She was last in line.

"Good morning."

Very softly, eyes on the ground, Nani said, "Good morning."

"My goodness! Your words are very clear."

"Thank you."

"You must be Nancy."

"Yes."

"Have you been to school before?"

She didn't answer. She didn't quite understand.

"Those words," the woman said, "how did you learn them?"

"My father."

"And what is your father's name?"

"Keala."

"Keala . . . Keala . . . You mean John Callahan?"

"Yes."

"Oh my goodness! . . . I never met the man . . ."

Something had come into the woman's voice—surprise, a kind of calling out. Nani looked up at her then, and saw that her white cheeks had turned as pink as the sky above the valley. Tears had filled her eyes. She reached out and took Nani's hand.

"Years before I came to California, John Callahan saved my husband's life. . . . Did you know that? . . . Do you understand?"

She did not quite understand the words. But she understood this touch and the suddenness of the woman's tears and the breaking in her voice.

She answered, "Yes."

"Well, Miss Nancy," said the woman, dabbing at her eyes with a small handkerchief. "You are most welcome here, most welcome."

Now Nani managed a tentative smile. "I happy meet you."

Inside, there was a room for boys and a room for girls. Nani sat next to one of her cousins, with a small desk to work on. There were spools of colored thread, needles held in patches of felt, and various cast-off dresses and scarves and caps scattered about. Each girl seemed to have a project. That first day she learned to thread a needle. When it was language time, she discovered that she already knew as many English words as some of the older girls. One word she had not heard was the name of the man in the picture hanging on the wall. He had long hair and a beard, wore a white, glowing robe and stood with his hands spread wide. His name was Jesus. The woman asked Nani to say it several times.

Her face beamed when she said, "Jesus loves you, Nancy."

They sang a song she did not yet understand, though the woman's radiant smile made her want to understand it.

> *Jesus loves me, this I know,*
> *For the Bible tells me so.*
> *Little ones to him belong.*
> *They are weak, but he is strong.*

After the song came the snacks, served each Friday to all who had a perfect attendance record for the week. An Indian woman wearing shoes, a white dress and a white apron brought in two trays, and Nani learned two more words that day.

"Sand-wich," said the General's Wife, handing her a plate. Handing her a glass, she said, "Lem-o-nade. Can you say that, Nancy?"

"Lem-o-nade."

"Again."

"Lem-o-nade."

"That's very good. Very good indeed."

She would stay five years at the rancheria, living in the house of her mother's sister, helping with the chores, the cooking, gathering wood, hauling water up from the creek, and taking classes at the school. While she learned how to read and write English, she did not forget her mother's tongue. While she went to church each Sunday and learned to sing a hundred congregational hymns, she did not forget the seasonal dances. That spring when all the families gathered to celebrate the new life in the land—the men in their feathered helmets, the women shaking their beaded pelts, singing and chanting to the thump of leather drums—she saw her mother join the dancers, bobbing among them with her eyes shut and her head thrown back as she had always done at this time of year. Nani believed then, as the bonfire crackled into the night, that she could always find her mother there.

While she learned the ways of the General and his Wife, she did not forget the teachings of her father. Her world now was part white, part Indian, part Hawaiian. Islanders still worked the merchant ships that plied the Pacific. They sometimes worked the boats and barges that carried supplies from San Francisco Bay up the river to Sacramento and beyond. Closer to the water now, Nani was closer to the ebb and flow of river traffic. Some who fished farther downstream had known her father. One was the Kinsman, who had also married an Indian woman, and who still visited from time to time. From him and others, news from the islands came trickling in. Nani didn't understand all that she heard, but she listened to the rumors, the gossip, the legends traded late at night, the tales of love and death, curses and miracles, the strange fates of Hawaii's rulers, who seemed to die too often now, and too young. In older times the rulers, the great chiefs in our homeland out across the big water, had died heroically, in battle. These days they died in beds, attended by missionary doctors.

How He Saved the General's Life

Little is known about the years Keala worked the Sacramento, those years before he met his wife. A lone event comes down to us, a near-legendary rescue that would later bind two families together.

The General was a self-made Westerner with a grip of steel and a rugged face that seemed carved of granite. As a young man he'd led a wagon party across the continent and through the Sierras. During the Civil War he would lead a militia unit and come away with the title he clung to for the rest of his days. During the Gold Rush he'd hit it big, made enough to buy a large piece of the upper valley. The management of his land, the crops and the ranching, often sent him down to Sacramento to mingle with his allies at the capitol.

Returning home from one such junket, probably in the mid-1850s, he took passage on a broad-decked schooner that was running late, pushing north against a heavy current. As it happened, Keala was in charge of this vessel's cargo. It was near dusk when they pulled in toward a dock to unload some sacks of flour and a couple of passengers. A large knotty tree hanging out over the water chose that moment to split away from its trunk. The General, who stood near the rail and also stood a head taller than anyone else, heard the crack but didn't see the limb in time, as it swung down like the arm of fate to catch him on the temple and toss him overboard.

Keala had his eyes on the dock, ready to leap out and secure the vessel. Hearing the urgent cries from other passengers, he turned and saw an inert body already caught in the current, floating facedown away from the boat. The limb had continued its rapid descent toward the water and now floated right behind the unconscious rancher, as if in pursuit. Keala didn't hesitate. He dove into the dark Sacramento and came up swimming. Those who witnessed this from the deck said they'd never seen a person swim so fast and with such powerful strokes. Like twin flywheels, his brown arms churned the water.

Keala reached the body just ahead of the limb, somehow kicking it farther out into the stream. With one arm clamped around the chest, he began swimming backward, stroking with the other arm, still kicking mightily. By the time they reached shore the current had carried them another forty yards downstream. Keala dragged him out onto a muddy bank, sat him up, and pounded his back until a choking cough came forth and the eyes sprang open, glazed with terror. Desperate for breath, the pallid rancher gagged and wheezed and finally sucked in the first wet, raggedy gasp of evening air.

For years afterward, in saloons and at dinner parties, the General would tell and retell the story of the tree limb that had a will of its own, how during all his years out west, years of being ambushed and shot at and thrown from horses and chased by bobcats, this was the one time he'd been knocked senseless, and without Kanaka John Callahan's fearless leap into dark and unknown waters, he most surely would have floated on down the river and through the delta and out to sea.

Fathers and Sons

San Francisco has always been my home base. Just for the record, I grew up in the Richmond district, half a block from Golden Gate Park. My mother still lives in the same house, and she's the one I have to thank for creating this path I now find myself on. I mean, she is the one who had eyes for my real father back in her teenage days, not knowing anything about him except that he played end on the football team and was, in her view, the best-looking guy in school. "We all had crushes on him," she told me, on the day this old history finally began to reveal itself, though it had taken years for that to happen, since having a child (me) "out of wedlock," as they used to say, was a shameful thing that a woman of her upbringing would never willingly confess to.

Among my earliest memories is the sound of Hank and Mother talking in the kitchen. I should say squabbling in the kitchen, her voice shrill, his low and clipped. I must have been about five because my younger brother was still a baby. I don't remember their actual words, but I felt the strain between them. It held me like darkness. For quite a while before she noticed me, I stood transfixed in the doorway. She wore a round yellow sun hat, so she must have come in from the yard. She took me onto the front porch, where we had some planter boxes and a little wooden bench, pulled me close and told me my first father was a very fine, wonderful man who was gone now and would not be coming back. He had died in the war. My real father was Hank, who loved me very much and would always love me. She tried to smile and not cry. In her voice and in her eyes there was a grief and a pleading, as if begging me for something that had no words, and around her mouth the pinched instruction that we would never talk about this again.

During all my growing-up years I suppose we had no need to talk about it. Only once or twice did I wish my father had been someone other than Hank, the devoted family man and raconteur, though I can't deny I wish I'd known the one she called my "first father." Twenty-five years went by before I had a glimpse of who he might have been.

I'd finished the course work at Berkeley, with only a dissertation between me and the degree. (I never did get back to the dissertation, by the way. It would have been in anthropology.) I had just parted company with a young woman I thought I was going to marry. One night she wanted to talk about when to have children, and before you knew it we were shouting questions at each other. I realized then I needed a change. I needed to get away from the Bay Area, where the traffic itself will break your heart. With enough saved for a month of low-budget travel, I was applying for a passport. It would be my first trip out of the country, and they had to see a copy of my birth certificate.

I searched my files and folders. I didn't have one. The fact is, I'd never seen one, so I wrote to the Department of Public Health and enclosed a check for four dollars. When the photocopy came in the mail, I saw my blood father's name for the first time. SHERIDAN WADELL.

People call me Dan, sometimes Danny. But Sheridan is my given name. I was stunned. How could I be almost thirty and not know where it came from?

The next afternoon I drove out to my mother's place. It happened to be one of Hank's days on the road. My mother was practicing the piano. She's always had something musical going on the side. In those days it was a gospel trio. She has a rich alto voice and near-perfect pitch nurtured by a lifetime of Baptist harmonizing. In her sunlit living room she leaned toward a song sheet, humming, working through some changes, and I didn't want to interrupt her. But she heard my step and turned, and her face brightened with a flush of girlish joy.

"Danny, what a surprise!"

"Something has come up. It couldn't wait."

"Well, sure, hon. Have a chair. I'll fix us some coffee."

She was off the piano bench, heading for the kitchen.

"Thanks, Ma. I'm coffeed out. Let's just sit down for a minute. Over here on the sofa."

Her face grew wary. "What is it, hon?"

"We have to talk. It's probably going to be hard for you . . . but the truth is, we should have talked about it a long time ago."

She looked away, as if she'd heard a noise outside.

"I want you to tell me about my father."

"He's up in Sacramento today."

"I don't mean Hank. Here, let me show you something."

When she turned to me again her eyes were naked, as if she were on trial for some grave crime. In her late forties at the time, she still had her looks. Now her face sagged. In ten seconds she aged ten years. I saw that I'd gone about this all wrong, come at her too fast. I didn't think I was angry, but I guess I was and wanted to elicit some such look. I put an arm around her shoulder and with the other hand held out the photocopy.

She forced a helpless little laugh. "Where'd you get that?" she said, as if I were ten again, holding a dead cat by the tail.

"The passport people said I needed one for the trip."

As she studied it, her shoulders slumped. Her voice dropped to a murmur.

"I always wanted to tell you, Danny."

"Well, maybe now is a good time."

"It was Hank kept it back."

"He must have his reasons."

"If it was me I would have told you years ago. It was Hank . . ." Her voice broke, as tears began to spill.

"It's okay, Ma. It's not worth crying about."

Though she loves to tell stories and talk away an afternoon, she will avoid or downplay troublesome matters for as long as possible. Take the subject of her own origins and early years. Her folks moved out here from Arkansas along with all the thousands of others blown west in search of better times. Her dad chased the crops, drove the long roads of the Central Valley taking whatever work he could find. She grew up in the hot farming country north of Sacramento and never liked it there, never liked working in the orchards as a kid, and never liked her family background much at all. When I was young, if someone asked her where her people had come from, she'd toss her head with a foxy little grin, as if she were Scarlett O'Hara, and say, "Oh . . . the South."

I think she was relieved to be trapped at last by the Health Department. For years she'd been waiting to unburden herself of a dark, shameful secret, which turned out to be not at all dark or shameful, though in her heart it had taken on that kind of weight. She talked at first in broken sentences, as if a broken rib gave each breath and bunch of words its stab of pain.

"Lord knows you have a right to hear about him . . .

"There never was a way . . .

"He had such dramatic looks. Like yours . . ."

He was her first boyfriend, the first one she'd cared about. She didn't think he'd even noticed her. Then out of nowhere he said let's go for a drive. And one thing led to another. When they started dating he told her he was crazy about her, and that put her in a daze for months. Maybe he was part Indian, though he only mentioned it once and wouldn't say how much, said it didn't matter. She never asked him about it. She never met anyone in his family, and she never brought him home. The truth is, they only went together three or four months, right at the end of their junior year. She wished now she'd kept some pictures or something, but after she met Hank she had to throw all those things away.

That summer the trouble started over in Korea. Before fall semester he was gone. Four of them joined the Marine Corps and went off to a training camp down by San Diego. He came home once, just before they went overseas. His beautiful black hair was gone, shaved down to a buzz cut that made his ears stick out. They went for one last drive in his V-8 coupe . . .

For an hour we sat on the sofa, until her tears subsided, until she said as much as she could say. In the years since then I have imagined them standing together in the Greyhound station in Sacramento, Verlene and Sheridan, waiting for the bus that will take him back to the troopship in San Diego Harbor, sometime in the fall of 1950, standing close, as you see the couples to this very day, every time there's some collision overseas, some police action or intervention or peacekeeping maneuver or short-term invasion that sends our young men strapping on their gear to sally forth. She is tearful and lovely in her tears, her classic Nordic eyes, the blue pools you could drown in, the silky golden hair, while he is tall and swarthy and smiling and stoic, already a warrior as he leans to hold and kiss her one more time and tell her he'll be back before you know it. Then he's climbing aboard the rumbling, fume-surrounded Greyhound, Private Sheridan Wadell, with a wink and a wave.

She waited for a letter, which never came. When her body began to change, she tried a folk remedy she'd heard about. It only added to her nausea. She couldn't hide the symptoms from her mother, who told her it was a sin to be unmarried and bear a child, but abortion was the greater sin, so she'd have to carry the baby no matter what and if need be give it up for adoption.

"We're going to get married," Verlene told her, "as soon as he's back home."

"We'll cross that bridge when we come to it," her mother said. "Is the father that Mexican boy I've heard about?"

"He isn't Mexican," Verlene said.

"Well, he surely is *some*thing," said the mother, who wanted nothing to do with a family like that, and who'd been looking for a good reason to flee Sacramento. She needed to put some space between herself and the husband who'd left her to take up with a younger woman. In San Francisco a beautician's job awaited her, if she could get to it. She pulled Verlene out of high school halfway through her final year, and they moved into the Richmond where no one knew them, where Verlene could tell anyone who took notice of her swollen belly that her husband was fighting in Korea.

After I was born she wouldn't hear of putting me up for adoption. She fought her mother over that, certain he'd be coming back, and she also fought her for my name.

"Can't a boy be named for his father?" she demanded.

"If it was me, Verlene, I wouldn't do it. You may never see that young man again."

All too soon her mother's prophecy came true. When I was three months old they learned that he had died in combat, the word arriving secondhand from the one classmate Verlene kept in touch with. She sent a clipping from the *Sacramento Bee*.

Verlene didn't believe it. She prayed that someone somewhere got the story wrong. She wept and she waited and fussed over her babe, who surely helped to fill the emptiness. I think Golden Gate Park helped too, a midcity forest just a block from their apartment, with glens and groves and shady paths for pushing the infant stroller and lakes where mallards cruised up close for feeding.

Eventually she took a job waitressing part-time. At nineteen, she was a melancholy beauty. On the days when she worked the Clement Street Grill, numerous regulars lingered for the third and fourth cups of coffee, among them twenty-six-year-old Hank Brody, a World War II vet trying to finish up at San Francisco State on the GI Bill. Like Sheridan, he too had joined right out of high school and crossed the Pacific with his rifle and his pack. But somehow this warrior had returned, he had survived, and he seemed to know the part of her she thought had died overseas. He brought her back to life.

Only after they were married, and after my younger brother came along, did she learn that Hank was raised in foster homes. For years he'd had a foster father who favored his own blood children. Hank knew the ache, he said, of being a second-class son. I'm pretty sure that's what they were arguing about when I was five, getting rid of any sign of a prior father, of another father, anything that might cause me to feel in a different category of sonhood.

Verlene was torn. What harm could a couple of pictures do, she cried, her one memento of a long-gone past? But Hank prevailed. His fears prevailed. That's my opinion. Fear of the one who preceded him. Primal fear of "the other." Having seen her teenage snapshots, he feared his own reactions to the idea of a stepson whose father had, in Hank's eyes, such an alien look, Indian, Mexican, call it what you will. Destroy the evidence then, and begin again. The first father would never be mentioned, nor would there be any photos or souvenirs in drawers to be uncovered later on, no basis for any pecking order as to who was a stepson, who a blood son.

I have to say this for Hank: he made it work. He was a good dad. He taught us how to catch and pitch and saw wood and drive cars. On weekends we'd sometimes walk to the park to watch seals cavort in the pools outside Steinhart Aquarium. He took us camping, took us to see the 49ers play. Even after we were grown, before the Forest Service moved my brother out to Denver, at least once each fall Hank would get tickets and we'd catch a game together, have a couple of beers and root for the home team.

So I never did mention the birth certificate to Hank. It would only stir him up, and it didn't really change anything between him and me. I told myself I'd show it to him one of these days, when the time was right, just as I told myself I would drive over to Sacramento to visit their high school campus, dig out the old yearbook from 1949 or 1950, maybe check the library for that back issue of the *Bee*. Though such a pilgrimage would often come to mind later on, I never got around to it. I was restless. I was eager to set out on another kind of journey. A few more years would have to pass before I had another glimpse of the man who died so soon after I was born.

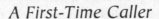

A First-Time Caller

Thanks to a price war that season, I'd picked up an amazingly cheap round-trip ticket. Thinking I'd be gone a month, I kissed my mother good-bye and set out for Bali, that soulful gem of an island just off the eastern tip of Java. Something clicked into focus for me there. I found an open-air bungalow with a view across rice fields that sizzled when it rained. Early each morning a woman whose family compound stood right next door would appear silently to set upon my porch a small offering, a fresh blossom with some grains of rice, held in a cup of woven leaves, to bless the steps and bless the bungalow. On one such morning, watching her, I saw how to revive my stalled dissertation. It came with a crystalline clickety-click.

Here's the idea I had once proposed to my advisor at Berkeley, a tenured professor: we need to take a long look at the traditional values of indigenous cultures and how they can offer guidance as we strive to balance the workings of the natural world with the hazards of technology and runaway corporate expansion.

With glum impatience he said, "It sounds sort of loose."

"How do you mean, loose?"

"Broad, then. Maybe broad is the better term. For a dissertation topic."

"It's a broad subject."

"For now you want to keep your sights on a single area. You can broaden out later. We all do that. What about those trips to Alaska?"

"That would be part of it, to be sure."

From my bungalow, in the early-morning silence, the approach came clear to me. It should not be academic in tone, or overloaded with footnotes and quotes from prior scholars in the field. It should not be scholarly. It should be grounded in the stories of specific people in specific places, whose lives offer guiding principles that can be instructive for us all—such as the Balinese, for whom there is no line between daily life and the sacred life, between the material and the mystical, the living and the dead.

In Denpasar I found a job teaching English while I studied the local language on the side. I bought a small tape recorder and started talking with anyone I could, and listening. As I look back I can see that this is what led me to the radio show and an audience from all around Northern California, with some calls coming in from as far away as Reno and Eugene. I did a lot of writing there on Bali—where I ended up spending an entire year—as well as in American Samoa, where I stopped for half a year, and in Honolulu, where I stopped again, teaching again, part-time, at a community college. I just kept talking with people as they appeared to me, as I leapfrogged my way across the Pacific and back to the West Coast.

I called the book *Sit Still and Listen.* When it was finally published, in simultaneous hardcover and trade paper, it seemed to strike a chord, especially with one of the producers at KRUX, across the bay. She was ignited by the range of topics that gathered around my interviews and stories: ecological wisdom, water flow, sustainable land use, pollution control, public health, the human immune system, the fates of indigenous peoples, how voices from the past can help us cope with the trials of the present, how harmony in the outer world begins with harmony within, and so forth. She became very animated about the prospect of a talk show that would dwell not on the most anxiety-inducing headline of the day but on a holistic view and the path of interconnectedness.

"I know there's a hunger for this," she said.

The call-in show, also titled *Sit Still and Listen,* started as a two-hour slot on Sunday nights. Pretty soon I was doing two nights a week, then three. In its heyday, I was doing two-hour shows on weekends and one hour three nights a week, and getting great guests from all walks of life—a couple from Sonoma who ran a twenty-acre organic farm, a fellow from the U.S. Geological Survey in Menlo Park, a solar power engineer, a woman who had mastered Iyengar yoga, an immunologist who had cross-trained in acupuncture, an elderly man whose ancestors once inhabited Yosemite Valley and who asked a question that had the phone-line buttons flashing like brake lights at rush hour.

"They say half a million Indians used to live in California. They were here for ten thousand years, maybe more. What I want to know is, how could that many people live here for that long and not deplete their food supply or trash their water? White people been here for two hundred years, and everybody's choking to death. Did those old-time Indians know something we don't know anymore?"

After he left the studio, the phones kept ringing. One of the last calls I took that night was from a woman in Sacramento whose voice was much like my guest's, that thick and velvety softness. Her name was Rosa.

"Welcome to the show, Rosa. Are you a first-time caller?"

"Yes. But I been listening to you for a long time. I like what you say."

"Thanks, Rosa. That's music to my ears. What's on your mind tonight?"

She took her time answering. She sounded up in years.

"That fellow who was just on, I'm not calling about him."

"That's okay. He had to keep moving . . ."

"I'm calling to ask about your name."

"My name? Everybody knows my name."

A quiver came into her voice. "I know you'll think this is crazy. It took me a long time to get up the nerve to call. I'm just wondering how did you get the name Sheridan? Not many people have that for a first name. I've only heard it once before."

If she'd asked me a month earlier, I couldn't have answered, on the outside chance that Hank might be listening. But in that very month he had passed away. My voice blurred with unexpected phlegm. I had to clear my throat.

"Well, Rosa, no one has ever asked me this, on or off the air. But as you know, here on *Sit Still and Listen,* we expect nothing less than an honest answer. It happened to be my father's name . . ."

"I had a son named Sheridan. That's why I called . . . just out of curiosity . . ."

"Wait a minute, wait a minute. Where'd you say you're calling from?"

"It's close to Sacramento."

"And your name is Rosa? Rosa what?"

"I probably shouldn't tell you that over the radio. I never do stuff like this. I hardly even answer my own phone anymore, there's so many crazy folks out there trying to talk you into things . . ."

"Of course, you're right. Look, we're just about ready for a music break here. But we don't want to lose you. Can you stay on the line?"

Julie, my producer, had cued up John Lennon's "Imagine." As she dialed it in, I punched the outside phone line. "You still there, Rosa?"

"Are we off the air now?"

"Absolutely."

"It's Rosa Wadell. Does that sound familiar?"

"Wadell," I said.

"Is your mother's name Verlene?"

I couldn't speak. My blood turned to cool air. I sat there looking at the clock's inexorable second hand making its rounds. When you have even the slightest bit of public notoriety people will try anything to wheedle their way into your life. With callers like this I had to be careful. But her voice was so slow and sweet you wanted to trust it, a voice both nurturing and seductive, trickling like brook water on a still summer day. I wondered how old she was.

She said, "Is this something we should talk about?"

"I only have a moment here. Is there a number where I can call you back?"

"I never give anybody my number."

"An address? A post office box?"

"Maybe in your case I'll take a chance, since you're only the second person I ever heard of with a first name like that."

Snapshots

Three days later I was driving across the Bay Bridge heading for 80, the eight-lane interstate that cuts through the Coast Range just beyond Vallejo. Bearing east across the valley I watched fields fly past, flat pasturelands and row crops laid out in enormous squares and trapezoids, thinking these were the fields where my granddad came looking for work fifty years back, cruising endless country roads in his battered pickup with dogs and kids squinting against the summer sun, my blond-haired mother squinting there, five years old and wishing they could find a scrap of shade. Think of it! Verlene spent her childhood somewhere out here, and years later Hank barreled along this freeway on his way to Sacramento in the days when he worked for the state. He must have come to dread it, the route he followed on the day he keeled over in the parking tower. And now, at seventy-five miles per, I was following the same wide road in search of another father.

I'd driven it a hundred times and more, a speedway cluttered with big rigs bound for Reno and points east. Yet on this day I was driving it for the first time. It's odd how such a mission can put a buzz on the atmosphere, make a stale road fresh and open-ended.

A few miles past Davis I spied the incongruous jut of Sacramento's midtown high-rises, the capital looming Oz-like from the agricultural quilt. North and east of the city I passed through some subdivisions and found myself on a semi-rural road that led into a scattered community of low buildings left over from an earlier time, set among high trees. Down a dusty side street I came upon a wind-blasted sign that had apparently survived from the 1930s. It said RIVERSIDE TRAILER COURT, though the nearest river was blocks away. A dozen mobile homes were arranged in a horseshoe, some with trellises attached or semi-permanent add-ons. Small signs said "Bide-a-Wee," "Trail's End," "The Gundersons." I passed pickup trucks and a long maintenance shed with tools stacked against it. Farther back, beside a stand of cottonwoods, a zigzag row of trailers sat at odd angles, like a derailed passenger train. One of these was a long silver Airstream, circa 1960, with its zeppelin curves of hammered metal. A faded orange awning ran its length.

When I turned my engine off, all was quiet, just the faintest breath of wind from the river to ruffle leaves overhead. I stood beside the car listening, wondering if this was the right place, or did I have the time wrong?—until a voice came at me, as if from beyond the trees.

"I'm over here."

I stepped toward the sound and saw her then, in the shade of a small patio. She sat in a white lawn chair of molded plastic, surrounded with well-watered potted plants and flanked by a pair of formidable dogs, some kind of cross. They had the muscular ribs of a German shepherd, the furred collar and pale eyes of a husky. As I approached they stood and growled in unison, more for each other than for me, as if to say, I'll bark if you'll bark. A murmur from her settled them down.

"Hello. I'm Sheridan."

"I know. Come. Sit."

She patted the plastic arm of another chair. I stepped closer and handed her the Peruvian lilies I'd brought from town. Her face lit up like a child's at a birthday party, a face full of grief and generosity and toil and wise acceptance, a brown and comforting face, remarkably smooth, the skin almost luminous, as if made of satin.

"Oh, these are really pretty. Do me a favor. Put them in that watering can over by the house. Just squirt a little in to keep them fresh. The hose is right there."

I was glad to have something to do. When I finished that task and sat down, her eyes were on me, glittering like black diamonds. She had poured out two tumblers of iced tea from a low table. After we sipped she said, "Interesting, huh?"

I wasn't sure what she meant. "The tea? It's good."

"I mean, a little brown lady like me maybe being your grandma."

"I guess that's what I came here to talk about."

"It always amazes me, even at my age, the way people's looks will turn up from one generation to the next, or skip a generation and turn up somewhere later on. I see the way you got out of your car. I see you sitting here. I see your face, the way your eyes are set . . . there's no doubt in my mind . . ."

Her voice caught. She didn't look away. She just sat there blinking, holding me with her eyes, warm and gentle now, and I was blinking with her, thinking that if things had gone another way I could have known this woman from childhood.

After a while she said, "You know, up north of here, on Highway 65, there is a little town called Sheridan. Back in the thirties my husband had a job there driving truck for a rancher. That's where we were living when our son was born. That's why we gave him that name. Now you have it too. Small world, huh?"

"When I first took your call I wasn't quite sure . . ."

"Another crank, right?"

She had an infectious laugh that said, Isn't this a crazy world we live in? Look at all the crazy things we do!

"Something like that," I said, laughing with her. "Until you mentioned my mother's name. That got my attention."

"I have a picture you ought to see. You want to go inside? You can bring your tea."

When she stood up I towered over her. She was five feet tall at the most, yet a graceful carriage gave her stature. She wasn't hunched. Her back was straight. Maybe she'd been a dancer.

"Watch your head," she said, as we stepped through her trailer door.

Inside it was cool and shadowy and smelled like herbs, a hint of sage. There was a tiny kitchen with a half-size Formica table, a couple of leatherette chairs, a somewhat larger sitting room with a figured throw rug on the floor, a TV set in one corner, and in another corner a poster board maybe three feet by four, thick with photos and newspaper clippings. She loosened two thumbtacks and handed me an old black-and-white print.

"There they are," she said.

It was my mother at seventeen, wearing a tight, short-sleeve sweater and a pleated skirt. They stand arm in arm beside a car that was surely his, a well-groomed V-8 with white sidewalls. He wears a T-shirt, jeans, his hair thick and dark and swept back in a ducktail. She is looking at him, and he is looking at the camera, staring right at me with a puzzled, reckless look. This time I couldn't blink away my tears. It was the first photo I'd seen of him, and to this day the only one I've seen of the two of them together.

"Turn it over," she said.

On the back, in pencil, he had scribbled one word. "Verlene."

I stared at this photo, compelled to gaze, though my impulse was to turn away. My mother's tearful story was one thing. This was something else. This was physical, his jeans, his car. I didn't need a new father. I'd been content with Hank. After he passed away the days we'd spent together had become more precious to me. I clung to the memory of those times. Where was I going to put this fellow I'd never met and could never know? I didn't say that to Rosa. He was her son, after all. As I stood there discovering my blood father, she was discovering me. Her long-lost grandson.

"I found it in his stuff," she said. "I knew he didn't like pictures of himself. It was the only one he kept. These others I picked up here and there."

Her souvenir board was a kind of altar, a family memorial lit by a dozen small votive candles set on a low shelf. This was where the sage came from. Savory herbs were clumped there, in among an arrangement of boxes, like jewelry boxes, lined with shiny cloth. One held a wedding ring. Another held Sheridan's Purple Heart, another his medals for marksmanship and special duty in a combat zone. Above the shelf hung a framed page from the 1950 yearbook showing Sheridan in his football uniform rising to catch an overhead pass. He had made All-League in his junior year. A clip from the *Sacramento Bee* showed him in his dress blues, the black-brimmed white hat, a Marine Corps press release sent to the hometown paper. He looks fierce in that picture, as if he has already walked through fire and is ready to walk through again. A letter to Mr. and Mrs. Thomas Wadell from a U.S. senator expressed condolences and praised their son's valor and service to his country.

An arch of snapshots and portraits curved across the top of the poster board, various relatives, I figured, with one at the top of the arch that caught my eye. From the sepia tint it seemed much older than the others—a striking, dark-skinned woman dressed in a nineteenth-century style, with sleeves to her wrists, the shoulders puffed, a very high collar, a brimmed hat with a tuft of something on top. Her eyes were like my father's Marine Corps eyes, fierce and uncompromising. I stepped in for a closer look.

"Is that you?"

"Oh no. That's too far back. That's my mother when she was in her twenties. Quite a gal, huh? You know that kind of milk that comes half and half, to make it richer? That was her. Half Indian. Half Hawaiian. You see this picture over here?"

She pointed to another aging photo, a luau scene with a dozen festive eaters gathered on mats around a spread of small bowls and serving platters and heaps of fruit. The moustachioed king of Hawai'i is there in a white jacket presiding over the feast, and nearby, though not next to him, sits this same young woman, her head raised, her eyes wide, as if just noticing the camera.

"That was in Honolulu," Rosa said with pride. "The first time she went roaming."

"The first time?"

"And both times it was a man old enough to be her father. Of course, I did the same thing, you know. I went around with a man old enough to be my father. I almost married him too. Guess who talked me out of it? Maybe she knew something I didn't know."

Her Mind Went Bingo

I'm not going to recount the long conversation that began that day. For now, suffice it to say that in the weeks and months that followed, I returned as often as I could to sit with Rosa and listen to her stories, ever more amazed that, after listening to so many stories from so many other places, this time the story was my own, or partly mine. Those seemingly exotic cultures that had called to me since college days were not so exotic after all. Before I knew what I was listening for, had I heard some calling in the blood, in the cellular memory some distant voice?

In time she told me all she knew about the short life of my missing father and the several histories that passed through him, from the Pacific, from the Sierras, from Wales and France and Germany. She let me make copies of all the clippings and photos she'd collected. When I asked if I could bring along a tape recorder she nodded and said, "There is so much to remember, and not everyone wants to do it."

Her husband was gone, a man who'd also had a Hawaiian grandfather like Keala. She had an older brother still living, my great-uncle, but he was in a convalescent home and these days could barely lift his head. There had been a daughter, who would have been my aunt, but she had recently passed away, at sixty-six. The daughter's children, now on the East Coast, near Baltimore, seldom came to visit.

"You just have to wait," she told me. "Sometimes you have to wait a long, long time for the right person to come along. When I heard your voice on the radio, something in my mind went bingo! But even then I waited. I wanted to be sure. I listened to your show a long time before I called in. I didn't tell you this yet, but you have his voice too. Sheridan's voice. Talking to you is like talking to him."

So we talked about his life, and her life, and her mother's life, and how strange it is that in each family someone will be chosen to make a record. No one appoints you to this task, nor do you stand up and publicly claim it for yourself. Yet by some process of selection you become the teller, the gatherer, the compiler of genealogies, the one obsessed with sketching in the forgotten journeys, the missing names.

She brought out other papers and souvenirs, more old documents stuffed away in drawers, photos, trinkets from her bedside table. One day she showed me a worn and stained notebook, its corners frayed, bound in blue fiberboard. She held it reverently, like a work of scripture.

"Take a look at this," she said, placing it on the Formica table.

I opened to the first page. Across the top, in elegant Victorian script, were the words "My Book of Days." Below the title, inside the rows of thin blue lines, was an entry dated March 2, 1881:

> She says my writing is getting good now. She wants me to keep a diary. I can write anything. She says it is not for school. Nobody can look at it unless I want them to. She told Edward to keep one because his writing is good too. But he says only girls do that.

What is it about old handwriting that can give a page its own light? Each stroke and flourish caught the flavor of a certain time, a moment, a life. I felt the whiffling, electric rush Hawaiians call "chickenskin."

"She was seventeen," Rosa said, "and by that time a helper in the school. Must have been her fourth year, or her fifth. She was working with the younger kids, bringing them along."

One by one I turned the brittle pages, saw the entries grow longer as the weeks and months went by, from a few lines to half a page to a page and more.

> *May 3, 1881*
> Edward is leaving notes for me. He wants to meet and talk. He wants to pray together outside church. After school he walks me back to the rancheria and he does not say one word. So I do not say one word and he does not look at me.

The pages were numbered 1 to 100. It was only the first volume. There were more, Rosa said, she wasn't sure how many. I looked at her. How could she not be sure?

"They're scattered around in boxes. Maybe seven or eight or nine of these big thick notebooks. I guess she kept a diary all the way up till her arthritis got so bad she couldn't write."

"Has anyone seen this?"

"Only me. She was kind of a private lady. Before she died she gave me all kinds of stuff I didn't even know she had. It was before Sheridan started school. With him and his sister both running around I had so much on my mind I never had a chance to think about it or even look at it. You know how that goes. You put things in a closet somewhere, years later you come across it."

"She keeps mentioning this fellow Edward . . ."

"Oh, Edward. Now he was a little older and helping on the boys' side. He was smart too. Her first boyfriend. I don't think she liked him much. She was pretty particular, you know."

I was startled, alarmed in fact, when Rosa suggested that I take this volume with me. There were three more just like it on the table, and she pushed these toward me too. I shook my head. In my view these all belonged to her, or should remain close to her. She felt just the opposite, that she'd been holding them in trust until someone like me should appear. I was honored and humbled by this gesture. There'd be more to come, she said, once she had a chance to dig them out.

Back at the apartment I secured them in a locked drawer, each volume in its plastic sack, years and years of entries in the flowing script of my great-grandmother's hand.

In the General's House

June 1881

From Nani's childhood foothills she had moved to the valley's edge, the valley shaped like an oval flapjack skillet between the long mountain ranges. Out of the place where the ranges curve toward each other and merge to make a tangled knot of peaks and canyons, the Sacramento River flows down into the valley. From east and west smaller streams and creeks feed its journey south toward the delta islands and the far-off bowl of San Francisco Bay.

Set back from one of these tree-lined tributary streams between the river and the hill country, the General's house presided over a small community spreading out around it, the white town, the Indian rancheria. If all the rancheria's little wooden houses were stacked together, they wouldn't have made a building as large as his, three stories high, with a lookout tower, balustrades and turrets, a circular driveway in front of its portico. For a hundred miles in any direction, there was nothing to match the General's house. From Sacramento north to Shasta, from Lake Tahoe west to the coastline, it stood taller than anything ever built in this part of the country, a grand and solitary monument to something . . . To his vision? To his empire? To his wife? Or to the woman he hoped his wife would be?

The General laid his plans before he was married, in the days when he hoped to find a woman who would join him out here on the farther side of the continent, an East Coast woman who appreciated elegance and expected it. He hired San Francisco's finest architects. No expense was spared. There was gas lighting, and indoor plumbing, and on the upper floor a ballroom, since the General enjoyed dancing, complete with hardwood floors, an atrium ceiling, an alcove for a small orchestra.

On a trip to Washington, D.C., he finally met the woman he thought he was looking for, still in her twenties, with the right sort of breeding and the necessary spirit of adventure. Only after he'd fallen for the radiant eyes and the inviting laugh did he learn of her desire to be ordained as a minister in the Presbyterian Church. The General hadn't counted on this but decided to make the most of it, since she was all in all a fine and remarkable woman and, at his age, pushing fifty, he didn't have time to travel east again in search of another young wife.

She came with many plans for bringing civilization and Christianity to this rough-hewn land. But his ballroom, alas, had no place among them. She did not approve of social dancing, a form of lewd and lascivious conduct that set a bad example, nor did she approve of social drinking. Occupied only by the orchestras of the General's dreams, the great room stood idle for many years, until his wife's classes grew too large for the whitewashed studio outside. The girls' class was moved up to the third floor, filling the ballroom with sewing machines and pattern catalogues, work desks, a portable blackboard, a shelf stacked with readers and arithmetic books.

It was Nani's job to escort the younger ones through a door that opened onto the back verandah, through the foyer lined with oil paintings, past the sitting room with its fireplaces of marbleized slate, and up the carpeted stairway. Sometimes she slipped away to wander alone, fingering the cut glass of decanters on the sideboard, the upholstered fabrics, the mahogany banister's sculpted curve. In the ballroom, she loved the glow of the floors as midmorning light spilled through the atrium.

She was a master seamstress now, able to hem and tuck and pleat, puff a sleeve, take a seam in, let it out. She had made dresses, blouses, jackets and skirts and sweaters and scarves, and each day wore one of these to class so younger girls might see the truth of the promise that you could keep all your handiwork. Nani showed them how to pump the foot treadle while they ran a straight stitch. Just as the General's Wife had taken her aside, she took each girl aside and read with them, word by word, sentence by sentence:

"Mother, may I sew today?"
"Yes, my child, what do you wish to sew?"
"I wish to hem a frill for your cap. Is this not a new cap? I see it has no frill."

Later on, Nani would take them aside for other reasons, to impart other lessons, much like the lesson once imparted to her at the end of a morning's class, as they stood together in the ballroom's dazzling light.

Nani wore her long black hair wrapped into a bun at the back of her head. A matronly dress covered her neck and arms and legs. In that little mission school of a dozen boys and a dozen girls, she was the star pupil. They were like mother and daughter, though Nani stood two inches taller now. They read the Bible together. They discussed the progress of the younger children. The General's Wife paid her five dollars a month to help with the class and to help around the house from time to time. In the kitchen she taught Nani how to make tea and serve it, how to set a table and roast a turkey and mix a salad. She also taught her how to greet someone, how to sit properly, how to conduct oneself in the presence of a young man.

On this day, as if a vivid memory had just come to her, she paused by a polished railing at the top of the staircase.

"You know, Nancy, for some reason I started thinking of what it was like when I was your age, turning seventeen, and boys were starting to notice me and pay attention to me. I must say I was flattered no end, I surely was. But I am happy to say that during the whole time I kept a level head, which is what a girl has to do if she wants to keep her virtue. You have become a lovely young woman, Nancy, and that is indeed a great blessing. But I know you understand that your virtue is your greatest gift of all. And it is a girl's duty before God to stay pure for her husband. Do you remember the verse we were reading the other day? I think it's from the first letter of Paul the Apostle to Timothy. 'Flee also youthful lusts: but follow righteousness, faith, charity, peace, with them that call on the Lord out of a pure heart . . .' You understand what I'm talking about, don't you?"

Nani had heard this before, numerous times. She was always moved by the change that came into the usually sunny face. The furrowed brow and blinking eyes told Nani that something about her troubled the General's Wife, and she did not want to trouble this woman who had been so good to her, who stood so straight and spoke with such a strong voice and was not afraid to laugh when she was happy.

Once again Nani said yes, she understood. And she was much relieved to see the furrows disappear. The light in the room filled the woman's unblinking eyes as she said, "Well, then, I don't know about you but I am getting hungry. I guess we'd better go off and get ourselves some lunch while we have the chance."

A Country Road

Later that day, as Nani stepped off the back porch, heading toward a stand of cherry trees beyond the house, Edward Steele appeared next to her. He was the reason for the brief sermon, a lanky, studious fellow who had lingered beside the doorway of the outbuilding where the boys' class still met, as if some busywork kept him occupied. He was eighteen, a mixed-blood, half Indian, half white. He hoped to be a preacher of the Gospel and wanted her to be his wife, though he had never shared this hope out loud. Walking next to Nani, who took her time, he had to shorten his long and eager stride, as if walking on railroad ties set too close together. For a while he didn't speak. They had reached the road to the rancheria when he said at last, "I have some fresh bread and some apples."

"So do I."

"Let's go down by the stream."

"It's too warm to go down there."

"I found a new place. No sun gets through. There is always a breeze. Come. I want to tell you something."

Why did she go down to the stream with him like this? Nani wondered. He always said he had something to tell her, and yet all he wanted was to put a hand upon her leg and an arm around her shoulder. At this new place he'd found, the bank was damp. Nani said it would stain her dress. Edward pulled off his shirt and spread it on the sand.

She was surprised to see his muscles, his arms much thicker than they looked inside the sleeves. She had thought of him as skinny, but the slabs of his chest were full and sharply edged. As they sat down on his shirt, he didn't look at her. He brought out a thick round of acorn bread and sliced it with the hunting knife he always carried at his waist. They began to eat, though Nani wasn't hungry. She wished something else would happen. She wasn't sure what. With Edward it was always like that. She wished something else would happen, or wished he were someone else.

The next afternoon, hoping to evade him, she left the big house by a side door and hurried across the lawn. The General's Wife had given her a message for one of the foremen, whose daughter had missed three days of class. She found him quickly, mending fence alongside the nearest wheat field. From there she cut through an apple orchard, toward a path she sometimes walked to take the long way home. In her shoulder bag she carried a reading book and her diary. She would find a place with no one else around, where she could sit still a while and think about what to write.

A quiet border between the orchard and a fallow field, the path put her in a thoughtful and meditative mood. She almost always had it to herself. But on this day her reverie was soon broken by the approach of voices. A couple of ranch hands were trudging along behind her, laughing softly. She could hear their words, in a tongue not hers but one she understood. A voice called, "Hey."

Nani kept moving, speeding her gait. She heard the boots speed up, crunching leaves and twigs.

"Hey, teacher girl."

She stopped and turned. "What did you say?"

"You are the teacher girl. Teach me how to talk right."

They were dressed like cowboys, in boots, jeans and wide-brim hats. They were not from the rancheria. They were from another tribe, two brothers her auntie had warned her to watch out for. Their father, Auntie said, had been a famous scout for the U.S. Army, a cruel-hearted man known to kidnap Indian children and sell them to whites. The father was dead now. These brothers had come down to the lowlands looking for work, and today they had probably wandered out of town to do some undisturbed drinking. Their eyes glittered. Drink had polished their cheeks. They were close enough that she could smell it. But they were also young, about her age. She would not let them frighten her.

She said, "Where are you going?"

"We are looking for you," the shorter one said, with a leering smile. "We want to walk along with you."

Waving a pint bottle, the other said, "You want a drink?"

"No. And you should not be drinking."

"Is that what you teach them at the school?"

"She teaches them how to be white," said the shorter one. "Say something white."

They both thought this was hilarious, giggling, shoving each other. They were too close to her, but so drunk she could surely outrun them.

"Maybe her skin is white too."

"I know it is . . . underneath that dress."

They fell against each other, their laughter high and crazy.

"Come," said the one with the bottle, "have a drink now, and teach us how to talk."

As he lifted it toward her mouth, she took off running, only to be brought down by the shorter one, who tackled her from behind with a wild shout and a headlong lunge.

"Get away from me! Don't touch me!"

To his brother he yelled, "I got a teacher girl!"

Kicking and punching, she squirmed out from under him. A powerful kick to the belly doubled him over, and she sprang free, but now the other one stood blocking her way with arms spread wide. As she moved toward the field, the shorter one leaped up in front of her. Whichever way she turned, they hopped and stepped to keep her penned, making it a game, a clumsy dance, taunting her with crazy laughter, until another voice came out of the orchard.

"Hey! Hey!"

Like a rangy colt, Edward Steele was loping between the rows of apple trees, Edward who had waited by the schoolroom door, and then set out in search of his sweetheart.

"Back off!" he shouted in their dialect, as the ranch hands straightened up, squinting as if awakened from a deep sleep.

To Nani, in English, he said, "Are you all right?"

"I'm all right."

"Come over here then, get away from them."

To the ranch hands he said, "Cowards! Two attacking one girl!"

"We were just having some fun," said the shorter one.

"Attack me! Come! Act like men!"

They considered it. They wouldn't mind a fight. They sized up the teacher boy. He was taller, a year or two older, and at his waist they saw the knife in its sheath. They were unarmed, but they were huskier and had him outnumbered. With a cocky smirk the shorter one took a step that said, "Okay, we're ready."

Edward stood firm, his knees flexed, one hand open, one on the handle of his knife, though it wasn't the knife that kept them at bay. He was on the other side of fear. In his eyes they could see this, and their smirks faded. Suddenly sober, they lost their will, turned toward the fallow field, stumbling away through summer-dry clods.

"I know who you are!" Edward shouted. "You are cowards!"

His voice rang into the afternoon, as they disappeared down a creek bank.

"They work at Spellman's ranch," he said to Nani. "They have only been there about two months."

"They are dogs," she said, slumped next to a tree, trembling, blinking back angry tears.

"Did they hurt you?"

"No. No. They tore my dress. Look at this. The dirt has ruined it . . ."

Sounding like a father about to scold his wayward child, he said, "Why did you come out here?"

She looked up at him, with eyes ablaze, ready to lash out. She wanted to lash out at someone, almost said, "Why can't you leave me alone!" but held her tongue. She too had seen the eyes that warded off her persecutors, the unflinching warrior look she would never have expected from studious and self-effacing Edward. Her heart brimmed with gratitude.

As they walked together along the path, heading home, they still did not talk, yet in the air between them hung a different kind of silence. Something had shifted. Touched by this rescue, she saw him anew, and Edward felt he had a larger claim on her affections. From now on he would pursue her more insistently, and she would not resist. She owed him something, after all, though she wasn't sure what.

Toward the end of summer they found themselves alone by the creek one night, with a round moon wobbling in the slow current, and their bodies at last pressed together. She felt his smooth muscularity beneath her hands and his urgent lips upon her neck. Pulling back, she told him, "No, it's a sin. We cannot do this."

"It's not a sin when you love each other."

"It's a sin if you're not married first."

With a prayerful voice he had learned in Bible class, he said, "If we do this, we are already like man and wife."

"No," said Nani, melting against him. "You have to get married in a church."

"First you get married like this, becoming man and wife in the eyes of God. Then you get married in a church, for everyone to see."

She knew it wasn't true, but she wanted it to be true. She wanted to yield to him there by the creek bank. As his hands groped beneath her clothes she saw the General's Wife, the furrowed brow and disapproving eyes. She heard her beloved teacher, while quoting the New Testament, drop her voice in a reverent murmur, to speak the word "fornication." That word always had space around it, silent space, moving Nani to sometimes say it slowly and softly to herself. "Fornication." "Fornication." With such a rich heat swelling in her loins, how could it be a sin to fornicate with Edward?

The Kinsman

His lust, once unleashed, was insatiable. In the weeks that followed, it was like a thirst that could not be quenched. He begged her to marry him as soon as possible. But marriage or not, he couldn't keep his hands away from her body. About half the time Nani too was eager to couple, resisting when she could, and giving in, resisting, and giving in. She didn't want to marry Edward. She didn't want to be a preacher's wife. She didn't want to marry anyone. Often when they made love she wept. Invisible walls were closing in around her, shaping a trap from which there seemed no escape. Her auntie watched, the way her mother used to watch when she was a child, making sure Nani did what was expected of a girl at this age, at that age. Seeing the flush in her cheek when Edward's name was spoken, Auntie asked if she planned to marry him, and Nani knew that if she intended to stay in this village, where everyone knew everything, her answer must be yes.

The General's Wife waited for an answer too. As both teacher and preacher, she would do the marrying, if it came to that. At the rancheria they no longer married in the Indian way, but in the Christian way, in a wooden chapel she had designed. Quoting the Apostle Paul's first letter to the Corinthians, she told Nani, "It is better to marry than to burn . . ."

By late September Nani had given in. To all the questions and questioning eyes she had answered yes. One by one the other questions were being answered—When would they marry? Where would they live?—when an unexpected message arrived from the Kinsman, who sent some astonishing news. Within a week's time she must get ready for a trip to the city of Sacramento. All the Hawaiians in the north country were gathering there to greet King Kalakaua, now traveling across America by train. On such and such a day he would stop at the depot. Every family must be represented. This kinsman, her father's cousin and an elder statesman in their far-flung community of islanders and descendants of islanders, made it a kind of order, one she was more than willing to obey. If this meant delaying the wedding plans, so be it.

A week later the message was followed by the Kinsman himself, cruising upriver by steamboat to fetch her. He was old enough to be her grandfather, a stocky fellow who'd worked hard and made a good living catching striped bass and catfish and salmon to sell to the wholesale markets on the Sacramento wharf. He wore a prosperous-looking traveler's hat, a lightweight summer suit, a white shirt open at the neck. Years earlier he'd lost three toes in a boating accident and so favored his left foot, rocking as he walked, like a sailor coming ashore after months at sea.

Like Keala, he got along well with Indians, spoke a couple of their languages. He persuaded Auntie that her niece must make this trip, assuring her he'd take good care of Nani along the way. He brought a weighty slab of smoked salmon as a gift, and also an extra traveling bag. Nani had already decided what she'd wear: a Sunday-service bonnet the General's Wife had given her, a full-length dress she'd made herself, in the Victorian style, high-waisted, long-sleeved, with a frothy collar to her chin.

The next morning when these two stepped aboard the downriver barge, Edward stood forlorn on the rickety dock, yearning to be with them. The General's Wife had insisted that she needed him at school. "Edward," she said, "how can I let both my helpers go traipsing off at once?"

Nani tried to avoid his pleading gaze. When at last their eyes met, she saw how her journey wounded him, and she wavered, but not for long.

"It is only for a few days," she said.

The Kinsman touched her arm. "Come now, Nani, time to push off."

She had taken these barges before, though never as far south as Sacramento, a city she'd heard of all her life. In early October the water was low, the river still waiting for the first autumn rains. She let its soothing flow muffle the voices from the rancheria, while the pale green surface, patched with blues and silvers, quickened her readiness for whatever lay ahead. At Colusa they stopped to take on cargo and four more Hawaiians, a couple of fishermen, a couple of ranch hands. Two had their Indian wives. Glad to see the Kinsman, they all began to joke and laugh. Soon they were singing Hawaiian songs. One cowboy composed a verse about this trip they were making together down the river to the state capital to see the king. He named the towns they passed. He called the river Muliwai Ulianianikiki (dark, smooth, swiftly flowing), and he called California Kaleponi. By the time they reached the Kinsman's riverside village, five more islanders had clambered aboard and the song had five more verses, which everyone had learned, Nani included, singing with boisterous pleasure as they pulled into the dock where his family waited, his Indian wife, his daughter, his son.

His house sat on a rise well back from the riverbank, a large ramshackle place where these travelers spent the night. They had all brought food—squash, yams, tomatoes, chicken. His wife laid out platters of fish. After eating, they sang more songs, then they sat up late to swap stories. For Nani some of these were new, some familiar, heard over and over again. She found a place in a corner where she could curl up and listen, the way she'd listened as a girl when her father was alive and this kinsman would come to visit the hill country.

His older sister had married an American sea captain, and their son, the Kinsman's nephew, was now studying law in San Francisco. He'd recently returned from Maui after a trip home to visit his mother. A reader of daily papers in both English and Hawaiian, this nephew was full of news. Leaning toward the flame of a kerosene lamp, he told them that King Kalakaua had traveled around the entire world, to Japan and India and Italy and France. He was the first ruler of any nation to do this, and at this very moment he was crossing America by train to complete his journey and head back to the islands. There he had many admirers and many adversaries too, the most vocal being white businessmen and politicians who said he was not fit to rule. Some were saying he had made this trip in search of a country that would buy the Kingdom of Hawai'i. Why? They say he needs the money to pay his extravagant debts, while his kingdom needs the protection of a larger nation. But Kalakaua denies all this. He says there is no teacher like travel, and it is the duty of any ruler to know as much of the world as he can.

The Kinsman, gazing proudly at his educated nephew, observed that the king was very brave to make such a trip. It is always dangerous for Hawaiian kings to travel, he said. Do you remember what happened to Liholiho, the son of Kamehameha the First? He and his wife sailed halfway around the world, all the way to England, to meet King George. Then Liholiho and his wife both died in London. He was a young man too, only twenty-four years old, and in good health when they first set out. The English said he died of measles. And yet for two months they held his body in the tunnels beneath a church. There were guards. No one could visit the bodies, until at last the coffins were loaded onto an English warship for the voyage back to Honolulu. "When I was a boy," the Kinsman said, "I talked with a man who sailed on that ship. He said to me, If King Liholiho died of measles, why did the English hide his body for two months? Why was the coffin lid nailed down with long copper nails so that no one could open it?"

He looked around the table. They all knew this story and agreed once again that it was very strange. The Kinsman's nephew said, "They were the first Hawaiians to die in Europe. Maybe their bodies were very valuable. Maybe the English doctors wanted to study their brains and hearts."

After a while another man spoke up. "White vengeance is long," he said. "Remember what happened to Captain Cook, after he died in the fighting at Kealakekua Bay. When his officers asked to have the body returned to their ship, only a part of it could be delivered. The head was gone, the hair, the legs and arms, given out to different chiefs. Maybe the English have not yet forgiven our people for doing these things to the body of such a famous man as Captain Cook. To this day they say a bundle of his bones is still hidden in one of the lava tunnels somewhere on the Big Island, though no one now remembers how to find it."

Again there was a silence, as heads nodded, as they sipped from their glasses and gazed into the lamp's steady flame. Soon another man spoke, his voice soft, almost a whisper.

"I have heard of tunnels," he said, "underneath the city of Sacramento, and they are lined with the doors and windows of buildings built there many years ago. I have not seen this, but I know a fisherman who is part white and part Indian. He was down there when he used to clean the streets. He tells me there is a city underneath a city, with streets and alleyways built before the great flood, and dark as tunnels now. Anyone who died in the floods, this is where their spirits go."

"I heard about that," said the Kinsman, taking in his guests with a swing of the head and refilling the glasses shoved toward his uplifted bottle. Making it a toast, he said, "I am glad we live up the river."

And so they talked and drank into the night, swapping news and semi-news, gossip, hearsay, tales of ghosts and old vendettas, until one by one they drifted away from the table to fall asleep somewhere in the house, in the bedroom, on the porch, on a couch, on a mat.

The Words Came

Though the last ones drank until after midnight, they were all up early for the final leg. In skiffs and launches they made a small fleet coasting south with the current, a couple of dozen Hawaiians and mixed-bloods, Indian wives, some children. They pulled into the wharf at Sacramento and from there walked three blocks to the Central Pacific depot. The king's two railroad cars, which had arrived overnight from Denver, had been shunted off to a siding where a crowd had already gathered, curious townspeople for the most part, here to get their first glimpse of a ruling monarch.

Nani stayed close to the Kinsman as he limped his way toward the side entrance of the first car. His nephew Makua, who went by "Mike," had taken her arm, as if assigned as a personal escort. He was thickset and sure of himself, and lighter than Nani, with skin the shade of cocoa butter. He leaned down to murmur, "This is a great day, you know. In Honolulu I have only seen the king from a great distance. They say he is a charming man."

More islanders stood waiting there, three or four dozen, some with families, called in from nearby ranches and foothill towns and river towns farther downstream. They waved greetings to the Kinsman and his followers, then fell silent as the car door opened.

With no announcement or fanfare, a large Hawaiian stepped out onto the loading platform. He wore a black broadcloth morning coat, sharply creased trousers, a necktie around a high starched collar, but no hat atop his black and curly hair. He sported a moustache and mutton-chops. At forty-four he looked ten years younger, a radiant and captivating man with unblemished olive-tinted skin, and his voice a melodious baritone.

"*Aloha!*" he said, with arms raised high. "*Aloha kanaka maoli o Kaleponi!*" (Greetings to my people here in California!)

While the white onlookers gazed in puzzled wonder, unsure what to make of this, the front ranks of islanders shouted out their loud reply. His voice itself was the sound of their distant homeland.

"Aloha, Kalakaua! Aloha! Aloha!"

In a burst of celebration they were waving, laughing and crying all at once, Nani among them, weeping for her father, who would have relished such a moment. This king was so much like him it was almost too much to bear—the same girth, the same eyes.

Gifts had appeared, to be heaped before him on the platform, flowers, fresh vegetables, a sack of walnuts, a box of apples, a cooked fish on a wooden platter. The Kinsman, who had left Hawai'i thirty years ago and never returned, was wiping his eyes as he stepped forward to chant in Hawaiian an *oli aloha,* a long chant of welcome.

As his last words dwindled, the celebrants waited for the king's response, but the king too had to wait, so moved was he by this expression of love, by these gifts, by the sound of Hawaiian, the pulse of the chant. Into this waiting silence another voice rose. It was the cowboy who had composed the song about sailing down to meet the king. He had brought along a battered guitar. He sang five verses, and the king's eyes were glistening. As a fellow composer and performer he clapped in loud applause, urging the crowd to join him.

"Hana hou!" the king called out. *"Hana hou!"* (Encore! Play some more!)

The second time through, others from the river trip chimed in, drawing a wider round of applause, a few hoots and whistles of approval. The exuberant king thanked them for this song and for this welcome. In English he proclaimed that on his trip across America he had stopped in many places, in Pennsylvania, in Lexington, Kentucky, in Omaha and Denver, but there had been no reception such as this, with such a show of his own people gathered together. Extending his arms and his smile to embrace the entire crowd, he thanked them all for coming to share his time in Sacramento, the capital of the wonderful state of California, a place he loved to visit for the beauties of its mountains and valleys and also because of its strong ties to Hawai'i.

Above the applause came a happy cry from one of the townspeople. "You better come back and see us, then!"

From the edge of the crowd another voice shouted, "But next time stay a little longer!"

Everyone laughed, including the king, and Nani was listening to his laugh, rumbling and resonant and full of delight. It could have been her father's laugh. His voice could have been Keala's voice, comforting, as smooth as honey. When the king spoke, it seemed he spoke to her alone. As he waved, ready to make his exit, he seemed to be waving to her. Some turn in the lifting of his hand was like her father's hand beckoning, and she had to speak. She didn't know what she meant to say, but the words came. A profound silence fell upon the yard and the loading dock as Nani's throat vibrated with Hawaiian words. She stood straight, her chin lifted, and names rolled forth as if drawn out or guided by her hands, which swam in front of her chest like dancer's hands. It was her family's genealogy, and the voice speaking was much older than her own.

Kalakaua, poised on the upper step, had stopped in midstride. With one foot inside the doorway he regarded this young woman attentively, transfixed by what he heard. The sound of these names and the music of these words ringing above the railroad tracks of a foreign land, and the look of sweet innocence on the face of one whose voice had such an ancient ring—it filled his heart. When at last her voice subsided, Kalakaua did not move. Nani did not move. She let the tears stream down her face. No one moved or knew quite what to do. Finally he waved again to the silent crowd, then beckoned to the Kinsman, who moved closer for a whispered message. Moments later he and Nani were following the king.

Inside, the royal car was furnished like the lounge of a fine hotel, with carpeted floors, cushioned couches, plush upholstery, velvet draperies, a velvet-topped card table, and at one end a small bar with silver fittings. Near the bar a large white man in military dress had been watching through parted drapes as the Hawaiians outside began to sing again. Now he approached the king.

"With all due respect, Your Majesty has a meeting in half an hour . . . the State Legislature . . ."

"Thank you, Charles. We will be there. They can't start without me. And of course you know those gifts outside will have to be collected. It would be an insult to leave them."

To his visitors the king said, "My chamberlain."

The Kinsman, overwhelmed by the pomp and royal presence, managed to say, "Hello."

Nani said, "I'm pleased to meet you," with a little curtsy that seemed to amuse the king.

"Your Hawaiian is very good," he said. "And I gather that you both speak English too?"

"Yes, we do," the Kinsman said.

Once Charles had excused himself, with an impatient smile, stepping through a door and into the adjoining car, the king urged them to sit down. He had a few minutes now.

"I did not expect to hear such chanting in the city of Sacramento. I am curious about your family. Are you this woman's father?"

"Her father was my cousin and my good friend, but he has passed on."

"*Au-we,*" said the king, turning compassionate eyes toward Nani. "Perhaps I know some of your people. Your father had several brothers. It seems we may have some ancestors in common."

"I know," she said. "He told me."

"Ah, he told you this. And is that why you spoke the chant?"

"I do not know why I spoke it. Not since my father died have I said those names."

For just an instant the king's eyes opened wider, and Nani held his gaze with a kind of fearlessness that ruffled his composure. What passed between them is best described by Nani herself, as she wrote about this day many years later:

> I often think of those first moments in his railroad car. When his eyes met mine there was a spark such as I had not seen before. His eyes were black as coal, but light came through them. Though he was older than me by nearly thirty years, at that moment he had a young man's eyes. I felt I knew him. In those days I did not know how to say such things or describe them for myself. I know now that he had the same feeling and was surprised by what he saw in the eyes of someone my age. I knew many young women, he would one day confess to me, but they were all trained to attend to me as the king and to do my bidding in any way I requested. I thought of them as birds who flew down from the sky and into my life and out of my life. You did not have the training to know what was expected of you in the presence of a king. But you knew something else. You were a bird from another heaven. And that captivated me.

He asked Nani if she'd been to Hawai'i. She said she'd only heard stories. Suppose you had the chance to travel there, he said, would it interest you? It was my father's dream, she said, but the islands are so very far away.

The king's broad smile returned, a warm, expectant smile.

"Something has occurred to me. In Honolulu I have need for a kahili bearer, someone who can carry the royal standard from time to time. It must be a person of a certain known family background. You could be this person."

Nani could no longer match his gaze, nor could she speak. His presence was suddenly overpowering, his physical size, the riveting command of his black eyes, which had taken on a conspiratorial glint. His smile filled the room. She looked down at the carpet, studying its floral swirls.

"We are a small party now," he said. "My chamberlain. My aide. A few retainers. We will easily have room for one more on the ship."

Still she couldn't speak. This was too much to think about.

He asked the opinion of the Kinsman—as speechless now as Nani—who'd never heard of such a thing, a woman of this age, hardly more than a girl, setting out to travel with the king of Hawai'i. She was like a daughter to him, and granddaughter too. He wanted to object, yet it was not his place to question or contradict Kalakaua.

"Is your mother here today?" asked the king. "Do you have a husband? Or family to care for?"

At the word "husband," her cheeks grew warm. The first thought of escaping Edward's constant attention came with a rush of buoyant relief. She didn't want the king to see her cheeks. With head inclined, still peering at the carpet, she said, "My mother also passed away. I have a younger sister who lives up the river."

Finding his voice, the Kinsman said, "We must talk of this among ourselves, Your Majesty. Nani teaches in the school. The younger children need her there."

"Of course. I can see that in her. She already has the look of a wise teacher. But perhaps there is also work for her in Hawai'i. We encourage our people to come home, you know . . . if only for a short time."

A door slid open, and the chamberlain appeared, officiously lifting a round silver watch from his vest pocket. "A carriage is waiting. We have fifteen minutes to get there."

"What about tomorrow? What time do we leave?"

"Eight a.m. Tomorrow afternoon we connect with the last ferry from Oakland across to San Francisco."

"I wish we could give you more time to consider this," said the king. "But if you can join us, you must be here in the morning at eight o'clock sharp."

Alarm filled the chamberlain's ruddy face. "If *who* can join us?"

"I want you to meet Nani Keala. Perhaps a relative of mine."

From the River to the Sea

That night was like a midsummer night, soft and balmy, with a breeze across the water to keep the insects moving. The Hawaiians who'd come downriver gathered in the Kinsman's yard to drink and celebrate—all but the host himself, who with his wife and nephew and a few others sat up late in the kitchen to consider Nani's future. How long would she stay? Who would look after her? Though they talked for a couple of hours, Nani didn't listen very closely. She already knew what she was going to do. She'd been thinking about her father. On the return trip from Sacramento, with the winds behind them and the sun blazing down, she had asked the Kinsman why her father left Hawai'i when he did.

"Keala was a young man then," he said, with nostalgic eyes. "Every week a ship sailed off for foreign ports. He was like me. He wanted to see the world."

"But Hawai'i is such a beautiful place. Why did he never return?"

"I myself never returned, Nani. When I was younger I didn't have the money. Then the family came, the children. . . ."

"And it was the same for my father?"

He glanced upriver. "Not quite the same. He almost returned once. He got as far as San Francisco, where he signed on as a deckhand. . . ."

"He did not tell me this."

"You were too young. Perhaps if he had lived to see you now."

"Well, what happened? He signed on as a deckhand, and then?"

"It was too late."

"Too late for what?"

Now he focused on the sail, tacking to catch a new wind. Again she waited, but he didn't answer. He removed his hat and smoothed a hand through damp silver hair.

At seven thirty the next morning she was there at the siding with a large basket of food, a suitcase of borrowed clothes, and numerous messages to be delivered to families in the islands. The Kinsman had given her some money, along with the address of his older son, and promised to take care of her good-byes at the rancheria. "What will you tell them?" she asked. With a guarded smile that couldn't conceal his many misgivings, he said, "I will tell them you won't be gone forever, that you will soon return."

The chamberlain's pinched face admitted her into an otherwise empty traveling car. "You can sit anywhere you wish," he said. "The others are still sleeping. The king is asleep, but he has asked me to give you this," and he handed her a flat white box from a Sacramento clothing store, tied with a blue ribbon.

Inside, after the chamberlain left, she found a knitted long-sleeve sweater. Having struggled to knit one of these, she was amazed by the expert workmanship. In its folds she found a sheet of notepaper with the king's royal seal at the top.

"You won't need this in Hawai'i," the note said, "but you may need it on the ship."

She folded the sweater, placed it in the box and set it next to her on the upholstered seat, glad to know the king was sleeping. Things were happening too fast. She needed time to think, or not-think, to sit and watch and listen. Maybe she would write a letter to Edward. Yes, that's what she would do. Later on. And to the General's Wife as well.

With a lurch and clank, a switching engine backed into the traveling car. As it began to move, she watched the rows of flat-topped buildings pass. How many stories had she heard about the city? Sacramento this. Sacramento that. Years ago Keala would talk about how this country looked in the days when Captain Crazy Eyes led them up the river and after many stops and starts finally decided where they should come ashore. As a young man, she knew, her father had lived not far from here, where so many blocks of buildings now stood.

"Sacramento is a famous place," he once told her, with a laugh. "The governor lives there. The leaders meet there. But in our time, nothing but grass. And the first houses to be built in the famous city were Hawaiian houses, covered with river grass."

The other night around the table they spoke of a city down below that no one can see, a place of dark doorways and streets. Under the streets you walk on, they said, there is another city where only spirits live.

White spirits wandered in that darkness, she was sure, and it eased her mind when the train passed the outer edge of the city, not a place her father's spirit would ever return to, the spirit he had breathed into her.

As the last buildings slid out of sight she opened a window and thought she smelled the ocean coming toward her. She wasn't sure. She closed her eyes and settled into the rocking of the train. It was like the chant she chanted yesterday, which chanted itself. She did not know why it came or where it came from. Now she was carried by this train, which took her toward the ocean. How far away was the ocean? And was she right about its smell? And would she soon be carrying her father's breath across the water?

PART TWO

Rosa's First Lesson

It was a godsend, meeting Rosa Wadell. When you're ready for a lesson, they say, the teacher will appear—a maxim you can apply in all kinds of ways. When you're ready for your relatives, the true grandmother will appear.

I was thirty-five, at a point in my life when I needed someone who'd lived a while and who understood what had happened along the way. My other grandmothers weren't like that—Hank's mother, Verlene's—decent, well-meaning people, but stuck somewhere back in the 1950s. Verlene's mother had never recovered from her husband's exodus with a younger woman. You can't fault her for that. At the time it was a devastating blow. But alas, it brought her inner life to a standstill, and to the day she died all she thought about was getting even. Being in the presence of her martyr's face and New Testament admonitions just wasn't rewarding at any level. But Rosa Wadell—now here was a relative you could fall in love with. You wait a lifetime to meet a grandmother like this.

When I first came visiting I couldn't tell how old she was. Somewhere between seventy-five and ninety. It didn't matter. She was not burdened by her own mortality, by the prospect that her time on earth might soon be coming to a close. She lived in what Suzuki Roshi used to call "the beginner's mind," which is what I now aspire to in my personal life. "In the beginner's mind," the Roshi once said, "there are many possibilities; in the expert's mind there are few." If this were a philosophy book I could stop right here. But I'll have to push on, because this is a story, a family story.

We'd been meeting for a couple of months when it occurred to me that I ought to bring Rosa onto the radio show, as a certain kind of elder who is not a celebrity, has no degrees or résumé or validated credentials of expertise in any recognized field, yet has lived a life that offers lessons for us all.

"Come on the show," I said, "and talk about your family. Talk about your mother as a California woman, as a mixed-blood woman, as a woman undefeated by the history of her people."

"Oh, I could never do that," she said, feigning disgust. "That's all idea stuff, Sheridan. That's anthropology. Nani Keala wasn't an idea. She was my mother. You are my grandson. Let's not get fancy about all this."

"Good," I said. "That's exactly what my listeners need to hear."

I told her I'd pick her up and bring her in to the studio so she could be there to take calls. She shook her head, as if I'd asked her to betray a close friend. She would never consider coming on a radio show, talking to strangers she couldn't even see.

And yet the next time we got together she was the one who brought it up.

"If somebody calls in, what if I don't have anything to say?"

"I'll handle it. That's my job, to avoid the great no-no of broadcasting."

She looked at me with lifted brows.

"Dead air," I said.

"Is that what they call it?"

"Silence. Everyone in radio is terrified of silence."

"Do you know why?"

"I have some theories."

"People are too impatient. They can't wait. They change the station. They want something happening around the house. If I was ever on the radio, that would be part of my lesson. People talk too much anyhow. Silence is when you learn things."

"Not on the radio."

"Tell me the name of your show again."

"Sit Still and Listen."

"Do people wear jeans?"

"You can wear anything you want."

"Nobody can see you, right?"

"It's the miracle of broadcasting. You talk, and they can imagine what you look like."

"Well, okay, Sheridan. Here's the deal, then. If I come on your show, whoever is listening will have to sit still and listen to some silence."

She wore her jeans, an old leather jacket, running shoes. A thick braid of silver hair hung halfway down her back. She had never been inside a radio station. Like a kid at a circus, she was wonder-eyed, yet worldly too. Everything was new for her and at the same time instantly familiar. "So this is where all the voices come from," she said as we walked through the door.

KRUX occupied a renovated warehouse dating back to the 1920s. Exposed wooden beams gave it a seasoned, rustic look. Over the years interior spaces had been reclaimed as needed, as the audience grew. It was now a perfect model of orderly clutter, the sprawl of magazines and weeklies around the coffee-stained sofa in the lobby, the soundproof cubicles where mike stands waited behind panes of glass, the miles of wire, the corridor walls a patchwork of broadcast schedules lost among bulletins and flyers for concerts, films, one-acts, readings, seminars and lectures on global warming, AIDS awareness, animal rights, tantric yoga, deep tissue massage.

Julie, my producer, was waiting in her booth, surrounded by LPs old and new, on long shelves stacked to the ceiling. She leaned back from the console to greet Rosa with a wide, happy smile.

"This is wonderful. Dan has told me about you."

"It all started on this program, the time I called in."

"I remember that call," Julie said.

"I never called a station in my life."

"A lot of people tell me that. It's what makes Danny's show so exciting." Julie looked at me with eyes flashing above a playful grin. "It *has* to be the people who call in. It couldn't be *him*."

"That's right," I said, faking humble self-effacement. "I am just a conduit. Rosa here is the one with a story to tell."

"I can't wait!" said Julie.

Her enthusiasm was genuine and catching, and it was not the bubbly kind. She exuded an intelligent vigor that drew you in. Julie loved her job, she was good at it, good with equipment, quick at the console, a flawless DJ when it came time to cue up transition music. She screened the calls with an uncanny instinct for who to weed out, who to put on the air.

Working with Julie was a dream, because she got all the details right. She was also the most captivating woman I'd ever known. I wouldn't call her beautiful, but if you ever saw her picture in a magazine you would study it long and hard. Her father's background was Mexican. Her mother came from Okinawa. She had these not-quite-definable looks that beguiled and haunted me, and maybe she was the real reason I had stayed with the radio show. I still like to tell myself it was the right thing for me to be doing at that time in my life, the best way to give voice to what I believed, with or without Julia Moraga. But could I have pulled it off alone? Probably not. *Sit Still and Listen* had been her idea after she'd read my book and heard my first KRUX interview. When she said, "People have a hunger for this!" there was such eagerness in her voice I fell for her on the spot. Much later, when we talked about that first encounter, I said, "You just wanted to get your hands on me," to which she laughingly replied, "My father always says if you have power, use it." Now she was the technical brains that kept the show together. And that was fine with me. At the station we had an ideal partnership. Outside the station it was not so ideal. But we were working on it.

She took Rosa's arm and guided her into the sound studio, chose a chair you could raise and lower and cranked it up until Rosa could sit comfortably and speak right into a table mike, though her feet couldn't touch the floor.

"Some people don't like the feel of these headphones," Julie said, "but they do let you hear what's going out over the air."

"I want to hear everything. Give me the headphones."

Julie is about five ten. As she leaned in close to slide the phones over Rosa's silver hair, they resembled earflaps on a big winter cap, and she a mother hovering at the breakfast table, getting a daughter off to school.

Rosa settled into the chair. "I feel like a rock-and-roll star."

"You *are* a star," Julie said. "I need to get a voice level. Then we'll be all set."

Back at her console, on the far side of a soundproof window, she spoke through the intercom.

"Say something, Rosa."

We waited. When Rosa didn't respond Julie said, "Can you hear me?"

"I'm practicing silence."

This didn't faze Julie, who'd heard enough to adjust the volume. Our current signature tune came in, a few bars of Ella Fitzgerald doing "I'm Beginning to See the Light." Julie chose it. Every couple of weeks she'd try something new. Her father was a jazz musician in L.A., and she grew up on that kind of stuff.

"Good evening one and all," I said. "It is the seventh of November, 1986. This is *Sit Still and Listen,* and I am your host, Sheridan Brody. As you know, we cut against the grain here, paddle hard against the currents of the mainstream, always on the lookout for something else to engage your mind besides the most nerve-wracking story of the moment.

Tonight, on other call-in shows not far from where we sit, they'll be debating the Iran/Contra fiasco, a subject that stirs the blood. But we let others spend the evening shouting at one another over the grim spectacle of a federal government selling lethal weapons to its own sworn enemies. That, in fact, is the easy way, the most obvious way to get through a night. We prefer to break new ground. We enter unknown territory. We are doing something never before attempted in the history of radio. Tonight for the first time, a host is bringing onto a talk show his own grandmother! Why do I do it? Because she has lived a long and amazing life. I won't tell you how long, since she might be sensitive about going public. . . ."

"Wait a minute, Sheridan."

Over the mike her shrewd eyes gazed at me as if we were sitting in her trailer having a cup of tea. "What's the big secret? My birthday is next month. I was born in 1899. You get to be my age, you don't care how old you are. You're thankful you can still sit up straight."

"There you have it, friends. Born in 1899 and still full of surprises . . ."

I filled in some of the background, how she grew up at the rancheria in a time when many believed California Indians had completely died out. She was twelve when Ishi, the famous Yahi survivor, had emerged from the canyon country above Oroville. After his death in 1916 he was often referred to as "the last California Indian." Whoever they'd been— so went the legend—the tribes indigenous to this part of the world were now gone, swallowed up in the inexorable flood called progress. The fact is—I reminded my listeners—they'd gone underground, changed their names, changed their clothes, kept low profiles and kept to themselves waiting for the great wheel to turn. Among them was Rosa's mixed-blood mother, who'd lived into the 1940s—dancer, linguist, master of traditional basketry. And here in our studio tonight was the daughter, a woman born at the end of the nineteenth century who'd lived deep into the twentieth and should be regarded as a national treasure. . . .

At these words Rosa shook her head, scolding me with slitted eyes.

"Okay," I said. "She thinks I'm sounding academic here. So I'll shut up and let Rosa speak for herself."

As I gave her a nod, her eyelids closed. Ten seconds went by. Was this going to be the long silence she had promised? Or was she, at the last moment, intimidated by the mike, by the wires and banks of dials?

Her eyes opened and she leaned in close as if she'd been doing this all her life. She had a kind of voice you seldom hear in the high-speed chatter of evening radio, a velvety purr, slow and deliberate, as if each thought was coming to her for the first time, with the sentences well spaced so that each one had its own weight.

"I learned a lot from my mother. . . . She took me out to find the different kinds of reeds and shoots you need to make the best baskets. . . . We don't need baskets anymore. . . . We have pots and pans and knapsacks to carry things. . . . You go buy them in a store. . . . You don't know who made them or where they came from. . . . Mama said each basket is like a blossom from the plant. . . . It is already there in the reeds growing up from the root. . . . After you gather the reeds and grasses and make the basket and carry it around, the plants are always with you. . . . They are still alive in the basket.

"I have one she gave me when I was a girl. . . . She wove it so tight it is as good as new, and she is still alive in that basket too. . . . She is always with me, everywhere I go. . . . Right here in the studio at KRUX she is with me. I can see her. . . . I can hear her voice. . . . It's a comfort to know your mother is always with you. . . . Her hair was very long, you know. When I was a girl her hair hung almost down to the ground. . . . Her whole life she never cut it. A black waterfall of hair, that's what it was like. . . . When she went over to Hawai'i everybody loved her there . . . the men loved her, the women too. . . . That was a hundred years ago, Sheridan, before I was born. . . . They loved her hair. That's what she told me. . . . I remember when she danced it would swing around her. . . . She learned the hula, and the hula is a very sexy kind of dancing. . . . That was something else she taught me. When I was young we used to dance together, me and my mother, at parties, at Big Times. . . . Can you imagine that? Way up north of here along the Sacramento, out in the middle of a field at night with a fire going, doing the hula. . . . I can't do it anymore. My knees are too stiff. . . . But this is how your life goes. Whatever age you are, some things you can do, some you can't do. . . . I don't mean that to sound naughty. Well, maybe I do want it to sound a little bit naughty. But I guess I have to behave myself because we're on the radio. . . ."

She began to hum a low, meandering tune, as if she'd come to a stopping place. In the control booth Julie was pointing at the message board, already lighting up. But Rosa had more to say.

"She used to talk about having a mother and father from different places. . . . It wasn't easy, she said, with people always trying to tell you to be one thing, or be the other. Or maybe, don't be anything, just hide your light under a bushel. . . . But she was tough, my mother. She saw a lot in her life, and she lived a long time. . . . Every road is hard, she told me, so you might as well be everything you are. . . . That's a good mother who will tell you to be everything you are. I told my own kids too."

Her brown cheeks were wet, cheeks creased by a beatific smile.

"It's why I came on your show, Sheridan. Mama told me to go ahead, you're eighty-six, what do you have to lose?"

She began to hum again, louder this time, the same tune coming from under her throat, working on me in a way I did not then understand, though I knew I didn't want to break the spell. Later on I would learn it was a kind of grief chant and message to the ancestors. Did that make for good radio? I didn't know. I didn't care. She wasn't a guest. She was my grandmother. I probably should have signed off then and let Julie play music for the rest of the hour, but callers were lining up. They had heard something too, something rare and true. They wanted to talk about her baskets, about being everything you are, and her mother being there in the studio ("Did I hear that right?" one caller asked), and about Nani's father. Why did he come to California way back then? Where did he settle? Did other Hawaiians make trips like that? Or was he a special case?

Gradually Rosa warmed to the task, responding when she felt like it, though if a caller sounded too theoretical she wouldn't say anything at all, just look at me with a cryptic, saintly smile. Someone called from the Oakland Museum, and a woman from Hayward who invited Rosa to meet with a hula troupe, and a botanist who collected stories on human dialogue with the plant world. This was the kind of hour I'd hoped it would be, with many voices chiming in. Connection, as always, was our guiding idea. From the outset Julie and I had agreed on that. "If we make this a regular show," said Julie the radio idealist, "it won't be about argument, not a debating society and who can out-fact the other guy. It won't be about winning, it will be about windows, opening a window here, a window there . . ."

The hour was three-quarters gone when a fellow named Quincy came on the line. I knew his voice.

"Hi, Sheridan. Great show."

"Nice to hear from you again. What's on your mind tonight?"

"I hope this doesn't sound too off the wall."

"Nothing is off the wall for us. Imagine a big room with no walls. Just you, me, Rosa, invisible wires of contact . . ."

"That guy a few callers back reminded me of something I heard the other day. I didn't mention it before, but I grew up in the islands when my dad was in the navy, then after they got divorced, him and my mom, she moved back to Honolulu, but she calls me all the time . . ."

I remembered him now, a fast talker who tended to get tangled up in his own excited rush.

"Quincy, slow down. Refresh my memory. Where are you calling from?"

"San Francisco, man, right across the bay, and I swear it was a couple of days ago she called to tell me she was reading about the last king of Hawai'i and he used to come to California all the time. She is part Hawaiian, see, a fourth or something, and a while back she got a bug about history for the first time in her life and she read somewhere that every time the king left the islands he stopped first right here in San Francisco and stayed downtown at the Palace Hotel, and I thought to myself, Wow!, from where I live I can *walk* to the Palace Hotel, so hearing your grandmother and all I thought I would call in to find out if this sounds true."

Rosa was nodding, but I could see she wasn't going to answer.

"As far as we know," I said, "I guess it does."

"Well, my mom, who belongs to a reading group, says he also died there and she thinks some kind of hanky-panky was going on, like maybe he didn't die of natural causes. . . ."

Rosa perked up. "Did he say 'hanky-panky'?"

"It's just a figure of speech," said Quincy.

"I haven't heard that one in years."

I said, "What kind of hanky-panky are we talking about?"

"I don't know the whole story. My mom and her reading group, they come up with all kinds of off-the-wall ideas. I thought maybe you might know."

His words caused my neck hairs to rise. A week had passed since Rosa handed me the diaries. Though I hadn't yet read all four volumes page by page, I'd been dipping in, skimming sections for an overview. That very morning I'd come across the entries for October 1881, brief and poignant references to their first stay at the Palace, where they'd stopped after ferrying from the Oakland depot across the bay to San Francisco.

In the midst of a show, with loose-cannon Quincy on the line, I didn't want to make too much of this. I tried to keep it light.

"What do you think, Rosa? Does this ring a bell?"

"I shouldn't talk about it on the radio."

"What about the hanky-panky part? Is the world ready for yet another royal scandal?"

Her eyes closed again, closing off the conversation, and she sat still as a statue, the mother of Buddha, with tiny feet dangling.

After five seconds went by, Quincy said, with a nervous laugh, "I hope I didn't say the wrong thing. I warned you. . . ."

"Hey, thanks for the call. Leave a number. We'll get back to you when we know more about this. We only have a few minutes left, and I get the strong feeling Rosa wants to move out in a new direction. She's our guest. She gets to call the shots."

Her eyebrows had raised, as if to say, "I'm ready now."

"Let's see if we can fill the time, not with talk, not with music, but with the sound of no-sound. . . . And please don't change the station. Nothing has gone wrong with the equipment, friends. We're not getting ready to practice the civil defense emergency alert signal. Every night we break new ground. Now we're joining together for perhaps the world's longest period of intentional on-air silence."

Glancing at the clock to note the time, I saw Julie mournfully waving, "No, no, no, let's don't do this."

But we were already doing it. Rosa's lesson. In the midst of our swirl of electronic gear, the wires and consoles and computerized transmitters, the filters and amplifiers and modulators linked up to countless receivers and car radios and portables between San Jose and the Oregon border— right there in the very belly of the techno-tangle we were having an interval of soundless calm, a zazen of the airwaves. Like Rosa, I had closed my eyes. Sit still and not-think, I told myself, though for me that seldom works. The mind will chatter chatter chatter like a monkey in its cage. I kept hearing "hanky-panky." What did Quincy mean by that? And what an uncanny bit of timing that I would note those pages—old ruminations from a time when Great-Grandmother Nani, at age seventeen, found herself befriended by the king at the peak of his vigor and charisma—and twelve hours later get this oddball call about Kalakaua's final days. Is that what my show was really all about? A way to pick up seemingly random signals that might otherwise have passed me by? I once met a psychic who told me if I wanted to understand what the world was like for her, just consider the nature of radio. "The atmosphere is full of signals," she said, "but most of us aren't tuned in to them. When I go into altered state, when my psychic mind kicks in, I start picking up stuff that is there all the time; I just wasn't getting it. Imagine the air around us filled with unheard voices from all the stations on your AM and FM dial, the songs, the sermons, the ball games, the weather, the six o'clock news. Every truck and car on the road, every room of every building, every kitchen and garage filled with voices you don't hear until you turn the radio on, and in an instant there they are! You pick one, but all the others are right there beside your ear waiting to be heard."

When I opened my eyes Rosa had lolled a bit, as if dozing. Behind the glass Julie held a phone away from one ear, while her free hand was aimed at me, fingers opening and closing against her thumb, saying, "Talk! Talk! Talk!"

An annoyed woman named Fran was on the line, another frequent caller.

"Sheridan, you know I love your show."

"Thanks, Fran."

"But this is nuts."

"Nothing ventured, nothing gained."

"If I want silence I can turn the radio off. But if I have it on to a station I like and everything goes blank. . . . It's just backwards. It's like watching TV with no picture! What's the point?"

As if roused from a light slumber Rosa said, "Sheridan calls it dead air. But I just figured out something. I been thinking about this all week. If air goes dead for a little while, maybe that's not so bad. It gives you a chance to catch up with yourself."

"I still don't get it."

Rosa started to laugh, unable to hold it in. Her merry chuckle spilled out as she said with pure delight, "Sit still and listen."

"Sheridan, I love your grandmother. She is wonderful. But you have gone too far."

Fran was the last caller. I ended with a plug for our next show— which would feature an expert on wetlands restoration—and signed off. Ella's wise and ever-swinging voice swelled forth: "But now that the stars are in your eyes / I'm beginning to see the light . . ."

Sandy

Julie met me in the corridor, her smile bent with concern, as she leaned against the wall.

"We're not supposed to do that."

"I guess that's why I did it."

"In smoother times no one would notice."

"Hey, it's an experiment . . . innovative broadcasting. Isn't that what we do?"

"You and I agree on that. But now Sandy has his panties in a twist."

"Did he call?"

"Twice."

"Shit."

"The first time I said what you just said. Take it in the spirit of adventure, Sandy. But he isn't happy. These days anything can push him over the edge. He wants you to call him at home."

As if we were alone on a verandah somewhere, she slid her tender arms around my neck and dropped her voice. "Otherwise it's one of the best shows we've done. Rosa was amazing. We should take her out to dinner."

"Yes, we should. But she's pretty tired, Julie. I need to get her home. If the traffic is with us it's an hour at least."

In her eyes disappointment flickered. As a single mom with a five-year-old son, her nights weren't always free. It was a niggling uneasiness, one we both tried not to talk about, since it only led to bickering that went nowhere. On nights when we took food up to her apartment, young Toby would be hungry too, hungry for pizza, hungry for games and stories and hugs. He was a sweet kid, a bright and eager kid, whose eagerness was usually aimed in my direction, as if I were already the man in his life, and I confess that this boyish hunger unnerved me.

I told myself I wasn't nearly ready to be the one Toby hoped for and waited for. When he called me Uncle Danny my heart would open toward him, then close again, and she would feel it and look at me and look away. But this wasn't anything I was ready to go into. Toby had scarcely known his father. I told myself I didn't care to know any more about him than the little I'd heard—a musician, like Julie's father, a guitarist, she said, "who could play everything, jazz, rock, country, blues, knew every tune in the book except 'Our Love Is Here to Stay.' " I'm not sure how long they lived together. After Toby was born they talked about getting married but never did. A year later he took off with his band on a ten-state tour and had only been back once.

This week Julie's mother happened to be in town, helping out with child care. Her eyes asked if I'd forgotten that Toby didn't have to figure in our plans. I tried to pull her close.

"Tomorrow night," I said.

"There's no show tomorrow night."

"Then I'll call. I promise. We'll improvise."

When I tugged again she eased up next to me. We stood eye to eye, almost mouth to mouth. Thanks to these Italian sandals she liked to wear, with lifted heels, I didn't have to lean for a kiss. Her lips on mine were so sweet and full, in a moment of utter and unexpected tenderness, I remembered once again why I was alive and roaming around the planet Earth. As her hair brushed my cheek, as our bodies pressed closer, I felt myself for the first time resenting Rosa, a twinge of regret that she was waiting in the lounge. Tonight I was the one with a relative who had to be attended to.

Once we pried ourselves apart, Julie headed for the women's room, while I found a phone. Sandy picked up on the first ring.

"It's me," I said.

"That last woman who called?"

"Fran."

"She was right."

"About what?"

"You went too far."

"C'mon, Sandy."

"You think we are running a wayside chapel here? Two minutes of not a sound? That's radio suicide!"

"It was ninety seconds."

"Whatever. You know what I'm getting at. That is the fastest way in the world to lose listeners."

"Hey, when we signed off, the phones were still ringing. Ask Julie. We had callers stacking up. . . ."

"We're under a lot of pressure here, Dan, you know that. We don't need grandmothers and mumbo-jumbo chanting nobody can understand."

"I can't believe you said that. You of all people."

"Never mind the sermon. Just listen to what I'm saying. These guys are breathing down my neck. A few things go the wrong way, we could all be out of a job. That's all I'm telling you. Please bear this in mind . . ."

His voice trailed off, but I knew he had something else to say.

"I'll still meet you for breakfast on Saturday, okay?"

"That's fine," I said. "But why couldn't we save this for the restaurant?"

"I didn't want to spoil the meal."

He hung up. I could see him sitting there in his apartment. He had a deeply padded tiltback lounger by the telephone. He drank scotch at night and favored loud aloha shirts, even when alone. Sandy had come out from Minneapolis in the mid-1960s when everyone else was heading west to be closer to the Grateful Dead and walk where Kerouac and Allen Ginsberg had walked. He got into guerrilla journalism, started a political weekly aimed at the Vietnam War, the Berkeley police, sexism, racism, right-wing politicians like George Wallace of Alabama and Ronald Reagan, governor of California at the time. He wrote profiles of Abbie Hoffman, Huey Newton, Janis Joplin and Cesar Chavez. Then the war was over. Watergate brought down the Nixon regime. All the street fighters went home. Sometime in the mid-1970s Sandy looked up and saw that half his paper was filled with singles ads and the back covers were devoted to color photos of rugged cowboys smoking cigarettes. The money was good. But the Cause, the Cause! What had happened to the Cause?

I give him a lot of credit. He sold the paper and started managing KRUX, an emerging voice in alternative radio. Everyone involved wanted to keep alive the flame of new consciousness. For ten years, with Sandy in charge, the audience had been steadily on the rise, so much so that the station finally caught the attention of Argonaut, a media conglomerate out of Baltimore. They owned some TV and radio stations, plus a dozen local papers, and were looking for a Bay Area foothold. Their timing was uncanny. As a listener-supported nonprofit, KRUX was just then suffering a crisis of cash flow. A foundation grant had dried up. A generous backer had died, leaving his estate locked in probate. Even so, three of the station's eight directors had voted against the buyout, and when it passed they resigned, unmoved by promises from the buyer that nothing would change. Argonaut claimed to like KRUX just the way it was. Why else acquire it? they said. Sandy would continue on as manager and, along with the remaining directors, continue to run the station.

But between the first and second round of negotiations, Argonaut had acquired a new CEO, who was now "rethinking" what our role would be in the larger corporate picture. Having watched his once radical weekly fall prey to Marlboro and the maestros of phone sex, Sandy was reentering his own dark night of the soul. With Argonaut would come a hefty salary increase, which meant among other things a hefty upgrade in the quality of his scotch. But he didn't trust a CEO who did his rethinking from afar, a fellow who'd never set foot in the studio and for that matter had never visited the West Coast. Sandy too was doing some rethinking. He was running scared.

As for me, as I look back, it's embarrassing to recall that I was *not* running scared. I had no idea what Argonaut was capable of. Improbably naïve, I figured they might tweak the programming here and there to satisfy some executive whim, but nothing a person couldn't live with. Why mess with success? In our little corner of Bay Area subculture we did, after all, command quite a following. So on that fall evening in 1986 I was able to walk away from the phone and shrug off Sandy's alarm as another overreaction fueled by his third helping of the single-malt Glenfiddich.

Healing Hands

Driving back to Sacramento I found myself once again in the middle lane and eastbound on Interstate 80, this time with Rosa by my side. She was a great companion. I gave her high marks in a silent character quiz I sometimes used to gauge personal chemistry: Can you imagine (I would ask myself) driving in a car with this person all the way across the United States? The answer is always instantaneous, a firm yes or a firm no. In the case of Rosa I could imagine with no effort just barreling on through the Sierras and past Reno out into the Great Basin, toward points beyond.

She was tired, but not falling asleep. Her mind was working. Mine too, with a dozen questions I wanted to ask, though I'd learned not to do that. If you asked Rosa something too directly, she would balk, give a one-word answer or hold her tongue. For her it all turned together, the present and the past, the dead and the living, the songs she knew, the stories she'd heard. She talked about what came to her, and I'd learned to have patience. If I waited long enough, sooner or later all my questions would be answered. And so it was on this night, as we sped through the wide valley darkness. When she finally spoke, it was as if she'd heard the very topic at the forefront of my mind.

"That last guy who called, it just wasn't any of his business."

"Well, he has called before. Half the time I don't think he knows what he's going to say until he starts to hear himself on the radio."

"I never told anybody about what happened at the Palace Hotel."

I waited, practiced silence.

"Years ago a guy came around with a tape recorder. I don't know how he found me. He was gathering stories, he said, for some university. I didn't trust him. He wanted to do all the talking. I could never get a word in. I made up some stuff so he would go away and leave me alone. But the things I told you are the same things I heard from Mama. She never talked about San Francisco much. She didn't like to. But one time she did. She told me the whole story. It was a sad one too because she still loved the king. She thought she could save him. She had healing hands, just like her mother. All those Indian women from the old time, they knew things. It was just a part of their life. Once when I was a kid I saw some ripe peaches high up in a tree the pickers missed. I was so excited to get those peaches I slipped off the limb and fell and landed on my arm. My whole wrist and elbow swelled up like my arm was broken. It was the worst pain I ever felt. Mama put her hands on the swelling, and I'll never forget the heat. The heat coming through her hands was hotter than a heating pad. She sat with me all night. She didn't sleep, probably ten hours she sat with her hands on my arm. The next day the swelling was gone, and the pain was gone. You can't learn that in the hospital. It comes from someplace else."

Her velvet purr was getting raspy, a low, compelling incantation, the words coming slow, and slower, each phrase lingering, with its own separate life, as I heard for the first time, in full detail, a story Rosa's mother once told to her, and only once, the longest of these stories I'd heard so far, carrying us all the way past Davis, through Sacramento, on out to the Riverside Trailer Court where her silver Airstream waited, giving off its own nocturnal glow. . . .

Nani had stayed close to Kalakaua for four days and nights in the royal suite, applying the heat of her healing hands. And in the course of a day she'd felt his body change from one that would live to one that would not. It wasn't right. She knew it happened after the Edison man came to record his voice. And it happened too quickly, as if he'd willed himself to die, or been prayed to death by an enemy.

Once the coffin-bearing cruiser returned to Honolulu, there were funeral ceremonies to complete. Soon afterward a machine was brought into Iolani Palace, said to contain the words of the dead king. Many gathered to see this strange device, or so Nani was told a few months later by someone who was there, or claimed to be there. Some held the ear tubes close and listened to a voice carried to them from across the water, a graveled and ghostly voice. *Aloha kaua,* they heard him say. Warm greetings. Some wept, while others fled the room.

The wax roll had come in a case lined with red velvet. According to Nani, the man who said he was there did not remember a second roll, did not remember a chant, and furthermore he'd never heard it mentioned.

. . .

At the Riverside Trailer Court the night air was cool and still. Rosa's neighbor, who kept an eye on the dogs, brought them out to greet her, saying only, "I wouldn't mind having me a couple like this."

I went around and opened her door. The dogs followed her into the Airstream and out again as she emerged bearing two weathered blue notebooks that had only recently turned up inside an old accordion folder marked "Bills." She'd meant to bring them to the station.

"I was sitting at my table the other day when something told me to look under the bed. I got down on my hands and knees and lifted the edge of the cover and there it was. Could be years since I looked under there. You don't know what it's like, Sheridan. You get to be this age, you have to have a powerful reason to get down on your hands and knees to do anything at all. You might never get up again. But that's how I found the rest of Mama's diary. And these are for you to keep. I bet there's a lot more stuff in here about the king, probably more than she ever told me."

Suddenly girlish, as if we'd been out on a first date, she added, gazing up, "I had a good time, son. You come back and see me when you can. And one of these times, bring Julie with you. She's quite a gal, you know. Just because I am your grandmother doesn't mean it is any of my business who else you might be running around with. But you take my word for it. She's a keeper."

On tiptoes she pecked my chin—my grandma, my good pal, my girlfriend, my godsend.

Ghosts

Back in San Francisco I stayed up half the night reading and rereading the flimsy pages. While her early entries had been written in fading pencil on one side of each sheet, ten years later she was filling both sides with neatly scripted loops and curves and dots of purple ink. I read until my eyes burned, but once in bed I couldn't sleep, my mind afire with curiosity about the life she'd led, the dreams she'd dreamed, with a new craving to somehow enter Nani's world, fill in the many spaces around what I'd learned so far, and wondering why her entries ended when they did. Was it the passing of the king? Was her hand stilled by his untimely death? Or had something else befallen her in San Francisco?

This is the final entry from Volume Six:

> *January 17, 1891*
> All this week I could not write, with my heart so full. This morning I can take up my pen again. Outside the window the city is quiet. The hotel is quiet too. The rising sun makes pink clouds over the buildings. He still sleeps. He sleeps too much. In the night he rolls and groans. The groans wake me, and I remember a dream I have dreamed many times but only now do I remember it. I dream about a little boy. He has black hair and large warm eyes like the king's. Hawaiian eyes. He is swimming. Maybe in a river. Maybe in the ocean. He swims toward me and I watch until he is very close. He ducks under the water like a playful boy will do and I feel my heart beat as I wait to see his face.
>
> Now the king must be awake. He calls my name. His voice today is frail but it is sweet to hear him call for me.

I must have dozed, though it seemed only moments had passed when my eyes sprang open. With the sun's rays glinting past the blinds, a destination popped into my head, a crosstown outing. All those years in the city of my birth and I'd never set foot inside what once was known as the world's largest and most luxurious hotel. In its heyday my great-grandmother had stayed there at least twice. It had been the frame, you might say, a site for the beginning and the ending of whatever had passed between Nani and the king.

I caught a bus, hopped off at the corner of Market and New Montgomery, at the edge of the downtown financial district, a five-way intersection where delivery vans and electric streetcars and cabs converged, and commuters rose by escalator from the BART station far below to join the sidewalk throng. The eight floors of the old hotel occupied an entire city block, its roofline a ripple of scallops and molded cornices, though overshadowed by the high-rises that had sprouted around it.

Through arching double doors—black wrought iron trimmed with floral gilt—I passed from urban clamor into an elegant calm. In the marbled lobby all light seemed to emanate from across a wide corridor, light from the vaulted atrium that spilled down upon a restaurant glittering with crystal chandeliers, goblets on white tablecloths. The early breakfast crowd sat in upholstered chairs on floral carpeting, among potted palms and Grecian pillars, while the Versailles-like corridor stretched away in both directions, from glassy doors on Market to faraway doors on Jessie Street, at least as long as a football field. Though empty at that hour, it was a palatial extravagance meant for leisurely promenades, and so I set out, not at all sure what I'd come looking for, some sign of Nani's tread, some trace of a long-gone wax cylinder that may have spent a few days here, or may never have existed anywhere but in her imagination.

Carpets covered the marble flooring. Overhead hung more chandeliers. Against the walls, glass cases displayed photos of the hotel when it opened back in 1875, made of thirty-one million bricks, they said, with bay windows all around the block, in every room on every floor. There were wine lists from decades past, and engraved invitations to legendary luncheons, a black 78 rpm twelve-inch disc signed by Enrico Caruso, who preferred the Palace whenever he sang with the San Francisco Opera. Photos and yellowed clippings chronicled the stays of other famous guests—Ulysses S. Grant, Lillian Russell, Harry Truman, Andrew Carnegie, Sandow the Strong Man, Carrie Nation, Oscar Wilde, Amelia Earhart.

Through the station I'd once acquired a press pass, which I now brandished at the front desk, wangling an audience with the assistant manager, a balding, pensive fellow with bushy sideburns who doubled as public relations director. When I described myself as a radio journalist researching the hotel's history, he told me he'd seen quite a lot of it, having started there as a waiter when Dwight D. Eisenhower was still president of the United States.

"My first banquet, Ike was the guest of honor."

My interests, I said, reached a good deal farther back. All the enticing memorabilia had caused me to wonder if any old records might be lying around from the early days, old guest registers, for instance.

"How early?"

"1880s, 1890s."

Handing me a pamphlet from his desk drawer, he glumly shook his head. "This will give you as much background as we have. For the small details, if it happened before 1906, your guess is as good as mine."

I told him of my particular interest in the royal visit of Hawaii's last king, names of those in his party, other guests registered in other rooms, perhaps a physician's log. The king did, after all, pass away while on the premises. . . .

Yes, he'd heard the story more than once, since the death of a king is no small matter, Kalakaua being the first royal death in this or any other American hotel, and he sincerely wished he could take me to a back room where documents such as these had been preserved. But as fate and firestorms would have it, he could only show me the photo of a burnt-out building, its walls scorched, blackened with flame-shaped streaks above the rows of exploded bay windows. All the hotel's records had gone up in flames after the earthquake and fire that wrecked so much of downtown San Francisco.

With a pained, apologetic smile, as if he'd witnessed it and still suffered from survivor's guilt, he said, "The walls held, as you can see, but the great blaze that came roaring toward Market just couldn't be stopped. Up on the roof we had our own hoses and our own water supply, but it wasn't enough. The whole place was gutted . . ." leading me then out of his office and back to the restaurant to show me the vaulting and translucent ceiling.

"This room is all that survived," he said. "In the early days, of course, it wasn't a restaurant."

He was a tour guide now, his right arm raised in melancholy tribute.

"Before the quake it was a courtyard, the ceiling much as you see it today, though a good bit higher. With six tiers of balconies stacked above the flagstone paving. There were pillars and arches on all four sides, and a wide entrance that opened onto the street, where horse-drawn carriages would roll in with travelers and their luggage, carriages of every type, as many types as we have cars—the hacks, the phaetons, the landaus, the barouches . . . you'll see them depicted in the pamphlet."

He paused and touched my sleeve, suddenly intimate, his voice almost a murmur. "You asked about the early days. Let me tell you something. I have always loved this room, the Garden Court. When I was still waiting tables I'd be working late, cleaning up after we closed, and there were times I'd be in here by myself. I'd hear hooves going clop clop clop. I'd hear the old wheels creaking."

His eyes roamed the room, head cocked as if through all the muffled chatter he could still make out the clink of harnesses. Something about his profile, his shiny scalp, his sideburns, the fleshy nose—up close you could see its web of broken capillaries—gave him the look of one whose service reached much farther back than Ike's banquet. He could have been a barman when the hotel first opened.

"One thing I forgot to mention," I said. "Before the king died, they say a recording machine was brought up to his room."

"Yes, I've heard about that too. Somebody from the Edison Company."

"What have you heard?"

"Only that it happened. But don't get your hopes up."

"Wouldn't the hotel take an interest in something like that? I mean, sooner or later? A king's last words?"

This seemed to test his patience. "Of course we'd take an interest. Please listen to what I'm telling you. Everything started over in 1906. The only things around here from before that time are the photographs . . . and maybe a few ghosts."

He turned toward me, his eyes, for just an instant, wistful and naked. "Do you believe in ghosts, Mr. Brody?"

"I suppose so, yes. It depends."

"Good. I think we need ghosts. They come in very handy now and then."

He stepped back a pace, formal again, the assistant manager excusing himself. "Welcome to the Palace."

I sat down in an upholstered chair and ordered eggs Benedict, cappuccino, half a grapefruit, and looked around trying to picture what he'd described, a carriage yard open to New Montgomery, rows of marble pillars separated not by floral carpets but by marble paving stones, and all lit from this basilica beehive of heavily leaded translucent panes that seemed to make the air golden. In those pre-earthquake years, before tremors split the gas mains that sent the fires roaring through town, when tiers of balconies rose above the courtyard like balconies at the opera house, how many drivers and animals with their harnesses had come jingling into this luminous space? And how had it all appeared to Nani on that January day in 1891?

Surely she'd stood somewhere in the courtyard-now-restaurant, perhaps close by the very table where I sat sipping coffee, stood there watching the horses, watching his body loaded into a black-ribboned hearse. Perhaps it had rolled over this very spot, the carriage that took him from the courtyard to the embalmers, then on to the church on California Street for public viewing, and finally led the long cortege past silent multitudes to the waiting ship.

Across the top of my scalp I felt a tingling, a galvanic buzz. Maybe it was ghosts. Maybe it was the cappuccino kicking in. At the Palace Hotel invisible carriages had surrounded me, my table somehow placed among them, out upon the flagstones where snorting horses waited for their drivers, and I saw standing near me two versions of my great-grandmother.

One was twenty-seven, with a band of black crepe around her sleeve, already knowing more of the world and its treacheries than she cared to know. Standing close by was the Nani of ten years earlier, the girl who dropped everything to seize the day and join Kalakaua's entourage. At age seventeen she'd left her north country terrain for the first time, following the Kinsman. Now she was in San Francisco for the first time, wearing a plump hat the General's Wife had given her and a dress she'd sewn herself, with shoulders puffed and high neck ruffled. From Oakland they had crossed the bay by ferry, and from the Embarcadero had come half a mile up Market to check in at the famous hotel. How had it looked to her? With eight stories filling a city block, with its thirty-one million bricks and myriad bay windows catching golden flashes of the afternoon sun, its bulk and glitter must have filled the sky.

After the trip downriver, and with the rancheria just three days behind her, what was it like to arrive at such a place, to clop clop clop through arches into a radiant courtyard where uniformed bellmen stood at the ready? One can only guess what went through her mind. Her Book of Days offers glimpses here and there, but her entries require a lot of reading between the lines. Her diary was still sketchy, not yet what it would become as the task itself, over time, sharpened her thinking and revealed perceptions that might otherwise have gone unexpressed. In later years she would begin to talk about her "book," as if she'd already found a publisher. But during that first adventure, writing was still, for her, almost an exercise in penmanship:

October 12, 1881

We are on the third floor. We ride the elevator. A man with black skin carried up our bags. He wears a black suit. His name is Milton. He calls me Miss Nani. I call him Mister Milton, and it makes him happy. Sometimes he whistles in the hall and I know it is him. He told us to make ourselves at home.

October 13

I have a big room with Malia and Leilani. They are my age. We speak Hawaiian, but I am too slow for them. I have my own bed. They go wherever the king goes, all around the world. Sometimes he calls them to his room. Malia will go. Or Leilani will go. They laugh about it. I hope he does not call me to his room.

October 14

Every day I see Mister Milton in the hall or in the elevator. He works hard. He carries all the heavy bags. But he winks at me every time. He says how are you today Miss Nani. When he whistles his lips stick out like he is kissing.

October 15

I went down the hall to sit on the big couch in the sun room. The king came and sat beside me. He asks me if I like the hotel. I tell him about the chicken salad. I tell him I can make it better. He laughs his big laugh. He says one day I want to taste your chicken salad.

We know they spent a week there. We know two carriages came to gather them up and take them back to the wharf, where they climbed aboard the S.S. *Australia,* an exodus with no fanfare, since the king claimed to be traveling "incognito" as he headed home on the last leg of his global tour. That long expedition had taken him to Tokyo, to Singapore, Bombay, Cairo, Paris, London, New York and Washington, D.C. Every stop and junket had been reported in full detail, along with frequent editorial speculation on his true motives. Was Kalakaua seeking out a new trading partner or two? Or did he perhaps hope to sell away his kingdom, or some valued piece of it, such as Pearl Harbor, in exchange for needed cash or military alliances? Or was this mere extravagance and indulgence, the kind of thing you'd expect from a carefree Pacific Islander who didn't fully grasp the idea of money and what things cost?

Society pages around the world had tracked his every move and utterance. And yet records of this final lap, his homeward voyage, are strangely in short supply. The *Australia* was not a private yacht, such as he maintained in Honolulu for trips from one island in his domain to another. This was a passenger ship on a regularly scheduled cruise, with others on board besides the royal party. Curious about who those others were, I called Special Collections at the city's public library, where I was referred to the Maritime Library at Fort Mason Center, only to learn that all passenger lists for ships arriving and departing from San Francisco during the 1880s and 1890s had been lost in the same quake and fire that consumed the records at the Palace Hotel.

Hula

Honolulu had become the largest town in Hawai'i. As the permanent capital of the kingdom it was the largest town between San Francisco and Manila, a mid-Pacific crossroads. There was nothing else like it for thousands of miles in any direction. France and England and the United States had consuls and ambassadors there. Its placid harbor was filled with sailing ships and steamers and outrigger canoes. But in those days, if you were approaching from the west, by water, you would not see much of the town itself. Trees rose above the buildings and the grid of streets to screen them from view, fan palms, coco palms, banyan, monkeypod and mango. A few white steeples poked higher than the trees, as did the central tower of the king's new palace. Beyond the steeples rose the extinct crater called Punchbowl, a bronzed and reddened cone of ash and cinders and weathered lava. And beyond the crater, soaring green peaks cut their jagged line against the sky, against rolling clouds with cotton edges and heavy undersides. The town was hidden, while the sky farther inland was always full of drama, moving and scudding, sending squalls and sheets of rainbow-painted mist into the wild, verdant places, into the rain forest valleys that notched the mountain range that made the long spine of the island.

Not far from town, at the lower end of one such valley, where the rain fell lightly once or twice a day, a sprawling two-story frame house stood next to a papaya grove. Early each morning, from her cot on the screened-in sleeping porch at the back of the house, Nani Keala would wake at first light to contemplate the sky, its slow turn from violet to indigo to a soft hibiscus red, or sometimes ginger-blossom yellow. Outside the screen a mottled coco palm sloped against the changing colors. At these times she did not think. It was a form of pure communion. Her auntie had given her permission to do this, her aunt-by-marriage, once the wife of her father's brother, her aunt Moana who owned the house and had taken her in. One evening, soon after she arrived in the islands, they were watching the sky at sunset, the way its light released something in the trees, made the blossoms of the flame trees glow like living fire. Moana's face was glowing with the same light when she said very softly, "*Ka leo o ka maka,*" just that phrase, letting it float in the air. "Let the eyes speak," she had said. Looking at her again, looking into the face of her auntie, Nani saw that Moana's eyes spoke the same message coming from the trees. After that, nothing more was said until darkness fell—falling early and quickly, as it does in the tropics—and it was time for dinner.

That had been Nani's first lesson from this generous and ample woman whose smile made you feel as if you alone were the one person in the world who could call it forth, and whose black eyes, when she was not smiling, were tunnels leading back and back to a distant time. Moana's lessons came in many ways, sometimes when they walked together to the open-air market, sometimes when Moana's yard was filled with dancers. She was, among other things, a teacher and master of the dance, a *kumu hula*. Young Hawaiian women would gather there and one by one drift farther back into the forest bordering Moana's land, past the papayas and the breadfruit grove, toward a low platform lined with lava stones where they would practice the dips and swings and startling moves of the style called *kahiko* (meaning old, antique, ancient), dances and chants Moana had inherited from her mother-in-law and grand-mother and the generations before them, dances and chants that in her time had to be practiced and passed on in secret, in places like this, at the far side of a piece of land where trees and layers of greenery would muffle the chanting and the slapping thump of the calabash drum.

Here Moana would chant the stories of love and war, of birth and death, of demigods and mortals and how the islands emerged in fire from a sea of darkness. She taught her dancers how to tell these stories with their hands and bodies, as knees popped and arms jutted skyward. As their supple hands became mountains and flowers and waterfalls and crashing surf, the dancers kept the stories alive, kept history alive. But into their island realm had come powerful foreigners who did not know these things, and did not want to know them. The missionary families from New England saw only bare feet and bare arms, provocative hips and breasts covered by loosely hanging vines. For decades now the preachers from their pulpits had been banning hula in public places, condemning it as crude, lascivious, pagan and barbaric. And who could blame them, coming as they did from such a demanding northern land, where the weather left no margin for error, where the body had to be thickly covered for much of the year, where clothing could save your life? Who could blame them, coming from such a place into a tropical world where clothing was a decoration to be shed at a moment's notice, where skin yearned to be touched by moist and feathery air? Join an uncompromising climate with the inclinations of the Puritan mind, and it is no wonder that those who came to save the souls of the islanders brought with them a terror of exposed flesh and a deep suspicion of gestures no decent woman should be allowed to make. They despised the hula, they mocked it, they called it "the Devil's Dance." Like the town as viewed from offshore, the bodies of the women were now concealed, covered from neck to toe by long, billowing Mother Hubbards the Hawaiians called *mu'u-mu'u* and the hula, as an art and as a calling, was kept well hidden by the trees.

What was Nani doing in such company? It had been the king's idea. It had occurred to him that Moana, one of his good allies, would be an ideal mentor for the extraordinary young woman who'd caught his eye, this distant cousin he now regarded as a protégée. Moana was a distant cousin too, by marriage. In this long-isolated string of islands, where clans had intermarried for centuries, where a chief, before the Christians arrived, might have several wives and multiple concubines, everyone was related one way or another, if not by blood, then by adoption, if not by an official genealogy, then by some covert and unofficial one.

In the Polynesian underground the king and Moana were accomplices, since he too had a passion for the hula. As a young man he'd been schooled in dance and chant. As the leader of his people he'd come to see all the ways their lives were threatened by the inexorable changes of the era. He wanted them to survive both in body and in spirit. For the Hawaiians, hula was a form of food. If the dances disappeared, he knew the legends and stories would gradually be lost, and the spirit of his people would wither away. He wanted Nani Keala to know this. He wanted her to know that the drumbeat they danced to was the heartbeat of her father's homeland.

On his global tour Kalakaua the Monarch had hobnobbed with dukes and earls and sultans and potentates and emperors, and he yearned to secure his place as a royal figure in the world of rulers. He coveted their satin sashes, the gold braid and sunburst medals splashed across the military jacket. Yet Kalakaua the Patriot still loved the old Hawaiian ways he'd grown up with, and so he sought out defiant chanters like Moana, whose foremothers spoke to her in dreams.

Soon after she arrived, Nani wrote this in her "Book of Days":

> He knows papa's family. He knows the wife of papa's brother. He says she will teach me Hawaiian things. The kahili is a long pole with feathers on top. One day I will stand beside the king and hold it high. You must stand very still, Moana says, but it is not hard to do. It is your blood that matters. Be proud of your Hawaiian blood. This is why the king chose you. We eat banana, papaya, breadfruit, fish cooked in leaves, sometimes roasted pig. Poi is mashed up root of a plant called taro. Moana says it is Hawaiian mashed potato. We do not use spoons or forks. The General's Wife would shake her head to see me eating with my fingers.

A while later, in another entry, Nani wrote:

> Across the yard a small house is made of grass. Moana sleeps out there. She says the big house belonged to her husband. But he is dead now. When she was a girl she always slept in a grass house. I tell her about the dome house in our village made of mud and curving branches. She says did Keala sleep in a house like that. I tell her yes. She says come, sleep one night with me. When I stay in the grass house, we talk in the dark. Moana says your papa took an indian woman. I tell her yes, my mother. She says was he happy. I tell her he was a leader in the village and had a big laugh like the king. I hear weeping in Moana's voice. I think she is going to tell me about him. But she only says when he left she knew he would never return to Hawaii. After that we do not talk. In the dark I smell the house. It does not smell like smoke. The grass has a sweet smell.

Moana still lived in the district where they'd all grown up together— her family, Keala's family, their compounds close by one another in the Honolulu of her girlhood. When Nani first appeared in her yard, welcomed with leis of ginger and plumeria, Moana's huge embrace was laden with so much joy and loss and reunion intermingled that Nani felt smothered, overwhelmed by a longing for she knew not what.

Whether she'd be staying a few days or a few weeks or a few months, she wasn't sure. She hadn't thought it through. She wrote to Edward right away, still regretting his wounded look, the unblinking eyes of a gut-shot animal, as her barge pulled away from the landing. She wrote to the General's Wife, whose reply, describing the progress of every student in the school, had its undercurrent of benign reproach: "We could have used some advance notice of what you planned to do, dear Nancy. But we all miss you nonetheless and look forward to seeing you at the Christmas party come December."

Such messages took weeks to find their way across the water, to steam up the Sacramento against the current and down again through the delta and into a mail pouch for the transoceanic passage. As Nani settled in, as one day folded into the next, that distant rancheria world, with its web of obligations, slid further and further beyond the horizon. She had stepped ashore wearing a Victorian dress the General's Wife taught her how to make. A shoe-covering traveler's dress with pleats and tucks, it hung in her closet now. She had found another family here, thanks to Moana, thanks to the king, who'd never regarded her as he seemed to regard the other young women in his entourage.

At the hotel, though he'd spoken with Nani several times and once commanded her to take his arm as they strolled the ornate corridor called the Promenade, he'd never summoned her to his room, which caused Malia and Leilani to wonder why she'd joined them. In their experience young women in the king's inner circle were there to provide whatever he desired. From what Nani wrote later on, it was the same on board the ship. She traveled more as a relative than as a retainer. Judging by what soon began to pass between them in Honolulu, she and the king must have spent a good bit of time together during the voyage. Evidently they invented a kind of game, a playful reenactment of the first time he came upon her scribbling in the diary.

If you weren't one of the crew, there wasn't much to do at sea but eat and drink and play cards and take the air. You would never have known, from the king's jaunty aspect, what awaited him once the ship came gliding into Honolulu Harbor: a legislature squabbling about the cost of his globe-trotting adventure, a small but growing opposition to his regime. He enjoyed pacing the deck in white shoes and skipper's cap and blue blazer with maritime insignia, with spyglass in hand for studying the birds and sea creatures that might appear nearby or in the distance, flying fish, the dolphins that often cavorted in the ship's wake.

Nani had found a cozy hideout between the railing and a lifeboat, where she could snuggle in and hold her notebook firm against her knees and write something if she felt like it, or watch the water which had no end, the boundless circle. It was her first time out of sight of land and far too soon to feel disconnected. She could sit for hours mesmerized by the great corrugated circle of blue.

One morning after breakfast the king spotted a corner of her dress, and stopped and leaned over the bow of the upturned boat and watched her a few moments before he spoke.

"Aloha, Nani."

Though soft and thick and soothing, his voice startled her. She turned to see him gazing at the open page and clapped the notebook shut.

"Have I caught you at last?" he said with curious amusement. "Do you have a secret I don't yet know about?"

"No," she said, studying the water.

"It cannot be a letter, in a notebook such as that. Did you bring some schoolwork with you?"

"I left all that behind."

"Well, then, this must be something very personal. You know, Nani, I myself have often thought of keeping a journal. But I could never bring myself to do it."

"Why?"

"I was afraid someone might find it. Then they would know too much about me."

She turned again and saw the teasing in his eyes and laughed.

"But I have a notebook just like yours," he said. "I have it with me, here on board the ship. Isn't that a strange coincidence?"

"Why do you keep a notebook?" said Nani, thinking of the General, the only grown man she knew who had one. She'd seen it on the desk in his study, and once opened it. There were columns of numbers next to a long list of things he'd paid money for.

"I gather stories and sometimes write them down. One day soon they will make a book."

"What kind of stories?"

"Hawaiian stories. We have many, you know, wonderful stories which should not be forgotten."

"I would like to hear one."

"If you will get up from your perch and walk with me, I will tell you one. I am supposed to be taking my morning stroll."

Nani stood and stuffed the diary into her shoulder bag. As they made their leisurely way along the weathered decking, he told her of Maui the trickster, who was part man and part god and loved to go fishing. Maui had a long fishing canoe that required several paddlers. One day while he was out in this canoe he baited his hook with the red feathers of a mud hen and cast it over the side at the end of a long, long line. This was a powerful and famous fishhook, and if it could catch a certain large fish called the *ulua,* Maui could pull up the fish and the whole bottom of the sea. He wanted to draw together the sea bottom and bring it up to the surface, where it would make one large island. And he did this. He caught the *ulua,* he pulled up the bottom of the sea. But then something unexpected happened. In the boat there was a hollow gourd used for bailing water. This gourd became a beautiful woman. When Maui's paddlers turned to look at her, the great island he had pulled up from the bottom broke apart and became eight islands.

"One day soon we will see them," said the king. "There will be nothing in front of us, then they will show on the horizon as if Maui has once again pulled them from the sea."

When she didn't speak for some time, the king said, "Well, that is the end of the story. What do you think?"

She had been reminded of another story, one she'd heard from her mother, who'd instructed her never to tell it to anyone outside the tribe. But from listening to her father and the Kinsman and other Hawaiians along the river, she knew it was the custom, when someone told a story, that sooner or later you must tell one of your own. She began to recite a legend heard many times when they lived in the village and many times in the years since then.

"In the beginning everything was dark. Everything was covered by water. Then there was a raft on the water, and on the raft there was a turtle. Then a rope of feathers came down from the sky. Spirit Man climbed down the feather rope. He is the one with power to make the world. But he needed some mud to get started. He told the turtle to dive down to the bottom and bring up some mud. So the turtle went down and was gone for six years. He found a lot of mud down there and filled his arms. But while he was swimming back up to the raft all the mud washed away. Only a little bit was left, underneath his claws. This was all Spirit Man needed. He rolled it into a ball as big as a pebble. After a while it grew into a ball so wide he could not get his arms around it. Then it grew as wide as the world, and the land rose out of the waters and made the mountains."

The king had been watching her, much as he'd watched her from the doorway of the train, when her chanted genealogy filled the railroad yard, once again transfixed by what he heard, the ancient note. He stopped walking. Having made a circuit of the ship, they stood again by the lifeboat.

"What a beautiful story, Nani. Where did you learn it?"

"My mother. My grandmother too. They both told it."

"And you say your mother was an Indian."

"Yes."

"Forgive me. I have read too many books. I have always imagined Indians wearing warbonnets and shaking tomahawks. I did not know they told stories such as this, with a turtle carrying mud up from the bottom so the mountains would be made."

"They are still there," she said. "You can see them to this very day."

"I believe you. We passed through them on the train to San Francisco."

The king's eyes, glistening with wonder, now winced as if he'd smelled a rotting fish. A silver tray had appeared in front of him, borne by a steward whose stealthy approach had gone unnoticed.

On the tray was a folded white page. Glancing at it he told the steward, "I'll be right there." And to Nani, "What a nuisance! A small reception in the captain's quarters. It completely slipped my mind. But we must talk some more of these things. . . ."

"Well," she said, with disarming sweetness, "you know where to find me now."

His delighted laugh bounced off the cabin, rolled along the deck and out across the churning wake.

In the days that followed, in their tiny quarters tiered with bunks, Malia and Leilani would want to know what she talked about each morning with the king. They could not conceal their envy, since he seldom said much at all to them, apart from brief and casual joking remarks. Though he might spend several hours with one or the other, he would never have walked beside them along the deck. Teasing Nani, they told her only Hawaiian girls can go with the king to his room. Half-and-half girls stay outside.

Meanwhile, in his suite, where the bar was kept fully stocked, the king would have long brandy-sipping conversations with the chamberlain about their moves and strategies after nine months away from the capital: how the carriages should be arranged for the grand welcome-home parade; and where to store the furnishings they'd ordered in London and in San Francisco until the palace was ready to occupy; and what to do about America. Having once again crossed from the Atlantic coast to the Pacific, he was reminded of how much he admired America, its large spirit, the expansive look of its terrain. Yet the politicians of America troubled him more than ever, and the dangerous smiles of the senators he'd met with in Washington, D.C., who clearly wanted a larger claim upon his kingdom. On board this ship, a thousand miles from land, as he drank and laughed and planned, he felt their ambitions pursuing him across the water like heavy weather bearing down from the north.

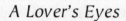

A Lover's Eyes

As the weeks turned into months, Nani made a place for herself inside Moana's compound. She could help with the cooking and the vegetable garden. She already knew about pigs and chickens. She learned how to roast a pig underground and how to strip a coconut. Moana's daughter and her husband lived in the house with their four kids, all Nani's cousins. Everyone was cousins. *Ohana,* they called it, the extended family, which included the husband's brother and his pregnant wife, and a young girl from up the road whose mother had passed away. Afternoons when the kids came home from school Nani would help them with their English. Sometimes kids from other families would join in because she made the lessons fun, she made them laugh.

Moana was like Nani's father. Learn English, she told her grandchildren. At school, she said, be good in English. But never forget Hawaiian. With all these whites taking over, you have to learn their tongue. Most of them only know one tongue. So you learn two, you have more power than them.

Like Nani's father, and like the king, Moana was a storyteller. It was part of her calling as *kumu hula.* In her grove, when the young women gathered, she would have them sit in rows and listen. To do the dance correctly, she would say, you must know the story. You must know the meaning of the story and the feeling of the story, so your arms and hands and feet can tell it.

At these times her face would grow stern, and you did not move. She would hold you with her black, black eyes. Not angry eyes. But fierce. Like Pele, the fire woman who lived on a big island far to the south. Many of Moana's stories were about Pele and her sister. They loved each other, but were rivals too. Pele was the keeper of the fire, her sister keeper of the forest. When you danced the story of the sister you had to become the forest, your body a tree, your arms the limbs, your fingers the leaves as they fluttered in the wind. When you danced the story of the fire woman your body became the mountain where the lava grows, and your arms became the flames.

Nani liked these stories. Though new to her they were not strange. She took to the hula and caught on quickly. It was already in her body, just as the words were already in her mouth when she first heard her father speak Hawaiian. She already understood how a story and a dance were one. She understood the nature signs, the pulse of the drum, the call of the chant rising from Moana's throat as she'd heard it rise from her father's throat and from her mother's too, from her grandmother's and grandfather's, as they danced and chanted for the harvest in the fall and for the new shoots and blossoms every spring. It was not at all strange when Moana said she must feel with her fingers the feathery softness of the ferns they wore and touch the long leaves woven into the mats they sat upon. They searched coves for small beach-rolled lava stones to be held and clicked together, each dancer finding the stones that fit her hands. Once you found them, you rubbed them against your face and along your arms. "These stones are in our family," Moana would say. "You must get to know them well."

In the big *ohana* of this secluded compound Nani was both Kaleponi cousin and apprentice, listening to Moana as the king instructed her to do. Yet she still was not sure what he expected of her, why he kept insisting she stay another month, then another three, and now to stay until his coronation, to be one of the kahili bearers and stand somewhere along the route of his procession, or perhaps march with the others.

He was an enigma, on one day protective and fatherly, on another remote and brooding, on yet another day a carefree and flirtatious youth. She once saw him at a lawn party sitting on the grass with a small guitar, singing Hawaiian songs, and later, just as the food appeared on sumptuous tables set across the grass, he was somehow next to her, whispering with delight, "Quickly now, while we have a moment, I must teach you how to play one of these. It is Portuguese, you know, small enough for sailors to carry on board their ships. It is so small we have called it *'ukulele,* jumping flea. All you do is scratch your finger up and down across the strings as if you are scratching at a flea bite. Yes. Like that. Oh, very good, Nani! And with your left hand place your fingers here," reaching in a near-embrace to set her wrist against the box, his hand upon her arm, his breath upon her neck, his rich scent suddenly close.

She had seen him in full military dress, stabbing his finger at a sheaf of drawings as he debated with the men who designed his palace—soon to be the largest building in all the islands, Moana said. Soon Nani would have the chance to step inside its doors and walk past the walls of polished wood, since it was her duty, whenever called upon, to stand beside the king and hold above his head the royal standard. She was but one of many kahili bearers who could be called upon at any time. A runner would come up the road, and gladly she would go, in a flowing white dress that made her feel important, to carry the short pole capped with feathers that gave her a reason to be near the king.

Was that why he'd given her this duty? Or was nearness to the king in the nature of the duty, which Moana called "a privilege of blood"? Or was it perhaps another of his lessons, to let her overhear what passed between him and his many visitors, the petitions, the debates, the greetings from foreign envoys coming to pay their respects and ask for favors? She didn't always follow what was said, but she listened and watched. From just behind his shoulder, observing him conduct affairs of state, she came to know his every twitch and gesture. Once, after a petitioner had stood before him to plead a case, bringing that day's royal session to an end, Kalakaua leaned toward her with an intimate glance and whispered, "Tell me, Nani, what did you think of that fellow who just walked out the door?"

As soon as he asked the question, she knew exactly what she thought. "His face is hard," she murmured. "But his heart is gentle."

"And why should that be so?"

"His heart is full of grief, as if a loved one has been lost."

"That is my impression too. But now I am curious. How do you know this?"

She looked him in the eyes, as she had in the railroad car on the day they met. "How do *you* know it?"

They were in an upper chamber of the courthouse, where he held hearings from time to time as he awaited the completion of his throne room and a grand receiving room such as those he'd seen in Europe. Nani held one of two kahilis, which met above the glossy black hair of the seated king. In front of them stood a fellow with a long-handled fan, stirring the sultry air. Beyond the windows, palm fronds hung like exhausted tongues, and beyond the fronds, across the street, enclosed by low walls of mortared stone, stood the two-storied palace, with its Florentine pillars and porticos, white balustrades along the roofline, turrets at every corner, all agleam in the blazing sunlight. It had been a particularly hot morning and with the last petitioner now gone, the king was eager to cool off somewhere, ready to push up from his cushioned chair when a loud voice was heard demanding an audience. In the doorway appeared the worried face of his aide-de-camp.

"Your Majesty . . . a Mr. Giles Peabody . . ."

"Yes. Yes, of course. Who else would it be?"

"I can tell him to come back."

The king shook his head. "You may as well show him in. He won't take no for an answer."

Without waiting for the formal announcement, a young fellow came pushing past the aide. "Giles Peabody THE THIRD," he said, with a careful smile and a bow that seemed to faintly mock the act of bowing. Handing the king his card he said, with the same hint of mockery, as if to protest all formality and pomp, "Your Majesty is most gracious to receive me on such a day and on such short notice."

A thick ruddy moustache spread out toward muttonchops covering half his cheeks, all the hair on his face and head the color of brick. Like the king, he wore a necktie and a dark morning coat buttoned to the top. It struck Nani that he did not sweat like most whites sweated in this kind of weather, in such cumbersome clothing, though his forehead shone as if polished with a light oil. For a young man he didn't have much hair.

"Well," said the king, "it's all in the family, I suppose, since I have known your father for so many years. And let me say how sorry I am to hear of his illness. I hope his condition has improved."

"Not by much, though I am grateful for your thoughts. I have just now come from his bedside."

"I suppose this will keep you in Honolulu for a while."

"This time I am home to stay. Just this week I have opened my offices."

"We can always use a well-trained lawyer, especially one who knows his way around these islands. I myself have studied law, as you may have heard, and practiced it. That was years ago, of course, before other opportunities came along."

Peabody's smile was broad and arrogant. His shrewd blue eyes were fixed upon the king. "I hope you're not suggesting that the law is one thing, while ruling a kingdom is something else."

"A little joke, Mr. Peabody, nothing to philosophize about. Please tell us what brings you here today. I am late for lunch. They say you were in Washington not long ago."

"Quite right . . . where there is much talk about the renewal of our treaty, a strong feeling that the advantages guaranteed to Hawai'i do not provide nearly enough benefit to the government of the United States. I have tried to no avail to bring this to the attention of your foreign minister . . ."

"On the contrary," said the king with uncharacteristic haste. He was known to be a patient man, willing to hear others out before he spoke his mind, but something in Peabody's voice annoyed him, disturbed his composure.

"On the contrary, the United States is the exclusive market for our sugar. For that we receive a sizable reduction in tariff. It's as fair as anything can be, and for seven years now it has worked quite well."

"I only repeat what I've heard on Capitol Hill, Your Majesty, where senators tell me the United States should now have permanent access to Pearl Harbor, that this should be a condition for any renewal."

Kalakaua sat forward, one arm pushing aside the constant fan. Peabody was not yet thirty. The king, at forty-six, began to lecture him like an elder. "You grew up in these islands. As a citizen of Hawai'i and a subject of this kingdom, you should know that what they propose is impossible! I cannot allow it. The Hawaiian people would not stand for it. Bad enough that their navy wants to blast away an entire coral reef to open it for larger vessels. When the time comes they can re-coal there, if need be. But while I have a say in the matter, no part of this kingdom will be given away to any foreign power!"

Peabody's smile was almost derisive. He held degrees from Columbia and Yale. He had practiced in New York and in San Francisco. He saw himself as the voice of right reason and common sense.

"With all due respect I should inform Your Majesty that I speak not only for myself but on behalf of the Sugar Growers Guild, which I now represent. It is their fervent desire that the Reciprocity Treaty be renewed in a timely fashion, since the economic benefit to these islands is enormous. Needless to say, the health of the sugar industry bears directly upon the funds required for running a government. And certain expenditures being what they are"—he turned then toward the open window for a long look at the nearly completed palace, its turrets, its opulent porticos—"we all have an interest in the ongoing health of our economy. Letting go of a rather marginal body of water such as the lagoon in front of Pearl River—a harbor in name only, I might add, seldom used by anyone but fishermen—seems a rather small price to pay. . . ."

At this Kalakaua rose from his chair and stepped toward Peabody, as if to take him by the throat. Large and brown and thick-boned in the Polynesian way, he towered over the smaller and paler but uncowed young attorney, who evidently figured that any bodily assault would be both unstatesmanlike and unmanly, since the king stood four inches taller and outweighed him by fifty pounds or more. For a few seconds their eyes locked. Then the king recovered, smiled his enormous, all-embracing royal smile.

"I would invite you for lunch. But I am meeting with some members of my cabinet."

"Of course," said Peabody, stepping back and out of range. "Perhaps another time."

"Yes. Another time. And welcome home."

"Thank you. It's good to be back."

With another cartoon bow, he was out the door.

The king sat down and signaled the fellow at his right to resume fanning. As currents of warm air flowed over him he spoke to the bare tables and empty chairs.

"What am I to do with such a man? He was born here, and his father too. Yet their loyalty is not to me. It is to a roomful of senators six thousand miles away."

After a while Nani's low voice poked a hole in the silence. "He did not blink."

Kalakaua turned to her. "What do you mean?"

"From the first moment until he left, his eyes were wide. He did not blink. He did not look at anyone but you."

With a wave of his hand the king excused the aide, the second kahili bearer, the wielder of the fan. Once they were gone, he said, "What else?"

"The way he gazed at you . . ."

"Yes?"

"He loves you."

"I am not sure I understand this, Nani."

"They are a lover's eyes. But . . ."

"Yes?"

"He hates you too."

For once the king seemed at a loss for words. His broad forehead bunched with uncertainty. Nani too was puzzled by her remarks. In the still and humid air of the room she stood next to the silent king as he sat gazing out the window at his palace, as if seeing it for the first time. Something in his profile brought to mind her father, as often happened on these days when she was called to wait upon the king, observing his gestures at such close range, hearing the honeyed cadences. He had the same way of laughing, pulling a hand across his nose and mouth as if laughter made his skin itch, the same glisten in his eyes when strong feeling rose in an instant, even as he tried to be the stern decision maker. Kalakaua was a softhearted king, much as her father had been a softhearted leader of their foothill clan. She liked him best when he had no affairs of state to wrestle with. She liked to hear him sing Hawaiian songs, hear his voice lift to a high falsetto.

"They call us primitive people," he said at last, speaking not to her but to the empty room. "We are backward and primitive, they say, and unfit to rule in our own land. And yet when we erect a grand building such as those one sees in Italy and in France, it offends them. They say it is a waste of public money. They cannot seem to understand that I do this for the Hawaiian people, who long to be proud of their king, and proud of their kingdom, to once again be proud of Hawai'i. . . ."

When he turned to look up at her his black eyes were wet and shining.

"I have to decide upon a name. The old palace was called Iolani. I have not yet thought of a better one."

"I know that word. Bird of heaven."

"Yes, and also a kind of hawk you sometimes see in the air above the Big Island. It can fly so high it is thought to be a royal hawk, the king of birds."

"Yes," she said, smiling like a bright student who knows the right answer. "Sometimes they fly without moving their wings."

"Why, yes," said the king, animated, leaning toward her. "They seem to float, don't they. But how do you know this? You have not been to the Big Island."

"In the mountains where my family lived. They ride upon the wind."

His manner had changed. His face turned smooth and his eyes eager. "Nani, I have to say that you are good for me. Perhaps we are good for each other. I want to see more of you"—speaking not like a king or a benefactor, and not like a distant cousin, but reminding her of Edward on the days when he hoped they might walk together after class. His nearness flustered her, and she wanted to pull away, but couldn't help herself. She had to touch him. She placed a hand upon his shoulder and felt his soft heart go softer. Who knows what might have happened there in the noontime heat of the meeting room had not the bearer of the fan returned just then, with an apologetic shrug, to fetch a straw hat he'd left behind.

Moana's Dream

I want to see more of you, the king had said, his sweet baritone unnerving her. Now she would have to wait a while longer to discover what he meant. The palace was going to require his full attention, the finishing touches, then getting himself and his queen moved into their furnished quarters on the upper floor. And with the completion of the palace came the thousand details of the coronation, which he intended to be the grandest event ever staged in the Hawaiian Islands. All previous kings had been anointed by a priest, as was the age-old custom. For Kalakaua and Kapi'olani, jeweled crowns were being shipped from London, gowns from France. There would be gold rings and gold braid, scepters and scabbards, bugles and snare drums, a grandstand to hold three thousand, and a crown-shaped pavilion where the royal couple would sit enthroned. There would be horse racing, fireworks, and two weeks of feasting.

For numerous Kalakaua-watchers, this was one more tribute to the scale of his insatiable appetite, for food, for drink, for partying and travel, for posturing and every form of pomp. While the king laid his plans, the leaders of the Sugar Growers Guild would gather in the downtown offices of their young attorney and dream of ways to circumvent a profligate ruler and secure the flow of trade. This extravagant and un-needed celebration of royalty gave them one more reason to get rid of him altogether, so that Hawai'i might one day be safely joined to the United States. It wasn't cost alone that troubled them. It was the ostentation, the filigree and fancywork, the pageantry and Parisian gowns, all these pretensions toward royalty and European show that their immigrant forefathers had left behind when they crossed the Atlantic in search of a land where no king reigned.

These sons and grandsons from the missionary families, when they heard that hula had been added to the program, took it as a personal affront. Hula had not been seen in a public ceremony for decades. Now it was announced that during the several nights of communal feasting, troupes from various islands would perform a cycle of traditional dances. The men in the Growers Guild could not decide which was worse, the costly and decadent self-indulgence of the crowning or the saturnalian wickedness of the dance.

When Moana's troupe was invited to perform, she gathered her young women in the grove beyond her house. The king himself had summoned her, she told them, saying the time has come for our songs to be heard again, for the stories of our dances to be told for all to hear and see. With pride she said, "His Majesty has honored us!"

Afterward two women came to her in tears, to say they dared not be seen dancing at the palace. Their father, a strict and upright German merchant, had forbidden anyone in his family to dance the hula. Only with the covert permission of their Hawaiian mother had they been able to join Moana's classes. But performing in public was too great a risk. They feared their father's wrath.

That night Moana told Nani she would have to be among the dancers at the coronation. She must prepare herself to practice long hours and in the weeks ahead give herself to nothing else but that. It was not an order or a request. It had the ring of an unavoidable family duty, filling Nani with confusion.

"I am to carry the kahili," she said.

"I will speak to the king. Others can carry kahili. He is the first of our kings to be crowned. Many will want to march in his procession."

"I know so few of the dances. I am only a beginner."

"You learn quickly. There is no one else. So many now are like the sisters. Afraid to be seen. Afraid to be criticized."

They were lying side by side on woven mats in the grass house at the edge of the trees, where Nani slept now most of the time. More cousins had moved into the big frame house, and a brother-in-law whose wife had passed away—cousins and friends of cousins sleeping on the porches and in the front room. It was quieter out there under the thatched roof, with layered grasses hanging low to the earth.

Nani said, "I too am afraid."

"Of being seen?"

She wanted to say, "Afraid of the king," though she couldn't say it. He'd been so good to her. It sounded ungrateful. She wanted to tell someone what he'd said. Instead she murmured, "I am only half."

"Half what?"

"You told me blood is what matters."

"So I did."

"Today I heard two women talking. They say to dance before the king you must be all Hawaiian."

Moana's laugh was a light and liberating ripple in the darkness. "Is this what worries you? Then listen to me now. . . ."

For quite some time Nani listened, waiting. At last Moana said, "It is blood. But not only that. It is also the spirit you bring, the mana. I have relatives, pure Hawaiian all the way back, who are now so eager to please the whites they will not dance the hula. Or if they do, they only dance with their bodies, no longer with their hearts. Those two sisters, they are gifted, and they are half German. Young Princess Kaiulani, the king's niece, she is half Scottish, yet the people love her, and she may one day rule the kingdom. You have a grace, Nani, that cannot be learned. I think it is time that I tell you where it comes from."

Again she listened, waiting, and what she heard is recounted in her Book of Days:

It was hard for Moana to speak. Her voice was so low I had to be very still to hear it. She wanted to tell me about her kumu hula, the one who taught her from the time when she was very young. It was her husband's mother who was her teacher for many years before they were married. His mother was your father's mother too, she told me. So it was my grandmother who taught Moana all the things she knows. She was a very strong woman, Moana says, born in the time before the missionaries. Every day Moana sees her in me. When she said this we both shed tears. She reached across to touch my hand in the dark and told me she sees Keala in me too. She says she knows I came to Hawaii to bring him back to her.

I said why did papa leave. *Pilikia,* she said. Big trouble. I waited for him. A long time. He told me he would return. I said to her how old were you. She said fifteen. This was nearly fifty years ago, she said. Now there is a song about a man like him, a man who sailed away to Kaleponi. Moana says she does not like to sing it. The song makes her sad. Papa still comes to her in dreams. She sees him in a big canoe in the middle of a wide stream paddling and paddling. His arms and shoulders are thick and dark. They shine in bright sunlight. Sometimes she is with him in the canoe but she does not know where the river leads.

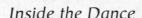

Inside the Dance

In Moana's grove they practiced the thousand moves of a dozen dances. They danced until Nani's knees burned and her bones cried out. All morning and all afternoon they danced. In the week before the coronation they danced through five days of unrelenting downpour. Day and night rain fell upon the town, to soak the earth and soak the grassy grounds around the palace, the kind of rain that makes you wonder. Was this a sign that the elements were lining up against the king's ceremony? Though people watched and wagged their heads, though some made dire predictions, it was too late to turn back. Too much food had been gathered. Too many had made their arrangements, the officials and dignitaries, envoys from Japan, from Britain, Austria, Hungary, the German Empire, and the United States—as well as common folk arriving from the backcountry and steaming in from the outer islands.

On the morning of the sixth day the skies finally opened. While sheets of foggy mist still blew across the inland ridges, a welcome sun blazed above the town. At ten o'clock a gate admitted the waiting multitude. Seven thousand, they say, pressed in to fill the grandstands on the palace grounds. At eleven the call of conch shells went out to the four directions. Their trumpet notes settled the crowd and seemed to summon more rain clouds.

Bejeweled, brocaded members of the royal family now appeared beneath the palace arch—Lili'uokalani and Likelike, sisters of the king, and the two sisters of the queen, and many bearers of the feathered kahili. A heavy overcast muted the glitter, muted the vivid show of red and white bunting above the archway and the king's pressed and pleated military whites, and the queen's gown of red velvet trimmed with ermine. Under lowering skies they made their slow, processional way to a crown-shaped pavilion where two thrones waited, where the king and queen received the prayers, the blessings, the proclamations, the ceremonial gifts, some European, some Polynesian—an engraved sword made in England of Damascus steel inlaid with gold; a yellow feathered cape once worn by Kamehameha the First, made of four hundred and fifty thousand feathers plucked a hundred years ago from underneath the wings of *o'o* birds.

At precisely noon a crown was presented to Kalakaua. Said to cost a thousand pounds sterling, it was made of gold and red velvet, with bands of emeralds, opals, rubies and pearls curving upward toward a Maltese cross. The king, upon feeling the full weight of it, couldn't resist an impulse to depart from protocol, from the way they'd rehearsed all this. In the manner of Napoleon I, whom Kalakaua much admired, he stood and crowned himself, and in that very moment, as he placed the crown upon his head, the clouds parted once again, more dramatically this time, causing a communal groan of wonder to rise up from the grandstand. The midday sun popped out, a cosmic searchlight shining down upon the palace and the pavilion, a radiant beam of approval from on high.

Kalakaua now crowned his queen, and this called forth a kind of thunder, as cannons were fired off down by the harbor, with an echoing salvo from American warships anchored offshore. After the sunny blessing, cannons provided the martial sound of triumph, a grand salute, and the announcement of an island-wide party, starting that night with the coronation ball. An orchestra set up inside the palace accompanied the mazurkas, the quadrilles, the Viennese waltzes. At the luau that followed, during night after night of outdoor feasting, the seldom-seen hula was accompanied by chanters and by the play of powerful fingers across polished gourd drums.

Moana's troupe had spent all day preparing. Early that morning Nani and the others followed her up the valley and into the rain forest where ferns grew thick, where vines and creepers and an overhead canopy dripped and gleamed in shadowy light. Giving thanks as she plucked each stalk, Nani wove a head lei for herself, fashioned a bunch to wrap around each wrist and ankle, then went searching for the fragrant runner vine called maile, giving thanks as she pulled loose each strand, to fashion open-ended leis that hung abundantly from neck to waist.

In the forest, while her dancers plucked, Moana spoke a long guttural chant that blessed each vine and clump of ferns and called upon Laka, the deity of hula, to bless each dancer and each dance. She reminded them that these plants came from the earth, which is our mother, and when we wear the ferns and vines we are one with the earth and in the dance we are one with Laka, who watches over us.

That night on the grounds around the palace they say five thousand gathered. While they ate and drank, their carousing chatter filled the twilight—until at last a space was cleared before the king and queen, who had spread out on mats, surrounded with bowls of poi, platters of yam and kalua pig and coconut pudding, bottles of wine and brandy. Into the clearing stepped a white-robed chanter who stood tall, with head held high, to speak a welcome, to bless the royal couple. While his throbbing voice quieted the chatter, it charged the air with high anticipation. As his last words subsided, two females voices rose, deep-throated, chanting in unison. Moana and a sister-in-law approached the clearing, wrapped in folds of the bark cloth called kapa, each carrying a double-globed gourd. On woven mats they sat side by side, calling the dancers who now moved out in three rows of seven, wearing head leis of fern, bracelets and anklets of fern, white blouses and wrap-around skirts of brown kapa, with strands of maile dangling.

Nani in the middle row tried to contain her fear of dancing before such a multitude. At the rancheria she'd danced in nighttime ceremonies, in the festivals each spring and fall, but in those times everyone danced. No one sat and watched. You didn't have to think about so many eyes upon you. She tried to think of nothing but the moves she had to make. Your back is like a tree, Moana told them, growing straight up from the earth. Nani had learned to become the tree, the mountain, the wave, the rainbow, the storm, and the lover too, since their dances were sometimes stories of men pursuing women, women pursuing men, stories of new love or stolen love.

"This song, this mele," she had heard Moana say, "is about waves lapping softly on the sand. It is about the sound of the waves and the beauty of the water. It is also about a woman caressing the body of a man she desires. The beach is his body. The waves are her hands. When the big wave rises and moves toward the shore, that is the strong feeling of desire rising up inside. Then it breaks and the spray and white foam, the *ehu kai,* that is the moment of love."

In this way Nani had learned to be the wave and also to make its swell a kind of invitation with the hips and a supple turning of the hands. As her body told these stories—sometimes bawdy tales, sometimes old dramas of the fire goddess and her sister, the keeper of the forest—she was inside the dance, losing her fear in a trancelike, unfettered flow that was not lost upon the king. From his mat, where he sat cross-legged sipping brandy, nibbling on roast pig, he watched with the close scrutiny and intense pleasure of the connoisseur, proud of what his trusted friend Moana had accomplished, captivated by his young cousin, her talent, her subtlety of gesture, by how much she'd learned, and moved by that which couldn't be learned yet was somehow released in the dancing.

What He Did Next

What he did next is not entirely clear, or rather, when he did it, since there's no public record of his movements during the rest of that festive week, nor is there any record of much else that happened in and around Honolulu. His prolonged coronation party was like Mardi Gras, like Carnivale in Venice, it was New Year's Eve stretched over fourteen days, with all formality forgotten, all routine abandoned, a season of carousing and gaiety, of chance meetings and matings and every form of liaison in the half-light of nightly fireworks.

As for Nani, her diary seems deliberately vague, as if she felt compelled to cover her tracks or protect someone—though modesty itself might account for the shortage of certain details. We don't know when he called for her, whether that very night, or the next day, or some days later, whether he called her first to the palace, as if to carry out a royal duty, or directly to the country house that, in the months to follow, would become their covert rendezvous.

In all likelihood a runner was sent to Moana's compound, as had so often happened in the past. Perhaps out of habit, Nani put on her long white dress before setting off on foot. Somewhere between the compound and the palace she was met by a fellow on horseback who instructed her to mount a second horse. Together they rode away from town, farther up the valley road and then along a narrower track that took them across the valley, through a mango grove, and up a short rise to a low gate that opened onto what seemed a solid wall of leafy rain forest. A nearly hidden carriageway of mossy brick led through it, lined with high-leafed hapu'u ferns that rose until their green arches touched overhead, bringing the riders at last to an elegant bungalow perched upon a bluff and framed on three sides by dense foliage. The fellow told her to go inside. If she needed him he'd be at the stable with the horses.

The house had a steep roof for shedding rain, in the Polynesian manner, with wide eaves to shade its wraparound verandah, and was lifted off the ground by round posts, allowing ventilation underneath. As Nani mounted the steps, what was she thinking, at age nineteen? What was she expecting? We can only guess. Had she asked the horseman where they were going? In this time of high festivity, would she be listening for voices, for the strumming of guitars? When she stepped through the open doorway, did she expect to see the king standing across the wide front room? One wall was open to the view toward town and the glinting bay beyond, and he stood there with drink in hand as if in contemplation. Did she look around for signs of other guests? Or did she already know it would be just the two of them? Perhaps Malia and Leilani came to mind, the many times he'd called them to his quarters. Had she secretly wondered if she too would one day be called? Had she dreamed of this? Or did she still fear the king? Or both at once?

Seeing him there, in the moment before he turned to speak, she could have backed out the door. No one was compelling her to stay. She could have commandeered a horse and galloped out of there. And yet she stayed. Sometime during the week of nonstop partying, when there could have been no official duties awaiting her at the palace, she'd answered his call, and there she stood, perhaps wondering why he did not turn. Surely he had heard their hooves upon the bricks.

"You sent for me."

"Ah, Nani, you are here at last. And how lovely you look. Come in. *Komo mai.* Come. Sit."

His smile was full of welcome. He wore a close-fitting white shirt with long sleeves, white trousers, his feet bare on the mat of woven lauhala.

We know they sat on the verandah, where food was laid out by a valet who moved noiselessly back and forth from some invisible kitchen. They sat side by side on a cushioned settee, and we know he persuaded her to try a glass of Riesling. He told her that after watching her dance he realized how seldom they had the chance to talk as they once did. Again he said he wanted to see more of her, his voice itself a warm and generous embrace, charming and endearing, a voice one wanted to trust. Yet she was wary. Once the valet came and went, they were alone as they'd been alone in the meeting room when she'd feared herself drawn toward him, toward the softness of his heart.

"You are the king," she said. "You have so many duties."

"But not today, Nani. And I want you to call me Kawika."

"Kawika means David."

"When we are sitting like this," he said with languid eyes, "I am not the king."

We know that after they'd chatted a while he twice asked her to dance for him. The first time she shook her head, causing him to sit up straight as if offended that anyone could deny him this request. Nani wanted to please—he had done so much for her—but his hungry eyes made her feel awkward, self-conscious. She understood that for him the dancing was a kind of foreplay. Later on she would learn that no young woman had ever dared to say she would not dance for him. When Nani refused a second time, he seemed oddly pleased.

She had whetted his appetite. There was about her an almost chaste reserve that was new for Kalakaua, thus all the more enticing. Women like Malia and Leilani were trained to serve his every whim—and here was Nani, who moved away each time he tried to touch her.

She said, "You are my cousin."

"Yes. But a very distant cousin."

"You have a wife."

As if bewildered, he wagged his head. "A very distant wife."

"I am a Christian."

"And so am I."

"Do you go to church?" asked Nani, who surprised herself with such a question, as if someone else spoke through her. She had not expected to be remembering the troubled brow and blinking eyes of the General's Wife, the small lips moving, the eyes full of warning and alarm.

"Sometimes I do," he said, "when it suits me. I honor our Hawaiian gods, but I try to honor Jesus too. Better safe than sorry, don't you think?"

"Then you know what the Bible says . . ."

Like the prim pupil she once had been, Nani was ready to recite the seventh commandment—Thou shalt not commit adultery—but before she could speak it, the king said, "Indeed I do, for you and I are much alike. I too attended a mission school and heard many of their teachings as a boy. Some made sense to me, some did not. Outside of school I had a Hawaiian teacher, a very wise woman who gave me some advice I have found extremely useful through the years."

Into his eye came a playful gleam, as he placed one edge of his hand against his stomach and drew a line across his navel.

"From here up belongs to God," he said. "From here down belongs to me."

His belly began to shake with impending laughter, and Nani could not help herself. This was too good. It was irresistible. They both broke out laughing, their eyes merry with desire.

He rose from the settee and began to sway, weaving patterns with his hands as he half hummed, half chanted a song. It was a slow and sensuous male hula, the knees jutting, the hips rolling, the arms and shoulders loose yet angular as he slapped his chest and dipped and turned, a large and nearly corpulent man now as light-footed as a child. He gestured toward Nani, his hands saying "Come, come now, join me here," and she could not sit still. She too left the settee, moving to this song she hadn't heard before yet seemed to understand. Reading his movements she could improvise her own, and they danced that way, as they faced each other, carving pictures in the air. Slowly he swayed toward her, step by step across the matting, until their bodies nearly touched, her bosom brushing the long curve of his belly. As he took her hands in his, the humming stopped, and this time she did not pull away. His eyes were warm and full and brimming, and his heart was soft again.

Though she stayed with him until nearly dusk, Nani would record almost nothing about how they spent that afternoon, entering into her Book of Days, years later, only these few lines:

> He was not like Edward who was always in such a rush. Kawika took his time with everything. Until that day I did not know the difference.

The part she wanted to record came afterward, as they lay together on a double-wide lounger out on the verandah, their unclothed bodies cooled by a breeze drifting up from the valley. He lay with his head in her lap and began to speak as if they had nothing but time and she had been sent to listen. He said he wanted her to stay in Hawai'i so he would always know she was nearby. Not daring to think then of what might lie ahead, she said, in the amorous quiet, that she would stay as long as it pleased him. He told her they were much alike. Mocking a wicked glance, he said, "We are both unconverted Christians. And we are both writers, Nani. We each have our secret notebooks. I still hope one day you will show me yours."

She shook her head, felt blood rising to her cheeks. With a reassuring touch he stroked her arm and began to tell another story he planned to include in his book of tales and legends. It was the story of a man from an older time who had traveled across the sea meeting every kind of obstacle, storms and thieves and demon spirits, but protected all along the way by a shark who was his *aumakua,* his ancestral guardian. . . .

Kawika's voice flowed on and on and somehow, before Nani knew when or why, he was telling yet another tale, the story of a man he'd never met but had heard of throughout his youth. Maybe it was the same man, the one who crossed the sea. Nani wasn't sure. All Kawika's stories were about heroic men:

It was late in the day. The sun was down. Perhaps I was dozing. When he said the name Keala my eyes sprang open. I was wide awake. He said many believed Keala would be a lawyer or a spokesman for his people. Many were filled with sadness when he left. From one day to the next he was gone, thanks to his cousin who was the governor of this island.

Kawika told me he himself had met this governor when he was getting old but when he still had a fine memory. The governor was the first one who told him about what happened to my father. In those days there was a fort inside the harbor. The governor hid my father in the fort because he attacked the son of a missionary. After that there was such anger in the town Keala's life was in danger and the governor helped him to escape.

This is what the governor told Kawika and what Kawika told me. He told me it was a warrior's act. And the missionary's son deserved what he got. You should be proud Kawika said. I wish I could have Keala in my cabinet.

She placed a finger on his lips. "You knew all this before you came to Sacramento."

"When I was a youth in the Chiefs' School it was already a famous incident that young Hawaiian boys whispered about."

"Before you took me to your railroad car, you knew it."

"I have wanted to tell you this, Nani. When I heard your chant I felt chills all through my body . . . but you are weeping now. Please forgive me. I should hold my tongue. . . ."

She waved her hand no, her throat so full she couldn't speak. His voice was much like her father's when she'd heard it at night inside the mud-covered dome of her childhood, yet his head in her lap was like the son's who has come to be caressed. As he lay there remembering what the Governor once told him, she stroked his hair.

Somewhere Downtown

While Nani listened, while the king reminisced and savored the calming touch of her fingers through his curls, a couple of miles away, in downtown Honolulu, perspiring typesetters composed copy for the weekly papers that would be ready for delivery whenever the shops reopened. Had Kalakaua known what was soon to be said of him, it might have brought this idyllic interlude to an early end.

During the luau no one had risen up to disapprove. After each dance the applause had been universal, punctuated by gleeful shouts. It was more than applause. Men and women wept at the spectacle of dances they hadn't seen for years, the blood-stirring throb of chants they hadn't heard in a public place since childhood. In time this night would be looked upon as a moment of reawakening, when new life was given to old ways nearly forgotten.

From the well-fed, well-lubricated crowd, calls of praise and satisfaction swelled up around the dancers and the chanters and the king's entourage. Only later came the cries of protest and condemnation—from the pulpits, and from the pages of papers like the *Growers Weekly Enquirer,* where Giles Peabody was a contributing editor. Whether he was somewhere near the palace that night taking notes, quietly checking out the program, or had come early to eat and run, or had boycotted the crowning, boycotted the ball and all events that followed (as had a number of his colleagues), and thus based this account on hearsay and third-hand reports, no one can say for sure.

A ROYAL DISGRACE
We have already expressed our dismay at the excesses of the Coronation. Last Friday his esteemed Majesty, David Kalakaua, once again tested the patience of every right-

minded resident of these islands. Taking it upon himself to retrieve from the darkest caves of barbarism the wretched and shameless native "hula," he has allowed it to be performed on the grounds of the very palace he claims will give his reign equal stature with other kingdoms around the world. If only this were true!

Can you imagine the effect if the Druids of ancient Britain, with their naked bodies painted blue, should suddenly appear in front of Buckingham Palace to reenact one of their pagan rituals? Can you imagine the effect if a tribe of wild Comanches should appear on the lawn of the White House in Washington, D.C., to beat their tomtoms and raise their primitive yawpings to the sky?

Indeed, all the efforts of this past century to bring some semblance of civilization and public order to the Hawaiian Islands seemed wiped away in an instant, as the grotesque pageant continued into the night. We beg the King to forbid any further display of such gross and bestial behavior, lest the very moral fabric of our citizenry be rent in twain.

The California Sailor

The story Nani heard Kawika tell that afternoon would merge with other versions heard during her days in Honolulu. A century later it would merge again with bits and pieces of her father's life that came to me from Rosa and from the books and articles I dug up.

Though he was never famous, he could have been. In travelers' journals, oral histories and memoirs from that era, his name appears—sometimes Keala, sometimes John Callahan, sometimes Kanaka John—known to be a man of skills and charisma, a man looked up to. From a sentence here, an anecdote there, his route begins to show itself. It still amazes me to think that at one point his travels brought him to within a mile of where I'm sitting, when what would become San Francisco was a clutter of shacks and sheds down the hill from my high perch above the water. Today Yerba Buena Cove is covered by landfill underneath the concrete towers of the financial district. But the blue bay still sparkles as it did then, as it has sparkled for a hundred and a thousand and a million years, framed by Coast Range ridges that haven't moved much at all. Today the water below me is alive with glints and morning sparks, each one the tiny marker and reminder of a trip, a crossing, the myriad sailings in and out of this nearly landlocked haven, among them the long ago voyage of my great-great-grandfather who left Honolulu in the spring of 1839 bound for Kaleponi.

For Hawaiians that meant Alta California, the northernmost province of Mexico. It also meant any destination eastward from Hawai'i. Anywhere in North America could be "Kaleponi," just as "Kahiki" could mean the island of Tahiti, three thousand miles south, but also, in their legends and genealogies, anywhere in the great oceanic realm below the equator. Kahiki was the ancestral homeland, the place we came from so long ago; Kaleponi was the new place, the next place, the far-off destination that once again sent us out across the water.

He was sixteen, dark and muscular, his skin the color of mahogany, black hair hanging to his shoulders. I see him surfing outside the entrance to Honolulu Harbor, at a famous break called Kekaiomamala—the Sea of Mamala—named for a fabled female surfer once married to a shark man. Keala's board is solid koa, nearly black from kukui nut oil rubbed deep into the grain. A wave rises and his arms dig in. One stroke. Two. He feels the lift, the forward surge, and leaps to his feet as the dark board skims over blue-green water, over coral heads a few feet down. With a sky now orange in the sun's last burst, the hissing of the board across this slide is an elixir like no other. He laughs with pleasure, riding as far as it will take him, then flattens out and paddles the long paddle into the beach, where two white boys stand as if waiting for something.

With one last stroke he picks up the lapping shorebreak, angling his board so that he steps into shallow water well down the beach from where they stand. He has recognized them and has no desire to know what brings them here at dusk. He knows their fathers have forbidden them to ride the waves, calling it the Devil's pastime. Only infidels would go into the ocean without clothing, the fathers say, both men and women together. In the mission chapel Keala has heard these admonitions and wears a pair of old trousers trimmed at the knee.

As he walks away from them, toward a grove of coco palms, one of the boys calls, "Look who's here!"

Keala keeps walking, until the boy speaks again. "It's our friend, the pagan!"

Now he stops and turns. "The headmaster says not to use that word."

"Well, the headmaster isn't here now, is he?"

"And your father was a cannibal," says the second boy, "just like all the other chiefs. Isn't that so, Giles?"

"Indeed it is. Just like all the other chiefs."

"My father was a leader. He was a warrior."

"Then that means he was a cannibal," says Giles with a malignant teenage grin.

"No. That is not true."

"He was a savage who ate the flesh of his enemies."

Keala drops his board and watches them approach. All three are sixteen, about the same size. Like Keala the white boys are husky, solidly built. With hands defiantly on hips, they figure they have him two to one. They also figure they're safe out here, with others scattered along the twilight beach—a family at the edge of the trees, another surfer heading for shore, a white couple in the distance, hand in hand to watch the sun drop. The boys don't see that Keala, whose father died young and whose memory is revered, has reached his limit. At the school, where the sons of missionaries mingle with the sons of highborn chiefs, Keala's mother is known as a widow who will send a son to learn the white man's language but won't set foot inside the white man's church, preferring (so the other boys have claimed) heathen rites known only to kanakas. They have called Keala "cannibal" and "nigger," and the headmaster has rapped their hands. "We will not have such talk in my classroom!" he proclaimed. After that, the schoolyard taunting subsided. But still they pursue him, wandering down here to the shoreline as if by chance. As the sun's last curve of flashing scarlet slides past the horizon, the boy named Giles speaks just loud enough for Keala to hear.

"This is what everyone says about your father."

"It is not true. He was brave. He was not a savage."

"It is true, and you know it."

Keala rushes him, grabs his shoulders, hurls him backward onto the sand.

Stunned and angry, Giles sits up. "You can't do that!"

"You cannot say what you said about my father."

From the side the second boy comes at him, in a headlong lunge that throws Keala off-balance, giving Giles time to get to his feet. It becomes a clumsy three-way wrestle as the two try to force him to the sand. They can't get the best of him, and there comes a moment when he stands free, with a clear shot at Giles. From men in his clan Keala has been learning the fighting style called *lua,* akin to boxing but more ferocious. His arm is cocked. His lightning punch catches Giles mid-chest, sends him reeling toward the nearest palm, where his head cracks against the prickly mottled trunk. As he slides to his knees, the bark lacerates his temple and cheek. His eyelids flutter, then close as he keels sideward. His face hits the sand, a streak of vomit spilling across his chin. Above him, blood darkens the curving trunk.

Keala's fist is still clenched, as if waiting for Giles to rise and defend himself. The other boy, Malcolm, is fighting back tears.

"I didn't want to come down here."

"Make him open his eyes."

"It was Giles wanted to."

"Make him wake up."

Malcolm kneels, leans in close, jostles a shoulder. "Giles, hey. Hey, lad, c'mon now. C'mon."

He looks up at Keala. "He isn't breathing."

"Yes he is. I saw his chest move."

"He looks dead."

"He cannot be dead. Run to the school. Find the headmaster."

"What if he dies?"

"He is not going to die."

Crying openly now, Malcolm seems paralyzed, his terrified eyes darting from the inert body to Keala to a man from the Hawaiian family coming toward them through the trees. He saw the scuffle.

Keala calls, "Please! He is hurt! Please stay with him. We are going for help!"

The boys take off running, Malcolm toward the mission school, Keala toward the nearby fort that overlooks the harbor, its chalk-white walls rising straight from the sea. His cousin, who is the governor of the island, lives inside these walls. He too is descended from a chiefly line, a diplomat who has traveled to South America and to England, and is now a kind of godfather to a web of interrelated clans. He tells Keala to stay with him here and not venture beyond the walls of the fort until they learn how the other boy is faring. He sends a physician down to the beach along with a trusted aide.

The next day word arrives that Giles is near death. In his chest they hear a deep rattle. His eyes have not opened. His chest bone is broken, maybe his skull. It will be a miracle if he survives, and the Governor knows that if he dies there will be no mercy for Keala. Giles Peabody Senior, known as the Pastor, is a powerful figure in the white community, one of the first New England missionaries to arrive in the islands. No matter how this fight began, Keala will be seen as the one at fault. Already some white citizens are demanding that he come out of hiding and turn himself in.

The Governor first proposes that his young cousin travel by night to one of the outer islands where it will be easier to remain secluded. Then, as if provided by the gods, another form of refuge presents itself, a chance to leave Hawai'i altogether. A European man has been trying to arrange a voyage to Mexican California, an impatient and talkative yet charming man who claims to have served in the army of France as a captain of the Swiss Guard. Just this week he has finally secured a place for himself as cargomaster on the brig *Clementine*. Twice he has called at the fort to negotiate for workers who can travel with him. The Mexicans, he claims, will give him land, thousands of acres, where he plans to establish some kind of town. The Governor has met many white men who reach these islands from faraway places with their mouths full of promises. But this man seems to have money, he has letters of credit, as well as other letters to recommend his character, more letters than the Governor has ever seen in one man's possession. He says he likes Hawaiians, knows them to be trustworthy and dependable, and his offer is fair—room and board and ten dollars a month for three years of service, after which they will be free to do as they wish. So far the Governor has contracted for seven men and two women, all young and strong, eager for the chance to travel and see some of the world. But none can speak English, or write it, and this European man, John Sutter, though he speaks several languages, knows but a few words of Hawaiian.

His weary face etched with the burdens of office, the Governor tells Keala, "I know how hard it will be to leave your family. But I fear it will be worse if you stay. If the white boy dies, his friend will surely testify against you, and you will have no chance. Even if he lives he will have injuries, his face will be badly scarred. There will be hardship for your people—unless I say I ordered you to leave. Then, with time, the anger may subside, and one day you can return. For now my advice is to travel with this man to Kaleponi. I have told him you speak English and have experience as a sailor, that your father was a chief and you have begun to train in his footsteps. He tells me he needs someone like you for this journey."

After three days hiding in a windowless room Keala already feels like a prisoner. Almost anything would be better than this. He trusts the Governor, a first cousin to his father, who has been like an uncle since his father passed away. Each time Keala thinks of the insult his anger boils up again, only to cool and give way to remorse. He didn't mean to kill the Pastor's son, he only meant to teach him a lesson. Fearing what awaits him outside the fort, he agrees to sign the contract, though before he departs he asks to see his mother, and it is arranged for her to visit him secretly for a sobbing farewell.

He asks to see the young girl, Moana, and this too the Governor arranges, allowing her to slip into the fort after dark. These two grew up together and for the past year have been sweethearts. They have one final night in each other's arms, much like my mother and father had their one night together before he went overseas, although Keala isn't going into battle, nor is Moana there the next morning to wave good-bye. Well before dawn he slides over the fort's seawall and into a waiting canoe that ferries him to the ship. Captain Sutter, having been paid something extra by the Governor for this service, allows him to stay below until they're well beyond the harbor.

The first days out he is lonesome for Moana, for the family he may never see again. But he's soon won over by the infectious gaiety of his mates, farmers and fishermen glad to be out on the ocean and bound for somewhere new. They've heard rumors about the fight, though they don't yet know who fought. They compose a traveling song about two warriors, one white, one brown who fights and sails away. Already they have made it a legend, something that happened long ago in the islands far behind them. And in the excitement for where they're headed, they send him into a land they've heard about from Hawaiian sailors on other merchant ships, where cattle have horns like wings and women dance in wide, twirling skirts. Day by day, verse by verse, it becomes the saga of Ka Holokai Kaleponi (The California Sailor), a heroic traveler who left Hawai'i for distant lands and after many adventures sailed home again.

Their course is north and east through moderate seas, with ample time between chores to make up songs, to trade stories, to joke about the names the white sailors give them: John Callahan, Sam Kapu, Kanaka Harry, Maintop. They talk and joke about this restless man who has hired them. He puts wax on his moustache. He wears a tightly buttoned military tunic and calls himself Captain, yet he is not the captain of the *Clementine*. His eyes burn, as if a fire inside is always burning, yet he will stand very still. He will stand for an hour in the ship's bow, leaning on the rail as if at any moment he expects to see an island. At night he does not sleep. In the darkness he walks the deck alone.

Each time the Captain speaks with Keala they want to know what he says. "He has made a picture of the Honolulu fort," Keala tells them. "We are going to build one like it in Kaleponi."

White Feathers

I see Keala standing on the deck as they sail through the straits toward the empty bay, and try to imagine what it was like back then, before the twin-towered orange bridge was built, before Alcatraz became a prison, before the dunes that covered half this peninsula were striped with avenues, rows of houses divided by a park three miles long and named for the soon-to-be-famous gate he'd just passed through. From the deck looking south he would have seen nothing but sandy drifts and hillocks sprinkled with tufts of dune grass. To the north he would have seen the blunt and verdant headlands much as they look today, while straight ahead he would have seen craggy Alcatraz capped with white like a mountaintop, named for the pelicans that flapped and hovered there and, through countless centuries, had layered it with snowy droppings.

They pass the crumbling Presidio, protected by a rocky point and overlooking the straits, its cannons so seldom used they no longer fire. Another mile around the peninsula brings them to the village, Yerba Buena, hugging a cove that faces east toward another island capped with white. Out from the curve of sandy beach, half a dozen ships rest in still water. Behind the cove, the hills where no one has ever lived, or needed to, are empty.

As the *Clementine* drops anchor, I wonder what Keala is thinking. As he takes in the sights of Kaleponi, what is on his mind, in his heart? There is cargo to ferry from ship to shore. But once ashore what does he do, what does he see? Little is known, since nothing of this brief sojourn was passed on to his daughter. There is a saloon of sorts, an adobe house where a Frenchman sells brandy by the glass. Other Hawaiian sailors are scattered about, mixed in with Mexican soldiers, American sailors and traders. Indians still come here to trade. John Sutter trades too. It is in his nature to trade, to barter, to cajole and bargain and talk people into things. He is an inspired talker, and he's the one in charge. His mission, his grand scheme has brought them here, Honolulu and Yerba Buena but stopping points in a pilgrimage that has taken him halfway around the world and brought him farther west than most adventurers have dared to travel, or cared to. Whatever young Keala imagined he would find, he and his fellow islanders are now joined by contract to the humors and passions and dreams that are still shaping Sutter's zigzag odyssey.

For one thing, he is on the run. He left a wife and five children back home in Switzerland and set out for the New World. Trip by trip, various trading junkets took him across the continent, west to St. Louis, south to Santa Fe, north into the Rockies and eventually out to Fort Vancouver near the mouth of the Columbia, where the Hudson Bay Company had its western port. By then, the fall of 1838, Sutter's goal was California, already, ten years before the Gold Rush, a mythical place. With heavy weather due, they told him, all routes south would soon be blocked, and he'd be well advised to stay put till spring. But he was an obsessed and willful man, thirty-five and dreaming of ranches, dreaming of an unspoiled country where land was there for the taking—or so he'd heard. He caught a ship bound for Honolulu, three thousand miles south and farther west, not at all sure where the Sandwich Islands were, but convinced he'd soon find a ship that would carry him to San Francisco Bay.

He had to wait four months, using the time to re-create his past and reimagine his future. In Switzerland he'd served briefly as a reserve lieutenant. In the islands he promoted himself to captain, one who'd served with honor in France, and somehow he fattened his already thick sheaf of character references. With such fervor did he speak of the new community he planned to establish at the farthest edge of North America that one merchant was moved to advance the cash for all necessary supplies, transport and payroll. Sutter hired his crew with borrowed money. Once across the water he made a stop at Monterey, the port town and provincial capital tucked inside another sand-edged peninsula that jutted into another empty bay, this one a full day's sail south from Yerba Buena. He met Juan Alvarado, Gobernador of Alta California, waving the thickest packet of reference letters Alvarado had ever seen, and asking him outright for a grant of land along the river called Sacramento.

In Honolulu he spoke English. Here he spoke Spanish, and Alvarado approved of this, drawn to Sutter, as were so many upon first meeting him. These two were about the same age, both ambitious and willful men. But Alvarado, like the Governor of O'ahu, had seen many foreigners landing on his shores with large plans and expecting favors. First, go out there and find what you are seeking, he said, go stake your claim, then come back in a year's time, tell me what you have found, and surely we can make it yours and make you a citizen of Mexico.

He knew Sutter's destination was part of the vast province under his command, yet it was still uncharted wilderness, a blank place on the maps, far from the string of ports and mission towns along the coast. If this Spanish-speaking Swiss with his crew of kanakas managed to push the frontier a bit deeper into Indian country, it would be worth a sizable tract of land. If he failed, or if he died trying and never returned, well, then, nothing had been gained, but nothing had been lost.

The eighty-ton *Clementine* is too deep-draughted to sail where Sutter wants to go. While it's loading up for the return voyage to Honolulu, he finds two schooners standing idle and leases them and stocks them for the next leg of his expedition. He buys a pinnace, a small double-duty launch with sails fore and aft and locks for four oars. He hires two young pilots, said to be the best in the region, though neither has sailed the inland waters. From the beach he hires five more sailors so that, with two German carpenters he met in the islands, he has a crew of nine white men and ten Hawaiians aboard three laden vessels setting out into an early fog.

They pass Alcatraz again and then, under clearing skies, Isla de Los Angeles (later called Angel), like the forested peak of an underwater mountain. The entrance to the bay's northern reach is marked by two points that almost touch and, as they recede behind the schooners, seem to join and make this basin a wide lake unto itself, a blue circle ringed with ridges. Where the northern bay begins to open toward the straits that will take them inland, they come upon a herd of elk, a multitude swimming toward an offshore islet, a herd so wide they cannot skirt it and so must push through. The elk, as if moved by some innate sense of purpose, press against one another to make a corridor, their snouts like black bobs on invisible fishing lines, their antlers the branches of a thousand chunks of driftwood. The vessels pass, and the herd closes together again, as if a gate to what lies ahead has been opened and closed.

Domed humps rise up to frame the narrow passage called Carquinez, named for the Indians whose villages still occupy its shores and who watch these vessels pass. The summer-dry hills and slopes of wild oat are golden, opening out to frame another nearly landlocked bay, where a small dock marks the lone settlement out this way, a ranch presided over by Don Ignacio Martinez. He commands his vaqueros to slaughter two bullocks as a welcome for these unexpected guests. His house seems not quite finished, a low-slung, two-room adobe, painted white with a tiled roof and surrounded by parched grazing lands waiting for rain. It's the last non-Indian shelter they will see. They sit at rough-hewn tables in a dirt yard where cattle bones and curling hides and skulls and horns are scattered about. In a balmy twilight they eat with their hands. "Twice I have ordered plates and knives from Mexico City," says Don Ignacio with an apologetic shrug. "For an entire year now we have waited."

Afterward Sutter shows him the only map of this route he's heard of or been able to find, hand-drawn some years ago by a British captain who brought a vessel through these same waters. Don Ignacio studies it and shakes his head.

"Who am I to judge? I have never been up there. All my travels take me the other way, toward the coast. If you seek that river, you are on your own. Perhaps you will find an Indian or two who can speak a little Spanish. They have been taken to the missions at Sonoma or San Rafael, you know, and then run away back to where they came from. And who can blame them? Some of those Franciscans with their intolerable piety—even I have run from them!"

The next day they depart at noon with the incoming tide and a good breeze from the west. Though the open ocean is twenty-five miles behind them now, the tides are strongly felt and rule a sailor's planning. Twice each day waters rush in through the gate to fill the bays and push farther inland past the straits to cover the mudflats around the inner bay as well as all the wetlands that edge the low-lying islands now confronting Sutter and his two young pilots. The water here is as blue as the sky and mirror-smooth. Tawny ridges form a horseshoe around the lake-like bay, with the mountain called Diablo making its singular thrust against the southern sky, a nearly triangular silhouette. They wish the delta islands would declare themselves like that. The scribbled map gives them names and outlines, but these are not like the islands in the Bay of San Francisco, made of rocks and humps. These are marshy, offshore meadows edged with brush and reeds. From the pinnace Sutter can't tell where an island ends and the shore begins. They have no contour. Everything is flat, layered with grasses that waver in the hot stillness.

At last a curving bank seems to show itself. Could it be the channel they search for? The lead pilot moves to steer that way, but Sutter calls to him, "No! No! Bear right a while longer!"

And so it goes, as the jigsaw world of low and reedy islands deceives and misleads and bewilders. For all of them the delta is unknown terrain, the map is useless. Every slough and inlet appears to be a river mouth.

They creep along until the light wanes, when they drop anchor, only to find they can't escape the mosquitoes that arrive with the setting sun. As they row ashore to set up tents, mosquitoes swarm around them. Some men try to stay belowdecks, but it's too hot there, too close to sleep. All night they slap and scratch and turn and twist, then rise early in a murky darkness, intending to push on. But now a fog has crept in from the west, dense and heavy, drawn from the ocean and sucked up from bays by the August heat. It shrouds the vessels, and Captain Sutter, ever restless, will not wait. He takes his pinnace, with four Hawaiians at the oars, and sets out on a scouting mission. Standing at the rear mast he commands them to pull ahead.

According to Nani, remembering the stories Keala would tell years later, this was the day they began to call him *maka lolo,* Crazy Eyes.

In the fog he muttered to himself. My father heard him. No birds flew. No wind. Father, who was steering, heard his low voice, his curses. Damn the river. Where is it hiding? Tell them to hold their oars, John Callahan. Is that a snag? Do you see it? No? You see nothing? What is it then? Damn this fog. Tell them to pull, damn you. Jesus Christ and Lord in Heaven . . .

All morning they row, searching ahead, as the fog slowly lifts and clears to reveal on their right a long, flat, unbroken shoreline, and on their left the same, as if they've somehow left all islands behind. South and west Mount Diablo stands against the sky, their only certain landmark, though it can tell them nothing about where to go, only where they've been. Up ahead all else is flat, as far as the eye can see. Each time they spot a break in the shoreline they try it, hoping for an inlet, a turn, a channel that can take them to the Sacramento. All day they search. With the fog gone the sun makes the air a furnace. That evening as the sun flames in the west, mosquitoes swarm again, clouds of insects that settle on their cheeks and hands and arms, a dozen at once. The men cover their arms and heads and faces and sweat in the insufferable heat below-decks or come topside and cover their skin, and still the mosquitoes bite through cloth and kerchief. One sailor, sleepless for a second night, begins to fire his pistol as if to shoot them out of the sky one by one.

"Blood-sucking devils!" he cries. "Goddam your eyes!"

Sutter shouts at him to put the gun away, stop wasting bullets, and the man fires a shot over the head of Sutter, who grabs him by the shirt and shakes him and tells him never to do this again. Frantic with itching, the sailor drags fingers across his bitten neck and face, wildly cursing the Captain and the bugs, so that Sutter has to hit him. He knocks him flat. In the long silence that follows, all you hear is the slapping of hands upon sleeves and foreheads.

On their third day in the delta maze they find a broad opening and sail into it with shouts of joyous relief, sure they've located the elusive Sacramento. It takes them a day and a long veering southward to admit this is the wrong river. It's the San Joaquin, which flows north through the great valley to meet the Sacramento flowing south. They have to turn around, tacking and rowing back the way they've come, and now the men, whites and Hawaiians both, are grumbling.

"The Captain is lost. We are all lost, and he knows no more about where we are than you or I. . . ."

With the pinnace still in the lead they lose another day in search of the opening. Under a brutal sun Keala and his Hawaiian mates take their turns at the oars, four on, four off, rowing between stands of tule. That night, after the vessels are secure, Sutter goes ashore to reconnoiter, tramping across one more contourless island layered with meadow grass, and comes upon yet another wide channel, one he couldn't see from the island's farther edge. Once again he's sure this is what he's looking for. As they set out early the next morning, once again the sailors curse and groan. But this time Sutter has guessed right. The channel opens at last into the broad and sultry waterway that will be a mile wide come winter when rains and early runoff make it a brown and surging monster. In late summer it's deceptively languid, gurgling along, holding close to banks lined with cottonwoods, elm, oak and alder.

Through gaps in the trees they see distant columns of smoke from fires that mark village sites. Though they see no Indians, the Indians have already seen them, according to what Nani wrote:

Clumps of white feathers were tied to branches above the water. Papa knew the feathers said we are watching you. All the Hawaiians knew it. They talked among themselves. Captain Crazy Eyes has come too far. We are going to die out here. Why did we not stay in the Bay of San Francisco where it is cooler and still the game is plentiful. Those feathers—does it mean they are going to kill us? The captain asked papa what they were talking about. He said they are worried about the Indians. They say we need a rest. This heat is new for us. The air is like steam. It sticks to you. The rowing now is very hard. We will have plenty of time to rest, the captain said.

When Keala told this to his mates, the one called Kanaka Harry began to compose a new verse to the song of the Kaleponi sailor, and he sang it to the rhythm of their oars:

> With a mighty stroke
> the paddler travels far
> to the land where leaves
> on trees are white feathers.
> The leaves of feather-blind
> the crazy eyes of the chief.
> They shake when there is no wind.
> And the paddler shakes
> his fearful shaft.

A schooner is in the lead again, as the vessels ply north through green water, between banks where wild grapevines dangle. Clouds of geese fly overhead, and take an hour to pass. They see more elk, in grazing herds, and clans of roaming grizzlies, and black-tailed deer and antelope and badgers. Lines of pelicans glide above the river, and cranes along the shore lift their beaks in curiosity. At night the crew moves inland, away from the river, hoping to evade the mosquitoes. From horizon to horizon the sky is a quilt of stars they cannot watch because insects pursue them and again force them to wrap their heads or sweat under suffocating blankets.

By day and by night they all grumble openly now. Their hands and limbs are sore, the heat relentless, and what does he hope to find out here? How long must we sail? One place is as good as another, Captain. The game is everywhere. The soil is rich. Why not stop here? Or here? Or over there in that little cove? Let us unload your precious supplies so we can find our way back to Yerba Buena where a man can sleep!

But Captain Crazy Eyes won't stop. He pushes northward like a man possessed, like Cortés marching toward Tenochtitlán, the difference being that Sutter claims no allegiance to any king or queen or nation, not Mexico or Spain or Hawai'i or the United States or Switzerland or the Catholic Church. The essential conquistador, he dreams of an empire all his own, and he is waiting for a sign, an inspiration.

Grass Houses

Five days up the river and they come upon another, flowing in from the mountains to the east to meet the Sacramento, causing it to swell and double its width to form a kind of bay, and at last they get a look at those who live here. A crowd of men stand on the bank, two hundred or more, armed with bows and arrows, their bodies painted yellow, black and red. Three sailors level their pistols, but Sutter tells them, "Wait!" A larger throng is emerging from the trees, women and elders, curious and chattering. Now a fleet of small canoes made of woven reeds has moved out, as if to surround these visitors.

From the deck Sutter calls down, "Adiós, amigos," stirring an agitated flurry among the nearest canoes, an exchange of startled glances that could be the first show of hostility—until a voice responds in Spanish more halting and inflected than the Captain's.

"Buenos días, señor."

With his hands and broken phrases Sutter tries to assure the Indians that he's not Spanish and has no desire to capture any of their people as the Spanish have done. We come in peace, he says, and the Indians seem to like this. The man who first spoke smiles broadly, and around him others smile. This could be a good sign. Where these two rivers meet might be a fitting place to stop.

The sailors ask Sutter if they should prepare to go ashore. But he isn't quite convinced. He is restless. He is not content. His eyes dart wildly from the fleet of reed canoes to the throng on the embankment.

"We will continue on."

"But why, Captain?" asks one of the white sailors. "You won't find a better spot than this."

Another sailor mutters, "He don't want to find a better spot. He's gone daft. We'll sail till we run aground and the next batch of redskins won't be quite so chummy. They'll just cut us into little pieces and fry us up for dinner."

Sutter whirls on him, with a hand drawn back. "I'll have no insolence!"

He catches himself, turns away, and up the river they go, the banks higher now, half a day's sail to a mighty bend that bears eastward toward the far mountains. Sutter orders the schooners to stay put while his pinnace scouts upstream. It doesn't take long, a few miles of rowing and tacking against the current, to discover that they've left the Sacramento and entered another tributary much like the one downstream. This one also flows west across the valley.

Reversing course, they head back to the waiting sailors, who've now agreed to sail no farther north. Weary and lost, fearful of the tribesmen who watch their every move, they're on the edge of mutiny. And Sutter himself is running out of steam, losing his will to resist the noisy, nonstop complaints of the white crewmen and the stoic displeasure of his Hawaiians. So they turn around at last, the water ahead of them as blue as the sky, while behind them it's silvered by the low sun, a flat sheet of gleaming silver between the trees.

They float a dozen miles or so, to the wide confluence where the tule boats surrounded them. Leaving the Sacramento they follow the second river until its bottom is too shallow for the vessels to continue. Not yet knowing this will be the last time he has to say it, Sutter says, "We'll drop anchor here and go ashore and find a suitable place to camp."

On the nearest bank they pitch their tents, while wary tribespeople gather again to watch. To the headman they offer gifts of beads and mirrors, and the Indians seem content for the moment. But the white crewmen are still not content. They are sailors, not trappers or mountain men; they haven't signed on for a stay in the wilderness. Late into the night they grumble and curse the rivers and the captain who has brought them to the very ends of the earth where they don't dare steal an hour's rest for fear the thieving redskins will take their scalps in the night.

The next morning Sutter has made up his mind. He'll stake his claim here where the rivers meet. Any who don't wish to stay can make their way back to Yerba Buena—meaning any but the Hawaiians, of course, bound to him by contract. And so the vessels are unloaded, all supplies are ferried ashore, then hauled from the beach another half mile inland. Having observed old waterlines across the tree trunks and erosion signs in the embankment, Sutter chooses a site with a bit of elevation, well back from the flow.

He bids farewell to the pilots from San Francisco Bay and to four of the white sailors. Remaining with him to set up a more permanent camp are the two German carpenters, a sailor from Maine, and the ten Hawaiians, who begin to gather reeds and high grasses from the river's edge. Keala and his mates cut saplings to make the posts, trim thin branches to shape frames, and layer the frames with thatching, to build two long shelters they call *hale pili* (houses made of grass that clings or sticks together).

As grass houses rise on an otherwise open and empty swell of land, you might call it the founding of the city that will one day take its name from the broad river that brought them this far north. But the *hale pili* won't last that long. Sutter will soon be making larger claims. Before his schooners depart he sets up two pieces of artillery, two six-pound cannons, and delivers a salute that is also a loud message to the hundreds gathering again to watch the movements of these strangers.

Sutter commands two men to load the cannons and point them away from the crowds. The first double volley shatters the air, causing all the Indians to leap and cry out in terrified alarm and bolt for cover. In a nearby grove of oaks slumbering deer leap as if startled from a long and vivid dream and gallop they know not where. With cries of warning and thrashing wings a thousand birds swarm up from the trees along the river. Geese and cranes flap helter-skelter above the camp, while wolves and coyotes bark and howl as if to fend off this unknown, alien roar.

After eight more volleys all the Indians have scattered. To his cannoneers Sutter says, "Well done, lads. They won't forget that for quite some time."

Aboard the departing schooners, men stand at the rail and shout their good-byes, their fading voices followed by an enormous silence in the river groves and across the plain that spreads beyond, where smoky columns rise from cooking fires, a long and wary silence as if the land itself has drawn inward.

Fifty years later the young fellow who pilots the lead schooner will compile his memoirs, an account of his rise from sailor to trader to investor and Bay Area real estate tycoon. Remembering the cannons' thunder that day, he will call it "the first echo of civilization in a primitive wilderness."

For him, looking back, the artillery fire was a welcome sound, a signal that this remote valley world would now be joined to the larger world and hence forever changed. But what about my great-great-grandfather? He was there among them. I have to wonder how that roar sounded to his ears. At age sixteen, could he have heard it as the pilot did, as the first note of progress in a benighted land? Or did Keala perhaps hear or see something Sutter and his pilot may have missed? These were his first Indians, most likely his first tastes of cannon thunder too. His grandfather had seen the ships of Captain Cook when they appeared in Kealakekua Bay, ships so large, with sails so tall, their size alone announced a new kind of power, striking a note of dread in the hearts of islanders who'd never had to contend with anyone but themselves.

In those hundreds of brown faces gathered by the river, would Keala have recognized their fear and consternation and confusion? He didn't join them then. He stayed on to work out his contract, to help Sutter build the fort that would magnetize the transcontinental wagon trains, then stayed to work his cattle and rise to head vaquero. But for all those years, he toiled side by side with Indians Sutter hired by the hundreds. In time Keala would marry a woman from one of these northern tribes, adopt their ways, become a village leader, and bequeath to Nani her double legacy. Though I will never know for sure what was on his mind, I know now that cannon roar has echoed through all the generations of his family, and it echoes still.

PART THREE

Myths and Legends

On an evening such as this, in early autumn, with mauve and silver twilight hues across the water, and the bridge a pair of pagodas outlined against a purple sky, I have to admit I owe a lot to John Sutter, still sometimes called the Father of California—pioneer, visionary, scoundrel and linguist, raconteur, boozer, womanizer, debt-ridden bon vivant. Long before he knew its shape and character, he heard the call of this remarkable bay and the waterways flowing toward it. Without Sutter's impulsive junket to Honolulu, and from there his incongruous return—heading north and east to reach the far west—Keala would have remained in Hawai'i. Keala would have secluded himself for a while on Maui or Moloka'i and sooner or later would have learned that young Giles the missionary's son had come out of his coma and healed and returned to school. He would have emerged from hiding and found a way to marry Moana, and I wouldn't be here. My mixed-blood father would not have been born. My mother would have been drawn to someone else on the football team—and finished high school in her hometown, and there would be no Sheridan Brody nor any trans-Pacific tale for him to delve into decades later.

During those days, when I first set out to track my itinerant ancestors, John Sutter was often on my mind. In this part of the world it's hard to avoid him. He turns up everywhere you look. A replica of his fort is now a state park in the very center of Sacramento. Forty miles up the American River, Sutter's Mill has been reconstructed to mark the spot where the first gleaming nuggets that triggered the Gold Rush were discovered. A county has been named for him, as are hospitals, and many schools, and a curious geological knot in the upper valley called the Sutter Buttes, and a long thoroughfare in midtown San Francisco presided over by the always crowded Sutter Street Garage, a parking tower that will send you spiraling upward floor after floor searching through the wilderness of cars for that long-awaited, long-imagined place to park.

Sutter is on my mind right now as I once again browse Nani's Book of Days, captivated by what she saw a hundred years ago, what caught her eye, what she chose to record or not record, as her first hours of intimacy with the king gave way to many such hours, as her months in Honolulu turned to years, as she bore witness to the ever-mounting challenges to his rule. She had her public place as *pa'a kahili*. She had her private place as mistress and confidante. And why did Kalakaua trust her? It was her rare and double nature. Nani was Hawaiian, yet not quite Hawaiian. She was there in the islands and knew her way around, yet never entirely *of* the islands. Though descended from a highborn, chiefly line, she was not yet enmeshed in the circles of intrigue that governed the lives of everyone else within his range. It was an odd role, one she only gradually came to understand, working it out in her diary page by page, a singular role, and not by any means an easy role.

Not long after the coronation she made this entry:

> Today I passed his sister on the outside staircase. She lives many miles away in another part of Honolulu. She came to visit the palace. She is short like me. Her name is long. It is Liliuokalani. If anything happens to Kawika she will be the queen. She walks like she is already the queen. Her back is straight like a dancer's. We passed very close and she looked at me as if she knows me. One time Kawika introduced me as their cousin from Kaleponi. That was a year ago. Maybe more. Today she did not speak. She did not smile.
>
> She wore a long dress made of taffeta. The General's Wife wears a dress like this when guests come to dinner. The sister is also a Christian. There is a church across the road from the palace. Every Sunday she goes there. Kawika says what we do is nobody's business. But it is like a village here. It is like the rancheria where all the houses stand side by side.

Was Nani seen far and wide as a royal lover? Like bearing the kahili, had this become a kind of public role? And was theirs a heated and prolonged affair? It's hard to know, since this part of the record she kept is told with a kind of Victorian reticence, as if some invisible censor (perhaps the General's Wife?) stood looking over her shoulder. We know she wasn't a kept woman. Moana's compound was still her home-away-from-home. Between her meetings with the king a week or two might pass, or an entire month, before he'd whisper a time, a place, or somehow get a message to her, and she would go, on foot, or on horseback. We know there was at least one trip to Maui on the royal yacht, in the company of some two dozen revelers, after which she almost headed back to California.

On board, or perhaps during a party onshore, she had come upon him giving a young woman her first 'ukulele lesson, his face close, the boyish and seductive eyes, with one arm reaching around to hold her hand and demonstrate the strum while she leaned lightly into his vast embrace, much as Nani once had leaned and averted her eyes as if held by the humming of the strings. The sight filled her with shame and self-disgust. Her sense of betrayal was what she thought a wife must feel, her pangs of jealousy mixed with a sudden understanding of the queen, Kapi'olani, who'd had to watch such scenes for years and somehow look away.

Nani let herself be drawn into the arms of a handsome fellow who'd been eyeing her, but she found no satisfaction in it. For two days she kept to herself, reading and rereading a recent letter from the General's Wife:

> Everyone here asks after you. What a blessing it would be to have you helping with the classes as you used to do. We have a few young ones coming along and could use a bit more room if we can find it. Your aunt is down with a cough and a chest cold that will not seem to go away, though the dampness that comes up off the river in the wintertime has just about run its course and the first blossoms are popping in the orchards now. Meanwhile I know it is surely gratifying to be there in your father's homeland. He was such a courageous man. We all know you will do what is best and return to us here in due time. For now, please know we all miss you, dear Nancy.

In her mind's eye she saw the orchards, the white petals opening, she saw the wide valley of her youth and the springtime shade of willows along the riverbank. She had stayed too long in Hawai'i. As soon as they got back to Honolulu she would book passage on a ship to San Francisco. She had a little money saved, not quite enough, but she could borrow what she needed from Moana, who would know why she was leaving, who had warned her about the king.

"He will want to play with you," she'd said. "He wants to play with all of us. In older times it was his privilege. With the *ali'i,* the ruling class, men always had many women and to this day some believe it is an honor to be chosen by the king. The Christians say it is *kapu* to sleep with more than one. It is forbidden, they say. But if you know the king," said Moana, with a sad, perhaps nostalgic smile, "not all the Christian things appeal to him."

As the yacht was leaving Maui behind, Nani received a note summoning her to the royal cabin. She ignored it, and a short time later came another. The king was ill. "His Majesty requires your healing touch," it said.

He lay wheezing, as if ready to pass out. Only when she'd laid hands upon him could she be certain nothing was wrong. He'd lied about his health. But by then she'd felt again the power in his shoulders, beneath the lubricated smoothness of his skin, and smelled the scent of coconut oil rising from his body. In his life, he murmured, there was no one else like her. All these other women, young and old, he said, were birds who had no names. They flew in from somewhere, flew in the door and out the door again. For all those others he was merely a king. Only for her was he Kawika.

So she stayed a while longer, trying not to think about the queen, whom she'd seen only at a distance, had never met, and didn't want to meet, having heard she was proud, sometimes haughty, could stab you with her eyes. Since the queen was a traveler, often away on trips to the windward side or to the outer islands, perhaps Nani found a way to imagine Kalakaua as a man on his own. Maybe she imagined that one day soon he would choose her over all the others, or take her with him on another long-distance voyage, just the two of them this time. She stayed a while longer because those hours when she had him all to herself were rich hours indeed. They danced, they sang, they traded stories. From time to time he brought her gifts, once a necklace of rare and tiny purple shells from the island of Ni'ihau, once a flat and lightweight shoulder bag of tightly woven cocoa fiber. "For carrying your journal," he said.

Here's an entry from the spring of 1884. She has recently turned twenty:

Each time we meet he wants to see my Book of Days. I tell him no. He pleads with me like a child hungry for a sweet. At last I let him read two pages where his name does not appear. When he tries to turn the page I snatch it from him. He says you have a graceful hand. I tell him I learned it from the general's wife. She must be a very good teacher he says. I like the way you notice things, did she teach you that? She said to write down anything I want but she never sees it. Only you see it. He says I am truly honored. Then his eyes grow soft.

My own heart is touched. I hold back my tears. He says what is it. Now it is your turn I say. Indeed it is he says. He opens his bag and shows me a notebook like mine, the same size, covered with blue cloth. You see Nani we think the same you and I. He laughs and says but I have nothing to hide. Read it. Start anywhere you want.

I open in the middle and see the lines of black ink, English words with many high loops and smooth lines but writing of Hawaiian things. It is a story of Pele the fire goddess and her search for a home. These are notes for my book of tales and legends he says. The story is much longer than you see here. And he tells it to me then.

It is a story of fire and water. Pele had stopped first on the tiny northern island called Nihoa and with her digging stick scooped out a pit and filled it with fire, but waters sent by the sea goddess soon rushed to cover it. Pele moved south to Kaua'i and dug another fire pit, only to have the sea rush in. And in this way she moved ever southward until she reached the biggest island, Hawai'i, where she finally made a home that cannot be reached by the waters of the sea, where her volcanic fires burn to this very day.

Nani watched the king as he told this story. From the verandah of the white bungalow at the edge of the valley that climbed into the mountains behind the town, he looked out into the forest and somehow past the forest, as if toward a place where the sea goddess might appear. It was a faraway gaze she'd seen in the faces of her storytelling elders during the firelit nights of her childhood. Yet it wasn't the same look, since it had been moistened by drink. On this day he'd started drinking early and went on sipping wine through the afternoon. Nani too was sipping from a glass, but lightly, wary of liquor. At the rancheria whiskey made her uncles crazy. A mad dog gets inside them, her auntie used to say. Their fighting, their lurching was the mad dog on the loose. As the months went by, Kawika was drinking more and more, though never enough to make him crazy or mean. The wine, the ale, the champagne, the brandy only gave him a larger laugh, sometimes a louder, more insistent voice, made his stories longer, his eyes more amorous.

He removed his shirt and lay out flat on the long settee, which meant he wanted to feel again her hands upon his back. As she dug her fingers in, Nani remembered a story she'd heard many times from her mother and her grandmother, of water rushing in to cover the land. It was another story she'd been told never to repeat outside the tribe. But she knew how much it would please him, and she liked to please him, because his enjoyment was so complete. He hungered for stories the way he hungered for food and drink and love.

As a child, Nani told him, she often went walking with her mother. Once they stopped on a high ridge where they could see the whole valley below, to the west the far mountains, and the long river shining in the sunlight. And her mother told her that in the early time waters rushed in to cover everything, making a great sea between the ranges. All the people drowned, except for two, who escaped to higher ground. From these two the tribe increased again, until one day there came a wise chief who began to wonder why water still covered the valley. For nine days he fasted, thinking about the water. In those nine days he was made stronger, so no arrow could pierce him, no enemy could kill him. This powerful chief called out to Great Man asking him to remove the waters. And when Great Man heard his call, he tore open the mountains to the west so the waters could flow out and rejoin the ocean, and the flowing of this water is how the wide river that still moves through the valley began.

The king's eyes were wide with merriment. "I have seen that river!"

"Yes."

"We saw it from the train!"

"Yes. Now it is the Sacramento."

He sat up and stepped to the railing, barefooted, wearing only his white trousers and a necklace of polished black kukui nuts, and addressed the lawn.

"And where the waters flowed out, we have seen that too."

"When did we see it, Kawika?"

"When we left San Francisco. Do you remember how our ship sailed through the place where the mountains are divided? Do you remember how we felt the tide and followed the waters right out into the great ocean?"

She hadn't made this connection. It lit a flame in her mind. Her scalp tingled. "Yes. You called it the Golden Gate."

"Americans named it the Golden Gate. But once it had another name. Do you remember it?"

"No. I never heard it."

"Ah, Nani, do you see how quickly things slip away? We must not forget the names."

He spoke now as if a crowd had gathered on the sloping lawn.

"We must not forget the stories! We must not forget the lessons of the older time! Our ancestors were wise teachers, and yet so many of our people are forgetting. . . ."

With arms outstretched he exhorted the trees beyond the lawn.

"They would rather listen to the white man's story. They believe the preachers who tell them there is only one true story and you only find it in the Bible!"

His voice grew louder as he proclaimed, "I have been to Egypt! Do you hear me? I have seen the Pyramids. I have seen where the Israelites set out upon their journey to the Holy Land. Their story is a great story. But it is only one story. Our people made historic journeys too! Do you follow me, Nani?"

She did not follow him. Not quite. Whenever he raised his voice she'd learned to be still and wait him out. It was the drink talking, she told herself. Only later, much later, years later, would she begin to understand what he said that day, when she finally took it upon herself to follow his example and try to make a record of all her mother told her. On that afternoon she scarcely grasped the meaning of his words, but she could read the sound. She joined him at the rail, curled an arm around his bare waist, and they stood a while in the upland breeze.

"In the church," she said at last, "the preachers always shout."

He looked down at her with narrowed eyes, as if ready to be hurt. "Why do you say that? Do I sound like a preacher?"

"On the street I hear men argue, the white sailors. They always shout. They think the one who shouts the most will be the winner."

He liked this. He laid an arm across her shoulders. "You are right. Preachers shout at us as if we cannot hear. It is the same in the legislature. There you have a room full of preachers."

"My father did not raise his voice. Yet when he spoke everyone listened."

"That is the Hawaiian way. But in the halls of government, can you guess who has the loudest voice?"

"Yes, I can guess."

"And who do you guess?"

She didn't want to say the name, but she said it. "Mr. Peabody."

"Exactly so! Giles Peabody will leap to his feet. He will shout and wave his arms and pound upon the table. Soon all the others give up."

"This is why you raise your voice."

Suddenly he looked sober, nodding. "Maybe so, Nani, maybe so."

"You want him to hear you."

"And yet he does not listen. What am I to do with him?" Searching eyes roamed the lawn and the verandah as if he'd forgotten something of great importance. "He is like a barking dog who cannot stop himself."

"You are the king, Kawika. You can do anything you want."

"Ah, Nani, if only it were so."

She smoothed a hand up and down his back. "Do not think about him now. He is barking somewhere else today. He is not here."

He pulled her close and looked long into her eyes, amorous again. She still wore a lei of pink carnations and the floor-length dress she'd arrived in, the high-neck *mu'u-mu'u* that a respectable island woman was expected to wear in public and that the king took great delight in. He liked to lift its hem and, as if for the first time, peek underneath, explore what lurked beneath the veils of propriety. Now he lifted off her carnation lei. He unbuttoned the top buttons at the back of her neck. His low and vibrant voice, a soothing murmur, enfolded her. "How do you know so much about me?"

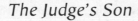

The Judge's Son

I am guessing that he took her advice that day and for a while put Peabody out of his mind, or tried to. Though he told Nani about the manic display, he didn't tell her why the red-haired lawyer had been shouting in the legislature, didn't tell her he'd raised his voice and slammed a fist upon his desk while faulting the king, as he regularly did. Once again it had been the treaty. Once again the senators in Washington had considered renewing it for another seven years. Once again they'd voted no, holding out for the long-awaited clause that would grant an exclusive hold on the Pearl River basin. This nearly landlocked lagoon was seen as a key to America's expansion farther west.

With balled fists and fevered eyes Peabody had marched up and down the aisle. "We need this guarantee that our sugar can be free of tariffs! One harbor is a small price to pay! I cannot believe my ears when I hear our beloved monarch say no! He vows to veto any such proposal! Over my dead body, says the king. And I have to ask you all, How are we supposed to govern? Of what use is a governing body when the king himself is a hindrance to the health and well-being of his own kingdom?"

At every session he fumed and fulminated, his tirades fueled by a resentment of the veto power, by the king's stubborn refusal to trade away any parcel of his homeland, by a personal resentment of the king himself.

I have said that John Sutter was often on my mind as I pored over Nani's account of her years in Honolulu. In those days the islands were awash with men whose dreams were much like Sutter's, men who dreamed of sprawling croplands and isolated fiefdoms, eager to control large and productive bodies of land that had long been occupied by native peoples.

By Kalakaua's time the missionary families had spawned many sons and grandsons, men who'd come of age with a sense of ownership that ran much deeper than the deeds of trust and writs of reconveyance their fathers had acquired as the congregations swelled. They came of age with a belief that these islands were theirs by a kind of divine right, not only the ranches and plantations they'd grown up on but the entire archipelago, its mountains, its plains, its forests and river valleys and sandy shores. In their hearts these sons and grandsons believed they alone, as chosen stewards, knew what was best for Hawai'i and its people.

And so by the 1880s a battle had been launched. It was not going to be a military battle, not yet, not for years to come, since neither side held any weapons to speak of, nor much inclination to resort to weapons. It started as a tropical tug-of-war between the palace and the back room of a downtown law office where a dozen men gathered every week or so, men who shared a vision of a new Hawai'i governed by the landed whites. While they laid plans to capture more seats in the legislature, they set out to undermine the credibility of the king, planting stories about him, his excesses, his pagan habits—whether true or half true or untrue, it didn't matter—and letting them spread like a poisoning mist.

One such story revived a dormant rumor that Kalakaua's true father was an immigrant from Jamaica. A few months after the coronation it turned up in an obscure journal published once or twice a year. Over time the story would evolve from a leak to an eyebrow-raiser to a widely whispered question to common knowledge. Much later, when the king was long gone, it came to light that this particular Jamaican had landed in Hawai'i some thirteen years after the king was born. By then the story had entered the swirl of popular legend and gossip traded late at night to become a shard of tabloid biography you hear repeated to this very day. Attributed to one Garrison Blade, "A Correspondent," the piece was titled "The Royal Line":

> It has come to our attention that the king's paternity may be in doubt. According to startling reports now in circulation throughout Honolulu, his actual father was not a chieftain with a long and venerable lineage, as has been repeatedly and noisily claimed. He was, in fact, from the Caribbean island of Jamaica, a barber by trade, said to be of African and Spanish descent, and notorious in his day for many liaisons with highborn Hawaiian women who found his advances too attractive to resist.

Among these—or so it has been more than once observed
—was the king's dear mother, God rest her soul, who soon
afterward found herself great with child. If true, this might
explain why our beloved monarch bears only the slightest
resemblance to any of his brothers and sisters. It might
explain, as well, his preference for the barbaric hula, which
resembles nothing so much as some depraved rite trans-
ported to these shores from the Dark Continent.

An impulsive and sentimental man, Kalakaua wasn't nearly mean
enough to cope with the guerrilla tactics of those conspiring to do him
in. He didn't mount a counterattack or demand a retraction. It appears
that he never gave them the satisfaction of knowing he'd even read the
piece. According to Nani, his first response was to chant a portion of his
own genealogy, his voice low and muted, as if chanting for himself, as a
way to reassure himself. In a characteristic move, he established a society
to preserve the lineages and lore of native families. It was the kind of gesture that endeared him to Hawaiians, another sign of his regard for their
traditions. For his white opponents it was a sign of weakness, another
meaningless show, more evidence of a soft-minded leader misusing public funds.

He was not a vengeful man. Trained in the martial arts, he loved to
reminisce about the warriors of old, but he didn't have the ruthless
nature that had allowed Kamehameha the First to unite all the islands
under a single rule. Kamehameha executed many rival chiefs. He had to
okay the slaughter of thousands of warriors and commoners. His bloody
campaigns wiped out whole villages. Kalakaua was incapable of such
strategies or anything close to them. He was a scholar first, a man of letters, inclining toward the study of law, the classics, philosophy and music.
As a younger man he'd published newspapers in Honolulu. He edited
the first Hawaiian language daily. Later on he made the first written
record of "The Kumulipo," the great Pacific creation story describing
the first swirl of light from the void, the naming of the many creatures
inhabiting his island world. He would have made a fine poet laureate. As
a king he was at the mercy of these tenacious and driven missionary
descendants.

Consider Giles. In all likelihood it was he who penned "The Royal
Line." While no one recognized the author's name, many recognized the
style, leading to speculation that he'd bribed the threadbare publisher to
run the piece. In my pursuit of Nani's story I've had to delve into his

story too, and I confess it is tempting to demonize Giles Peabody, his attitudes in our day seem so harmful and extreme. Yet how far can you really fault a man for inhaling something that had been in the air he breathed since infancy?

He grew up on Maui, the son of a feared and land-rich judge, the grandson of a fire-and-brimstone sermonizer, the one they called the Pastor. At thirteen he took an interest in a large-eyed Hawaiian girl, daughter of a field hand who worked on one of his father's sugar plantations. Giles was not a rebellious boy. He knew she was forbidden fruit. He couldn't help himself, his young body melting with delicious and uncontainable lust. They flirted back and forth, met covertly a time or two, and at last were discovered swimming together, their laughter rippling across the placid waters near Lahaina.

Taking his son aside the alarmed father said, "Listen to me, Giles! You cannot ever be seen with this girl again. Do not go near her. If you do, I will fire her father and have the family sent to another island. You don't want that. I don't want that. He is a good worker. I hope you understand my meaning here."

With head bowed, the boy stood as if on the gallows awaiting a noose. His chest ached, his breath came in agonizing gasps.

"They are not like us," the Judge went on. "Your grandfather tried mightily to bring them closer to God, devoted half his life to the task, and you can see them filling up the pews on Sunday morning. But in the end they are a wanton and careless people, and one truly wonders what God has in mind for them. It has been our calling to be sent here to lead them out of the darkness and into the light, if they can see it—if they *will* see it—though nowadays I often ask myself what it will take. . . ."

In his study, high on a slope above the town, looking out through latticed windows toward the nearby island of Lana'i, the Judge quoted Exodus, as he often did, just as Giles's grandfather had quoted it from the pulpit, likening his fate to that of Moses, sent by God, burdened by God, with the task of wandering forty years in a desert in order to deliver his people to a Promised Land. His grandfather, the Pastor, had a thundering voice and a face like Moses must have had, sunburned and bearded white. Now the father's patriarchal eyes held Giles, as the Pastor's eyes once held his congregation, demanding to know if forty years would be nearly long enough to redeem these islanders from themselves.

"You have seen this scar across my forehead," said the Judge. "But do you know from whence it came? It is the handiwork of a kanaka lad who challenged me when I was not much older than you are now, a brutal and cowardly fellow who ran away rather than face the consequences of his action, ran off to California and came to no good there, or so we've heard. Though your grandfather yearned to bring him to justice, it was a welcome riddance. His uncle was Governor of O'ahu at the time, a big beefy kanaka who brought gifts to our family in a feeble attempt to make amends. But I nearly died from the attack, you see. For weeks I lay at death's door. And my father knew the Governor all too well, a scoundrel who used his position to line his pockets and never had a thing in mind but advancing his own interests."

Giles had heard of this episode, though never in much detail. Now the time had come for the Judge to tell him the full story, to hammer home its lesson. For the first time he heard the name. *Keala.* In his father's voice he heard the contempt, the condescension. He saw the tightening jaw, as the serrated, shining scar took on a rosy tint, the bright print a palm's trunk had left upon his father's temple. He watched the Judge's hand rise to touch the scar, as he explained a lifetime of blinding headaches that ever since had flattened him once or twice a month.

A few years later, as an eager law student at Columbia, Giles would hear the chair of the political science department praise the Anglo-Saxon race, its superiority in all areas of law and governance. Example after example would be cited, from every corner of the globe. According to this celebrated professor, the theory of the survival of the fittest, recently put forth by Charles Darwin, applied to both biology and social evolution. "If history has taught us anything," Giles would scribble in his notebook, "it is the successful advance of Teutonic and Anglo-Saxon peoples as the rightful civilizers of the world."

As a specialist in maritime trade he joined a firm in San Francisco. From there he could oversee the West Coast end of the family's investments, the shipping of sugar, the contracts with Bay Area refineries. He thought he had settled in the city. But everything changed with the news that his father had suffered a crippling stroke. Giles reached the islands in time to sit with the Judge and grasp his hand and gaze into eyes beseeching him with some final, unvoiceable plea.

A blood clot had led to a swelling of the brain. For days he drifted in and out of consciousness. The Judge was only fifty-seven. It isn't fair, thought Giles, it isn't right.

After the funeral the physician told him an uncanny pressure had built up just behind the temple, "some sort of vulnerability there, though without an autopsy we can't be sure." In Giles's mind, there was no mystery, no autopsy was required. At the moment of death he'd been seen to lean forward and kiss his father's ever-wounded brow. "Farewell," he murmured. "Fare well."

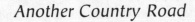

Another Country Road

I'm still not certain how he learned of Nani's background. In a town like Honolulu, where everyone knew something of everyone else's business, it was probably just a matter of time. Sooner or later he would have heard her name. Nosy fellow that he was, it wouldn't have taken long to put two and two together: a mixed-blood woman from California, living with the widowed sister-in-law of the man who'd injured his father, the same widow being a niece-by-marriage to the Governor, who'd helped the assailant escape.

But having learned this much, however long it took, what then was running through Peabody's mind? The boys who'd wrestled on the beach at Honolulu Harbor so long ago were both gone, as was the fort where Keala had found refuge, torn down years back to increase warehouse space beside the busy port. Yet in his mind an old score was still to be settled. Someone should pay. Kanaka treachery had done his father in. And here, by improbable chance, was the daughter of the culprit, consort to the decadent and irresponsible king.

The first time she noticed him watching her he stood alone by a banyan tree on the palace grounds. She recognized his ruddy moustache and muttonchops underneath the wide plantation hat. Even outdoors in the midmorning heat he did not appear to sweat. He stood at ease with one hip cocked, watching her ascend the stairs. She offered no reaction, looked straight ahead until she reached the verandah and stepped into the foyer, the cool protection of polished koa paneling.

Late one afternoon, while downtown shopping for a new notebook and some cloth to make a skirt, she saw him the second time. He stood across the street next to a fruit stand, in the same white suit and white hat, making no attempt to hide, his blue eyes glittering from underneath the brim, seeming to challenge her.

Nani had also put two and two together. From Kawika she'd heard her father's story. From Moana she now heard the story of this famous missionary family, Moana who knew where all the bones were buried, who remembered that the Pastor had been like Jehovah himself, a man of wrath and vindictiveness, traits passed on to the Judge, and then to the Judge's son. Beware of him, Moana told her. "All these years Hawaiians try to share our aloha with this family. All these years they reject it. Sixty years in Hawai'i, and they learn nothing. Look at their faces, Nani. The mouths all pinched, the eyes like shiny stones. They judge you for everything you do, and no forgiveness. The old man, he preached about Jesus and asked us to forgive. But he did not forgive. Keala's uncle, the Governor, came to him with gifts, and he took the gifts, then he stood up in his pulpit and told the story of Cain and Abel. I still remember it. I was fifteen. Keala was gone. Everybody thought the Pastor's son was going to die, everybody in the whole church crying . . ."

With trembling voice the Pastor reminded them of the original fight, as described in the Book of Genesis. Cain, the firstborn of Adam and Eve, was a farmer. His younger brother, Abel, was a shepherd. One day Cain brought an offering to God, the fruit of his field, some vegetables perhaps. Then Abel brought a sheep to offer. And God looked upon the sheep with greater favor, with more respect, which made Cain very angry. And so he killed his younger brother with a club. When God asked Cain what had happened to Abel, he said he didn't know, he said, "I am not my brother's keeper." God said, "The voice of his blood cries out to me from the ground. And now you, Cain, you are cursed from the earth which has opened her mouth to receive your brother's blood."

With tears burning his parched pink face the Pastor repeated, "The voice of his blood cries out to me, said the Lord! And he punished Cain. He sent him away to wander the earth as a fugitive and a vagabond!"

The Hawaiians knew he was talking about Keala. They watched him lean forward, his grieving eyes ablaze, to proclaim that if any one of them thought another had more favor in the eyes of God, he must not be angry. Do not commit Cain's sin and turn to anger. Try harder to be worthy, he told them, lest God cast you out. And the Hawaiians knew he meant try harder to be like whites, since they too, like Abel, were more favored, and for no reason except that it was God's will.

"You see, Nani, I know this family from way back. That is how the Pastor thought. That is how the Judge thought. Now the Judge's son is next. He is a small man who lives in the shadow of his father. He has no wife. Everybody hoped he would stay a long time in San Francisco. But he did not stay. *Au-we! Au-we!*"

One weekend in early summer a brief report appeared in that same infrequent political journal, under the same byline, "Garrison Blade, A Correspondent":

YET ANOTHER ROYAL WHIM

It comes to our attention that His Majesty has befriended a young woman now residing in this city. Born in California of a Hawaiian man and a Digger Indian, she has been seen waiting on him at Iolani Palace.

Strange as it may seem, she is rumored to be the daughter of a kanaka who fled these islands some years ago. In a violent rage typical of his kind, he had brutally assaulted and left for dead a man who went on to become one of our most distinguished jurists, a man only recently deceased, whose reputation for public service was Jeffersonian in its scope and indeed beyond reproach.

If this report stands the test of further inquiry and proves in the end to be true, it would indeed be another deplorable comment on the already questionable judgment of our monarch, that he would see fit to welcome to these shores the half-breed daughter of a vagabond, a fugitive and a felon.

Someone passed a copy of the journal to Moana, who passed it on to Nani, who had to read it several times, slowed by unfamiliar words. "Vagabond" and "fugitive" were Bible words, Moana reminded her. This was how God cursed Cain.

In the shady cool of her grass house Nani leaned against the motherly bosom and closed her eyes and saw the healer's headband of yellow feathers the day he came to dance around their hut. She heard his piercing birdbone whistle, a mournful note because it didn't rouse Keala from his bed of rabbitskins. She saw her father lying there, calling "Come close, come close," his watery eyes commanding her to place her nose against his nose, her mouth upon his mouth. Once again she tasted his breath, and it occurred to her that Moana too had tasted Keala's breath. She wanted her to talk again about him, Moana who knew things no one else could know.

"I feel robbed," she said at last.

"Do not believe this, Nani."

"I feel too much shame."

"It is just another white man's story."

"Why does he do this? Why does he write these things?"

"He wants to shame the king, not you."

"Others will read it too. The king's sister, she will read it. She does not speak to me. I know she does not like me."

"She knows the true story of your father and why he had to flee. All the Hawaiians know it."

"But how can I stay here now?"

"Do not talk like that. Nothing has changed. Words on the page cannot hurt you."

"He will want me to go away."

"Who? Giles Peabody? Who cares what he wants! These things he writes are all lies!"

"I mean the king. If I go away, then Mr. Peabody cannot write these things."

"Stop it! I will not hear this kind of talk. Come. Today is the day for the *halau* to meet. Help me gather ti leaves to prepare the grove. Under the trees I will chant a healing chant. The dancing will cure you of his lies."

They danced all afternoon and into the night, danced to the drum and Moana's pulsing voice. The next day Nani began again, giving herself to the dances of loss and death and rebirth and renewal, of crashing waves and forests and soaring cliffs and cleansing fire. When Kawika finally summoned her, three days after the article appeared, she had passed through her shame. She knew what she was going to do.

Riding out from Moana's place she took her time, let the horse find its path. What would she tell him? He would smell of drink. He would pace the floor and denounce the journal and curse those conspiring against him, and she would want to be invisible. She had another letter from the General's Wife, with news that her aunt was bedridden now: "We all pray to see you back here in California, sweet Nancy." And that was where she wanted to be, where there were no haughty queens to watch out for, no imperious sisters, no Peabodys to taunt and pester her. She despised Honolulu. Could she tell this to Kawika? I must go home for a visit, she would say. Would he allow it? Would he once again say how much he needed her? Or would he be relieved to have her gone so he could turn to the young woman he'd flirted with on the trip to Maui? Was he already spending time with her in another house, in another valley?

She ducked under a low branch and far ahead saw a patch of blue. All morning it had rained. Now the clouds were passing, rolling on down from the high peaks and across the valley, heading for the lowlands. From overhead the road was shaded and sheltered by its canopy of broad leaves still glistening. She loved this country road with thick-trunk mangoes keeping it cool all day long. It would be hard to leave such a road, to leave Moana's house, hard to leave Moana and the evening fragrance of her grass house, and the troupe of dancers who all were sisters to her. Nani had two families now, one here, one in Kaleponi. Hard to choose which way to go. Maybe she could simply avoid the town and spend all her days out here. Yes, maybe she would become a country girl again.

She was near the trail that cut across the valley when another rider rounded a bend in front of her, a white man cantering along on a horse she hadn't seen out this way. She didn't recognize the rider until she was close enough to see the square jaw, the trimmed whiskers, the arrogant smile. Giles wore riding boots, an open-neck shirt, his wide white hat. He lifted his hat and turned his horse to block her way.

"*Aloha ahiahi.*" (Good afternoon.)

Something insinuating in his voice mocked the language and mocked her. She didn't want to speak to him in Hawaiian, didn't want to speak to him at all.

As if surprised to meet her he said, "Nani Keala."

She shook her head.

"Am I mistaken, then?"

His eyes gleamed with a dark satisfaction. She knew he wasn't on this road by chance.

"Let me pass."

"I beg your pardon?"

"Please move your horse and let me pass."

"Ah, you speak some English."

She tried to push toward the trail but he nudged the animal a pace closer. She glanced past him, up the road leading inland where a foggy drizzle blurred the highest peaks. Looking back the way she'd come, she hoped to see another rider, remembering then a Chinese boy who three times followed her from town, walking far behind. Yes, of course. Peabody had been tracking her, and it would be risky to continue on across the meadow trail. Who knew what might happen if he followed her into the glade beyond the high grass, or followed her until he saw the bungalow—or had the Chinese boy already followed her?—and found a way to bring more shame upon the king, more shame upon the two of them?

She said, "Why are you here?"

"A very good question."

"What do you want?"

"Perhaps I should introduce myself."

"I know who you are."

"In that case I am flattered. Just the other day I came across an article about the king and his Indian girl, and I have hoped we might one day meet."

His sarcasm was too much to bear. She had to fight back tears. "That article was written by you!"

"I believe the author was a fellow named Blade."

"You lied about my father!"

"Ah, you *are* a lively one, just as I have heard."

His appraising and lascivious look filled her with disgust. She tried to turn and head back the way she'd come, and again he moved to block her path. He had a young, fast horse and the skill of a cowboy working a herd. On her steady but aging mare she would never outrun him.

"Let me pass."

"I have a better idea. On such a day as this we should ride together a while. You might help me find my way."

"Find your way!"

"Your English is surprisingly good, you know. I wasn't prepared for that."

"You are crazy."

"The article in question makes reference to my father, and if I am not mistaken, to your father as well."

"How could you call him a vagabond? He was not a vagabond. . . ."

"Such a long time ago. And both of them gone. Yet we two are somehow bound by their youthful deeds. Don't you agree? Do you feel that bond?"

He was leaning forward in his saddle with a cruel smile that filled her with confusion. Everything he said seemed to mock and diminish her, the very sound of his words.

She shook her head. "My father died many years ago. Now yours is also gone. We have both lost our fathers. Why then do you insult the dead?"

This caught him off guard. In his face nothing moved, his gaze like shiny stones fixed upon her, his thin smile carved in wood. On that country road by the side of a rain-bright meadow, nothing moved until Peabody blinked. In his blue eyes she saw a skin of moisture, and in that moment she saw him, she saw through the smirk. She knew his loss. She knew what it was to lose a father, to sit beside him in the final hours, to see the last light leave his eyes. She saw that Giles had not found a way to speak his grief. He still carried all of it.

In spite of her wariness Nani said, "I loved my father. I know you loved yours."

She spoke so softly he had to lean closer to hear her say, "My father called me to him and into me he breathed his breath. I sat by him until he died. Then I had to leave our village in the mountains. I was twelve years old. It was the end of my childhood."

Now the man who never blinked was blinking back the wetness. The man who seldom broke a sweat turned away to wipe his brow. As he gazed toward the misty peaks he inhaled deeply. She watched his shoulders rise. She felt his heart move, and within herself she felt a sudden, unexpected willingness to do as he suggested, to ride with him a while.

As she would record years later, she sat there trembling, afraid of what he might say next. Evidently he could not look at her again. Perhaps a minute passed. He didn't move. Nani flicked her reins and turned around, heading away from the meadow, listening for the clop of hooves on the trail behind her. She heard nothing. She urged the mare to pick up speed. She didn't look back.

From the moment I saw him I started to tremble. I tremble again as I write this. What a narrow escape. When he said those things in the paper it was like stealing. He wanted to steal my father. By the meadow he wanted to take something else but he did not know how to do it. He was frozen. For years when I thought about Giles Peabody I would see him on his horse like a man carved in stone. He could not move. I thought I was afraid of him. Now I know I was afraid of myself. I did not want to be in the same town with such a man. I did not want to be on the same island, or in the same ocean.

Sometimes I think about the first day I saw him, when he barged in upon Kawika. I remember the blue eyes that wanted to pierce him and wanted to devour him too. He believed being white gave him the power to do such things. The first white man I ever saw had those eyes. They made me tremble. Men like that want too much. They want everything. Kawika knew this though he never spoke of it to me. It was too soon for him to tell me of the threats against his life by men who thought the islands belonged to them.

Kawika needed soldiers to protect him everywhere he went. I see that now. He would not live that way. What is life, he used to say, if you must be ruled by fear? One time he made me laugh. He pranced back and forth like a captain on a deck and slapped his hands against his chest and said I am the only king in history to travel all the way around the world and I did so without a bodyguard.

Articles of Faith

San Francisco

Not long after my ghostly breakfast at the Palace Hotel, I paid another visit to the public library, the main branch downtown, the square granite edifice across the plaza from City Hall. Up on the top floor, beyond the farthest reference desk, I came again to the Special Collections Room, where the rarest, most fragile and treasured documents were shelved behind closed doors. I asked the clerk what they had on Thomas Edison and the West Coast branch of his General Electric Company. Five minutes later he presented me with three folders, a pamphlet, and an early biography, from which I learned that when Edison invented what would become the phonograph, the recording of music was an afterthought, a by-product he himself never took much interest in. Much more important, in his view, was preserving famous voices.

In one folder I came across an address for the Edison Historic Site in West Orange, New Jersey. The next day, by Express Mail, I sent off a letter, wondering if they might have a file somewhere on the contents of early cylinder recordings, or perhaps the actual recordings cut by Mr. Glass in San Francisco in January 1891. "Any information would be greatly appreciated . . ." etc., etc.

I was fishing for whatever I could find. On the day I'd basked in the luminous Garden Court, as I lingered over my second cappuccino, an idea had begun to jell, a suspicion, an as-yet-unanchored hope that the fate of those wax cylinders held a key to the entire story Nani had to tell. If the hotel's records had gone up in flames, that didn't discourage me one bit. If anything, it spurred me on. But why? Why dwell on the final words of a long-dead king from a long-gone kingdom? A century later, what difference did it make? I knew the Hawaiian Islands had been stolen, the monarchy overthrown by force of arms. I knew his role in that theft was still debated, as was every other feature of his mercurial career. But in the fall of 1986, when I embarked upon this quest, his message was but one piece of what intrigued me. There was also Nani's message. I felt compelled to verify her memories. I needed them to be true. I wanted to trust each word in her Book of Days, having come to believe her history was mine too, or a part of it. And then there was Rosa, my newfound oracle, the guide I'd been waiting for years to meet—like her mother, raised part Indian, part Hawaiian, part white—opening for me a legacy I hadn't known was mine. What was I to make of this? What did it mean, halfway through your life, to come upon an unreported gene pool? Would it change me? Was I to be a different person now?

A bizarre linkage was beginning to glimmer, like the glint of an air-craft's night lights moving through the dark, still so far away you don't know if it's a plane or a star or a satellite making its rounds or a visit from another galaxy. These foremothers had become my muses and my beacons. Their stories had become articles of faith. I was like the Bible Belt archaeologist searching Mount Ararat for a place not yet shown on any map.

As I was posting my letters a name sprang to mind, someone I hadn't thought of in years, a fellow halfway around the globe from West Orange who might well have the answer to all my questions. He was a research specialist at the Bishop Museum in Honolulu. During my island-hopping days I'd spent a few hours in his reading room, and we'd ended up having coffee a couple of times. Fussy and methodical, he tended to keep the public at a distance, but he'd warmed to me once he'd learned I'd done some graduate work and knew a bit about the Pacific. When *Sit Still and Listen* was published, with his name prominent on the acknowl-edgments page, I sent him an inscribed copy. I'm still not sure if he liked the book. "You have raised the bar," he said cryptically in his note of thanks, adding that if anything ever came up he could help me with, just let him know.

Early afternoon on the coast is still morning over there in the islands, making it a handy time to call. We chatted a while, catching up—it had been five years—as I trolled for a way to phrase my query. I didn't want to sound underinformed. The Bishop is the major repository for Polyne-sian and Oceanic lore, a brownstone Victorian monument rising from a bluff on the city's outskirts, and Frank the Specialist, who'd grown up on O'ahu, was a fixture there, a master of artifacts, a human encyclopedia.

When at last I broached the reason for my call, his voice lifted with true and almost giddy enthusiasm. I could see him at his desk removing from his fleshy nose the rimless spectacles to clean them with a square of cloth, as he always did when the conversation called upon his expertise. He was a broad, beefy man with the body of a wrestler, thick arms, thick neck, and the card-catalogue habits of a librarian, a possessive shepherd of the museum's many precious holdings. He wore gabardine slacks and extra-large aloha shirts, not the flashy, flowery polyester kind you find in Waikiki but the subtler kind, the floral patterns subdued, made of cotton, for the Honolulu professional who prefers a casual style yet wants to be taken seriously.

Not only did he know about the king's recording session, the cylinder itself, he gloated, was right there inside the museum, one of their treasures. I asked if anyone remembered how it had reached the Bishop, and Frank had the whole story in his head.

It had followed the king's coffin by a couple of weeks. At the time only one person in all of Hawai'i knew how to operate Edison's elaborate machine. Thanks to him the recording was played back and heard several times, then somehow it became his, perhaps after the fall of the monarchy and the gutting of Iolani Palace, when so many royal possessions disappeared, to be dispersed throughout the city. For thirty years the cylinder sat on a shelf in the home of this early audiophile, unplayed, forgotten, until he finally donated it to the museum, where it had remained ever since, safe and secure inside a locked cabinet in a locked storage room that was climate controlled.

"And what about the sound? Anything still audible?"

"When we first acquired it," said Frank, "the grooves were so worn you could barely hear a word. But as I'm sure you know, there's been a lot of new interest over here in the last days of the monarchy, the transfer of power, whether it was legal or illegal, who stole what, who said what to whom and when, and where. Not long ago we sent the cylinder to a high-end lab in Syracuse, New York, to have it tested. They put their best people on it and according to them the sound was gone. In any event, the king did not really say that much. '*Aloha kaua*' and a couple of other things, general greetings, nothing very dramatic . . ."

"When you say 'a lot of new interest,' what does that mean?"

"Oh, you know—local people looking again at the historical record, looking at who wrote the books we read today, looking at whose stories got told and whose didn't. There was pressure to check out the cylinder because wild rumors were circulating about what Kalakaua said in San

Francisco. His words had been suppressed—some folks were claiming—or mistranslated. The winners always get to write the history books, people said, and the haole translators only tell us what they want us to hear and leave out all the meat. . . ."

Across my arms I felt a rush of chickenskin, an electric chill, and a rising of the neck hairs. "What if there'd been another recording? Would that make a difference?"

"Another what?"

"Suppose Kalakaua recorded two cylinders for the Edison Company, but only one of them reached Honolulu."

"I'm not sure I follow this, Dan. . . ."

"Just tell me if you've heard anything like this, seen it mentioned anywhere, even as a mad and reckless guess."

I could see the skepticism bunching his librarian's brow, as he sat beside his wall of wide, flat drawers with prints and maps of all the archipelagoes, as he faced his wall of old-time oaken cabinets with their rows of card-sized drawers where catalogued knowledge of the Hawaiian chain was laid out in alphabetical order, a century of cards, an ocean of cards.

"It's an interesting idea," he said at last. "Now that I think of it, a fascinating thought. But no. It's nothing I've heard about or read about. Where the hell is this coming from anyway?"

Could I tell him it was a family story that had turned up in a low-budget trailer court outside Sacramento?

"I have this talk show now. In Berkeley."

"No kidding."

"One of my callers brought it up."

"Talk shows," said Frank with a knowing chuckle. "Today's litmus test. Our new polling booth. I'll bet you're good at it."

"I'm having a good time."

"But this isn't much to go on."

"It's why I called you."

"Well, I'm intrigued, needless to say. If you hear any more about this, you let me know. That would be a bombshell over here in the islands. That would be like finding the bones of Captain Cook."

I asked him if visitors were ever allowed into the climate-controlled storage room. There wasn't much to see, he said—a brown roll of wax in a cardboard tube with Thomas Edison's name on it—but in my case he might give me a peek, next time I was over there.

Her Floating Mind

For Frank it was a point of honor to know where every arcane document was stored, to have the backstory on every loose fragment of Pacific memorabilia. If he hadn't heard of a second wax roll, then no one had, and this was not a good sign. I needed to talk again with Rosa. Had she told me all she knew?

It must have been a couple of weeks after she came on my show when I drove out there and took her to a place called Shorty's Diner, her favorite hangout. Shorty served up a smoked salmon sandwich that she liked and kept a few Hank Williams tunes in the jukebox, along with some Elvis and Merle Haggard and Patsy Cline. One booth by the window—red leatherette with stitched padding—might as well have had a permanent placard saying RESERVED FOR ROSA. I brought along a volume from the Book of Days and read passages aloud to her, entries she'd never found the time to read but now savored and consumed, listening with eyes shut like a child at story hour as the words of her mother came channeling through her newfound grandson.

"Yes," she said, "I think I heard about that once before."

And, "Hey, Sheridan, this is news to me."

And, "Thanks for reading that. I just remembered a picture she showed me once. Let's go back. I wonder if I still have it in a box somewhere. . . . No, wait . . . did I put a shopping bag in the car?"

"It's right there next to you."

A near smile crossed her face, amused, apologetic. "I guess my mind floats around a lot. I thought we left it in the car."

I'd been waiting for her to get to this. Twice I'd almost asked, "What's in the bag?" but held my tongue, remembering that with Rosa it was better not to ask, better to allow the unchartable flow of what could be said or not-said.

Two words were printed on the heavy, wrinkled paper:

MAMA'S STUFF

I didn't ask her where she'd found the bag or how some picture of its contents might have come floating into view.

Inside were six smaller paper bags, so brittle the first began to tear as I lifted it. They held six blue notebooks, their fading covers scuffed and worn. As I scanned the topmost volume, I was floating too. Nani had numbered them Seven through Twelve, each containing a hundred pages, both sides covered with lines of script in purple ink, the first entry from February 1891, a month after the king died, continuing off and on for over forty years.

"Rosa, what an amazing find!"

"That mother of mine was a busy girl."

She sat next to me on the leatherette seat. Half-shut Venetian blinds screened out most of the midday sun, striping her brown face with light and shadow, a face that showed the long journey of her eighty-six years, but in her eyes there flickered a glint I hadn't seen before. Was it a schemer's glint? For an instant I wondered if this shopping bag full of Nani's "days" had actually been "forgotten."

She said, "Read some of it."

"Right now?"

"Pick out a page. I like to hear you."

Flipping through Volume Twelve I had opened to an entry with the dateline, "Sheridan, California. October 10, 1932." I began to read:

Tom and Rosa had a baby boy. They named him for this town. I gave him a Hawaiian name too. Sheridan Keala Wadell. Keala means the way or the path. I hold him in my arms and walk out into the yard where the wind is warm today and the mountains are clear on both sides of the valley. Tears of joy come down. My first grandson. I already see papa in his face. I see papa's hands. Sheridan Keala.

The entry ended there. In the diner it was suddenly quiet. All the lunch customers but us had left. The last quarter had played its way through the jukebox. Shorty was out back having a smoke. It was a reverent quiet, as if we sat alone in the shaded research room of an empty library.

At last she said, "Thank you, Sheridan."

"You want me to read some more?"

"Not now. That's plenty. I have to think about that. I remember those days when she came down to stay with us a while. My dad had already passed away, so she had plenty of time to help out. I remember she had her notebook and would write things in it but I never knew what, I was so busy with the kids and Tom working such long hours at the ranch . . ."

I saw moisture under her eyes. A faint quiver burred her voice. "You keep all these," she said. "Keep them with the others. You can come back another time and read me some more."

"This could be the whole story of the rest of Nani's life."

"Well, then, you come back as soon as you can and tell me what you find."

The same hooded sidelong glance caused me to wonder again if old age and forgetfulness accounted for the rediscovery of this shopping bag and its unexpected treasure. Or could it be something else? A matter of trust, perhaps? Was Rosa passing things on to me as they came to her attention? Or was she parceling them out, a photo here, a package there, a piece or two at a time, while she watched and listened?

Though she loved me and saw me as a rightful heir to all this family lore, was there still a need to measure my intention? Perhaps this was what I saw in my grandmother's eyes: a hint of the trickster. I wasn't sure. Before I met Rosa, I'd never spent much time around a person of her age. I couldn't quite tell.

The floating mind?

The wily mind?

Some of both?

The Man from Baltimore

I wanted to open any door or window that might shed light on Nani's story and on the king's last days. I'd written to the Edison Historic Site. I'd picked the brain of Frank the Specialist. I'd gone again to the Riverside Trailer Court, hoping Rosa might have more to tell. Now six more volumes in Nani's hand were stacked beside me on the passenger seat, and as a kind of bonus, almost by chance, I'd learned the rest of my father's name—Keala, the way, the path. But was it chance? And was it mere coincidence that as I barreled south on 80, bound for Berkeley, I happened to be crossing the bridge at Carquinez Straits, right above the water where my great-great-grandfather once steered John Sutter's pinnace through a thousand swimming elk, when it came to me: Why can't I put this to my listeners? "Imagine the air around us," the psychic said, "filled with unheard voices from all the stations on your AM and FM dial." I could send out a general call for any kind of lead, old or new, a plea for rumors, hearsay, scholarly opinion, fading memories no matter how sketchy, feeble or deranged.

This was, please remember, at the very end of what many now regard as the primitive era of communication, when letters were still being written on paper and callers expected an actual person to answer the telephone. I'd only recently had an answering machine installed in my apartment. According to Julie, the personal computer was soon to become a household appliance, and the Internet too. Before long, she said, we'd all be able to enter words and names at random and get free information from a galaxy of sites. It was a heady thought. Punch in "Kalakaua," "Thomas Edison," "talking machine," "wax cylinder," "Palace Hotel," up come the search reports and you never have to leave the house. But meanwhile, and in advance of that, I had another kind of database, thanks to KRUX. I had come to rely on my wide web of listeners to give me what I was searching for, as well as what I did not yet know I was searching for. Hadn't Rosa come to me this way, unsolicited yet eagerly welcomed? Hadn't the Palace Hotel come to me this way, thanks to Quincy, whose part-Hawaiian mother called him once a week? Who knew what else was out there waiting to be summoned?

I'd given myself an early start from Rosa's, hoping to meet a man who was flying in from Baltimore. His name was Roy Wurlitzer, the new CEO of Argonaut Media Group, in town to visit the station, meet with our board of directors, and be around for most of the afternoon, or so I'd heard. As it turned out, I almost missed him.

A black Chrysler with tinted windows and an escort driver was parked in the No Parking slot. The fellow then moving across the sidewalk toward the open rear door had to be him. I introduced myself. His direct and never-blinking gaze came with a ready handshake, and in his hand I felt a strength I hadn't expected. A low-key muscularity pushed at the sleeves and sporty collar of his Italian silk shirt. I figured he played tennis and swam a bit, had a weight room somewhere.

"Sheridan Brody," he said. *"Sit Still and Listen."*

"You know the show."

"I've heard some tapes. Intriguing stuff, I must say. And what's the word? . . . Eclectic?"

He could have been a model for an *Esquire* fashion ad, a dapper and Napoleonic fellow with glistening dark hair combed straight back from a high forehead, and eyes of a startling and unforgettable blue. A thick black moustache was trimmed to arch his mouth, adding more drama to an already dramatic smile, a magazine cover smile.

"I suppose we cast a wide net," I said.

"And so your audience must be . . ."

"They come from all walks of life. I don't mind saying we've built up a sizable following."

"That's what we like to hear," said Roy with an approving nod and something playfully fraternal in the lift of his black moustache. "Should I get your autograph while I have the chance?"

"No autographs until after the show. I have to save my strength."

His light laugh was charming, intimate, as if drawing me into a chosen circle.

"And you're on tonight," he said, "if I'm not mistaken."

"In about an hour and a half."

"Maybe I'll have the chance to catch some of it."

Inside the car the driver, waiting stoically behind the wheel, glanced at his watch.

"In that case," I said, "I'd better get moving. I have some setting up to do."

As they pulled away from the curb I saw him lean forward and speak to the driver. Then they were gone, heading for San Jose, as I soon learned, to check out another station he'd recently acquired. Alone beside the now vacant No Parking zone, I was strangely shaken by this brief exchange. It occurred to me that Roy moved like a boxer, like a welterweight who'd been working out relentlessly and was ready to climb into the ring, his arms swinging at his sides, his hands thickened by laced-up gloves and held away from his body. I imagined that every moment of Roy's life was like that: ready to climb into the ring.

When negotiations began, Argonaut had promised nothing would change but the letterhead. And Sandy had trusted the guy who made that promise, a man who'd grown up in broadcasting, older than Roy by thirty years. He'd taken over his father's hometown station, parlayed it into a midsize media empire, and still believed in radio, enjoyed the company of what he called "radio people." The buyout was all but completed when that fellow lost control of the company it took him a lifetime to build. He'd been reassigned as acting chairman, while Roy Wurlitzer moved over from marketing to replace him as CEO.

Roy was not a radio person. He had an MBA from Wharton. Under his command Argonaut was already poised to merge with another, larger conglomerate, leaving Sandy with a case of the jitters, hovering over every feature of our programming like a mother hen worried that one of her chicks might scamper off. He hadn't forgotten the night I brought Rosa onto the show and tried ninety seconds of on-air silence. In his memory that loomed as a warning sign, flashing red. Unmoved by the calls and thank-you cards that followed (enough to fill a manila envelope), he still called it "risky radio," too far "over the line."

"And what are we risking?" I would ask, trying to tease him toward a lighter mood, tease out the brave and unflinching Sandy I'd once known. "Where exactly is the line?"

He would never say for sure.

I knew his salary was going up. I did not yet know all he had covertly agreed to. I did not then know he'd been on the phone daily to Baltimore, fielding memos on changes in format and personnel. While three of our directors had resigned in protest when the buyout was first agreed to, I did not fully grasp how power within the board had shifted, the new chair being a fellow Sandy had never liked, a loan officer from a local bank brought in for his "fiscal discretion." I did not yet know board members were receiving market reports and poll results, softening them up for their first audience with the new chief exec. I have called Roy Napoleonic. "Sutteresque" might be closer to the truth, since he too saw the West Coast as a certain kind of wide-open terrain. He too had cannons at the ready, to be fired at the optimum moment. And he too had made no promises to anyone.

The Yoga of Radio

Inside the station it was too quiet. I stood still and listened. Something was missing. Usually you can hear the muted voices, the studio chatter, the Bay Area report, the touring author, the jazz DJ reminding you that Django Reinhardt, the great French/Gypsy guitarist, had only two usable fingers on his fretting hand. With the in-house speakers off, it was like the lobby of a funeral home. I stuck my head in the office door, where Lorene the receptionist was labeling some file folders, Lorene from Austin, in her rodeo shirt and snug jeans. My honky-tonk angel.

"Are we off the air?"

"Not yet," she said.

"What's that supposed to mean?"

"You'll need to ask Sandy."

"And is he here?"

"He just left."

"Is he coming back?"

"He wouldn't say."

"How about Julie?"

"Just waiting for you, darlin'. Just waiting for you."

And she was—at her station, surrounded by all the LPs of the past thirty years, her headphones, her eyes shell-shocked and angry.

"Where were you?" she said, like a wife to the husband sneaking in at 2 a.m.

"Where *was* I? I'm an hour early!"

"Why am I always the one?"

"The one what? You look like somebody just stole your car."

"You are *never* here when the shit hits the fan!"

"What's going on? Did Sandy have his meeting?"

"That spineless bastard is selling us out. And I was the only one here to listen to it. All he cares about is his condo and his parking privileges and his portfolio. . . ."

Her eyes were blazing. She was ready to execute him. I'd seen this look before, knew it was pointless to try calming her down, though I have to confess these eyes still took me by surprise—due in part, I suppose, to some latent notion I'd once had. I still don't know where it got started, this legend of the docile and submissive Asian female. In all my travels I have yet to meet one, and certainly there was none of that in Julie. It's tempting to think it had been canceled out by something on the Mexican side. But her mother was the same way, having left Okinawa and come to the U.S. when she did because none of the prevailing legends of female behavior fit the way she wanted to live her life.

Julie had to talk it out, shout it out, and I was there to be shouted at. It's an important role, once you come to understand it, once you see it's nothing you have to take personally. With someone like Julie, shouting back will get you nowhere. You listen. You wait her out, maybe you learn something.

After Roy met with the board they'd all gone around the corner to the Last Resort for drinks, then Sandy and Roy came back to the station, Sandy to start Lorene putting a staff meeting together, Roy to meet his driver. Though he seemed to be in a great rush, the sight of Julie's lissome stride through the lobby slowed him down. When Sandy—pale as ashes—told him she produced the show they'd just been talking about, Roy began to fill her in on what was soon to happen at KRUX.

"It was like he thought I'd be flattered to hear all this coming straight from him!"

Nothing radical, Roy told her. Just a few modifications to expand the core audience. Musically, we move toward the center. For instance, no more jazz. No more classical. No more blues. There'll be more soft rock, along with more current-events features feeding in from Argonaut's news hub back in Illinois. And a number of shows will have to shift their focus, or perhaps be replaced, or dropped. Not the movie review, of course. That stays. Everybody loves the movies. But *Sit Still and Listen* is a good example of what he's getting at. A bit "slippery," in Roy's view, "outside their new parameters."

Julie was waving her headset like a cat-o'-nine-tails flailing invisible necks and shoulders. "Can you believe it, Danny? New parameters! The next thing I know, he tells me his marketing people think we need a new kind of host, somebody who can handle a different range of material. I said, What kind of material? We already have great material! Then he aimed his blue eyes at me, filled with heartfelt sincerity. If it was entirely up to me, he says, I wouldn't change a thing around here. It's our people in marketing. And please understand that what I'm saying doesn't necessarily involve you, Julie. The way you handle things on the technical side, everyone's happy. It's on the content side. They have done audience polls all across the land and what builds the listener base is cooking and restaurants and sports personalities and above all controversy. And I say to him, Roy, we have plenty of controversy. Just the other night we had a big debate on selenium leaching into wetlands over in the Central Valley, into a game preserve where it's killing off the wildlife. Roy shakes his head. You want to have an ear for the topic that will touch a nerve, he says, and stir the blood. Aha, say I, you mean the outrage of the day, the story that gets everybody shouting. And with his winning smile he tells me it's about meeting people where they live. No, I tell him, you mean where their worst anxieties live. Then he is looking at me like a casting director or something and I am auditioning for a part. This will have to be Sheridan's last week, he says, though he'll stay on the payroll for one more month. We're not punitive people, we just want to bring radio into the late twentieth century. I was trying to be cordial, but I was ready to strangle him. I could have. I should have. I could have hurt him too. I'm taller than he is. I said, That sounds like tabloid radio. You open with today's case of police brutality, you fan the flames of urban dread, then soothe the nerves for a while with a new way to pep up the marinara sauce! And all he does is smile again, this time with a look—I swear, it was one of those looks of appraisal you get at a cocktail party, checking me out like a suit of clothes he has finally decided to buy and now he's ready to make his move—and he says, I like your spirit, Julie. I wish I didn't have to run. Depending on how things work out here, maybe we could bring you back to Baltimore. We're going to need some new people in production. I'll be in touch, he says, slipping me his card. Then he's on his way across the lobby, and it's me and Sandy, who is on the verge of tears.

"I say, Sandy, *Sit Still and Listen* is your best show. We can't just roll over for this dude. Julie, he says, I'm trying to stay afloat here. You have no idea what these people are like. Then buy back the station, I say, tell him your listeners won't stand for this. He can't look at me. He looks at the blank wall like it's a window with a view, and you know what he says next? Roy has already found a new host! I don't know his name yet, Sandy says, but he starts on Monday. Goddam it, I say, you can't do this!

Dan has a contract. Not with the new ownership boys, he says. It's a whole new ball game, according to Roy. Tell me what happened at the meeting, I say. Who voted on all this? It was close, he says, it was three to two. And where were you, I say. He still won't look at me. He won't answer. That's when I lost it, Danny. I'm screaming at him, and he stands there like it's what he deserves, his eyes pleading for forgiveness, or maybe pleading with me to keep screaming till he falls over in a heap.

"When I calm down he can hardly talk. Julie, he says, Julie, Julie, Julie, this is the worst day of my life. You can see what kind of a guy Roy is. We thought there was going to be some give-and-take. But that sonof-abitch did not come here to give anything. All he said was this is what we're going to do, then he put it to a vote. If this makes your life more difficult, Roy says to me, if you want to look for work somewhere else, well, Argonaut would understand completely. So they got me by the nuts. I mean, I love Danny like a brother, I really do. But I am not as young as I used to be. Pretty soon I'll be fifty. I have to think about what's up ahead. Then Sandy was gone too, about ten minutes ago, out the side door like a thief in the night."

She slumped back in her chair, her brow damp. The sense of betrayal was so complete, for a moment neither of us knew what more to say or do. How many times had Sandy and I talked about the role of radio, the dialogue between you and your listeners, how profit for its own sake would be the ruin of us all? I thought of calling his apartment, giving him a chance to explain himself. I knew he wouldn't be there, or if there, wouldn't answer. The last thing he wanted to hear was the sound of my reproach. I saw Roy again, out on the sidewalk, the firm grip, the smile, the unswerving gaze, the fraternal banter—his way of saying, "So long, sucker."

A while back I'd met a fellow from the English department at UC-Berkeley. "I have been around campuses for years," he told me, "but I've never seen a place like this. I mean, you're used to people stabbing each other in the back. That just comes with the territory, I guess. But here, they walk right up to you and make eye contact and stab you in the chest."

That's how I was feeling. Stabbed in the chest.

I blamed Roy. He'd forced Sandy into this. Roy was the most dangerous type of profiteer—deceitful, and shameless too. Incapable of shame. Sandy, on the other hand, was consumed with shame. I give him credit for that. At least he could acknowledge what he was doing to me and to the station, and it would surely weigh on him, add another layer of shadow around his burdened eyes. But he could learn to live with the fallout. He wanted his job, his raise, his bonuses, his perks, his leased car.

And what did I want? Well, sooner or later I wanted some satisfaction. Don't get mad, my first dad used to say, get even. (Hank, who'd come out of the war with a Bronze Star and two oak leaf clusters, said don't be ruled by anger.) I also wanted to keep my show. I wasn't giving it up without some kind of stand. Julie felt the same. She didn't have to say it. We were still idealists. We both needed the money, but there was more at stake than a check every couple of weeks. Her head tilted with anticipation, as she waited for me to say what move we should make. In an unvoiced and subliminal way I knew it had to start with the show. Somehow the show itself would be our weapon.

"We're on in thirty minutes."

She nodded. "That's right. We have three shows left. We should use them."

"I'm going to get some audience input."

"After the staff meeting tomorrow we might know more. Plenty of people around here are going to be upset, ready to rebel."

"I can't wait that long."

"Neither can I."

"I am pissed off, Julie. I really feel shit on."

"Tell me about it."

"One thing I know. In times like these you go public."

"I'm with you on that. Go public as soon as possible. For your own protection."

"Prudence, of course, would say give it some time. Give Sandy time to rethink what he's getting himself into."

"Fuck prudence," Julie said. "We don't have that much time. Roy is a hit man. Sandy can't think without some help from us."

"Okay. Okay. I see it now. We have a great guest coming tonight. We start with him, we work with that, make it the best interview we've ever had, remind them why they care . . ."

"Good, Danny. You were born for this."

"But wait. Wait a second. According to Roy, I'm finished here, I'm history. You still have a job. You could lay low, ride this out . . ."

The way she looked at me, I felt my heart expand. The righteous anger in her face dissolved or transmuted into a sweet and naked vulnerability, such as I'd seen only a few times, in those moments of surrender when her clothes fell away in the bedroom and her eyes said, "Here." After two years of overt lust and seductive glances and flirting around and eagerly coupling now and again—wildly coupling, I might add, a fiery igniting that always seemed to come as a miraculous surprise—I saw her as if for the first time. My voice caught in midsentence, thirty minutes before showtime, and my heart opened like a full moon coming out from behind the clouds.

She knew it. Her eyes were embers. Her touch on the back of my hand was like a live wire. She said, "Danny, let's not forget how this show started. We imagined it together. We'll see it through together, I promise you that."

I'm not sure how long we sat looking at each other in the soundless sound studio. It was blissful while it lasted, an interlude of pure communion. No one else around. Nothing in the way. No place to think about making love, so it wasn't about warming up for that. Nor did we kiss. We had kissed hundreds of times, short kisses, farewell and hello kisses, long kisses with tongues roaming all around each other. This was the other kind of touching, a kind I'd only known with her. I wondered if the studio had something to do with it, the surreal intimacy of the task we shared, in these mike-filled spaces, sealed off by acoustic paneling.

I remembered Rosa saying, "She's a keeper, don't let her get away." I didn't want her to get away. Long ago Julie had passed my private companionship exam: could I imagine driving with her all the way across North America in a car? Of course. It would be heaven. But . . . suppose young Toby also came along. What then? Could I imagine crossing the continent with a five-year-old strapped into the backseat? That would make it another kind of expedition. That would be a test. That would turn a lovers' cruise into a family trip.

There was a time when the very talk of starting a family could send me halfway around the world. When I was twenty-seven it came between me and another woman I imagined I might one day marry, and suddenly I was on the plane to Bali. But eight years had passed, and this was different. Whatever roaming still awaited me I wanted Julie by my side. I was ready for Julie and could imagine spending a life with her. I was pretty much ready for fatherhood and family too. I guess biology had caught up with me at last. And yet I was not ready for the glistening and innocent hope in Toby's eyes whenever he saw me coming. When the three of us went somewhere I usually knew what to do: lift him onto the swing and push, buy ice cream cones, skip rocks at the lake. He was hard to resist, a striking kid, with mixed-blood looks that one day would make him quite handsome, the Okinawan and Mexican from Julie's side, some kind of Anglo-European blend from the long-absent guitar player. But the truth was, Toby scared me. At the time I didn't know why, or how much I feared falling for him.

The studio was a kind of rendezvous, a place apart, where we two could be alone together in close proximity for moments like this, when no talk was required, partners and allies in the heat of an evening show when each caller marked another step along what we viewed as "the path of consciousness." That was Julie's phrase, and I thought it sounded right, our agreed-upon goal, our common vision. What was the alternative? Roy had described it perfectly. Controversy for its own sake. Polarize every situation. Provoke loud argument on all sides, and heat the blood.

Roy was right, of course. That *is* what draws the biggest crowds. Polarization is always good for ratings. And hadn't Sandy and I talked about this time and time again? KRUX was not about making a killing. It was about offering another take, another sound, another kind of dialogue. Just the previous night, our guest had reminded us that "yoga" is an ancient word meaning "union." Through control of breath, he said, and regular practice of the asanas, the postures, the mind and body and spirit can find their proper balance. When I asked him, "Can there be a yoga of radio?" he chuckled in a friendly way and said, "Everything in life has its yoga dimension."

When he said that, was Roy Wurlitzer perhaps listening from afar, thinking to himself, "Am I actually paying for this?" Would he be listening tonight, in his tinted-window Chrysler somewhere in Northern California? I hoped so. The very thought quickened my resolve.

Listening to Jazz

Behind the wall-size pane of glass Julie's finger said, "Go."

Music up: "How Long Has This Been Going On?"

Zoot Sims on tenor, Oscar Peterson on keyboard, giving new swing to an old ballad, with only a moment to wonder who's asking the question, Ira Gershwin, who wrote the song, or Julie Moraga, who chose it tonight? Here was something else that drew me toward her: she remembered lyrics, and she thought about them. Phrases stayed in her mind, titles and couplets from the great songs she'd heard her sax-man father play and sing all through her early years. Listening to such stuff is like growing up in a Bible-reading household, as I did. Somewhere on the side of your mind a sound track of verses will be running for the rest of your life. For Julie it was a sound track of jazzy standards: "Paper Moon." "Ain't Misbehavin'." "My Funny Valentine." "How Long Has This Been Going On?"

The tenor fades . . .

"Good evening, folks. Sheridan Brody here. It's the nineteenth of November, 1986, and this is *Sit Still and Listen,* a show we thought would be running well into the next century. For reasons I'll share a little later on, our days here at KRUX are unexpectedly in short supply. If the station has its way, there'll be a new voice in this slot come Monday, with a new show, a new concept. If you want to find out more, stay tuned. Our policy, as always, is full disclosure. Leave no stone unturned, no question unasked, no listener un-listened to. No story half told. It's an all-too-familiar tale that is sure to hold you spellbound, or perhaps have you writing to your congressman. Who knows? But I'm going to save that for a while, since we have a rare guest with us tonight, or soon to be with us.

"Dr. Elwood Perot is a physiologist newly returned from a year in the highlands of central Mexico. He was down there studying tribal uses of chant, incantation and ritual song. His special interest is how such practices affect us at the cellular level. Not so much what the words mean, but what those vibrations can do to us, the voice alone, the voice in concert with other voices. His research has taken him all around the world, to Nepal, to Mongolia, to mosques in Mecca, to Benedictine monasteries. I want you to hear what he has to say because it's about cell chemistry and healing and sense of community, and general settling of the nerves. I like to think he's the kind of guest who gives this show its special character and, as some of you have pointed out more than once, gives KRUX its special place on the radio dial, its verve and its mojo.

"Dr. Perot is on his way. At this very moment he's probably outside parking his car. While we wait, I think I'll pose a question I was also saving for later. I'll just put it out there right now, in the spirit of our ongoing journey through the cultural borderlands. It has to do with our nearest neighbor to the west—which is? You guessed it. The Hawaiian Islands. And by a happy coincidence, it involves a chant that may or may not have been chanted, depending on who you talk to, a chant with words and long-range vibes. . . ."

I glanced at Julie for some sign of how much time I had. She shrugged, with a "who knows?" face, and rolled her hand, which meant "keep talking." And so I did, telling them more than I'd set out to tell, reminding them of Quincy's call, how that had led me to the Palace Hotel to investigate a little-known San Francisco story that was starting to have the feel of an international mystery—Hawaii's last king, en route to Washington, D.C., meets Thomas Edison's earliest talking machine, the original wax cylinder now preserved in Honolulu, with the outside chance of a second message—a chanted poem from a dying monarch— heard once or twice in January 1891 and never heard again.

"This may seem far afield," I said. "But indulge me, folks. It's a personal crusade. It's like the legend you get glimmers of from time to time about the brain of Ishi, the so-called last wild Indian, being preserved somewhere in some anthropologist's basement in a jar of formaldehyde. Call it a research project with unpredictable results. If what I've told you touches any kind of nerve, if anything at all comes to mind, no matter how improbable or dubious or remote, please call. Or in the event I'm not around much longer to answer the phone here at KRUX, drop me a line. I'm counting on you, folks. You are my reference desk and my almanac. I send this along, maybe my final salute, like the fellow on the desert island who scribbles a note on his last scrap of paper and stuffs it into a bottle and tosses it into the wide, wide sea."

The tenor sax was fading in, Julie's sign to take a break. She killed the

studio mike and said over the intercom, "Nice, Danny. An open letter to
your fans and followers. They'll love you more than ever."

Then she told me Dr. Perot was stuck behind a twelve-car pileup on
the northbound Nimitz Freeway. He'd finally made it to an off-ramp and
just called from a Texaco station outside Hayward. They'd considered trying a pay-phone interview, but the line was full of crackle.

I said, "I wonder what tribal chanters do when they're stuck in traffic."

"They keep on chanting. We already have callers wanting to know
what you mean when you say your days are numbered."

"How many?"

"Six. Eight. The board is lighting up like a pinball machine."

"Okay, then, let's go with that."

"Five seconds."

Zoot Sims fading out . . .

"Yes, we're back, and we have Norm on the line from San Mateo.
Norm, are you there?"

"Hello, Sheridan. I'm a first-time caller so I'm a little nervous. But I
listen to almost every show and when I heard you say you might be leaving . . . hey, I couldn't believe it!"

"Thanks for saying this, Norm. I need all the support I can get.
Maybe you can help us with something."

"You name it."

"Maybe you can give us some idea of why you listen."

"Why I listen?"

"What keeps you coming back to the show?"

"I guess it's . . . I hope I don't blow this . . . like I said . . ."

"You're doing great, Norm."

"It's always something I'm interested in. Take this guy coming on
tonight, with the voices and the body chemistry. I know exactly what
he's getting at. I'm a software engineer. But nights and weekends I'm in
this choral group, just amateurs. We love to sing. We do big production
numbers like the Hallelujah Chorus, and sometimes my whole body tin-
gles for hours. It's like being inside a huge organ. Is he there yet?"

"Not yet. Poor guy is still caught in the automotive quicksand."

"Well, what's the story, Sheridan? Are you sick? Are you retiring?
You don't sound that old. Are you moving to another station, or what?"

I tried to keep it brief, capsulizing what might be in store for
KRUX, how *Sit Still and Listen* was one of several shows about to be
revamped or phased out. This news left Norm baffled and muttering. I
took a few more calls, all from regular listeners asking the same ques-

tions, all baffled, troubled, alarmed. Who's behind it? they wanted to know. Who would be replacing me? And didn't listeners count for anything at a time like this? What about *us?* one woman demanded.

I tried to take the high road and voice both sides. Here's the way I see the station and the show; here's the owner's point of view. "It's not about me, folks, it's about marketing. You can't take that personally. Mega-marketing is the Manifest Destiny of the modern world."

Well, of course they *did* take it personally. Maybe I went too far. I was feeling reckless. Whenever I glanced at Julie behind her console, knowing she was with me, I felt shielded and bulletproof. Sandy himself was among the callers, as I later learned, telling her I was way out of line, didn't know what I was talking about, and she should cut me off, go to music for the rest of the hour. She wouldn't do it. "If he's still talking five minutes from now," Sandy threatened, "you're both fired. I'm coming over to the station." "Good," said Julie. "There's a lot more we all need to rethink here." I guess that scared him off.

After thirty minutes the mood was shifting from lament and alarm to indignation and outrage. One woman said, "I feel like something is being stolen from us." Another woman, a fifth-grade teacher, said, "We can't let them get away with this. It's bigger than radio. This is what you find everywhere you look these days. TV. Magazines. Clothes. Books. Music. Everything moving toward the common denominator. Pretty soon we'll all be wearing the same pair of jeans and driving the same car and listening to the same song at the same time!"

Finally one frequent caller, a fellow named Larry who'd lived in Berkeley since the sixties, who remembered marches against the war in Vietnam, and perhaps had never again felt so fully energized, proposed some kind of street action. "Strike before the iron gets hot," he said—a gathering, a rally, a sit-in or teach-in or a guerrilla radio call-in—something to galvanize opinion and protest what sounded like a faceless corporate entity coming in from afar to silence our community's voice.

And this was how it started—THE PEOPLE VERSUS ARGO-NAUT—as outcries first heard that night spread through the city and through nearby towns and cities like a windblown grass fire.

We signed off with ten callers still waiting. Julie was high from the show. We both were. We'd been true to ourselves and straight with our listeners.

"I don't know where this is going, Danny. I just feel like we should celebrate."

With her mother in town and willing to keep an eye on Toby, she still had a bit of space in her crowded life. She wanted to make the most of it, since her mother might soon be gone. Some relatives were flying in from Okinawa, cousins, and a brother the mother hadn't seen in thirty years. "The one who stayed with me in the cave," she told Julie, "during the war, when the Americans were landing, and we thought they were cannibals." She might have to cut short her open-ended visit and get back to L.A. in time to meet them at the plane.

For Julie it gave the night that extra savor, the one last apple plucked from the highest branches of the tree. She wanted to go out for margaritas, order Caesar salad and some pasta, maybe head back to my place. We set out for San Francisco, thinking of a North Beach bistro we both liked. She was so amorous we almost didn't make it past the station. In the lobby we kissed like newlyweds. We kissed again in the parking lot, leaning against my car, and again in the front seat.

Past the Bay Bridge toll plaza I was going fifty in the middle lane as we nuzzled and fondled. We laughed about Dr. Perot marooned in the phone booth at the Texaco station and wondered if we could book him for another show—if we still had a show. We'd know more after the staff meeting, but that was tomorrow afternoon, and we were tired of thinking about Sandy and his perfidious ways.

I dialed in KJAZ out of Alameda, another station that would soon fall prey to bottom-line thinking and changing times. Sarah Vaughan was singing "Midnight Sun" with a tight trio behind her. Julie knew the lyrics and hummed along. Half singing a few bars she leaned in next to me and whispered, "Don't you love listening to jazz in the car?"

My foot slipped off the pedal. I veered, almost taking out a little VW bug. Luckily there was no one behind us for a hundred yards.

"That song you picked tonight," I said, "I liked it. I'm still wondering what you had in mind."

She reached for the dial, turning the volume down, and again leaned close, with her lips beside my ear, as she whisper-sang some lines, taking her time between phrases, letting each one sink in:

> *What a kick. How I buzz.*
> *Boy, you click as no one does.*
> *Hear me, sweet. I repeat,*
> *How long has this been going on?*

That was it. Dinner would have to wait. We came straight up to my place and gave ourselves to an exquisite desire. In times past our unions had been wild and bawdy. This was different. This time was new. She had never been so pliant, so generous. We wept. We laughed like children. Our bodies melted as we swam together in a molten river, fire water spilling in all directions, through my thighs and calves, upward through my chest, my arms, my neck, fingers and rivers and waterfalls of fire and sparks. At last we reached a precipice of spilling water. If we could hold it there, hold on, hold tight and not let go maybe we could swim forever in this flow of melting sparks.

She Chose the Water

I have a place to sit where no one will disturb me. The rowboat is my backrest. I cannot take my eyes from the ocean. Papa told me it was bigger than any lake. It is a lake with no shores. It makes a ring all around the ship, a wide blue ring. The ship throbs and moves through the water and white waves roll away from the ship. But the blue ring does not move. It stays the same. It stays the same. It stays the same.

October 5

Kawika loves the ocean. He says I will have my sea legs this time. I think he is right. The ship rolls with the swell and I am not sick. Very few are sick. They walk the deck. They play games on the deck. The ocean is good to us this time.

He said I will miss you Nani, do not stay away too long. I won't I said. I do not want my bird to fly away forever he said and held me and my tears came down. I was filled with sorrow. I did not want to leave. Today I feel the sorrow. I miss Moana. I feel something else too. What is it? I have to stand up and think about what I feel.

And yes now I know. It is being free. On the ship I feel free.

October 6

After breakfast a man called out to me. He looked strange until he said his name. He is my kinsman's nephew. He has a moustache now, the long kind with pointed ends. He puts something in his hair that makes his forehead shine. His clothes look very costly. He is half and half like me. On one side he is white, so his skin is lighter. He says we must sing some songs together like the day we sailed down to Sacramento to meet the king. He remembers that day and all the songs.

He says many remember how I went back to the train and rode away. They wonder am I ever coming home. I tell him how Moana took me in and taught me hula and how I was paa kahili too. I tell him Moana has a grass house where we used to sleep. He says his mother has one like that and she sleeps there when his father is away at sea. He shakes his head and says his mother is crazy to sleep outside when she has a big house made of wood standing empty.

This nephew, Makua, had put on weight, the fleshy poundage of early success. Running into him was both a blessing and a burden. In a brotherly way he began to watch over her, as a kind of family duty (somehow they were related, the Kinsman, Makua's uncle, being a cousin to Nani's father, though whether first, second, third or fourth, no one had ever seemed to know). But he'd become a boastful young man, full of himself and the kind of money he expected to be making. "They can't get along without me," he crowed, speaking of a firm that had hired him two years ago, right out of law school, as a specialist in trans-Pacific trade. Soon he would step in as their bilingual liaison with the Kingdom of Hawai'i. Before long he hoped to meet the king himself, "the Merrie Monarch," Makua called him, with a derisive smile.

October 10, 1884

Every day he wants to talk about Kawika. He wants to meet him. Do I like the king he says. I tell him yes. He hears the king is a stubborn man. I tell him I don't know. I think you do he says and a look comes on his face. It is the wrong smile for a man with a Hawaiian mother. It is a crooked smile. Like Mister Peabody. When we all met at my kinsman's house Makua did not have this smile. He did not have this pointed moustache. He did not have this fancy jacket. He was like a schoolboy then. Now he is a lawyer in San Francisco. Maybe it is a look the lawyers have.

Yet once they stepped ashore he was gallant, as if attuned to her silent apprehension. As their ship neared the West Coast, she'd imagined herself a solitary woman down there by the wharves where she'd have to spend at least one night, a dark-skinned woman in a city of strangers. Loading her bags into a carriage he took her to a small hotel where Hawaiians were known to be welcome. Early next morning he returned to meet for breakfast in the dining room and escort her back to the fan of wharves in time to catch an inland steamer bound for the delta and points north.

He gave her his card—

MICHAEL "MAKUA" FLYNN
Attorney at Law

and placed upon her shoulders a garland of fresh carnations, followed by a Polynesian kiss, nose to nose. The scent and his soft "Aloha" called back for Nani her farewell at the gangplank in Honolulu, with Moana there and all her relatives from the compound, her daughter and four kids, and the family from up the road with their kids, and all the women from the hula troupe, some with husbands and boyfriends, all bearing leis they piled one by one around her neck until she could scarcely breathe, leis spilling from her shoulders and into still water beside the ship. Their eyes shone with such light, it was as if the islands themselves had assembled there to see her off, eyes shining while the voices called, "Aloha, Nani! Aloha! Aloha!" (Good-bye. Hello. Safe journey. We love you. Wherever you go, our hearts are with you.)

So far away—those words, those faces—as she stood by the rail on the last leg of her second voyage, in her traveling coat, her high-button boots, the sturdy dress with puffed-out sleeves, the prim straw hat atop her piled nest of ebony hair. It was one of those dazzling fall days when the water sends up blue-silver light. Once before she'd crossed the bay, and she knew this light. She knew the cobalt blue of ruffled water. As the city's skyline receded behind the ferry, she surveyed the ring of northern hills. Nothing was strange this time, yet everything was new.

She could have taken the train, since the tracks stretched out from Sacramento in all directions now, south toward Fresno and Bakersfield, north toward Shasta. She chose the water, remembering her father's stories about Captain Crazy Eyes searching for a place to build his fort. Surely this was the way they'd sailed.

From San Francisco the steamer seemed bound straight for Sonoma, until it swung east through Carquinez Straits and on through the maze of islands, now well known and charted, yet still mysterious, with no contour, nearly invisible. At last the channel appeared that led them north again, onto the broad green flow of the river Nani thought of as her father's river, as she felt its pulse beneath the ferry. Before long she would learn from the Kinsman why Keala had spent so many years out here as barge hand and helmsman. Knowing the Hawaiian side of Keala's story she could swap that for the rest of the California side. She would tell him about Moana, about the fight on the beach, about the song she'd heard, and a heroic sailor who in times past had to leave his homeland and came east across the water with a shark to protect him, then sailed back to Hawai'i, after many years, to defend his honor and rejoin his sweetheart.

"Yes," the Kinsman would say, "Ka Holokai Kaleponi. I too have heard this story."

"Someone told me it is about Papa and his voyage."

"Sailors are dreamers, Nani. This is what they wish would happen. Your father was one of them. For many years he dreamed of going back. When we were young this was what all of us wanted. . . ."

He would tell her how Keala left the Captain and the fort behind, as did everyone else when gold was found glinting in the American River, promising riches farther upstream and in all the other Sierra streams. When he'd had his fill of mining, Keala came back down to the lowlands only to find the fort taken over by squatters and desperate argonauts, the fields empty and unplowed, the herds scattered, and the Captain gone, bankrupt, they said, hiding out at his country place north of there, beside the Feather.

Having made a bit of money, Keala decided to return in style to Honolulu and find Moana, his dream girl for all those years. It didn't take him long to land a berth on a merchant ship bound for the islands. On the night before he was to sail he met some other Hawaiians in a Barbary Coast saloon, one of whom knew the family, knew Moana had waited and waited and finally married Keala's older brother, with two children now running around the yard. So he came back to the Sacramento—in his late twenties by that time—and worked it for the next ten years, living on the river, sleeping on the river, learning its bends and snags and sloughs, its colors and its moods. *Muliwai konaola* (turbulent water). *Muliwai ulianianikiki* (dark, smooth, swiftly flowing water). And he hummed the verse Kanaka Harry sang when they came paddling upstream from the delta, composed on the day Keala and his mates thought they'd reached the very end of the world and had lost their way forever:

> *With mighty strokes*
> *the paddler travels far*

to the land where leaves
on trees are white feathers

. . . . . .

All these years later the river was still a lime-green corridor, its banks still tangled with trees and vines, the willows and alders and cottonwoods and oaks. But feathers no longer hung from their branches. The myriad villages that once dotted the wide plain had long since disappeared, their cooking fires extinguished. Ranchlands and croplands now spread across the valley. The river was busy with skiffs and barges, a waterway north to the state capital, where the opulent homes of railroad barons rose, though none yet rising as high as the mansion the General had built, which Nani was about to see again.

Varieties of Love

From Nani's letters no one could calculate the precise day or time of her return, but they were ready to welcome home their long-lost, wandering girl: the auntie, her mother's sister, still laid up with some chronic ailment of the lungs; and her daughters, the cousins who'd first led Nani to the schoolroom, now grown and married; and the young girls she'd taught to read and sew, three years older, willowy and shy; and the General's Wife, her pink face radiant with true delight; and the General too, who remembered her as the daughter of Kanaka John, the one who'd saved his life; and Edward Steele, of course, the long-legged and patient suitor who once thought he was seeing her off for three or four days, then had to wait three years. Each afternoon for a week Edward had been walking to the store to meet the wagon that hauled passengers and cargo up from the General's dock. When she arrived at last, he was there to offer his hand, and Nani was glad to take it. Stepping down from the wagon she was stepping back into a web of duties that once had seemed nothing but a trap. Now it felt like a haven.

For many nights she sat up with her aunt, laid hands upon her wheezing chest, the ribs and belly, talking quietly in her mother's tongue of what she'd seen, the dances she had danced. She learned that her younger sister had moved far up the valley where her husband found work closer to his tribe. Then the auntie said she knew Nani would be home soon because Nani's mother had been coming to her in dreams, still a young woman, a mountain woman, wearing her willow skirt, carrying her burden basket, walking toward her as if she had some news.

In the big house, at the kitchen table, Nani took a cup of tea with the General's Wife, whose small hands fluttered, eager, as she said, "to know everything," though after she'd heard about the churches in Honolulu and what women wore in that kind of climate, and some of the exotic recipes Nani had picked up—for baking fish in the earth, for chicken in the Shanghai style—she turned her conversation toward the progress of her pupils, the fortunes of some older ones Nani might remember, and the throng of younger ones who'd appeared to take their places.

"Oh, Nancy, as you can see, I have my hands full here. I can't tell you what a thrill it is to see you in our midst again. You're so . . . grown up now. Your English is so much better now. And your writing. My good-ness, how I looked forward to your letters. I've kept them all, you know. I have to confess, I was afraid you'd come back speaking some Kanaka language none of us could understand. When we have more time I want you to tell me about that king. It's not everybody these days gets to hob-nob with real royalty!"

Nani began to take long walks with Edward, who was the same fel-low she'd left standing helpless on the dock, yet not the same fellow at all. Tall and fit, no longer gangly, he'd filled out in every way, shoulders broader, dark hair thicker, with smoky eyes that seemed to say, "I know my mind."

He too had been gone a while, across the valley and over the western hills to a school for Indians the U.S. government opened south of Clear Lake. His new goal was to be a teacher, not a preacher, if only he could find a place to start. The government school was already running out of money. Public schools wouldn't hire a mixed-blood. For the time being he worked long hours as a teamster, hauling grain for the General, guid-ing his wagon in tandem with the mower, when the wheat was ripe. He still tutored older boys. In his room he had a shelf of books and always kept a book nearby, under his arm or under his wagon seat, as a badge of his profession.

Nani's legendary train ride with the king had been as mysterious for him as for all the others at the rancheria (for months afterward they wagged their heads, shrugged their shoulders; some prayed for her; some joked that Hawaiians had kidnapped her). When the first letter arrived from Honolulu, Edward had gone looking for the islands on a map of the world, gazed at the curving row of tiny spots in the great circle of blue. If Nani had spent those years in Sacramento, it would have fueled a dark resentment. But Hawai'i was another kind of place, a form of outer space, as remote for him as the Milky Way. The seventy-five miles south and west to the government school was as far as he'd traveled (and that was farther than most of the villagers had gone). For all his reading, the world he knew was the wide valley and the nearest ranges east and west. While he was curious about her family in the islands and the details of her voyage, it was enough, it seemed, to have her by his side again. He'd saved himself for Nani, dabbling with a few other women, but keeping his distance, refusing to believe she'd stay away forever. Her return was a sign that their courtship had merely been postponed, a signal that she was ready to complete a plan they'd agreed upon three years before, ready to marry him at last, settle down and start a family. He didn't voice this in so many words, yet from the moment he took her hand, it was in the air, in his face, in his eyes, in the way he linked their arms, a reclaiming of what had all along been his.

She didn't resist. His brooding possessiveness appealed to her. Hidden in her baggage was a round-trip ticket from Kawika, with the return passage open-ended and good for a year. By the time she was home a month she knew she wouldn't be using it, a ticket that would only carry her back into the sultry climate of intrigue and rivalry that surrounded the king. She'd had her fill of that, had her fill of the islands. She knew the story of her father now, and the story of those who'd challenged him. Here there was no Giles Peabody to watch her from across the street or block her way; nor were there any young girls hungering for Kawika's next music lesson. At the rancheria she was ready to move along the path of least resistance. Edward expected it. The General's Wife expected it. The men and women of the village expected it.

Edward was the opposite of Kawika, plainspoken, slow to smile, already set in his ways, at twenty-three. But he would be true to Nani, this much she knew. He was neither a flirt nor a drinker. And his passion for her had not subsided, with three years of stored desire waiting to be released. This time his eagerness to make love ignited her, and frightened her too. It was like the great river at flood time, overflowing its banks. Yet for all his heat and urgency Edward knew only one way to do it, what Moana had laughingly called "the missionary position." Kawika's lusts had taken many forms. Under his tutelage she had learned the varieties of lovemaking. One by one she would pass them on to Edward, whose missionary mind resisted for a while, though not for long. She was a capable teacher, having learned from Kawika that respect for a higher power can happily coexist with the pleasures of the flesh.

Imitating him, she drew an edge of one hand across her belly and told Edward, with an inviting grin, "From here up belongs to God. From here down belongs to me. And now to us."

With a sour face he tried to disapprove. But all in all he was a good student, willing to test himself at the borderlands of sin. "Move this way," Nani would tell him, in the darkness. "Roll over. Place your hand here. Yes. Like that . . ."

Two-Minded World

They were married in the wooden chapel the General's Wife had designed. In her ministerial frock, small and erect and proud as a mother, she stood before them, Edward in his black suit, Nani in a white dress she made herself. The pews were full, with villagers spilling out the doors, peering through the windows. Nani's Kinsman came upriver with his Indian wife, their sons and wives and children, bearing slabs of smoked salmon for the wedding feast. The Kinsman's nephew, Makua Flynn, came all the way from San Francisco bearing a calabash bowl of polished koa. As surrogate father the Kinsman gave the bride away. The rancheria's brass band played exuberant marching songs—cornets, trombones, snare drum, bass drum and fife—and the General, the tallest man for miles around, who attended all such gatherings with the patriarch's pleased and watchful attentiveness—the General announced that in memory of a long-ago heroic deed by his good friend Kanaka John he was giving these newlyweds a house he'd recently added to the two rows of small frame houses that lined the main street of the village.

And so they set up housekeeping, Edward driving his teams by day, bent over his books at night, while Nani rejoined the women of the rancheria. She dressed in calico and spoke with them in her mother's tongue, kept a garden, and in the springtime joined them at the river to gather sedge root and willow shoot for weaving the baskets they used for sifting and storing acorn meal. She went to church to sing with fervor all the gospel songs, and before long she took her auntie's place in the women's dance society.

The rancheria was a two-minded world, where two buildings competed for the souls of the people, where villagers were pulled both ways, yearning for some path through these years of unfathomable change. On Sundays they gathered in the whitewashed chapel with its pews and pulpit, its organ loft and belfry, to hear the General's Wife read, to hear stories of the Prodigal Son, of miraculous healings of Lazarus raised from the dead. When the time came for a tribal ceremony, they gathered in the wide pit of the roundhouse, a dirt-floored theatre with a long log drum and a fire circle in the center. Its dome of soil and timbers was supported by two posts, the larger known as "the spirit post," anchoring the house and all the dancers, a column linking the constant earth to the heavens and the spirit realm.

For church service Nani had a white dress, and for the dancing a buckskin dress her auntie had stored away for her, along with the shell pendant and beaded necklaces passed down from Nani's grandmother. Inside the roundhouse, sometimes the men would dance to release the spirit of the coyote, or the deer. Sometimes the women would dance, and sometimes everyone together, to the log drum and the clicking of the clappersticks and the piping of the birdbone whistles.

Nani danced the bear dance and the dance to fill the oaks with acorns. One night as she gleamed with sweat she thought she saw her mother in the smoky shadows, sitting by the wall, and in the midst of all the grunting chants called out to her. When the figure called back she thought it might be another old woman from the village. Inside the dome of moving shadows she wasn't sure. Dancing all the harder, dipping and bouncing, she let herself be carried by the drum and the droning chant, let her mind drift and fall away, to make a place where her mother could enter and reveal herself.

This roundhouse, as sacred as the chapel, was a sanctuary the dead sometimes returned to, where shamans came to find the voices of the spirits. Men of the rancheria had built it in the proper way, observing the season, blessing the space and the wood, selecting with care the tree that would become the spirit post. And through the years the roundhouse had remained intact because the General understood the tribal need for ceremony.

As Nani would record much later, thinking back upon this time:

The elders said he once kept an Indian wife called Miss Graciela. This was years before he brought his wife to the ranch. Miss Graciela taught him to respect the old ways. Thanks to her, our rancheria was the last place we could live the way we lived and not move a hundred miles to a reservation. We had our own community. We all worked for the general. And somehow he protected us.

He had lots of land and lots of money. So all the men were loyal workers. And other ranchers envied him. They called his place the Plantation. They said he kept us like slaves for cheap labor. But now I see that the other tribes around us were almost gone. Their tongues were gone. Their ways were gone, just like the place in the hills where mama and papa used to live, where we would sit together weaving baskets in the shade. That place was gone. She was gone. The old times were gone. But at the rancheria some small part lived on. We still buried our dead in the old way, in a pit deep enough to hold the treasures one needed for the next life, the baskets and the belts.

At candlelit dinner parties in the mansion's dining room, the General would sometimes feel compelled to stand and speak on his own behalf: "I bought this ranch fair and square, paid good Yankee dollars to a friend of mine who had a land grant signed by the Gobernador of Alta California himself. I have done right by these Indians too! I pay them a fair wage, by God, and let them keep on living where they have always lived. I ask you all—in this day and age, who else *does* this? Who else lets them chant their chants and wail all through the night when a loved one passes on?"

At such times it was hard for his wife to hold her tongue. Like the men in the Sugar Growers Guild, she viewed all these ancient practices as regrettable ties to a savage past. God-fearing Christians should put dancing and the shaman ways behind them. "It's not just the praying to their own native spirits," she'd been heard to say. "Lord knows it's bad for their health! Going into that smoky dancehouse and working up such a lather, then going back outside into the cold of the night? It's no wonder so many come down with the flu!" If the General's Wife had her way, the roundhouse would be demolished and her chapel would become the rightful village center.

Edward Steele agreed with her, having sat in her classes as a youth, having heard her preach on hundreds of Sunday mornings. Her lessons were reinforced by zealous instructors at the government school, where the stated goal was to replace all native languages with English, to wean promising Indian students away from the corrupting and backward influences of their parents. This was why Edward wanted to teach—somehow, somewhere. There was a movement abroad in the land, to guide young Indians out of the dark ages of the eighteenth century and into the bright light of the nineteenth. He wanted to be part of that.

As of their wedding day Nani and Edward hadn't talked much about his dream for the future. He still was not a talker, not in the personal way, not outside the classroom, where the lectern and blackboard and pointer seemed to free his tongue. In bits and pieces he'd told her some of what he'd studied: the war with Mexico, the names of all the presidents, the names of tribal chiefs who'd started wars against the United States. He told her how steamboats worked and how springs of water rose from reservoirs within the earth, and she let him talk whenever he was in the mood, listening to the sound, to the pride he found in his new knowledge. She had to agree that teaching the white man's way was good and necessary work. She herself was a teacher, after all, spending her mornings in the mansion again, up on the third floor, under the skylight, in the ballroom crammed with chairs and desks and sewing machines and racks of clothing and shelves of dog-eared books.

The full shape of his ambition came clear when he began to wonder why she wasn't pregnant. Eager to start a family, he'd already waited too long. Others in the village kept their eyes on this young couple, and maybe they were wondering too, not openly, but wondering with their eyes, with tilts of the head that told Edward perhaps his manhood was being discussed.

One night, when woodstove crackle was the only sound in their two-room cabin, he closed his book and said, "Nani, I have been praying for an answer."

Re-hemming a dress by kerosene light, she kept her eyes on the stitches. "I too have been praying."

"When a child comes, it is a blessing from God."

"Yes."

"When no child comes, it must be that there is no blessing."

Her belly gathered in upon itself. "You think there is no blessing in our house?"

"This is why I pray."

She waited, pushing against the sense of shame.

As if speaking part of his prayer he said softly, "I am worried about the dancing."

"You mean our dance society?"

"I think you should leave it."

"I cannot leave it."

"I think God frowns upon it and thus withholds His blessing."

"Please do not say such a thing."

"One day soon it should all be disbanded. It is un-Christian."

Her tears welled up. "All the women in my family were dancers."

"I know that," he intoned, his voice lifting a notch, emboldened by what he'd been able to say so far. "My own mother was a dancer. But these are old practices, Nani. You call out to pagan gods."

"My aunt. My mother. My grandmother . . . I have their beads. . . . They danced all their lives, and God did not frown upon them. They all had children. . . ."

"But don't you see? That time has passed by. They did not hear God's word. They lived in ignorance. 'And the times of this ignorance God winked at.' So says the Apostle Paul in Acts 17 and 30. But the Christian God has come to us, and we can no longer claim to be ignorant of His truth."

Edward was in the pulpit now, delivering his sermon. "We should be grateful to Him for the gift of His truth and His love, and we should be calling out to Him and *only* Him, not to the coyote, not to the spirit of the oak tree to make the acorn grow. God makes the acorn grow! Why do you think we were married in a church? Did you want me to purchase you with animal skins the way your father purchased your mother?"

Again she fell silent, her throat so tight she couldn't speak. What did she hear in his voice? It was another's voice. From Edward's mouth, she heard the strident sound of Giles Peabody, the same righteous and accusing voice. She saw Giles in his morning coat, with his dry brow and his rooster's chest, lecturing to the king. She would not let Edward shame her.

"Why are you so quiet?"

After a while she asked, "Why only Him?"

"Why only Him? Because Jehovah is a jealous God."

"When we go into the roundhouse and call to the Creator for a good harvest, we do not make the Creator bigger than Jehovah."

"You cannot worship two gods, Nani. Jesus said there is no other way to heaven but by me."

"But why is Jehovah jealous? The Creator is not jealous of Jehovah. If you pray to Jehovah, the Creator does not punish you."

He hadn't thought of this. As he searched for an answer, she could see his anger rising. She could smell it. On his neck the veins stood out. On the day, years ago, when he rescued her from the drunken ranch hands, she'd seen his anger rise. Just last week she'd seen it in the fields, with his horses, though the horses had done nothing wrong. The white grain merchant had cursed him for something and walked away, and Edward had cursed the horses then, whipped them and would have whipped them till they bled, but another teamster grabbed his arms.

She stood and went to him and touched his shoulder. "All right," she said. "I have many things to do. I can leave the dancing for a while. We will pray some more for God's blessing."

Standing beside him she felt his anger melt. When he looked up, his eyes were warming with another kind of heat. His arm went around her hips, pulling her close.

"We'll start tonight," he said, rising from his chair to press against her, to press into her a sudden hardness spawned by this surrender. His eager hands roamed her curves as he eased her sideways toward the bed, and she moved with him, aroused by how quickly his desire broke through the sermonizing. As the clothes fell away, their bodies joined in certain acts too delicious to be condoned by a punitive and vengeful God. In lamplit privacy Edward seemed always willing to take the risk, as Nani gave herself to what lurked just behind his preacherly restraint.

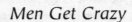

Men Get Crazy

Six weeks later she missed a period. She missed a second, then a third. When she told him she was carrying a child, he smothered her with kisses. Each day his affection grew. On their knees they prayed together, thanking the heavens for smiling on them both.

She was four months along, and bent over the washtub behind their cabin, scrubbing a pair of trousers, when she was gripped by excruciating cramps, the pain so sharp she couldn't move. Her flesh went cold, then a feverish moisture covered her. Hunched against the cramping, which would not let her go, she felt her insides slowly spilling out. She knew what was happening. It had happened once before.

When it was over she stood gripping the tub as if she stood at the railing of a drop-off cliff. She knew it was a boy. She'd seen his face. Auntie had told her it would be a boy. She sobbed for him and for the empty hole in her belly, sobbed with gratitude that the stabbing pain was gone and with dread for what Edward might say or think or do. She considered running, but where could she run to? She went to see her auntie, no longer bedridden but frail now, with a constant cough, spending most of her days indoors by the curtained window, her eyes gaunt, her gray hair hanging loose.

She told Nani of a poultice that would help to stop the bleeding, and of a tea made of twice-boiled herbs. Nani told her how Edward viewed the dancing, and her auntie smiled.

"I think that school made him crazy. Men get crazy anyhow. Sometimes a baby is not ready to be born. Another one will come. Do not grieve too long. Edward is a little crazy, but you must tell him right away. He will look at you and know."

At first he seemed to share her grief, his tearful eyes bewildered, beyond consolation. Frantically he paced the floor.

"You must lie down. I will take you to a doctor. Don't cook tonight. I will cook. Tonight. Tomorrow night. Tell me what to cook for you!"

He held her, stroked her shoulders. Again her tears flowed, as she felt the heaving of his chest, as Edward sobbed long and hard, sobbing away everything that might have been expressed in words.

In the days that followed he spoke less and less, as if slowly losing his powers of speech. And Nani tried to read his looks. From his eyes she knew this silence was heavy with a blaming he could not speak. One night, almost offhandedly, as if to get it out of his mind, he said, "Did you dance again, Nani?"

"Why do you say this?"

"It is a sin, you know."

"I told you I would stop. I have been with you every night."

"Why would God take away His blessing?"

"Auntie says it is not a sin. She says sometimes a baby is not ready to be born."

His eyes were fixed upon her, and she saw again the blame she could not challenge, the same blame she put upon herself. In Hawai'i she had not told Kawika. She only told Moana. Now that it had happened a second time, she feared she had a weak womb, feared she'd never be able to carry a child, feared she could not be a good wife. And yet . . . and yet a part of her was glad. Yes, a secret part of her was glad she'd lost the boy, though this was a truth she could not yet think. Many years would pass before she allowed herself to say it.

(Over forty years later, while holding a new grandson in her arms, Nani would tell her daughter how she was already wishing she hadn't married Edward when she did, in such a hurry. "And even then it was hard for her to talk about such things," said Rosa, as we sat inside her Airstream. "Almost fifty years gone by, and tears came down mama's face while she held your father in her arms.")

The miscarriage fell between them like a thick and weighty curtain neither one could push aside. On the nights when they coupled, the heat was gone. For Nani it was as it had been in the days before she left. An obligation. Or worse. A task. Sometimes in the darkness, as he mounted her, she squeezed her eyes shut against those same walls closing in.

It's still not clear when he first heard about the teaching job, whether before or after they lost the child. One has to wonder at the remarkable timing, since it forced upon them a choice that might otherwise have been postponed for years. His former headmaster had been transferred to a government school farther south, near San Jose, where there was need for an assistant, "someone in tune with the Indian temperament." The final letter broke his long and brooding silence, seeming to open a door he'd feared might never open. Edward was the ideal candidate, the letter said, if he could get there for the start of a new semester.

It meant packing up and leaving right away, and Nani didn't want to leave right away. She didn't ever want to leave. She had learned to like their little house. She had her students at the mission school, where the General's Wife counted on her more and more. And there was her auntie to look after.

"She has two grown daughters," Edward said. "They can care for her."

"But they have their own children to raise," said Nani, the childless niece, for whom family duty was also a form of penance.

"You don't have to leave when I leave. I will take the train to San Jose and find a place for us to live. Then I can send for you."

"Are you sure, Edward?"

"Am I sure?"

"If you quit your job and leave the rancheria, the General will not let us return. This is his rule."

"I am tired of the General and his rules! He gives us a house, and we can never leave. I cannot spend my life driving horses, Nani! I have the chance to be a teacher now. Do you know what that means? I can share the things I know. I can help other Indians learn English and history and how to follow in the path of Jesus Christ, and one day there will be no need for a rancheria where the General holds us captive!"

His eyes flashed with such evangelical zeal, she was almost willing to follow him then. But something struck her wrong. Where Edward wanted to take her, there would be no roundhouse, no dance, no chanting, no speaking of her mother's tongue. If these things were gone, her mother would soon be gone. She couldn't go with him, and she didn't know how to tell him. For days afterward Nani was the one immersed in brooding silence.

Then came the time for the women to prepare for a dance to bless the acorn crop. She unfolded her buckskin dress and her apron made of rabbitskins. She laid out her strands of beads and her clamshell pendant. When he ordered her to put those things away she didn't answer. He'd been telling her to get ready for their move, but she had made no preparations. She dressed for the ceremony, which began at dusk. In the roundhouse she danced for hours, leaving at midnight, exhausted, ecstatic.

She found Edward slumped over their kitchen table, his head on folded arms, next to a half-empty quart of whiskey. He wasn't moving. He looked dead, until she jostled his shoulders. "Edward. Edward!" His eyes popped open, bloodshot, blinking, as he sprang to life, nearly knocking her over. His face looked made of clay, a mask.

She said, "Where did you get this?"

His thick tongue took a while to move. "None of your business."

"You are my husband," she said, stepping back from a menace in his voice.

"Yes . . . yes, and you are my wife. But you will not do my bidding. What kind of wife is that?"

"What do you want? You want me to go with you? Is that what you want?"

He didn't hear. "What good are you, Nani? You will not do my bidding! You cannot carry a child!"

He rose from his chair with a lunging reach. Before she could evade him he had her by the shoulders, shaking, shouting in her face. "What good are you! What good are you!"

He shoved her across the room and against the wall with such force, her beads flew back and the pendant too. The pearly square of clamshell hit the boards and split apart. She stood there stunned by the sight of the pendant passed down from her grandmother now in glinting pieces at her feet. As she stooped to gather them up, he raised his arm in a wild swing. She ducked under it and fled.

"Come back here!" he thundered.

But she was gone, sprinting down the midnight road. Inside her auntie's house she latched the door, pushed a chest of drawers up next to it, while from her bed auntie called out, "Who is there? What is it?"

He was outside pounding on the wall. "Nani! Nani! Open this door or I will break it down!"

"Go away! Get away from me!"

He pushed at the door but she braced against it, and soon he gave up, his voice young and desperate now. "Nani . . . come out . . . please . . . I have to talk to you."

When she didn't answer, his pleas trailed off. He dropped down onto the stoop with his head in his hands, temples throbbing in the aftermath of drink, while in windows all along the road oil lamps flickered briefly, and one by one went dark.

An hour later she opened the door, stepped out, looked down at him and stroked his head. She stroked his arm and his hand and drew it away from his face.

His red eyes were wet. "I'll find another one."

"Another one."

"A pendant. I will find one for you. Don't worry."

She tugged his hand, and this time he stood. "Tomorrow I have to leave."

"I know."

"I want you to come with me."

"I know."

She led him to their cabin, put him to bed, then climbed in next to him, arousing him, and in the deep silence of early morning they made love. His body at ease, Edward fell into a dreamless sleep, slept off most of his hangover, slept till nearly noon, waking to find himself alone. She was not outside. Her auntie hadn't seen her. He asked all up and down the road. No one had seen her.

He had to finish packing. The next morning, still hoping she would appear at the last moment, he begged the wagoneer to wait ten minutes, and another ten. At the General's dock they almost missed the ferry that carried him downstream to Sacramento. He caught the train to Oakland and from there the train on south to Santa Clara Valley, where the headmaster's buckboard was waiting to take him out to the government school in the foothills east of San Jose.

Her Dream

Nani spent a day and a night in the tack room of the General's stable. The groom, an old Indian man who'd known her mother, kept his silence and cadged her a plate of food from the kitchen. When she knew the wagon had rolled away toward the river, she walked to her cabin, picked up the shiny fragments of her pendant and laid them out like a jigsaw puzzle, trying to fit them back together.

If she and Edward were ever divorced, it must have happened years later. We know some letters were exchanged. When he finally found a house, he sent for her, and she agreed to travel down to San Jose to give it one more try. After a couple of months she was back at the rancheria. The General bent his rule a bit, since his wife counted on Nani to help manage the classes and keep her school on track. Around the big house she'd come to depend on Nani's newfound grace and cultivation to handle domestic duties large and small.

A year passed, and then another, and another, as she settled into life at the enclave shaped and guarded by the General's will and by the spirit of his Indian wife, at the edge of the wide valley shaped and guarded by mountain ranges east and west. In the chapel she sang "Rock of Ages." In the roundhouse she danced for the bear and the coyote and the clover.

In the winter when consumption finally took away her auntie, she attended two services—one in the chapel where prayers were heard and verses from the Book of Psalms and one by the grave, which the General's Wife disapproved of but could not prevent. Auntie was one of the last elders to be buried in the old way, knees bound to the chest, accompanied on her journey by precious belongings such as the cone-shaped basket she'd had since childhood, woven by her grandmother, tossed into the pit by Nani, as she looked one last time at her mother's older sister. Her mourning voice joined all the others, wailing for the lost aunt and for the lost mother too, calling the mother to visit and comfort her, wailing through the day into the long winter night.

In the classroom she became a mentor to the girls of the village, teaching them all she'd learned in the big house—how to make clothing, how to read English and write it, how to make tea and serve it, how to eat with knife and fork, how to set a table. On certain days, when she had them to herself, when she knew no one was looking, Nani reminded them to honor their ancestors and respect their parents, to listen to the stories and to remember the language they heard at home. Like her father, and like Moana, she would tell them, "Learn the white man's tongue. But do not forget your mother's tongue. Speak both, and then you have more power."

If she went with other men—and others surely came along from time to time, given Nani's age and pleasing looks—her Book of Days never mentions it. My guess is, in her mind this wouldn't have been the proper subject for a married woman to write about. The man who turns up most often is the one three thousand miles away and seemingly beyond reach.

Though I can't verify it, I still suspect that somehow, after she returned to Kaleponi, she was in touch with the king, if only a carefully worded note, addressed to His Majesty, to inform him of her marriage, or to explain that she'd be staying away longer than expected. No evidence of this survives, no notes from him among her papers, no letters, nor is there anything from her or any mention of Nani Keala in the Kalakaua file at the State Archive in Honolulu. At one time there might have been. We'll never know. Like so many features of his plentiful life, she remains a shadowy presence in the public record, hard to trace. A great many of his personal manuscripts, letters, traveling notes, and the memorabilia of a lifetime were deliberately destroyed by his opponents during the looting of Iolani Palace.

Among her known souvenirs was the shell necklace he'd given her. While living with Edward she'd kept it out of sight, in a drawer, in a small cloth bag folded into a scarf. Inside the bag was the bark cloth wrapping printed with squares and diagonals of brown and black. And inside the folded bark cloth called *kapa* was the long necklace, strands of tiny purple shells from Ni'ihau, an island Kawika said he'd never visited, but he knew the shells were hard to find and precious. Now she added these strands to the ornaments she wore to the roundhouse, much to the amazement of the other women, who marveled at their delicacy and rare glow. "It was a gift," she told them, "from a Hawaiian dancer, from a relative of my father who himself knew Hawaiian dances but was also a leader of our village in the old days and a member of the men's dance society."

It was this gift, now uncovered, that stirred the first of numerous nostalgic entries:

February 7, 1888

Each shell is like a tiny ear listening for something. Kawika said they wash up on the beach. Every morning women search the beach and comb the sand. This many shells might take a year he said. I still hear his voice when he said it. So much like papa's voice. I hear his laugh. Why did I leave when I did? He always said he needed me. Why did I tell him he was wrong? I thought I knew his fear. Now I think I did not know it at all. Only a dull king has no enemies he said, and I laughed with him. So many times we laughed. I was still a girl. I wanted him to love me. He loved everyone. That is what I saw. Now I see that no one had a heart as large as his.

A necklace. A curve of bead-size shells. A link to the islands. Another way of remembering Kawika, a larger and fonder way. Does it mean she was yearning to get back over there? Maybe so. A distant yearning. From time to time a tug from the long line that had never quite been severed, stretching out across the water now. At some point she took another look at the round-trip steamer ticket, only to find that the return passage had long since expired. Once she counted her money, only to find she was far short of what the trip would cost.

Once she took a barge downstream to visit her kinsman, perhaps to talk about borrowing some money, though they also talked about Edward. The Kinsman nodded and stroked his silver beard and told her his own first marriage hadn't worked out either. "I had to wait a while longer," he said, "to find the right woman for me."

The hazards of domestic life didn't seem to interest him as much as his recollection of the king. Seeing Nani stirred his memory of their meeting inside the royal railroad car, a story he'd told a hundred times, and how her chant revealed a common ancestor. Someone had brought him a clipping from a Honolulu paper, a story of the king as honorary fire chief, leading one of the city's brigades into Chinatown to quell a massive blaze that eventually leveled several blocks. "King Kalakaua did excellent work"—so went the story—"urging on the willing men and exerting himself to the utmost to stay the raging flames."

"He is indeed a brave king," said the Kinsman with familial pride. "I knew it when we met him."

Back at the rancheria Nani wrote:

In my dream I saw him. There was smoke all around and ashes flying in the air. Horses pulled his wagon. In Hawaiian he called out to them to hurry toward the flames. The island was on fire. I heard my own voice. I called to him Wait. He turned to me. His hair was burning. His hair was made of flames. He raised his arm. Come he said. Come. The fire was moving toward him, rolling down the mountain. I said go the other way. Come he said again. My horses are very brave. They rose up in front of him kicking at the flames. I called his name. Kawika. Then I was awake. In my chest my heart was beating. I lay very still and heard the frogs croaking in the creek and the beating of my chest slowed down. Today I wish I could see Moana and be in her grass house again. Sometimes we would lie side by side and tell our dreams.

In the General's Study

It was December 1890, and the school had closed early for the holidays. The way things were going it might never reopen. Every couple of weeks a blinding ache in her neck and shoulders would leave the General's Wife prostrate for a day, sometimes two. "Nervous trouble," she called it, and in search of a cure had spent three months with "a specialist" who ran a therapeutic ranch in the desert near San Diego. It didn't help. Drained of energy, she'd cut the classes from five days a week to four, then to three, and now to zero, leaving Nani time for many tasks inside the mansion.

Each morning she straightened up the General's study, a sacrosanct retreat even his wife was not allowed to enter without asking. On certain days the floor would be littered with periodicals that arrived in bundles, dropped upon the front verandah—the *Argonaut,* the *Atlantic Monthly, California Agriculture,* the *New York Times.* The General, it seemed, tried to devour them all at once, and on such days Nani gathered up these papers and magazines and placed them in their proper stacks against the wall.

She first came upon a picture of Kawika while stacking a week's supply of the *San Francisco Examiner*—a line drawing of his head and shoulders and the upper half of a military jacket bristling with medals. That is, it looked like Kawika, his hair, his mouth. And yet it didn't. Something was missing. The light in his eyes? The glow of his skin?

It appeared halfway down the front page, below the lead story's headline:

HIS MAJESTY THE KING
ARRIVAL OF THE HAWAIIAN MONARCH
On These Shores
The Ceremony of Reception

Though she'd seen many newspapers, it had never occurred to her to pick one up on her own and begin to read. Under the high ceiling, amid the glass-paneled cases and shelves of books, she took her time, discovering that she understood almost all the words. She read it twice, then again, listening for footsteps out in the corridor, as if she'd broken into the house without permission. It was a moment in late morning when the mansion was empty but for her, as she stood alone in a hushed and carpeted silence:

> The bay was full of government powder smoke yesterday in honor of the visit of David Kalakaua, King of the Hawaiian Islands, who arrived during the forenoon on the U.S. Cruiser *Charleston,* nine days from Honolulu. It was 11 o'clock when the *Charleston* passed through the Golden Gate and met the cutter detailed for escort duty up the bay. The latter vessel inaugurated the salute, running the Hawaiian flag to the mainmast head as the first gun was fired. Alcatraz and the other forts took up the salute. . . .

At the wharf, the story went on, carriages were waiting to bring the royal party to the Palace Hotel, where a great crowd filled the courtyard. After a stay in California, the king would travel by train to Washington, D.C., to meet with the president. His chamberlain was with him, and his aide-de-camp, but not the queen, whose duties required her to remain in the islands.

In her mind's eye Nani saw the hotel, the courtyard, the king alighting from his carriage. She saw him wave to the throng and wondered if any Hawaiians had gathered to welcome him as they once gathered at the siding in Sacramento with gifts and songs. Surely her kinsman would have sent such news. She wanted to be there waving back, waving until he spotted her, seventeen again, and Kawika the dashing celebrity in tailored coat, though this time they would already know each other. This time their eyes would meet and his kingly smile, his parade smile, would open wider with the private smile he saved for her.

She thought of sending a letter, then wondered how long he'd be staying. After all this time would he even remember her? In her diary she wondered too about the queen, who never seemed to travel with Kawika:

She went to England once. And he did not go. He stayed in Hono-lulu. When he traveled all the way around the world, then she was the one to stay behind. But why did she not join him for such a voyage? Did she stay to rule the kingdom until he came home? I do not think so. She never takes the throne. They say she can be shy. She will not speak English. When the king is gone, his sister takes his place, Liliuokalani. While he is here in Kaleponi she will rule Hawaii. I know she likes to rule. It is in her nature. She is not shy.

A week later another headline appeared on page one of the *Examiner*:

HIS ROYAL MAJESTY
WILL TRAVEL TO LOS ANGELES
AND OTHER POINTS OF INTEREST

After a restful stay in the city, the story said; Kalakaua's spirits were high, his health was good. Not eager to make the long trip east during the Christmas season, he would head for Santa Barbara and points beyond as a guest of the Southern Pacific Railroad. He'd never visited this region and looked forward to the ranches, the orchards, the harbors, more of the famous coastline. "America is a vast and glorious land," he said, "and I want to know it all!" Sometime after the holidays he would return to the Bay Area and from there press on to the nation's capital.

For a week she'd been playing with the picture of greeting him at the Palace Hotel. Once she placed around her neck the strands of precious purple shells from Ni'ihau. It was a kind of dreamland picture, a wistful might-have-been, sweet and distant, since in her mind he'd already come and gone. But no, he had not yet gone anywhere at all. He was still in California, and now that distant picture filled her with giddy panic. If he was coming back to San Francisco, maybe she could be there to meet him at the depot. She knew the way. No delegation of Hawaiians this time. Just Nani. By herself. And he would . . . hold her. He would . . . take her . . . in his arms?

She sat down in the General's easy chair. It was too much to imagine. Her head was light, her stomach fluttering. She read the story through again, telling herself it was crazy to think such things. At the station he would be surrounded, saluting everyone, embracing everyone, loving everyone at once, as he always did.

She folded the paper, set it on its stack, told herself to stop scanning the pages of the *Examiner*. But of course she couldn't stop, and ten days later another headline appeared:

KALAKAUA'S SOUTHLAND TOUR
CUT SHORT BY ILLNESS
HIS MAJESTY EXPECTED SOON

Somewhere near Santa Barbara, during a side trip to an olive grove, he'd caught a cold, perhaps the flu, and was being rushed back to the comforts of the Palace Hotel, where he would take a week to rest and recuperate and finalize some kingly obligations before heading east at last.

> As a man of the tropics, the King does not look forward
> to January weather in Washington, D.C. But he feels that
> an eye to eye encounter with President Harrison is worth
> the risk.

This time Nani's dreamy, fearful thoughts could not be shoved aside. She stopped thinking about what he would do when he saw her, what he would say. She reread the story and looked at the calendar. He'd be at the hotel until January 16, which gave her enough time, if she took the train. She had the money for a trip like that. It was too late to send a letter. In his office the General had a telephone. She'd heard him using it, shouting as if at someone across an open field. Could a person hear you as far away as San Francisco? What would she say? She didn't know what to say. She didn't know what she expected. She would have to take her chances. If not, how else would she ever see him again?

Any lingering doubt about such a plan was soon erased by the General's Wife, who pushed both palms against her brow as if pushed to some final limit.

"Good gracious, Nancy. You could not have picked a worse time."

"It is the king. He is returning."

"Surely you know you can't travel alone to San Francisco."

"Someone has to welcome him."

"Yes, and what if you are gone again for another three years?"

"It will only be for a few days."

"You know how much I need you here."

"I know."

"You know about the dinner party on Saturday."

"I know."

"The mayor of Sacramento will be here, and we are counting on something special. The General himself is counting on it. The mayor's wife still talks about your Peking pork dumplings. . . ."

In times past she would have said this with twinkling eyes and a girlish smile designed to draw you in, make you want to please her. Now it came like a threat. With her eyes narrowed against some spike of pain, it sounded like a task Nani would have to fulfill to perfection in order to avoid harsh punishment. For weeks it had been like this, for months, and today she couldn't bear standing near the General's Wife. She needed relief from her oppressive instructions. On the pathway that led to the mansion's back porch, Nani studied the gravel and thought how everyone in the village needed relief, needed to get away for a while, but couldn't, afraid to work elsewhere for fear of being evicted, afraid to cross the General or his wife, once so kind, so gentle and generous, and now, wracked by ailments, a kind of overseer. Even her Sunday sermons suffered, as she lashed out at older villagers who refused to come to her church, lashed out at their stubborn refusal to hear the words of Jesus. Like drowning men, she said, they clung to the sad wreckage of their pagan ways.

Nani looked up. "By the weekend I will be back. Perhaps sooner."

"Well, then," she said, eyes heavy with regret, as if betrayed, "you are a grown woman now. I suppose I can't forbid you."

Looking into her tortured face, Nani remembered the day she'd tried to touch it, tried to lay her hands upon the neck and forehead and how the whole body drew back, voice full of alarm. "What on earth are you doing?" "It is my mother's way," Nani had said, "an Indian way of touching." But the General's Wife would have none of it. "Just pray for me, Nancy. That is all I ask. Pray for me when you can."

PART FOUR

Fathers and Sons (Continued)

Berkeley

In the *San Francisco Chronicle* they have a "Bay Area" section, to cover news coming in from all parts of the great megalopolis for which this city is the hub. It's a world of stories from around the shores of the long and nearly landlocked bay where multitudes have gathered, from Silicon Valley in the south to the vineyard country in the north, to the narrow plain and range of hills the Spanish named "La Contra Costa"—the opposite coast—referring to what they saw looking east across the water from their tiny outposts at the Presidio and Yerba Buena Cove. That farther shore is now an urban corridor, with only city limits signs to tell you where one town ends and the next begins. On any day of the week, much of the *Chronicle*'s "Bay Area" section will be given over to this sprawl of neighborhoods and malls and boulevards strung along between the bay and the first ridges: Richmond, El Cerrito, Berkeley, Piedmont, Oakland, Emeryville. And so it was, two days after Roy Wurlitzer of Argonaut had come and gone, that Sandy's picture took up most of the section's first page, Sandy in his square-rim wire glasses, his buckled jeans, the frayed denim shirt (from Ralph Lauren) that was his gesture to the working class, Sandy in his office backed by a treasured photo, blown up to poster size, of a very young Sandy with a very young Bob Dylan.

A Berkeley stringer had picked up my show, heard the voices of dismay and agitation. Then he'd sniffed out a staff meeting set for the next afternoon. "This is an internal matter," said Sandy when the stringer called. "There is no story yet. We're still negotiating."

That's not what the stringer heard from me or from others who attended, who heard Sandy lay it out pretty much as Julie had laid it out—the dollar squeeze, the restructuring at Argonaut, the program cuts, the homogenizing and dumbing down of news and music, a new commitment to "broadening the audience base"—all of this punctuated by murmurs from around the crowded room, long exhales of disbelief.

I sat near the back keeping an eye out for Julie. She wanted to be there to maintain our united front and if need be stand up to Sandy before the assembled staff, but she'd called to tell me she might be late, having come home from my place to find her mother by the door with a suitcase, the mother who'd moved in for a few weeks to lend a hand with Toby now threatening to shame her daughter and take a cab to the airport. They'd squabbled before, and I tried to keep my distance, though of course I couldn't, held in that strange place between lover and not-yet-mate, the holding zone between boyfriend and not-yet-daddy.

Up in the front row an engineer ran out of patience. "Can somebody tell me what this meeting is about? Is it a done deal, Sandy? Do we have any input at all?"

With a helpless shrug, palms toward the ceiling, asking the heavens to explain his fate, Sandy looked straight at me.

"Thanks to Sheridan Brody back there, we have suddenly reached a point of no return. Certain things are going to have to change, and there's no way around that. But it is far too soon to open this up for a public debate. . . ."

What was he doing? Making me the culprit? Yes! That's exactly what the desperate Sandy had in mind.

By his account our preemptive strike was not a reaction to Roy Wurlitzer and his new policies. We had jumped the gun. Unwilling to bend with the times and listen to those who'd tried to offer some serious fiscal advice, we went out of our way to stir the pot of controversy, pushing the situation to an all-too-early flashpoint. His face was bright with indignation.

"Telling people on the air about personnel matters that have not even been finalized—my God, that is way, *way* over the line! I hate to say this, but it leaves me no choice. I am going to have to suspend Sheridan until further notice."

I was on my feet. "Wait a minute! What the hell, Sandy! Last night you said we get to finish out the week!"

"Sit down, Brody!" someone cried. "You've already done enough damage!"

A woman across the room called, "What about the rest of us? We still have jobs? Or is this the big Aloha?"

Whatever had been gathering and bubbling now spilled forth, a barrage of charges and countercharges, the shrill voice of Lorene from the office among them.

"This is treason, Sandy! You promised us! You promised nothing would change!"

"Hold it! Hold it!" cried the newscaster whose avuncular reports were familiar from shore to shore. "Give him a chance! Sandy, you finished yet?"

He wasn't. But anything else he had to say was lost in a rising chorus. Two directors walked out. I saw a man and a woman, a couple who co-hosted *Short Story Classics,* break into tears. An ordinarily peaceful vegetarian, a very tall, ponytailed and saintly fellow who came in twice a week to do the organic gardening show, rose from his front-row seat and, without touching Sandy, somehow forced him back against the acoustic tiling. Hoping he'd break character and land a blow on my behalf, I watched two friends pull him away, all the while calling out for calm.

My own disgust welled up. I would have rushed Sandy then, taken him by the throat, had not the board of directors closed in around him like a squad of security guards.

I was near the door when another volunteer, a guy who came in on weekends to DJ an hour of world music, glared at me from under his Oakland A's ball cap.

"Thanks a whole hell of a lot."

"What's that supposed to mean?"

"For making things worse than they already were, that's all."

"Did you hear my show?"

"I'm glad I wasn't listening."

"You dumb shit . . ."

I have thrown few punches in my life, but I was ready to go after this guy I hardly knew. I couldn't get at Sandy. I had to get at someone. When I swung the first time, a half-swing, he ducked and I caught his temple, twisting the cap.

"Hey! For Christ sake!"

I wanted more, wanted to feel a solid blow. I swung again, realizing too late that he was on something and ready to be reckless, coming back at me with both arms flailing. A friend of mine who boxed Golden Gloves in college once told me the most frightening person in the ring is the total amateur because you can never anticipate what he's going to do or where his next punch might come from. That was us, in the cluttered lobby of KRUX, two absurd amateurs willing to draw blood. By the time others pulled us apart I'd cut his cheek. My eye was dark and my right hand swollen.

A child's voice called "Uncle Dan!" and Julie's boy was running toward me, with Julie right behind him. "Toby! Toby, you come back here!"

She'd just walked in the front door, her face a scowl of motherly concern, maybe scowling at me too and at herself for being late, though I have to say she still looked wonderful, the way she entered. In the confusion of grappling hands and arms this was not lost on me, her light step, her supple stride.

"Uncle Dan," said Toby, grabbing my leg. "Your eye looks funny."

His small voice broke the tension, released a smattering of nervous laughter. Someone said, "Looks like you got at least one fan left."

As my opponent let himself be hustled away to the men's room for some in-house first aid he called back, "I'm going to sue your ass, Brody!"

"Good! I'm counting on it!"

"What's going on, what happened?" said Julie, close enough now to check out my face, my hand.

"Nothing. A little disagreement."

"Are you hurt? You look terrible."

"C'mon, let's get out of here."

"What about the meeting?"

"It's over."

"Already?"

"You didn't miss anything."

"San Pablo and University, that damn light is out. It took me forever . . ."

"C'mon."

As I lifted Toby I was suddenly aware, intensely aware of how much he took after his mother, not in a feminine way, but in a boyish transmuting of her exotic features, the cast of skin, the angle of eye, even in the heartbreaking openness of his five-year-old grin. It was a great comfort to feel his arms around my neck. I needed a hug of some kind just then, and I wanted to hold him closer but wouldn't let myself.

Once on the sidewalk I put him down, asked Julie where she'd parked, and as we walked tried to explain this muddled day, explain my wounds, my self, while she went on and on about the San Pablo traffic light, a stalled delivery truck, her mother's pride and sorrow, the cherished relatives soon flying in from Okinawa, and how Mama wanted

Julie and the boy to be in Los Angeles when they arrived, insisting they all be together at the exit gate to greet the long-lost cousins, the legendary uncle. "He's my older brother," Mama said, "the one you never met, the one who stayed in the cave with me during the war." She wanted to show off her full-grown daughter and the grandson too, and when Julie said it wasn't a good time for her, the mother didn't hear it. When Julie said, "It's a madhouse at work right now, I really have to be there, so how about we fly down next week or the week after?" her mother didn't hear it. "This is your uncle," she said, her eyes brimming with old griefs.

"You should have heard this, Danny. She talks about World War II like it ended yesterday, and she is still nine and they are all still living in caves and can't decide who they're hiding from, the Japanese or the Americans, and when the rice was gone it was this brother who went out and found some, crept down the hill below the cave and on that hillside she says they still find mortar shells and bullets—to this very day!—sometimes American bullets, sometimes Japanese. Forty years after the war, this is what she's telling me, and now this same brother who has never seen his family in America is coming to L.A. 'You can stay out all night in San Francisco,' she says, 'but you can't be there to meet your uncle. He is fifty years old, Julie! You think he is going to live forever?' "

Sometimes, when she passed these stories on to me, her eyes would challenge mine, just a flicker, inside an apologetic glance. Julie never made demands in so many words. But her eyes would say, "If you care about me, if you truly care about us as a couple, you'll find a way to support me here and share this task." To which my inner voice would reply, "Why now? Why today? She is not my mother-in-law. Toby is not my kid."

In the parking lot, around the corner from the station, we stood beside her car, very near where we'd stood the night before, jazz lyrics in our ears, kissing like hungry high school kids, but separate now, with Toby between us looking up, waiting for someone to pay attention to him, hoping for another lift from me, or a loving glance from his exhausted mommy who'd hoped this day could be devoted to our common cause, our podium and our pulpit, and meal ticket too. Along with our high-minded principles, income was at stake. We both needed our jobs, though her juggling act was more precarious than mine—part-time lecturing at the community college, freelance gigs when she could get them, the occasional check from Toby's father.

"Where's your mother now?"

"She went for a walk."

"You hungry? Thirsty? You want to get something?"

"I do, yes. But I'd better go find her. She was pretty upset. We were both upset."

"I'll come with you."

"Not with that eye. You need to get that taken care of"—shaking her head like a teacher in the schoolyard. "You know, Danny, sometimes you overdo it."

"Punching out Roland?"

With a shrug she flung her hands wide, as if to say whatever had befallen us was somehow all my doing.

In self-defense I blurted, "You should have heard the sonofa-bitch . . ."

I caught myself, glancing down at Toby, whose blank face told me he hadn't missed a word. I knew that face, knew it too well. For an instant it was the day I heard my mother and Hank exchanging strained words in the kitchen, the air around them charged with things unsaid and all they couldn't say, the day she took me out onto the porch to tell me I had another father, who had died in the war. I was five again, looking up with an empty face at Hank whose fierce words made me cold inside. Then I was Uncle Dan again looking down at Toby.

Pay Attention

On Friday morning the *Chronicle*'s "Bay Area" section led off with a headline designed to agitate and prickle:

KRUX: SOLD TO THE HIGHEST BIDDER

The end of the story noted a demonstration planned for the next afternoon. By the time I got there, five or six hundred people had already moved into the parking lot behind the station, spilling across the street where two motorcycle cops sat waiting, watching.

Larry, the frequent caller and veteran protestor, had cobbled together a citizens' committee and backed in a flatbed truck. Over the cab flapped a hand-painted banner with tilted, cartoonish mikes beside bold red lettering:

SAVE OUR VOICE

Channel 2 was there, a cameraman, a soundman, the glossy van parked around the corner. If they followed the usual script for rallies and marches, the news editor would single out a tattooed, shirtless figure shaking his fist at the heavens and crying out for justice. On a blue-sky Saturday when the sun was unseasonably warm and the scene magnetic, such fellows were surely part of the mix, but far outnumbered by the mothers with kids, the senior citizens bearing homemade signs, teachers and nurses, lawyers and carpenters who couldn't have found time for this on a Wednesday.

The committee had invited a dissenting board member, who said his heart was with them but by-laws prevented him from speaking at a public event, at least not yet. They invited Sandy to speak for management, and he promised to give them a statement, but he hadn't sent it and that was a mistake. Sandy needed a PR man. He truly didn't know how to handle his new role: the guy who once wrote profiles on Abbie Hoffman and César Chávez wasn't used to being grouped with "The Man." Any gesture from him could have diluted the swell of mistrust in the air. Silence from Sandy and from the rest of the board was read as further proof of backroom collusion.

Larry himself was the first speaker. I'd only heard him as a caller. Now here was a seasoned face—bushy beard, bulging eyebrows—to go with the raspy, seasoned voice. He wore a black T-shirt, black leather jacket, wraparound shades. You might have taken him for a dealer, or a film director. Later on I found out he was a county social worker who moonlighted weekends as bouncer at a singles club.

As he mounted the truck bed I was once again looking around for Julie, hoping she'd make it back in time from Oakland International. Her mother had chosen that day to fly home. "She can't wait till tomorrow," Julie'd told me on the phone that morning, "and I don't want to set her off again. At this point, the sooner the better. So yes, I *will* try to catch up with you at the rally."

It gave me hope, the way she loaded the word "will." If she showed, I would read it as a sign of . . . what? A new beginning? On bright days she wore a big white hat with a flat crown, something you'd wear in Palm Springs if you hoped to be taken for a celebrity. On her it looked outrageously glamorous. I was scanning for that hat when Larry raised his hand, calling for quiet. With his own money he'd rented the bullhorn, which gave every word from the flatbed a weird authority and hint of crisis, as if it came from the top of a patrol car telling you to pull over.

"Just call me a listener," Larry announced, "a devoted listener. As soon as I heard from Sheridan that this station might be in trouble, I said to myself, 'We can't let it happen.' It isn't just a bunch of chatter and background music to get you through the morning commute. It's a big voice in our community. You mess with KRUX, you mess with our soul!"

A cheer rose from the parking lot.

"What you have to understand is, back where I came from they didn't have anything like KRUX. I remember catching an interview maybe fifteen years ago, with a Zen roshi, and he did what roshis always do. They hit you with some kind of riddle that turns your head around. He says, 'One day someone asked the master, if you knew you only had three days to live, what would you do? And the master says, Pay attention.' "

A murmur of approval rippled through the crowd.

"Pay attention! Maybe it sounds simple. But it changed my life. You see, I'm telling you this because back where I came from you never heard roshis on the radio. The news was about wheat futures and the price of hogs. Sometimes you could get the ball game. Gospel preachers are going all day long. I have nothing against the gospel either, don't get me wrong. But there's a limit. Go look up 'gospel' in the dictionary. Originally it meant 'the good tale,' 'the good news.' Think about it, people. Aren't there many kinds of good news? On KRUX you hear them all."

Another cheer.

"So we want to bring up some of the people who make it what it is, folks from the station you hear all the time but never get to see, starting with the guy who blew the whistle. You know who I mean. We all know him as the host of *Sit Still and Listen*. Please welcome *Sheridan Brody*!"

They gave me a rousing ovation. From cards and letters that soon came in I learned I was seen not only as a whistle-blower. I was a first casualty in the battle to save the station. In that crowd no one yet knew I'd been let go *before* I blew the whistle. This was okay with me, a little misperception I could live with. Every cause needs a poster boy. I let myself be swept away by what felt like an outburst of approval, laced with a current of respectful pity. And I welcomed their pity, telling myself I was there to serve. To reveal my darkened eye—which appeared to them to be a well-earned badge of honor—I removed my shades and actually raised my arms high in a power salute, triggering another swell of applause, a chorus of whistles, a brief and good-humored chant.

"Bro - dy! Bro - dy! Bro - dy! Bro - dy!"

As things turned out, that Olympian salute was all I had to say. Poised like a demagogue prepared to storm city hall, I found myself at a loss for words, and I wasn't ready for that. Talking off the cuff had never been a chore. Five nights a week it was what I did, field the comments as they came. But a sea of eyes and faces watching me in high anticipation—this was different. Inside the studio you knew somebody was out there, but you never knew quite who or how many or what they looked like. As a talk show host you're a public figure, but seldom in the public eye. You don't have to get your teeth straightened or have a wardrobe consultant or worry about your hair.

Out of habit I looked for Julie, as I always did at the start of a show, for her cue to start talking. I wanted her to be up there with me, to share this odd moment of sunlit notoriety, my cohort, my coconspirator. Again I scanned the crowd for her wide white hat. I scanned the rows of booths and tables at the lot's far edge, hoping I might spot her among the gypsy vendors and petition bearers who showed up at every kind of public gathering with T-shirts saying SOLAR POWER and GREENPEACE, with sign-up sheets and handouts for Planned Parenthood, mass transit, the Big Sur Marathon, tai chi and acupuncture. One tall poster with a missile turned into a dollar sign said IRAN/CONTRA: TELL THE TRUTH. Lifting my eyes, looking farther east, beyond the crowd I could see the campus bell tower, the campanile standing white against the Berkeley hills. Toward the west a narrow view opened through staggered rooflines of the neighborhood with just the peak of Tamalpais showing from far-off Marin, its penumbra made of light rising off the waters of the bay. I couldn't see the water, but I could see that light. It was one of those rare fall days when the skies are stunningly clear, all forms of smog and haze erased, so that reflected light coats the towns around the bay with an atmosphere of silvery gold. That Saturday, even the scuffy, oil-stained parking lot had its luminous edge. In that westward glance I saw a day like this a hundred years earlier, with no smog yet, no haze, no refineries or Texaco storage tanks, no all-day, all-night cavalcade of cars and trucks and vans and buses across the bridges, up and down the freeways that follow all the shorelines, back in the days when the only screen between you and sunlight was an early-morning fog that on most days pulled back outside the gate or disappeared and let the inland sea glitter and shine and send up its salubrious aura to fill the air from Santa Rosa to San Jose.

Envisioning that smog-free harbor, I saw a ferry pushing through this same kind of light, an afternoon of wind-chipped water, each chip a spark, the ferry surrounded by leaping sparks, an old double-decked side-wheel steamer that once plied the Sacramento River but now puffed back and forth across the bay, this time bound for San Francisco. Something came to me then, and I should have started talking. On the air I could have talked for hours. I wanted to call out the words on the sign behind me. "Save Our Voice." I wanted to tell them about my great-grandmother and how she came to be aboard this ferry, the unspoken history threaded through her stories, her diary. I wanted to tell them more about the floating memory of her daughter Rosa and all the family souvenirs crammed inside her Airstream, tell them about Rosa's son, my missing father who never had a voice and didn't live long enough to gather any souvenirs, save for one Purple Heart and a snapshot of his high school girlfriend. When Larry handed me the bullhorn I thrust it toward the sky, drawing another roar from the expectant crowd. But when I held it to my lips, nothing came.

In my eagerness to speak I'd lost my powers of speech. I could only see pictures. I was like the blindfolded guy before the firing squad in the instant before the triggers are pulled. In that loaded interval between "Aim!" and "Fire!" his whole life passes before him, though in this case it was not my life, it was Nani's. Larry was trying to save the station's voice. I was trying to save Nani's voice. Nani didn't know it yet but she would soon be trying to save Kawika's voice. I saw where he had been. I saw where she had been. I saw where she was going, or thought I did. I'd been rushing through the trove of volumes passed on to me by Rosa, devouring pages no one else had ever read, gripped by her account of those days as she lived them and as she revisited events that seemingly took half a lifetime to understand.

I passed the bullhorn to Larry, but didn't leave the flatbed. He wanted me to stand with him as others came forth to testify, to bear witness, to lash out at management, call for public hearings, call for a letter barrage to the station and to Argonaut, to state and federal officials, call for volunteers to blockade the building. It was more than a rally. It was a war party, and I listened. I had to. My job was on the line. Yet I wasn't there, and I did not listen. I was two places at once. In my body. And out of my body. Standing on the flatbed like a revolutionary. And floating out over the silvery lustre of the bay . . .

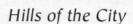

Hills of the City

I saw islands poking through the glitter, where clouds of seabirds swooped, pelicans and gulls, and in the burnished distance the headlands of the unbridged Golden Gate. Out in the middle of the water, on the brave side-wheel steamer ploughing west, I saw Nani in a deck chair with her hands in her lap, atop a small cloth traveling bag. She wore gloves, a pillbox hat, her heavy coat buttoned to the neck. At age twenty-seven she was on the move again, on the water again, feeling cleansed by a hard and briny wind, a winter wind.

Ahead of her rose the hills of the city, set against a cloudless blue sky coated with gold. Off to the right, behind the row of wharves, stood the rocky heap called Telegraph Hill, where Morse code signals were once received from lookout posts above the straits to alert the town that a ship was about to enter the bay. Right in front of her the bulging nob of Nob Hill was studded with mansions like the General's. And farther back, where the city had yet to reach, rose the pair of mounds they called Twin Peaks, once a single mountain (so went the tribal legend) composed of a man and wife who quarreled so much the Great Spirit finally sent down a lightning bolt to split the mountain apart. Did Nani know this legend? Not yet. Not on this day. But later on she'd hear of it and enter it into her Book of Days, followed by this remark:

> Kawika is right. Every mountain tells a story. Every river sings a song. Every bay. Every island. We must not forget them.

In the flats, where downtown buildings spread and spread, the tallest was still the Palace, eight stories high, a small mountain unto itself, a mesa topped with parapets and flags on poles. As her ferry neared the wharf she could see it, and from its roof she could see the tricolored flag of

Hawai'i, striped red, white and blue, which meant the king was still in residence.

She'd kept the address of the small hotel where Hawaiians were welcome, the one Makua Flynn took her to, and she would stop there first, to pay for one night. She had the money for two or three, if need be. If she somehow missed Kawika, or couldn't reach him, if he refused to see her, or if his chamberlain barred the door—if all else failed she'd spend a night at the small hotel and head for home on the morning ferry. That was her backup plan, though she wasn't thinking of it as she made her way along Market Street, through city air charged with a thrilling and threatening uncertainty, as if at any moment some unseen hand could dart out and take her by the shoulder.

She sighted her destination five blocks ahead, a monolith above the scurrying crowds of late afternoon, the hacks and carriages, the rattling of wheels, the clatter of horses' hooves, the clerks and shopgirls spilling out of doorways, and tradesmen heading for saloons, with paperboys at every corner, their urgent voices cutting through the hubbub. And in the very midst of this throng of strangers appeared a man she thought she recognized but did not want to recognize, the bowler hat, the brick-red sideburns and muttonchops sprouting from his jaw. As if this were the unseen hand she feared, a tightness gripped her throat. He'd stepped from an office building and now moved briskly along Market not four feet ahead of her. She tried to make him be someone else, tried to see another nose, another cheek, but couldn't. It was Giles Peabody in woolen scarf and overcoat with fur lapels.

She slowed her pace, let the crowd surge past, following him first with her eyes, then with her feet. She followed him to the intersection with New Montgomery, where five streets met, where a tall policeman stood like a blue tree at the center of a traffic snarl, his arms two waving branches, his shrill whistle adding the highest note. The hotel stood half a block to the south, but Giles turned north toward the business district. Screened by pedestrians she continued to follow him, and why she did so, why she tracked this man she should have been running from, is still something of a mystery to me. In her diary she would describe this day with uncharacteristic confusion:

Why is he here? Is he with Kawika? The news did not mention him. He has not changed. He walks like a man walking into the wind. I almost called out to him, almost said his name. How could

I think of doing that? He should not be here. I should not be here. The city is too big. All the pushing and fast walking makes me feel alone. It makes me crazy.

When he turned again, a couple of blocks down New Montgomery, she watched from a corner, watched him walk half a block along a street busy with carriages and cable cars and step into another building. She wanted to wait there, watching, to see if he might step out again, but it was too cold to wait. New Montgomery was a tunnel of icy wind. She walked toward the building, studying its line. From the opposite sidewalk she could see a plate-glass window on the second floor with gilded letters lined in black:

PEABODY TRADE AND MARITIME
EST. 1874

As she gazed at this, he appeared at the window, without overcoat, a drink in hand. Was he looking down on her?

She dipped her head and hurried back the way she'd come, shrugging against the cold. She hadn't noted that gilt lettering across the third-floor window spelled out EDISON GENERAL ELECTRIC COMPANY. There was no reason to notice, since Nani had not yet heard of Thomas Edison or his wondrous machine. Nor did she yet know that Peabody was passing through this city on his way home to Honolulu, after a hectic trip to Washington, D.C. Only later would she learn, as she looked back, trying to solve the puzzle of these days, that he was here to prevent the king from traveling any farther east. She didn't know this yet, but maybe she felt it and, for these few blocks, had followed the same look of dark intent that once had repelled her and also drawn her toward him.

In the Nick of Time

She ran the last block, slowing only to pass through the archway and into the Garden Court with its tiers of balconies, its soaring atrium. Past the carriages lined up on marble paving, and the patient horses breathing steam, the heaps of baggage, she found the lobby just as she remembered it and fell into a padded chair. She didn't want to move for quite some time, hoping in this way to remain invisible, as again she asked herself, What is he doing here? And, what was *she* doing here, where she had no good reason to be? Why had she come to this city? What did she imagine would happen today? She didn't know. She couldn't remember. She was ready to run back through the archway, though she had no idea where she would run to.

A voice called out, "Miss Nani?"

Like a thief caught on the doorstep, she froze, listening. Had he somehow followed her here? No. This wasn't Peabody's voice. But she'd heard it before.

"Miss Nani, is that you?"

A black man in a black suit and a black bow tie was sizing her up from across the corridor, a man from times past.

"Mister Milton?"

"Well, I'll be. I will be. Saw you walk in here and said to myself now how do I know that pretty lady? Then it came to me."

He stood beside a narrow desk, the very fellow who'd handled bags for the royal party back in 1881. Now he was head bellman, hair a bit grayer, but his face lit with the same rascal smile, as if they shared an old secret.

"Mister Milton," she cried, as if he'd traveled a hundred miles to rescue her. He had stepped out from behind his desk, and she threw her arms around him.

"Whoa now! Like to knock me over."

"You used to whistle songs. . . ."

Under his breath he piped a few notes. "Still do from time to time. . . ."

"I remember how you made us laugh and laugh."

"Have to be careful, Miss Nani. Can't cut up quite like I used to, bein' an executive now." He winked. "Maybe later on I'll whistle up a tune or two. But first tell me something. You been here all along? Didn't see you come in with the Hawaiian bunch."

She couldn't answer, but he didn't seem to need an answer.

"I was kinda hopin' you come back to see ol' Milton. I guess I can't hold it against His Majesty now, can I, laid up the way he is. They say he's fightin' off a cold or some such thing and not takin' callers. But I reckon he won't mind having you around, since you're not just any ol' caller, after all. C'mon, I'll ride up with you. There's a fella outside the elevator just in case somebody gets off by mistake, if you know what I mean."

As they ascended he kept talking. "I know if I was laid up with the croup or whatever I'd feel a whole lot better seein' you walk through the door." Another wink, another flirting chuckle. "No ma'am, wouldn't need no patent medicine or any such as that if ol' Milton knew *you* was headin' his way."

She was giggling now, as if ten years had fallen away, a happy, giddy, nervous giggle, wishing she and Milton could just ride a while inside this upholstered elevator where it was safe, up to the top floor and down and up again. But the door slid open. Another, younger black man was standing there, and Milton was all business, telling him with a somber face that his good friend Nani was on her way to see the king.

"You need anything else while you're here," he told her, "you let ol' Milton know. Most of the time I'm there at my station . . . unless . . . unless . . ." His chuckle broke through again. "Unless I take sick myself, come down with something so you'd have to look in on me and lift my poor ol' raggedy spirits up to a new level."

Far down the corridor she could see a soldier with a pistol at his belt. Again she yearned to run back the way she'd come. But the elevator door had closed behind her. Milton was gone. Reaching the soldier seemed to take an hour, her steps noiseless on the plush carpeting. He was an officer from the Hawaiian Royal Guard, an aide-de-camp. Before she opened her mouth he was shaking his head. The king is resting, he said, on physician's orders, and cannot be disturbed.

In Hawaiian she said, "I am a relative of the royal family. Please tell him it is Nani Keala."

He regarded her closely, as his eyes relaxed, perhaps not entirely persuaded, but amused by her bravado. With a smile and a nod he stepped inside, closing the door, and returned a while later with a respectful bow of welcome.

"His Majesty will see you. But remember, this visit must be very brief."

He led her through one room, then another, then a third, rooms that hadn't changed at all, each with its fire grate, its chandelier, its figured carpeting. The king had taken six rooms that wrapped around one corner of the third floor to make an L-shaped suite. In the farthest of these his bed was placed to take the sun that had poured all afternoon through one of the high bay windows. Now an orange twilight tinted lush draperies and upholstered chairs, and for just a few moments lit the king's face. It was hard to tell whether the flush across his pallid cheeks was put there by the sight of Nani or by the setting sun.

His hair was thinner. He looked like an older brother of the Kawika she remembered. But the same voice reached out to her, rich and resonant, filtered by a stuffy nose.

"Aloha, Nani. How wonderful to see you. I am overwhelmed."

"Aloha," she said, stepping toward the bed to place her nostril next to his, touch forehead to forehead.

His hand went up. "Better not come too close. They say I may still be contagious."

"Is it the flu?"

"A fever. A slight condition of the chest. Nothing serious, or so they say. Please sit down and let me look at you. What a treat this is!"

"I am so glad you remember me."

"Remember you! I have thought of you a thousand times and wondered if we would ever meet again, though I wish of course I could give you a proper greeting."

A lift of his eyebrow gave this a playful, suggestive edge, and she had to smile, though it was hard to smile, seeing what he had become. Something had happened to Kawika. A bad cough had sent him to bed, but the sadness around his eyes was more than fever or the watery look of a cold running its course. On the ferry she'd been remembering how he looked the day she saw him step from the railroad car to greet the welcoming contingent, so large against the doorway in his morning coat, his hand held high, his broad, bronze face so youthful, full of confidence at the end of his trip around the world. Seeing him propped on pillows in the orange afterglow was like the drawing on the front page of the

Examiner, the outline of his head and shoulders. What was missing? Was it the whiskers? His black side whiskers had been shaved away. Is that what made his cheeks look thin?

A white-haired man in naval uniform stood in the doorway. "Excuse me, Your Majesty . . ."

"Come in, doctor. I want you to meet my cousin and my very good friend. . . ."

This was the medical officer from the U.S.S. *Charleston,* mightily displeased, regarding Nani as if she'd just climbed in a window. "This is to be a day with no visitors."

"Well, doctor, I am to blame. We are having a bit of a reunion here."

"Your dinner is coming up. In advance of that I need to check your temperature and your pulse and a few other matters. Alas, I'm afraid we must ask your friend to leave. . . ."

"On the contrary. I think Miss Keala is joining me for dinner. Isn't that correct, Nani? Do you have other plans? No? Excellent. Let us call room service and have something sent up. As I recall, you never did approve of their chicken salad. So we'll simply skip that. But the fish this week is quite good. What do you think? Some grilled salmon? Some russet potatoes? Some string beans? Perhaps a half bottle of Pouilly-Fuissé . . ."

The officer's jaws were bunching, as his cheeks turned red. "You know alcohol is not recommended. . . ."

"It's not for me. Nani is having some. I don't know where she has come from, or how far she has traveled. But I'm sure it has been a long day."

The physician slipped a thermometer under the royal tongue and left without another word, causing the king to lift another bawdy eyebrow, and again Nani had to laugh. With the thermometer dangling like a cigarette he laughed too—getting away with something—a little salute to who they used to be.

After that it was easy to talk, to begin the catching up and reaching back—"Have these been happy years for you, Nani?" . . . "Are you still writing in your journal? That's important work, you know" . . . "I still remember the day we met"—while she revealed, to his delight, the necklace underneath her coat, the purple strands from Ni'ihau, while twilight faded and electric lamps came on below to light city streets still busy with the faint rattle of trolley cars and carriages.

Their food came on silver trays, the entrées under silver hoods, the wine in its silver bucket. White tablecloths were spread. With great flourish a black waiter opened the bottle, filling Nani's glass, and would have filled the king's but it was upside down.

"What is it the French say? Abstinence makes the heart grow fonder?"

The waiter laughed. "Not quite the way I heard it, Your Lordship. But I guess it's close enough."

With the food and the drink, the litter of goblets and cutlery, they were soon talking in the manner of old friends who haven't met in years and can pick the conversation up as if no time has passed, the comfort of familiar companionship that loosens the tongue and opens the heart. It was almost the same. And yet it wasn't. Somehow their roles had reversed. Once famous for his many appetites, Kawika didn't eat much, drank only water. In times past he had been the mentor, she the protégée. Now he seemed to feed on her, as if she reminded him of something almost forgotten. In his eyes she glimpsed a sorrow no laughter could erase. Had his wife passed away? Or his beloved sister?

The officer reappeared, this time with a pitcher of water and a sedative and a face so sour she rose from her chair, searching for her coat.

With true alarm Kawika said, "Where are you going?"

She didn't know. All she could say was, "I have stayed too long."

"Indeed," said the officer. "His Majesty needs nothing so much as an undisturbed rest. . . ."

"On the contrary, doctor. I am inviting Nani to stay the night."

"Surely you are joking."

"We have not worked out the details. But this is my desire."

"Your Majesty, if I may, as your personal physician, speak frankly . . ."

"Forgive me, doctor. But my precious rest will not be endangered. We have other rooms here. We have nothing but rooms, with beds and couches of every type. What do you think, Nani? Will you stay a while longer? Do you have other plans? You can make yourself comfortable, order food, whatever is needed. Seeing you again . . ."

As if the officer had already made his exit, as if they were alone again, Nani and Kawika on the breezy verandah high on their slope above the distant town and the gleaming harbor, he said with intimate ardor, "Seeing you again . . . well, you were always good for me. And now you have arrived in the nick of time. I don't want to lose you. I need to know you are close by."

"Yes," she said at last, her voice catching. "I can stay, if it please you."

"Your Majesty, I must protest!"

"As well you should. Protest away. It is your duty to protest, and I salute you for it. But Nani will be with us here a while. I assure you, for my affliction, whatever it may be, there is no better remedy."

In an adjoining room she stayed the night, and spent the next day beside the king, while the grim and disapproving medical officer came and went, while a consulting physician came and went, and the gracious waiters, and while the aide delivered bouquets and cards from other callers who'd been turned away—the vice president of a lumber company, a member of the city council, a reporter, a fire chief—while messages passed between the king and his chamberlain, fighting off bronchitis in a suite across the hall, having picked up a similar bug during their side trip to the olive grove near Santa Barbara.

On her way to the city Nani's dream had been to see him, simply that, to be with him one more time. Now that she'd seen him, her dream was to see him strong again. Her instinct was to heal whatever had weakened him. The first night she listened to his voice. The next morning she placed her hands upon his body. She would start with his ribs, his back, his forehead. As she pulled a chair up next to the bed he said again, "Do not come too close." But once he felt the heat upon his skin and passing through his skin, she wasn't close enough.

"Lie beside me, Nani."

She shook her head.

With a smile both weary and cavalier he said, "I am too indisposed to take advantage of you. But I would give anything to feel you next to me. Our bodies once made such a perfect fit. Please, Nani. I will behave myself."

She took off her dress and hung it in a closet. Wrapping herself in a hotel robe, she lay down next to him, on top of the spread, while her hands heated his chest and his face and his eyes, like flat hot stones from an earth oven.

Only one caller was admitted into the royal presence that day, a Mr. Louis Glass from the Edison Company, who claimed to have a talking machine.

"Does he mean a machine that talks?" asked the king.

"Forgive me, Your Majesty," said the aide-de-camp. "I am not sure what he means."

"Well, if he works for Thomas Edison, I want to meet him. By all means, show him in."

From his suite across the hall the red-eyed, wheezing chamberlain was summoned. The ship's physician and the aide stood by, as curious as the king. During his global tour Kalakaua had gone out of his way to stop in New Jersey for a visit with the world-famous inventor who, in those days, had recently developed the first lightbulb. As he followed Edison around the lab, he'd been full of questions, already scheming to bring this miracle out to Honolulu. But that was ten years ago. Before Glass finished explaining his new device, with its wheels and pulleys and flex hose and rolls of wax, the king was dozing off, his enthusiasm muted by a sudden fatigue. A patient man, Glass asked if he might leave it on a table in the corner. With a courteous nod to the assembled staff he said, "Please tell His Majesty I will return."

Gifts

Sometime later they began to talk again, lying side by side as if they were still lovers in the lazy aftermath of making love. She had just appeared to him in a dream, he said. "You were dancing, with your hair hanging loose, and maile vines around your neck."

"Were there other dancers?"

"You were all alone on a grassy point above the sea. What a delicious dream. I did not want it to end."

"I too have dreamed of you," she said, telling him then of how he rode on horseback toward a fire in the mountains while all those around him were shouting to turn back.

"Your hair was on fire, and sparks were in the air."

"Not such a happy dream as mine."

"You showed great courage."

"But fire was everywhere, you say."

"Yes, your horse reared back and kicked his legs."

"Ah, Nani, this was indeed an accurate dream. Every day I feel that I am riding into a fire. Touch my forehead. Is it hot? No? Even so, I am burning up. I am burning alive. Please, place your hand there again, right where it was. Yes. Thank you. What a blessing to have you here. Can I tell you what is in my heart?"

"You must always speak your heart."

"I am afraid, Nani."

"I know."

"How do you know?"

"We are all afraid."

"It is a curse to be king."

"Do not say that."

"I only want to be Kawika."

"Do you fear your death?"

He rolled his head and looked at her, as if astonished by this question, then reached to draw her close. She held back. But he wasn't being amorous. It was only to bring his lips next to her ear, to impart a secret history he felt compelled to share. Almost whispering he told her that during his lifetime four kings of Hawai'i had died, each death surrounded by rumors, mysteries and questions that still awaited answers.

When Kawika was eighteen the younger son of Kamehameha the First had passed away at the age of forty-one. He was ill and unconscious when an English physician came to look in on him and, after an hour alone with the king, emerged from his chambers to pronounce him dead. No one who'd seen the king in recent days thought him anywhere close to death. Yet somehow, during his hour alone with the Englishman, he had given up the ghost. And this was only one of several stories Kawika could tell her, of Hawaiian leaders taken before their time.

His own life, he said, had been so often threatened he knew not whom to trust. Not long ago in Honolulu a rattle of shutters had awakened him from a restless slumber. Damp with sweat he'd rushed to the window in time to see a hunched figure hurrying across the grounds and into the darkness. As he cried out for guards, he noted a scrap of paper pinned to the casement and by lamplight read the crudely scribbled warning, "Next time you won't wake up." Now here he was at age fifty-four, confined to his suite, wondering why this ailment had come upon him, and pleading with Nani yet again to stay nearby, his lips beside her ear whispering, "Do not leave me. I never wanted you to leave. You are my ears and eyes. Help me see what surrounds me here."

With one hand on his forehead she lay close and listened. Like a student with photographic recall she seemed to remember everything he said that day, whether or not she fully understood it at the time. Years later she would still be looking back:

I almost told Kawika who I saw in the street. But I could not say the name. I did not want him to be in the city. I was hoping I only dreamed him. If I said the name it could make him real. But Kawika already knew what was in my mind. He said the missionary boys are still after me. They want me gone. They want me gone so they can give away the islands. That is why I go to meet the President. Make me well so I can do it Nani. It is not too late to save Hawaii for Hawaiians. This is all I want to do. Yet some of my people think I am owned by the missionary boys. A powerful kahuna puts a curse on me, a kapu, for giving away too much. He thinks I go to Washington to take a bribe and sell my people out. This kahuna says you give away your land you give away your soul. I want to tell him yes. Yes. I want to tell him put a kapu on the missionary boys not on your king.

His aide knocked on the door and came in with a big package. It was a book. The king told him bring a pen. I watched him open the book and write. Then he handed it to me. I had to sit up to hold it. Open it, he said. This is for you. They sent it up from a shop around the corner. It was a thick book with many pages and yellow covers and gold letters that said Legends and Myths of Hawaii by His Hawaiian Majesty King David Kalakaua. The letters were bright and glowing and made my hands feel hot. I could not speak. I want you to have this he said. Last year it was finally published. The stories are here the ones we used to talk about. I opened it and saw a photo from years before in his uniform with all his medals and a wide sash. His chest was thick and black side whiskers covered his cheeks. On the next page were the words he wrote. For my bird of another heaven, with Aloha.

My tears came down. Such a beautiful book. And I had no gift to give Kawika. I leaned and kissed his forehead and his eyes and his smooth cheeks where the whiskers used to be. I could see from his eyes that his heart was full. He said I want my people to remember. So many have died. So many are forgetting. The same kahuna curses me for giving away our stories. He says our soul is in the stories. You give away our stories you give away our soul. I want to tell him stories are different from land. Never let them take away the land. But the stories must be heard.

One day you will understand what I am talking about. You are a writer too Nani. Your people have a story that must be told so others can know their spirit. Many will tell you do not speak. Don't be afraid to tell it before it disappears.

I saw my mother then. I heard her voice telling of great man coming down to make the world from mud carried by the turtle from the dark sea bottom. I heard her tell how soldiers came and rounded up the people and marched them across the valley and into the far mountains. I listened to her voice. She was a young woman. In my mind she is always young. But her voice is old and wise. Again I heard the stories she told and I knew then what I could do.

. . .

By this time it must have been late afternoon, with the sun's last rays slanting in to tint the king and the wall behind his bed. As Nani closed the book and folded back the blankets and set her feet upon the floor he said, "Don't go far."

She stepped around the bed, into the middle of the room, so that her hair was backlit by a late sun. She stood still, waiting for the movement to come into her legs and arms, gradually easing into a slow hula, though it wasn't quite a hula. It was a rolling, random warming up, and Kawika's eyes were instantly brighter. His hungry eyes followed her as a low hum rose from his throat. Inside the humming lurked a subtle tempo, and she gave herself to that, her liquid hands drifting into it. When his hum trailed off, she waited, marking time.

"Are you going to dance for me?"

"Yes."

"Ah, Nani, this is so much more than I could have hoped for."

"And you will sing."

"Yes, I will sing. But first, I think your robe . . ."

"My robe?"

"Is too thick . . . and heavy . . . for the hula."

"It feels heavy."

"And too long."

"You are right."

"You should take it off."

"But the door is open."

"Close it."

"The doctors . . . the waiters . . ."

"Close it. Lock it. Lock both doors. And pull the drapes. Take everything off."

"Everything?"

"All too confining . . . for the hula."

She locked the doors and drew the drapes across the high bay window, shutting out a dusky twilight. She removed her robe and underclothes, all but the strands of purple shells, which hung from her neck and lay against her bosom. She undid her hair and let it fall. From his bed Kawika's hum eventually became a string of words. It was the song called "Kaholokai Kaleponi," The California Sailor. But he wasn't singing it. He was chanting verses in a guttural cadence. Her arms and hands followed the words as her gestures depicted the undulations of the sea, the rocking of the long canoe, the wind, the guardian shark who crossed the ocean behind the canoe, the fin of the shark a flat hand slicing air above the languid rise and fall of her smooth brown hips.

Verse after verse her body told the story. When his canoe reached the far land to the east, her fierce eyes said she was a demon creature waiting on the shore. She was fire. She was flood. As water spilled from her hands, she became the bays and rivers. Then her arms were dark trees along the river, and her fingers the white feathers hanging from the trees in the stillness above green water.

Kawika's voice faded. Around her the walls dissolved. Nani was alone above the river, and through clumps of white feathers her mother's eyes were watching the canoe and watching Nani, the mother young, speaking her name as she stepped through the trees to join her daughter, be one with the daughter, move with her, dancing as she used to dance in the roundhouse, in deerskins and necklaces, her head bobbing, her feet stomping as she shuffled forward, shuffled back, and in her hands the rabbit pelt, shaking, shaking, to keep the grizzly at bay.

Other elders entered Nani one by one and danced their dances, elders who watched and also danced and breathed their breath back into her body. She had not seen them before, yet she knew them by their moves, by their watchful, knowing eyes. Reverence flowed through her, the rush of ancient breath, and it must have passed into the eyes and limbs and shoulders of Kawika, who sat up straight in his bed, arms opened wide as if to breathe it in, chanting louder.

She heard his words again, as he urged her with a voice full and throbbing, until the California Sailor at last came back home from his journey. Nani was the Sailor, then she was the lissome lover he returned to, her hands shaping the valley between her legs that could also be the valley of his homeland, the lush lowlands, the damp slopes furred with greenery, the hands then fanning wide as she dipped her knees in a final bow to end the dance.

Through a long silence the king regarded her with wonder.

"Beautiful," he said at last. "Never have I seen such dancing."

"Thank you."

"You have revived me, Nani."

"It is my gift to Kawika."

"Now you must come back to bed."

She shook her head.

"You cannot say no."

"When you are well . . ."

"Nani, you have made me well."

"We have to wait."

"I have not felt so good in years. I am born again!"

"Maybe tomorrow."

"Have you only come here to torment me?"

"We have to wait."

She put on the robe, gathered up her underclothes and the volume of myths and legends. Unlocking the door, she left him there.

For years to come she would be haunted by this day and night. In her diary she would return to it time and time again, trying to account for what had passed through her, what had passed between her and the king. She said it changed her, but she could not say quite how. It haunts me too, the extraordinary nature of this gift to him, in the locked room on the third floor of the world's largest hotel, with Thomas Edison's new invention on a table in the corner, and trolley cars and carriages rattling down below, while other rooms in the royal suite were cluttered with other gifts, candy, crystal bowls, cards and flowers sent to the visiting monarch. Nani's was of another kind, just for Kawika, coming to him once again from outside the loop of politics and royal intrigue, a hula girl who danced her own kind of hula. The gift of her nakedness had stirred his loins, raised his erotic hopes, held his rapt attention as his eyes feasted on the lamplit skin, yet the subtle motion of the dance stirred more than that.

How hard it was to leave him. I feared he would be angry. He wanted me. I wanted him too. I thought we could wait. It was not that kind of dance. I did not want that to be the reason for the dance. I wanted him to be strong again.

I remember the words of Moana. Your ancestors are always watching she said. Our stories are their stories she said. You dance for them. At the rancheria the women say it too. The elders are always with us. In the room I saw them. They were there. Kawika knew it. The next day he thanked me. He told me about the story he chanted. When I see you he said I think about your father. I think about Keala. Once this story was Keala's story, he said. But when so many sing the song it is everybody's story. Now he is everybody's sailor. Be proud of him Nani he was a courageous man.

We did not yet know when the Edison man would come back. We did not yet know Kawika would chant the story one more time and it would be the last story he would tell. We thought he would soon be well and traveling again. This is what he said to me. He said your touch makes me alive again. Your dance makes me alive. He said let us run away together Nani. Let us run away to Washington D.C. His eyes were happy. He grabbed my hand like a young man would grab it. He said we will take the train as we did once before.

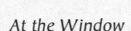

At the Window

In the second-floor offices of Peabody Trade the vice president and general counsel could not sit at his carved mahogany desk. He had to pace. In Prince Albert coat and dark cravat he crossed and recrossed the carpet with thoughtful, measured steps, chin outthrust as if about to address a jury. Now and again he paused to look down upon the busy midday avenue, the horse-drawn rigs, the crowded trolleys pulled toward Nob Hill by invisible cables clattering below the street. Ordinarily he liked the clang and clatter of San Francisco, the sound of progress. But on this day it did not satisfy. From the teeming city he wanted something else. After a month of travel he was still in a traveler's mode, anticipating the next stop, the next turn, bristling with the restlessness of expectation itself, and trying to shake his memory of a young woman he saw gazing up at his window as if ready to cross the street and climb the stairs.

It was his first day in town. He'd poured himself a drink, stepped to the window to consider the view, and he was almost certain he recognized her, though it had been years—how many?—and she was muffled in a thick winter coat. It took a moment to recall her name, the Indian girl with the Kanaka father who'd fled to California after that long-ago wrestle on the beach. Though she too had fled, or so he'd heard, left the islands in haste, she'd never fled far from his mind. He'd thought of her more times than he dared to count, a secret thought. Though he often bragged to other men of his liaisons, this was a day he'd never mentioned, their meeting in the country. He had no way to speak of it, only wished he could have it back. He'd figured her to be another simple-minded consort like all the rest of them, and yet she'd left him unhinged by some quality he could not name. If only he'd found the words to hold her there, it might have turned out differently. He wanted something from this day; he'd wanted something from that day too. As she rode away how it galled him that she belonged to Kalakaua, that she'd be riding back to the one who least deserved such a companion.

He'd almost waved, imagining something more than chance had brought her to the sidewalk outside this very building, imagining she might actually have come in search of him. After all these years perhaps she too remembered that day. It would be vain to think so. Yet he allowed himself to think so. In Honolulu he could not be seen with such a dusky woman, but here in San Francisco, where they don't watch your every move, who knew what might occur? He'd almost raised the window to call down, then stayed his arm, thinking he might be mistaken, it might not be her. From where he stood, as she ducked against the wind, he couldn't be entirely sure.

So let that go. Yes, let it go and keep your sights trained upon the king, the king, the incompetent king.

Allies

Wherever Giles went, it was always the king, his calendar, his entourage, his hollow remarks. In Honolulu. In the pages of the *Examiner*. In Washington, D.C., where Kalakaua's arrival was now much anticipated. Or so Giles had been told, in confidence, by a very influential senator. Almost ten years had passed since the last royal visit, toward the end of his famous global tour, yet many there still remembered his charm, his erudition, his good humor, his ballroom skills.

"He was so well received," this senator said, "he is sure to be saluted again, wined and dined again, perhaps given the chance to speak before a joint session, since a king here in the capital is rare indeed."

"Remembered!" Giles had exclaimed. "Dammit, man, he has no right to be remembered!"

"Perhaps not. But he is. And he will be listened to. I would not underestimate it, Giles. Kalakaua will be listened to. The mere fact that he has come so far, by ship and by rail, in the dark of the year—this will not be lost on my colleagues. This in itself will have considerable effect."

What an intolerable thought. Giles didn't want the king to have any kind of an effect. He wanted him to dissolve, to disappear and be forgotten. Going over well in Washington would not only advance his standing there, it could improve his stature in the islands, something Giles had worked all these years to undermine. He had no intention of stopping now, which was why he'd left Honolulu in such a rush, to be the first to arrive and speak for Hawai'i, speak out against the new and unjust tariff bill sponsored by this McKinley fellow who wanted to remove all protections for imported sugar. It would be a disaster for Hawai'i, a disaster for Peabody Trade and Maritime, and a disaster for the king, who'd also set out for Washington to speak against the bill. But Peabody dared not let Kalakaua's views prevail, since he was too big a fool, too backward in

his thinking, too full of himself to understand what was in the best interests of his own kingdom.

In his long campaign to disqualify and unseat the king—though it
was painful to admit—Giles had been losing ground. In the Honolulu
legislature his party had lost its edge. In the U.S. Senate, men thought to
be trusted allies had seemingly turned against him—though now that
he'd met with them he felt certain they still *were* his allies. Hadn't he
brought them around once again to recognize his own forward-looking
grasp of the subject, just as he'd done four years ago?

My God, he thought, it was less than four years ago! And how could
things have so suddenly gone topsy-turvy? Giles wanted that time back,
to be onstage again on that triumphant night when he'd leaped to
the podium wearing the militia's tunic, the braided epaulets, the rows of
brass buttons, and likened their cause to the revolution of 1776. He had
likened Kalakaua to King George III and the king's followers to the
British colonial army, while the men who filled the hall around him, the
assemblage of growers and missionary sons and rifle-bearing merchants
from Düsseldorf and Bristol and Baltimore, embodied the spirit of the
minutemen who'd taken their brave stand at Concord and Lexington.

"Gentlemen," he cried to their five hundred white faces. "We are the
new patriots! Like our forefathers we must rise up against the insufferable abuses of this profligate monarch and take a stand for the democratic
way of life!"

Oh, it was glorious, the thunderous roar that swelled to shake the
walls, further proof that they'd done the right thing, "the missionary
boys," by joining forces with that band of citizen/vigilantes who shipped
in their own rifles and fashioned their own uniforms. They weren't born
in the islands. But they were white, and they were useful.

With weapons to back them up, Giles and his colleagues had their
way at last. They rewrote the law of the land, stripped away most of
the king's authority, his infuriating veto power, his control of cabinet
appointments. They let him keep his yacht and his palace, his medals, his
staff, his letterhead, but the day-to-day managing of the kingdom would
be in other hands. They changed voting standards, set levels of income
and property value that excluded most ethnic Hawaiians, giving landed
whites, men like themselves, civilized men whose opinions could be
trusted, a stronger voice in all elections. Then they forced the king to
sign it, threatening his life, relying on superior firepower, relying on his
reputation as a softhearted man repelled by all forms of bloodshed.

In that tiny kingdom, where thousands of warriors once sailed from one island to the next to settle old scores, to avenge the crimes of a rival chief, the royal army had shrunk to a couple of hundred men. To save himself, to save his troops—outmanned and outgunned—Kalakaua signed what came to be called "the Bayonet Constitution." Under duress he also signed a long-overdue renewal of the Reciprocity Treaty, guaranteeing that Hawaiian growers could continue shipping sugar to the U.S. duty-free—this time with the clause the senators had been holding out for, an exclusive lease to Pearl Harbor.

Since the king had vowed never to relinquish control of any part of Hawai'i to a foreign power, it was seen as a form of abdication. After that, Giles and his colleagues figured they had him where they wanted him. Gladly they watched Kalakaua begin to drink as never before, sometimes putting away—or so it was rumored—two or three bottles of champagne in an afternoon.

But that was three years ago, and the tide in the islands had turned again. Ethnic Hawaiians began to organize, something Giles had not expected. He didn't think they had it in them. They wanted their voting rights back. Their newspapers railed against "the white power grab." They wanted their old constitution back, one ratified by a vote of the people, not by rifles and death threats. The Missionary Boys were in disarray, squabbling among themselves. The militia had disbanded, some members saying they'd gone too far, some saying they hadn't gone far enough, others saying there were U.S. warships in Honolulu Harbor with marines on board who could surround the palace at any time and settle things once and for all.

Then this news from Washington—could it have come at a worse time?—Congress backing out of the trade deal Giles and the Growers Guild had lobbied for so long and hard. "Why are they doing this?" he cried, as if the very heavens had turned against him. "And why now? Why now?"—though he already knew the answer.

Growers from the American South, tired of competing with Hawaiian sugar, had persuaded William McKinley to sponsor a bill that would reimpose the import tax. Expansion-minded senators loved this bill. They seized upon it as one more way to push Hawai'i into the American orbit. For them a coaling and repair station at Pearl Harbor was just a wedge. They wanted the entire kingdom. It was all connected, southern sugar, import tax, a mid-ocean base, trade with Asia, backroom deals on Pennsylvania Avenue. And Giles had made it his business to be there first, to tell them that if annexation was the desired end result, there was no need to break the treaty.

"Let it stand," he told them, "while we work together to join Hawai'i with the United States."

In his view, this couldn't happen soon enough. Then goods would begin to flow back and forth across the water as if from state to state. The American frontier would take another great leap forward. And statehood could not be far behind.

This made such marvelously good sense, the king's bullheaded resistance filled Giles with a cold rage. Only one part of his vision was shared by Kalakaua. He too opposed the McKinley Bill, since "even he" (as Giles put it) could not deny how much Hawai'i now depended upon tariff-free sales to the U.S. But the king was dead set against annexing his whole kingdom. What Giles saw as a new beginning, Kalakaua saw as the end. In a recent speech he'd called it "the death of our culture"—to which Giles had replied, in a letter to the *Growers Weekly Enquirer,* "If this be culture, then the sooner the better."

In haste he'd crossed the water, and crossed the continent, to reassure his allies in Congress.

"Whatever else the king may say," he told them, "it is only a matter of time before we are ready for territorial status. An annexation bill brought to the Senate this very week would not be premature. There is abundant support for this, take my word for it. And once Hawai'i becomes a territory, unlimited military and commercial access to our harbors will of course be guaranteed!"

He'd liked the sound of that, and liked it more in retrospect. Pacing his office he spoke the words aloud, remembering the attentive faces of the half dozen men he'd invited in for drinks. Yes, he was well satisfied with that mission. And yet . . . and yet he wondered now if they might still be reserving some final judgment, still waiting upon Kalakaua's arrival. He wondered how long they'd have to wait. He wondered too about the king's "effect," should he ever reach the capital. Some said he was too ill to travel. Others said his trip had merely been delayed, by weather, by the season, by fatigue. If at last he continued on, what then? If he were actually granted an audience with President Harrison, or invited to speak before both houses, who knew what damage he might do?

This restless reverie was interrupted by a knock.

"Giles. Are you there?"

"What is it? Yes. Come in. Come in."

It was Mike Flynn, his chief West Coast attorney, in shirtsleeves, spectacles hanging loose against his chest, his cocoa-butter skin polished by the midday light.

"I've just had a most interesting telephone call from our neighbor, Mr. Glass. He invites us to come upstairs, if we have a moment. . . ."

"Does he mean right now? I'm rather occupied. . . ."

"He says he has a message from King Kalakaua. Evidently a recording of some kind. . . ."

"From the king, you say."

"In Hawaiian. You've no doubt heard of his new machine. He's asking me to translate. Not a very long message. 'And if Giles can spare the time,' he says, 'I think he might enjoy this too.' "

Mike "Makua" Flynn was one Hawaiian Giles fully trusted. "Half kanaka," he had confided to Louis Glass, "but all in all not a bad fellow. He can think like a white man. Gets it from his father, I suppose, a sea captain from Nantucket who took up with a Maui woman. That's where I was born, as I may have mentioned. Years ago I met the father, a nicely buttoned-up and nautical fellow who made sure his son got into the proper schools. So he is very useful to us here, speaking both tongues. He moves with ease back and forth across the water."

In the oak-paneled offices of Edison Electric, one floor above, a decanter waited on the sideboard. Glass brought out three gleaming snifters. They sipped, commenting on the age of the brandy, the heady lift of the fumes themselves, as Glass described how he'd captured the king's voice and now hoped it might kindle some interest in his talking machine. "It would greatly benefit my customers, of course, if they knew what he actually *said* . . . which is where Mike comes in."

"And how fares the good king?" said Giles, weighing all this like an intelligence officer weighing an espionage report.

"Confined to quarters. Alert. But needing rest."

"Do I understand he is still too sick to travel?"

"Not for long. Not from the look of things. He's quite well attended to, you know, with a ship's physician close by, and one of his handmaidens seemingly at his side day and night."

"Well, yes, it goes without saying. His Majesty is famous for the company he keeps."

Giles shared a knowing wink with Louis Glass, a man he liked, a man from Maryland who enjoyed being out here on the farthest shore, which he regarded as the frontier of new possibility. Glass lived in a world of ingenious devices that were changing the ways people did things, changing their habits and their horizons. From their first meeting he and Giles had recognized each other as comrades in this new era, on the cusp of what they were already calling "the Pacific Century."

Flynn had moved to the talking machine, eager to get started, flattered to be called upon. His animated face was full of curiosity. "You've told me about these, Louis, but I have yet to see one work. What do you do? Put these things in your ears?"

"Come, gentlemen. Please take a chair. Let's get down to business."

He had a separate table for the machine. Above it, attached to the wall, two shelves were lined with short canisters, some labeled, some yet to be labeled, each displaying Edison's name, each containing a roll of wax like the one already installed. He handed Flynn the ear tubes and lowered the stylus.

Flynn gazed at the stylus, the revolving roll, the pulleys, the sleek bottles of battery acid, as if a ghost lurked somewhere within this intricate contraption. He had met the king in Honolulu, had heard him speak at receptions and public ceremonies.

"Unbelievable," he murmured. "Quite unbelievable."

"Why?" said Glass. "What does he say?"

"Well, it's just a simple greeting . . . but the sound . . . so hollow and far away, yet unmistakably . . . him. Aloha kaua, he says. Warm greetings. We all soon will go to Hawai'i. Tell my people what you hear me say. . . ."

Glass waited, expecting more. "Is that it?"

"I think so." Flynn removed the tubes. "Now it's simply a long hiss."

"It would be typical of our fearless ruler," Giles said, sipping. "He has the chance to record his voice for posterity, and all he can think of is hello."

"Well, hold on now," said Glass, "hold on. We do have another roll. I'm certain he spoke a bit longer. Shall we give it a listen?"

This time Flynn sat gazing out the window, across the rooftops of the city. "It's another greeting. Another aloha. . . . No, wait. . . . This could be a chant. Yes. In fact, it is a well-known chant. . . ."

"What sort of chant?" said Glass. "What does he say?"

"It's a sailing song. . . . I have heard it many times. . . . But never like this. . . ."

"Never like what?" said Giles.

"Well, let me listen now."

Two minutes passed, and the stylus reached the final groove. Extracting the tubes, Flynn said, "This is quite fascinating. If you want the fine details I should listen again."

"You have been more than generous with your time," said Glass, already losing interest, hearing nothing that might be salvaged for the benefit of promotion or sales. "All I hoped for was the general sense."

But Flynn had more to say.

"This is very Hawaiian, you know, and yet a bit surprising, coming from the king, or what we know of him, that is, what has been said of him of late. This is not at all what I would have expected."

"And what has been said of him?" Giles asked. "Is there some recent news?"

"I mean only what we all have heard—that he is less and less effectual, no longer his own man, as he once was."

"And in this chant you hear what? Another note?"

"It's an old song, but with a new twist, as far as I can tell. A sort of rallying cry. Almost a call to arms . . ."

"Good God, man! What's that supposed to mean?"

To Glass Flynn said, "What is to become of these recordings?"

"I believe I told the king I'd give him one. Now I suppose I'll give him both. This whole enterprise has turned into a kind of wild-goose chase."

Like his boss, Flynn had specialized in maritime law and Pacific trade. He too believed annexation was the key to Hawaii's future, the key to ever-expanding trade and profit. "I wonder," he said, "if you'd want this to get back to the islands. Given the mood over there, something like this, coming from the king . . . it could be inflammatory . . ."

Giles sat forward. "Something like what? Get to the point, man! What are you driving at?"

"It's a chant, Giles, a kind of legend, about a heroic sailor who travels to Kaleponi, which is to say the land to the east, and after many adventures he returns home again. But in this case—and I'd have to give another listen or two to be absolutely certain—it's in the very play of the words, you see; each word, each phrase can have several meanings—in this case the sailor in the song, I'm almost certain, is the king himself who has traveled far and now comes home to reclaim the land he left behind and to urge his people to join with him. . . ."

"Well, I'll be damned," said Giles, rising to his feet.

"I should listen to it one more time."

"It's another kanaka trick!"

"Gentlemen, gentlemen," said Glass, hoping to calm his agitated guest, "there's half a decanter of rare brandy here. If we don't finish it I'll have to pour it down the sink."

Giles accepted a refill and took a long swallow. "He's trying to put one over on all of us. Mike is right. If this gets back to the islands it can only stir them up, when things are already too stirred up."

"You should listen yourself, Giles. The voice coming out of a machine like this, it has, well, a certain magical quality. It's absolutely uncanny. When the Hawaiians hear of it they will be captivated. Once heard, these words would surely be repeated. They could spread like wildfire. And I'll tell you exactly how his words will be heard. The king we thought we'd lost has come back to us. . . ."

Now Giles was pacing the room.

"And we do not want this, do we, gentlemen? We want to nip it in the bud. We get rid of the recordings, and we get rid of the king's song before it becomes a hindrance. Is there any harm in that? What say you, Louis? I'm sure you appreciate what's at stake here."

"I'm not sure I do."

"Then let me bring you up to speed"—another refill, another swallow, and he paced now as if pacing the stage at a convention of the Sugar Growers Guild, as if lecturing a multitude.

"Hawai'i is on the verge, on the very verge of a great new partnership. We cannot afford any more mistakes. The Hawaiians who oppose us have become more vocal in recent months. Who knows where it will lead? But this much is certain, we cannot give them any ammunition. From what Mike says, this chant would underscore all they want to believe about their king. It is simply too great a risk to take!"

His wide, unblinking eyes regarded Glass, who had withdrawn to his liquor cabinet, wary of this outburst.

"On second thought," said Glass, "there's no harm retaining one of the rolls, for the company's collection."

"Aren't they made of wax?"

"Yes indeed."

"Why can't we simply melt them down?"

"Hold on now, Giles . . ."

"Light a fire and drop them into the stove."

"That's easier said than done. Each roll is numbered and sooner or later must be accounted for."

"To whom?"

"Within the company there are procedures. . . ."

"And the company is three thousand miles away! Here in San Francisco, aren't you the company? Tell them . . . tell them anything. You lost it or . . . or you were caught in a burning building and had to flee for your life."

"Melting down a roll . . . I need a bit of time to think this through. As I mentioned, I have a certain obligation to the king. When I know he's heading home I'll present him with the shorter version, the greeting, together with a machine to play it on. I promised him that. Who knows—if he returns with one of our machines and a good opinion of the Edison Company—it can't hurt, you know, the royal endorsement can't hurt at all. And as for the roll in question, I assure you, Giles, this will not leave my office. It will go into this drawer"—he patted a knob at one side of his polished desk—"which is always locked, the key residing in this opposite drawer, used only by myself and my secretary. The king will never see it again. Only we three have heard its contents . . . and perhaps . . ."

"Perhaps what?"

"In his quarters, at the time, as I noted, there was one other person who might have followed what he said, though I'm guessing here."

"Not the physician."

"The young woman lying by his side, apparently an island girl. I hadn't thought of it till now. She heard him speak the chant, then listened through the tubes and afterward offered some brief remark which at the time of course made no sense to me. 'Everyone should hear this.' "

"And does she have a name, this cozy bedmate to the king?"

"He called her Nani."

Peabody's pacing took him to the wide window, where he stopped, peering out at the street.

"Nani? Nani? Does she have a second name?"

"I believe it starts with a K."

He leaned closer to the pane, as if distracted by the scene below. "Was it by any chance Keala?"

"That could be right. I only heard it once."

"In his bed, you say. Under the covers?"

"Partly."

"With black hair."

"Very black."

"And well endowed."

"Quite."

Flynn chimed in, as if to make light of this, but with a mouth oddly bent, half smile, half frown. "His Majesty's health must be somewhat better than has been reported."

"His Majesty's health indeed," said Giles, turning from the window, and not at all amused. "For the time being we will entrust these rolls to your safekeeping, Louis. But what can be done about His Majesty's health, that is the larger matter? This young woman, if she's who I think she is, is quite a rare creature, not at all your fawning handmaiden. She may well be very useful to us in what we now must do."

"Must do?" said Glass.

"Mike and I. What Mike and I must do. Nothing we need to trouble you about. Thanks very much for this audition. It has opened our ears, opened our eyes."

Glad to see them go, Glass reached for his decanter. "One more sip then, to speed you on your way."

Again, Giles accepted a refill, tossing it back. "Yes, yes, and thanks too for your boundless hospitality," as he took Flynn by the arm, guiding him out the door and down the stairs, speaking in tones subdued and urgent.

In an Upper Room

I woke from a dream. All these years later I still remember it. Men were shouting. I could not see them, yet I knew their voices. There was smoke. We had to move Kawika. We could not see the flames, but we could smell smoke and hear the shouting. In my dream I said Kawika, Kawika. He slept so soundly I watched his chest to see if he was breathing. I said Kawika the hotel is on fire.

Then my eyes sprang open. I was lying next to him in the hotel bed. I heard an angry voice. Kawika did not hear it. He was snoring.

A window had been left open. From somewhere smoke was drifting in. She slid out of bed to close the window and heard someone say her name, a voice she thought she knew. Over the hotel robe she pulled on her winter coat, for the warmth and to cover herself as she made her way through three rooms of the royal suite, now strangely empty in the middle of the day. Just inside the entry door she stood and listened to the aide-de-camp arguing in Hawaiian with a man who demanded entrance, not to see the king, but to see her.

"Here is my card! I only ask that you present it . . ."

She opened the door and said, "Makua?"

"Nani, please tell this fellow I am a friend, a kinsman."

"How did you know where to find me?"

"I did not know. But now that I see it is really you, I beg you to come with me. I must speak with you right away."

"We can talk inside."

"Not here."

She hadn't seen him in years. His face was heavier, the skin around his eyes much darker. He acted like a fugitive, a man on the run.

"Are you in trouble?"

"No, no, nothing like that."

"Then what? I am not dressed, Makua."

"Button your coat."

"And the king is here. I cannot leave him."

"We won't go far. We won't leave the hotel."

"But why?"

"Just come, please. And I'll explain."

Some desperation in his voice persuaded her to hurry along beside him, down the corridor toward the stairwell, and listen to his double message. He worked for Peabody Trade and Maritime, he told her, and his boss had ordered him to bring her to an upper room. It was a good job, with uncomfortable duties like this one from time to time, but he made the extra effort to get along with his employer, now that he was married and ready to start a family.

As they climbed the stairs he was a man divided, talking too fast, babbling. "A very sweet woman, Nani. I know you'll like her. White. Did we send you an announcement? One may now be waiting for you at the rancheria. Are you recently arrived? I have often thought of paying you another visit. The wedding here was very small, very small indeed, and we have just returned from Maui, from our honeymoon and a grand reception there, a luau with all the trimmings. Mr. Peabody does not know I am your cousin, by the way, but rest assured I have not forgotten it, I have not forgotten it, and no harm will come to you. . . ."

On the fourth floor the company kept an apartment for employees and guests and for certain conferences and conversations that called for undisturbed confidentiality. An open doorway joined two rooms, exactly like the king's rooms, to make a small suite.

Makua seemed embarrassed now. "Please sit down, Nani. Be at ease. How long have you been in San Francisco?"

She couldn't sit. Like a deer on full alert she stood just inside the door listening, eyes darting from cousin to sofa to high bay window.

"Why do you bring me here?"

"Simply to hear what you can tell me about the king."

"And then?"

"It depends."

"You are going to harm him."

"Don't think that."

"Mr. Peabody always wants to harm him. How can you work for such a man?"

"Is the king sick?"

"Why should I answer you?"

"You are a good judge of such matters, Nani. Some say the king is very sick. Some say . . ."

"I want to trust you. . . ."

"You have to trust me."

"But you have changed so much. . . ."

"Is he too sick to travel?"

"I don't know you now. . . ."

"Anything about his health, his habits. You know his habits."

"It was wrong for me to come."

"Nani, please . . . his journey has been so long delayed, is there any chance it might now be canceled? Have you heard him mention this?"

"Let me go back!"

"This morning he spoke into a talking machine, and you were there. You heard what he said. . . ."

"Forgive me, Makua. I am leaving now."

As she turned away from him, reaching for the knob, a key turned in the lock. The door swung open, and Giles was standing there, so close to her their bodies almost touched. His eyes expanded with surprise as he drew back, summoning a guarded smile.

"Well, well. Miss Keala. We meet again."

She ducked her head and would have pushed past him into the hallway, had he not shut the door and leaned against the jamb.

Makua looked as if a small bomb had exploded. "Giles, Giles, I thought . . ."

"I know what you thought. Things have changed. We had an unexpected call. The Trade Bureau called. They want their report by noon tomorrow."

"They said Monday."

"I know. Now they say tomorrow. You'll have to get on this right away. It's crucial. It's more than crucial."

"But you said . . ."

"I know what I said."

". . . to stay with Miss Keala."

"I can take over here, Mike. We have already met, as I mentioned, some years ago in Honolulu."

Evidently Makua had not told Giles that he too recognized her name—perhaps to protect Nani, or perhaps to protect himself. Knowing

how Giles regarded most Hawaiians, maybe it seemed safer on this particular day not to remind him that his lead attorney had dark-skinned
relatives. Makua stood there flustered, sputtering, pinned between loyalty
to his boss and the unspoken duties of kinship.

As for Giles, from what is known of his maneuvers that morning and
afternoon, it's still hard to say quite what he had in mind, how much he'd
thought through in advance, how much of his thinking he'd shared with
Makua. My guess is, he was making it up as he went along, propelled by
his own excitability, by brandy fumes, sipping steadily through the day,
sipping and scheming, taking each moment as it came. As they left Louis
Glass behind he'd told Makua, "We have to keep Kalakaua in the city.
This woman is a key. You will speak with her. You're the one who can
talk your way past their security. Apart from the daily papers, how else
are we to know the true details of His Majesty's condition, his state of
mind?"

Now Makua said, "At the very least I should escort Miss Keala back
to her quarters . . ."

"Yes," she said, "I am ready . . ."

Giles cut them off. "She is not finished!" And his face fixed around a
thin curve of a smile, a warning sign Makua understood.

He handed Nani his card, eyes brimming with regret and apology
and turmoil. "You can always reach me here."

Like a castle's gatekeeper Giles allowed him through the door. When
she made a move to follow he closed it and bolted it.

"So we will not be disturbed."

She backed across the room.

"Come, Nani. Are you afraid of me?"

"No. Why should I be?"

"Good. Good, then we can talk. It has been too long. We have some
catching up to do. I'm sure Mike explained why we're here."

"I have nothing to talk about. I should be with the king."

"Indeed. We know of your affection. We too are concerned for his
welfare, deeply concerned. Something is afoot today. It is hard to know
quite what."

He spoke with the insinuating tone she remembered, wore the
mocking smile.

"Afoot?"

"He could be in danger."

"What danger?"

"As I'm sure you know, he has many enemies, and at the moment he is highly vulnerable."

"Do not make fun of me. You are still his enemy. What are you going to do to him?"

"Not me, Nani. I am but a messenger, here to say that you can be of service. You can help protect the king. Perhaps we can find a way together, you and I."

In fear she hugged her arms across her chest, as if a cold wind blew through the room, and Giles caught himself. Abruptly his manner changed. He tried to smile an honest smile.

"I don't mean that to sound the way it did. What I mean to say is . . . what I mean to ask is, what brings you to the city? Have you been here long? And have my eyes deceived me, or did I see you just two days ago in the street below my window?"

Blood rose to her cheeks, and she looked away.

"I was almost certain I saw you, though of course I could not be sure, so much time has passed since our paths last crossed. But it *was* you, was it not? Dressed in the very coat you're wearing now, gazing up at my office window on a bright and windy afternoon."

She shook her head. "It was not me."

"Ah, Nani, this is music to my ears. In the end you and I are much alike, willing to bend the truth from time to time if it suits our purposes. Come, let us sit here on the sofa and be comfortable, perhaps have a little something to drink. Would you like a drink?"

"Who is going to harm the king?"

"We'll speak of that, indeed we will. But now we have a rare chance to talk about old times. Do you recall a day many years ago when we happened to meet on a country road? We were both on horseback? We talked about our fathers?"

Again she shook her head, though she recalled it all too well. His eagerness confused her. He was like a suitor now, an awkward suitor.

"This much I know. Between us two there is still a special union. I let you get away once. I cannot let you get away again."

He seemed to see this as a compliment, a form of flattery that would endear him to her, give him license to reach across and touch her at least. But Nani wouldn't allow it, stepping farther back.

Poor Giles. He yearned to close the space between them but didn't know how. Whatever he'd had in mind when he first walked through the door had now been blotted out by the sight of her, the scent of her at such close range. In desperation he began to pace, wringing his hands like a man who felt his time was running out. "And then he was like an animal" (she wrote years later) . . .

> . . . like a lion getting ready to pounce. His brow was wet and pale, and his eyes were dry like stones. Blue and dry. I saw no way to escape them. He smelled of brandy and the other smell that comes with drink when a man is going to have his way no matter what.

Before he stepped toward her she felt the movement pushing at the air between them, felt the force of it. Backed against a cabinet, she had nowhere to go. In the sudden grip of his hand around her upper arm, the painful squeezing, she felt an unexpected strength. She knew she could never match it with her own. Then he had her other arm, as if to pull her, though whether toward the sofa or toward a bed or toward himself to force a rough embrace she could not tell. She dropped down into her body then, not in surrender but to a deeper kind of readiness.

Closing her eyes, she saw him as she'd seen him so many times, in his long-sleeve white shirt, astride his white horse, behind him the green ridges, steep and rugged, capped with mist, the veils of mist so close she could see water dripping from the trees, and his face so close to hers she could see the bristles of his stiff moustache. His lips wanted to move but couldn't. In his eyes she saw the grief he could not speak, and in this vision, as he turned away, she remembered how softness had disarmed him.

She let her arms relax. With a rough yank he pulled her close, pressing his hips against her.

"Don't make me hurt you." It was almost a plea.

"You do not need to hurt me."

"If you cry out it will do no good. No one will hear you. This hotel is built to muffle every sound."

He expected her to cry out, to kick and plead for mercy. Since his university days Giles had known only two kinds of women—bawdy and foulmouthed and raucous; or on the verge of running, to be taken on the run. He wasn't ready for Nani's hand, now reaching toward his cheek.

"Don't do that."

"Your face is hot."

"I said no."

Her fingers grazed his cheek and temple like the feathered wings of a small bird, and his eyelids, until this moment wide open as if fixed in place, began to flutter and squint.

I wonder if any woman had ever touched him in this way. Maybe his mother when he was young. He said you can't, I will not allow it. I let my hand slide down by his neck and held it there and felt muscles hard as wood, the kind of muscle you press with your fingers and nothing gives. I remember that Kawika's neck was thick and strong but at ease, sometimes as smooth and firm as the flesh of a dolphin. I thought I hated Mr. Peabody but I felt sorrow for this man who had a neck like that. I watched it turn pink. All his white skin turned pink from his neck to the top of his forehead.

She said, "Please do not harm the king."

"Help me save him, then."

"How?"

"Take off this infernal coat."

He let go her arms and seized the topmost button as if to tear it loose. She drew his hand away and quietly said, "I can do it," unbuttoning the coat, letting it drop to reveal the robe beneath. Between white lapels some cleavage held his greedy eyes. His hand hung in the air where she'd left it. She took it again in both of hers and stroked his hand as if it were a small creature needing care, and watched his greed turn to another kind of longing, watched color rise again, the skin rosy, the ears, the eyelids rimmed with red. On the verge of tears he shook his head, as if to shake off sleep or chase away a buzzfly.

"Now take off your robe," he said, without conviction.

"No."

"You must."

"Not yet."

"What's that you say?"

"There is a better way."

"What better way?"

"A better way to start."

He blinked. His mouth opened, but for once he had no words. Her hands rose to touch his cheeks, pressing soft as silk against the heated skin, lingering there, as if to coax his head closer. But the neck wouldn't bend. Her fingers glided up to cool his eyes, to close the fevered lids, her voice as cool as creek water.

"You must lie back on the bed."

Obediently he did so, without protest, as she unbuttoned his trousers and unbuttoned the fly of his white long johns, then stood between his legs and regarded his flaccid member. It lay limp against his thigh like a wilted carrot.

I see them there, both still clothed, Giles in cravat and vest and fitted shirt and cuff links and trousers and shoes and socks, while Nani in her hotel robe still sashed is ready to submit to him, or wanting him to think she is. But why? As I try to trace the twists and turns of my great-grandmother's life, this has been the hardest part to comprehend. I still ponder how she could come to be standing between his outspread knees in the Peabody Trade and Maritime suite.

Did she reach down to try and revive him? Or had she hoped he would go limp and stay limp? Perhaps it was a tactic she had counted on, to undo him with a feathery caress.

But if he had not gone soft, what then? With no other way out of that room, was she prepared to bargain, to make an outright gift? Or was there something else between these two smoldering through the years? Part Puritan herself, was Nani drawn to whatever lay coiled behind his cravat and vest and Protestant veneer? I can't help suspecting there was some urge to be taken by that, as a way, perhaps, to make amends for the old wound inflicted by her father. She never wrote about this, never mentioned it to Rosa or to anyone, so far as I've been able to discover. These are my musings on that day, not hers, my reading into the few remarks she left behind, as I try to be the witness (not the judge):

> Why do I still think of him? Why does the thought fill me with shame? Why do I think of Miss Graciela who slept with the general? He had all the land where her people used to hunt and fish, where they had their villages and cooking fires and dancehouses. The land that once was theirs was his and yet she gave herself to him as if he owned her too. Did the general buy Miss Graciela? Did he force her? I don't think so. She slept with him for many years. He hungered for her dark skin. Did she hunger for his white skin?

The blow that almost killed Peabody's father was not Nani's doing, and at this late date Giles no longer blamed her. But he had blamed her once, and called her savage, just as his father had called Keala savage. And these labels can leave another kind of mark. Nani's instinct was to heal. Maybe it was her legacy to absorb a blame not hers, and so she'd prepared to give herself, as if she owed him this, an old debt still to be collected.

As things turned out, it was an offer Giles could not accept. He closed his eyes in self-loathing and would not open them. His chest began to quiver. His voice was low and husky.

"Get away from me."

She watched him roll onto his side, draw his knees together, his small body shuddering. He was docile now. It would have been easy to lie beside him, extend a comforting embrace. She might have considered this. But he said in a near whisper, a near sob, "It is done."

She waited. When he didn't speak she said, "Do I have your promise then?"

His small laugh was dry and cynical. "My promise?"

"You will not harm him."

"Go. Leave me. I will not harm him any more."

She put on her coat and buttoned it to the top, unbolted the door and stepped into an empty corridor, hurrying back the way she'd come, down the stairs, along the silent carpeting. Outside the king's suite the aide regarded her with questioning eyes, but made no comment.

"Did anyone come while I was gone?"

"Only the waiter."

"Henry?"

"A white one this time. A haole waiter."

"All the waiters are Negro."

"He said he was new. He brought some tea."

"Was it hot?"

"I felt the kettle. I saw steam coming out."

"Good. He likes it hot and strong."

In the bedroom, Kawika, sipping the last of his tea, asked if she'd been bathing.

"I had to step outside. A relative was at the door, and you were sleeping. I don't know how he found me."

"Don't leave me, Nani. You know I want you beside me all the time."

She crawled back into bed, comforted by the smooth and hairless limbs. She touched his neck, his cheek. With all the weight he'd lost there was still warmth and fleshy appeal. She thought of all the times she'd been with him, the different ways they'd been together. Never had he treated her roughly, grabbed her arms or raised his voice. She wanted to stay right there, pressed against him for the rest of her life.

A Theory

On the following day something inside Kawika changed, picked up via the radar of Nani's healing hands. According to her, that's when death came into the body. As for how or why, we can only surmise. Piecing this and that together I have come up with a theory, and this is partly mine, partly hers. It seems very likely that Giles had sent Mike Flynn on a false mission. Extracting information about the king was only a cover. The main intent was to get her out of his suite, to remove her from his bed so that an unfamiliar waiter could deliver a cup of tainted tea.

The chamberlain and the aide-de-camp were both known to be loyal. And from all I've been able to learn, the ship's physician was a humorless but honorable man, a career naval officer with an impeccable record. From his personal log, preserved at the Maritime Library, I learned that on this particular afternoon a phone message had come to him from the hotel desk, calling him back to the U.S.S. *Charleston,* though it turned out to be a false emergency.

Perhaps it was coincidence that during a period of about an hour, with the physician gone, Nani removed to an upper room, and the congested chamberlain still confined to quarters, an unfamiliar waiter found his way to the king's bedside. Did someone bribe him? Did someone deliberately clear the suite and thus clear the way? And why—as Nani wonders in her diary—did this white-skinned waiter appear only once and never again?

Eventually I came across another curious detail. It was in a letter sent to my box at KRUX, after I'd broadcast my plea for any information no matter how remote or dubious. Dozens of responses had come in, calls and cards and letters. "Remote" and "dubious" are good words for describing most of them. But one leaped out at me, from a fellow in Marin who called himself a longtime listener. He sent me a grainy photo from the 1890s showing a covered walkway that had once passed over New Montgomery Street, connecting the Palace to another, somewhat less prestigious hotel—the Grand—which stood directly opposite:

> This is how the ladies of the evening would come across to visit businessmen who kept rooms at the Palace. It was very handy because it connected at the second floor, so you didn't have to go through the lobby or come up the elevator. I don't know anything about what happened when King Kalakaua was staying there. But if a person was stealing something or up to anything at all, this would be the way to do it.

On my next trip to San Francisco Public I stopped at Special Collections, looked again at the Palace Hotel file, and found several glimpses of this elevated walkway I'd missed the first time through. Never a subject in and of itself, it will show up as a peripheral detail at the edge of some panoramic shot of the great building in its glory days. This walkway too was destroyed in the 1906 earthquake and fire and never rebuilt. Its memory survives only in these photos, a hundred years old and more, and needless to say, they don't prove much. Yet they do suggest a possibility, open a little window on what may have been a clever and successful scheme.

Whether or not Giles Peabody was behind it can never be verified. Indeed, whether or not the king was actually poisoned is now impossible to verify, one way or the other. Even at the time, had some nosy hotel detective harbored a suspicion or two, the prime sources of testimony soon left town. Like the steam from the teacup, they all quickly steamed away—Peabody, the medical officer, the chamberlain, the aide-de-camp.

The official medical report to Hawaii's minister of foreign affairs noted "there was probably a suppressed secretion of the kidneys, due to disease of those organs," and "interstitial nephritis with uraemia" and "the heart greatly atrophied." If you'd only read this report, it would be easy to believe his entire system had broken down and his body was falling to pieces. Yet ailments such as these seem oddly out of sync with another picture that turned up during my second visit to Special Collections.

The caption says it's the king's last photograph, taken at the Palace in January 1891 by one Theodore C. Marceau of San Francisco. He is sitting in an ornate, high-backed chair with carved arms and a leather seat. He wears a dark suit, the double-breasted morning coat buttoned to its high lapels, the top of his cravat showing at the neck. His hair is short, his moustache trimmed, his sideburns gone, so his face is thinner than in early years, but still well fleshed, not gaunt. His look is somber, reflective, but no bagging shows around the eyes. His posture is good. He looks alert and dignified, his gaze clear and direct, his skin remarkably smooth and free of blemish.

Whatever had befallen him, some ten days after this photo was taken, and three days after his voice was recorded for the Edison Company, Kalakaua lapsed into a coma. A day later he was gone. According to witnesses his final words were, "Tell them I tried."

A Love/Hate Thing

San Francisco, 1986

Every night a flaming sky turns orange, then rust, then turns quickly indigo as time-lapse footage takes in the panorama of a darkening sky. Black waters, seen from high above, are ringed with urban light, strings and streaks of moving light along the freeways and from a thousand office windows gleaming from their many downtown towers. Like the eye of a great seabird, the soaring camera swoops and glides to catch the electric glamour, as if all this is one with Las Vegas and Rio at carnival time, aglow and alluring, while a generous male voice welcomes you to Northern California's award-winning number one newscast. . . .

Alone in my apartment, exhausted and spent, I watched the bay-shaped megalopolis swirl and bend upon itself, a kaleidoscope of cities and bridges and waterways, and then the anchor, an impeccable Asian woman, was offering a foretaste of stories to be covered later that night—a drive-by shooting in Vallejo, a seven-car pileup south of Oakland, the budget showdown in Sacramento, new names in the Iran/Contra scandal, a sports roundup with all the scores. But first the night's lead story:

> In Berkeley today a peaceful rally took an ominous turn. Reports that station KRUX had been sold to an East Coast conglomerate drew an estimated one thousand demonstrators to a parking lot rally. With their investigations still pending, Berkeley police won't release details. But our camera team was on the scene to bring you this eyewitness report.

I saw Larry again, his black jacket, black T-shirt, his unruly eyebrows above the thick black beard, with a bullhorn out in front of his face like an exploding party favor. Behind him stood the Rolling Thunder Boys, a cowboy-hatted bluegrass band who'd just finished tuning up, and behind them two young fellows who climbed onto the flatbed to wave a hand-lettered poster saying SIT STILL AND LISTEN. Though I was up there next to Larry in my aviator's shades, I didn't recognize myself. I never wore shades. I never wore the KRUX ball cap. I was watching someone else play the mute martyr with the injured eye, the whistle-blower whose job was on the line.

Between us stood a bearish fellow from the university's communications department, and Larry was introducing him when the flatbed that was our makeshift stage shuddered, as if the Hayward Fault, which underlies all the cities strung along that side of the bay, had at last begun to make its long-predicted move. But this was not a tremor of the earth. It was coming from the truck. Someone had switched on the engine. Dense exhaust smoke billowed out upon the nearest listeners, who recoiled with cries of distress and outrage. Then the flatbed of the one-time lumber truck began to tilt. We turned to see who was in the cab, but the wide banner proclaiming SAVE OUR VOICE blocked the view, and now that banner was rising. The boys in the band were staggering down-hill, lunging toward us, trying to find footing and not let go of their mandolins and banjos and guitars, while their microphones slid out into the retreating crowd. As the slope steepened, Larry and I and the communications prof finally had no choice but to leap clear. For just a moment all three of us hung in the air like rag dolls, arms flung wide, the prof's notes floating overhead.

The truck's front end had been pulled up close to a chain-link fence. Whoever started the engine and hydraulic lifts had climbed out of the cab to scamper over that fence before anyone could lay a hand on him or get a good look at his face. I thought Larry would have used the bullhorn to call for pursuit, but he was calling for another kind of action. A veteran of many such campaigns, he seized the moment, raised high his bullhorn to indict "the people who want to steal KRUX right out from under us!"—urging the crowd to regroup outside the station. They didn't need much urging. It was a warm Saturday afternoon, the atmosphere now both jittery and buoyant. They were ready for something, and I was in the midst of it, having landed on my feet, though a bit off-balance, pitching sideways into a middle-aged couple who broke my fall, shook my hand. Mothers with kids were pulling back, and some of the senior citizens, but most of us headed for the street, prodded along by Larry's bullhorn, as he tried to push his way across the lot and take the lead, a bit like Gandhi, who once remarked, "There go my followers, I must hurry and catch up with them." They had their own momentum, with an anthem rising:

"What do we want?"

"Open radio!"

"When do we want it?"

"NOW!"

Somehow the newscast got a fresh angle on this approaching crowd. Whether a savvy cameraman had rushed ahead, or whether a second camera was already placed to catch any possible action outside the station, I was never sure. But as this coverage rolled on, I saw something I would not otherwise have seen.

The front rank was rounding a corner half a block from the bold call letters above the station entry when, at the edge of the frame, a gleaming black escort car with tinted windows pulled into the No Parking zone. As the camera zoomed past, moving in for a closer look at the signs and determined faces, a female figure stepped out of the car, hurried across the sidewalk, and my heart dropped. In that minisecond of a glimpse I saw Julie's build, Julie's stride, Julie's wide-brim hat.

What the hell? Is this why she was late getting her mother to the airport? Late for the rally? No. She wouldn't do this. It doesn't make sense.

Then students were sprinting toward the car. They didn't know who was inside, but here was a perfect target and focus for their cause. Too sleek for that neighborhood, it had arrived in time to offer fitting evidence of what we all feared the station would become. They were pranksters rapping knuckles on its darkened windows until one slid down to reveal the agitated driver, a Syrian or Pakistani, worried about dents and scratches and also in a hurry, with no patience for this uncalled-for blockade.

"Get away from the door! Leave me alone! Don't stand so close!"

"It's a No Parking zone," said one young fellow with mock authority. "We're going to call the cops."

His tone was lost on the driver, who shouted, "Get away! Let me pass!" With angry, almost arrogant pride he said, "I'm working for the guy who just bought this station! I can park anywhere I want!"

It was all they needed to hear. As this news percolated back through the crowd, twenty demonstrators, as if they'd spent weeks training for such an event, locked arms around the car. The nearest leaned down, demanding to see the driver's boss. Was he inside the car? Inside the station? The driver wagged his head. As the crowd thickened he opened all the windows so they could check to see that no one lurked in back.

"It's not his car!" the driver cried. "It's my car! This is my business! He hired me to drive him around! I don't even know the guy! What's going on? Who are all these people?"

From the steps Larry was urging them to block the entrance, block all traffic, block the path of the company car until they could get some satisfaction from the manager or from the CEO himself, if he had the guts to come forth and speak. In front of him stood a dozen men and women with locked arms. Radiating from the car in concentric circles, dozens more stood in silent, nonviolent solidarity, while the hapless driver, the centerpiece, frantic now, shouted for police to come and clear the street.

After that the scene played itself out almost as if scripted and rehearsed, as a sergeant's stern voice came through the bullhorn, "Please disperse, please move back onto the sidewalk and open this right-of-way!" and as Larry the ecstatic demagogue cried from the station steps, "We want some satisfaction!" On cue the riot-ready cops moved in to disperse a retreating multitude, while half a dozen students with arms still locked waited to be dragged to the detention van.

Now the newscast caught up with Roy Wurlitzer, near the ticket counter at Oakland International, carrying a thin attaché case, black hair combed flat against his scalp like a celebrity from the 1930s, blue eyes regarding the camera as if he owned it: "Of course we're disappointed by this kind of welcome. But I think people out here on the coast will soon come to see that our support can be a virtue, not a drawback. Argonaut isn't a predator. We simply bring a new kind of business model to media at a time when technology is changing, demographics are changing. I believe we can take the essential style and appeal of a station like KRUX and give it new life, not to mention a longer life. . . ."

They cut to the communications prof, a burly guy with shaggy hair in a rumpled seersucker jacket, sitting in his office backed by shelves of books: "Okay, I'll tell you exactly what I think. I have been following this right from the get-go, and there's a lot more at stake than the fate of one FM station. There's a sense here, not just here in the Bay Area but all across the land, that we are losing something of great personal value. We are losing our opportunity to hear and be heard, a sense that we are being swallowed up by . . . let's call it the packagers. What I hear right now is one of the deepest fears of modern times, and that is the fear of the pack-ager, a fear of the impulse to take something that is authentic and convert it into a commodity that can be bought and sold for profit. It is a love/hate thing I hear. Everybody likes profit. We respect it. We revere it. But we also fear the packager who has less and less regard for whatever the content of the package may be. . . ."

Then we were tumbling side by side again, the seersuckered prof and Sheridan and Larry in midair with arms flailing, with the tilted truckbed as a backdrop—Are they agitators? Demonstrators? Burlesque victims of a faceless saboteur?—footage to be run and rerun in the days to come.

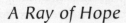

A Ray of Hope

In a fragile silence, with the set off, I kept seeing her Palm Springs hat as she crossed and recrossed the sidewalk. I saw the polished black sedan with no passengers. And Roy at the airport, full of purpose.

But none of this computed. For half that afternoon she'd been with me, finally caught up with me as the crowd milled. Side by side we'd watched the cops move in and afterward picked up Larry at the precinct station where they booked him for unlawful assembly and obstructing traffic, set a court date, and released him on his own recognizance. From there we went out for drinks, talked about how to keep the pressure on, Larry ignited by the day's events, and Julie, after a couple of margaritas, a vivacious revolutionary who left the bar only because she had to fetch Toby. As we hugged and kissed and promised to talk tomorrow I fell in love all over again—which made it unthinkable that she could have somehow stepped out of that black sedan. I must have glimpsed another woman wearing the same kind of hat. Yes. Only a paranoid would see it another way. I didn't want to see it at all, or talk about it. And yet, of course, I had to, and my hand was reaching for the phone when a startling jangle filled the room.

I hoped it was Julie. And I hoped it was anyone but her. Hearing Sandy's voice I was oddly relieved. I hadn't seen him or talked to him since the staff meeting and thought then I'd never want to talk to him again. I felt obliged to sound hostile.

"What the hell do *you* want?"

"I fucked up, Dan."

"Is that what you called to tell me?"

"I was watching the late news. I saw the rally."

"We missed you."

"I should have been on the truck. In the old days I would have been up there."

"Well, it's not too late."

"Plus, I said some things."

"We all said things."

"Things I never should have said. About your grandmother coming on the show. Calling her chanting mumbo jumbo. That was way out of line. It fills me with shame. . . ."

His voice broke, on the edge of a sob. Was this true remorse, or the scotch speaking? Or some of both? By that time of night he'd had two or three shots. Or four. Which is not a judgment on my part, just an observation. After a margarita with Julie, I'd switched to red wine for some solo tippling, a couple of glasses. Maybe more. I could feel forgiveness already welling up. I could see Sandy tipped back in his recliner, his shelves of LPs and tapes and paperbacks, on the wall above his desk a plaque commending him for excellence in broadcasting, on the desk a photo of his daughter, now off to college in Seattle, and next to it a photo of Sandy with his wife. They'd split up after twenty-two years together, but he said he still loved her. They were talking again, talking every other night. They'd probably been talking for half an hour just before he called, and he was letting me hear a sob that was meant for her.

"Don't apologize, Sandy. Everybody does what they have to do."

"That's just it. That is just fucking it! I didn't do what I have to do. I saw you and Larry on the truck with the bullhorn and the signs, I almost shot myself. I have a pistol here in the closet, you know, a forty-five. . . ."

"I didn't know that. You never told me that."

"I loaded it. I thought about using it."

"You want me to come over?"

"I'm fine now. That's not why I called. But maybe it is. We have talked about death before. It's like I didn't have to shoot myself. I had already died. You know what I mean? I threw the I Ching."

"What did you get?"

"The hexagram for Break Through. That's what came up."

"Break Through. That's a good one."

"Listen. I have it right here in front of me. Listen to how it starts. 'This hexagram signifies on the one hand a breakthrough after a long accumulation of tension, as a swollen river breaks through its dikes, or in the manner of a cloudburst . . .'"

"Someone is watching over you, Sandy."

"After that, things started falling into place. I have been rethinking my whole life."

"Me too. Me too. Year by year. Maybe we're on the same wavelength here. We should get together for breakfast and talk all this through."

"I'd love to do that. It's been too long. I have not been straight with you for months. I'm ashamed of myself. I want to clear the air. It is so easy to forget all the things you started out wanting to do. You get addicted to all this meaningless shit that just clutters up the place. . . . Did you see Roy on TV?"

"I did. How long has he been in town?"

"All I know is he called this morning from a hotel. He has this telephone tone, this way of drawing you in, like you are his new best friend. He reads the papers and he hopes all this disturbance isn't going to slow things down."

I saw him again at the airport, his fashion model smile. I saw the escort car again, a woman stepping past the open door, her wide-brim hat, her pipestem jeans, almost asked Sandy if he too had caught that glimpse, but my throat bunched around the question.

I said, "This is just the beginning. Did you tell him that?"

"I lied, Dan. In my chickenshit way I told him yeah, don't pay any attention to the papers. They never get it right. This is why I called. This whole week has been a nightmare, my stomach burning all the time. I'll tell you what really got to me. That guy from the campus. What he said cut through me like a sword. Ten years ago I lost my newspaper to the homogenizers and the packagers, and I didn't learn a goddam thing."

"Sure you did. Or you wouldn't be talking this way."

"I want to get out from under Argonaut. After I watched that rally, those people in the street, those are my people, Dan, not these arrogant fuckheads from the other side of the world!"

Oh, this was sweet to hear. This was the Sandy of old, who had died and was now coming back to life.

I said, "Let me tell you something about those people. They were energized. You could feel it. And they will be back. They are going to the city council. They are going to write letters and make phone calls. They are going to march again, and next time we'll see twice as many in the streets."

"So you're with me on this, you think it's doable."

"It's the only way to go. Those folks out there today, they still want to believe in something they hear from your radio station. They believe in the stuff we've always talked about."

"And they'll be hearing more of it. We're not changing anything. I want you to get back on the air. It's the least I can do. This new host I hired, I'll call him, I'll wake him up in the middle of the night if I have to and tell him to stay home, I made a mistake, I overreacted. Your show, you and Julie, you're the heart and soul of what we do."

"According to Roy, my show in particular rubs the wrong way."

"Fuck Roy. Maybe he will get the message that muscling in here is going to be more trouble than it's worth. He already has fifty other radio stations, for Christ's sake!"

"Maybe that's why he wants fifty-one. Maybe that's why he hired some guy to sabotage the rally."

"You think Roy had something to do with that?"

"Who else?"

"You're right. Who else would bother? He is not a guy who takes no for an answer. If we back out of this, he will surely try to cut us into little pieces. But hey, what else is there, if you can't be true to your own gut-truth. Here's the thing, Dan. This is why I called. Thanks to all the publicity, some people have come to me, I can't say who, not yet, but people with dough who want to bail us out."

"You mean it's not a done deal?"

"It's an almost done deal. We have letters of intent. A kind of deposit was supposed to go into a holding account, a good-faith advance."

"Can't you just give them that money back?"

"It's out of reach. We had to borrow against it. But now I think we can raise at least that much. The lawyer says he found a clause in the agreement—not even a paragraph, he says, just a clause—that gives us about three inches of wiggle room. So there is a ray of hope, a thin ray, which today, tonight, is all I need. I am already starting to feel like a guy I saw downtown the other day who looked like he was in recovery from nine kinds of self-abuse and wearing a T-shirt that said, 'I used to think there was no light at the end of the tunnel until I realized I was looking in the wrong direction.' "

Lemon Light

I poured myself another glass of Zinfandel, one I didn't need. With the first sip I felt above my left eye the low ache of red-wine overdose, while another pang kept digging deeper, the Julie Moraga pang. I sipped again, tempted to call Sandy back, ask him about the woman in the hat, if he'd noticed her. Once upon a time he and I had talked about everything, life, death, women, money, the ups and downs of radio, the daily news. An ally I'd feared lost to me was now found again. If I called him I knew I wouldn't bring up the woman in the hat. I wanted to talk about breaking through, breaking past, breaking out. I envied him that guidepost of a hexagram. "I've been rethinking my life," he said. "Me too," I said. "Me too." It's what can happen when someone pulls the rug out and from one day to the next your job is gone.

I had mine back, of course, I had my show again. Sandy gave me his word *Sit Still and Listen* would last as long as he did. Call it a foothold, a handhold. All the more reason to fight the good fight. I should have been shouting Hallelujah. But his chances of salvaging the station were slim indeed, and the questions I'd started asking hadn't gone away. How did I get here? How did the zigzag trail of my so-called career put me in the ring with a welterweight tycoon like Roy? At any moment I could find myself out on the sidewalk. And what then? What happens next? Should I be feeling around for other gigs at other stations? Or some kind of teaching post? Or go back to the department and finish up my abandoned degree? When your job is in danger it can derail you, rattle your self-esteem. It can also be a blessing, open up some unexpected space, a breakthrough.

I sipped again and dialed. On a night like this Sandy wouldn't mind reading again the meaning of that hexagram.

When six rings went by I figured he'd turned off his answering machine. Then I heard the click and a soft, inquisitive female voice, "Hello?"

Did he have some company? I couldn't speak.

In the silence her guard went up. "Who is this?"

I knew the voice. I knew then I had dialed Julie's number.

"Just me," I said. "Were you in bed?"

"Almost."

"I was sitting here thinking. . . ."

"Good. I'm glad you called."

"It was an impulse."

"That's the best reason. There's something I should have mentioned."

"You happen to catch the late news?"

"I missed it. Did they cover the rally?"

"I think they caught you on camera."

"Really? How did I look?"

"Maybe it wasn't you. Hard to tell from behind, but with the hat and all . . . stepping out of a black sedan?"

After a heavy silence she whispered, "Shit."

In my heart I too whispered "Shit," for the panicky disappointment running through me like cold rain.

"You want to tell me what's going on?"

"This is what I started to say . . ."

"How could you get into the same car with a creep like Roy Wurlitzer?"

"He's not all bad, Danny."

"You yourself called him a son of a bitch."

"I think that was Sandy's word."

"I can't believe I'm hearing this."

"I'm not saying I trust him all that far."

"Trust him! About what? What in hell is this, Julie? I don't want to have to play detective all through the night!"

"Well, that is sure how you sound."

"How do you expect me to sound? What's the big secret? This afternoon you didn't even bring this up!"

"I couldn't figure out how to do it. I knew how you'd react."

"React? React like what?"

"The way you're reacting! Listen to yourself!"

"Goddam it, I have a right to react!"

"Roy wasn't even in the car!"

"But you were. Don't you know how that looks? You have any idea what's running through my mind?"

"You don't own me, Danny!"

I took a couple of deep breaths, yoga breaths, aimed my attention just below the navel, trying to project a wise, transcendent calm.

"That's true. I don't. Whatever you do is your business. You want to ride around in the corporate limo, so be it."

Now she was inhaling, searching for her center. It was so quiet I thought the line had gone dead.

"Julie?"

"He offered me a job."

My carefully modulated calm fell to pieces.

"A job? Jesus Christ! Doing what?"

"I didn't say yes, I didn't say no. But I had to talk to him, Danny. There's no harm in talking. If this came through, I could make enough for both of us. We could both go and all you'd have to do is work on your book."

"Go where?"

Roy had called that morning just as she was rushing off to the airport with Toby and her mother in tow. Bad publicity, he said, had brought him back to the Bay Area, added a day to his West Coast junket, and could they meet for coffee. When she said no, her day was pretty full, he said he had in mind for her a very good position with Argonaut and was hoping for a few minutes to talk about it before he caught his plane.

And so they met at Java Junction on University, after she'd waved Mama good-bye, after she'd left Toby at the preschool's weekend crafts program run by mothers who took turns volunteering. The nonstop round of parental strategies such as this, of course, had much to do with her readiness to hear him out, since he was talking about quite a bit of money, more than she'd ever made. It was a production job that would bring her back to Baltimore, to Argonaut central, where the equipment was state of the art.

" 'Think of this as a preliminary talk,' he told me. 'I'll have to run it past my personnel people and maybe fly you back for an interview.' Don't groan, Danny. I heard you groan. I know what you're thinking. And you're probably right. You know how he got my number? From Lorene at the office. He is completely transparent. But guess what I found out. He likes Miles Davis and Dizzy Gillespie. In college he played trumpet. He still has a huge record collection. Which sounds weird since he's talking about cutting out the jazz show at KRUX. You know what he says? He can't let his personal tastes interfere with programming decisions because they are not about him, they are about audience. And that is cold. That is very cold. But where I am on this, if he's taking over the station I'll be working for him anyway. A couple of years with Argonaut I could learn things, everything I need to know on the technical side, then come back to the Bay Area at another level.

"And that's all there was to it, Danny. I swear that is what we talked about. I didn't want to move my car again so I asked him to drop me at the station, mainly because I had to pee. If you saw me hurry across the sidewalk it was a bladder run. He already knew about the rally. He'd seen the papers and wanted to check it out incognito. He wanted to mingle. 'Get a feel for where they're coming from' was how he put it. He's a very quirky guy. He showed up at the coffee shop wearing a panama hat and shades and a denim workshirt he'd just bought. 'Do I look local?' he asked me, like a kid in a Halloween costume. Then he says, 'Have you ever seen *Henry the Fifth,* when he takes off his crown and dons the garb of the common soldier and wanders among his men on the night before battle to speak with them as an equal and in this way learn more about how they think of him and measure their states of mind?' It was all a kind of game. I think he has more money than he knows what to do with."

The driver had dropped him across from the parking lot, then come around the block, waiting out two long stoplights, by which time the flatbed had tilted and the crowd was on the move. With his car surrounded he probably let the driver fend for himself and caught a cab.

Was she making this up? I didn't think so. She wasn't given to flights of fancy. As I think back, everything she'd ever said to me was true, or pretty close to true. Julie was an honest person, with a practical mind, and Roy was a stepping-stone. At least at the outset, that's how she saw him. By the time we hung up—well past midnight—I told myself I wasn't worried about Roy. I'd watched her fend off advances of every type. What silenced me were the hints and intonations that crept in, as if she expected me to talk her out of this new job and the prospect of a move across the continent, or to make a counteroffer. And I wanted to. Don't even think about going anywhere, I almost said, Roy may never call again. I don't want to lose you, I almost said, stay here and we'll get married.

"I have to think of what is best for Toby," she said. "He's in kinder-garten now. I'm not saying I'm going to move, or that I really even want to. If Sandy gives us our show back, that's great, it really is. We should do that for as long as we can, it's such important work. But I have to be real-istic. If I was going anywhere, or if we were, this would be the ideal time, don't you think? For Toby's sake, I mean . . ." as if we were already mom and dad working this out together, her voice loaded the way her eyes sometimes were loaded when Toby was the subject, or her mother, that expectation hovering around the words, and never quite voiced because, I think, she faulted herself for having such a mother, for having a father-less son, bore that fault though she was not the one who'd walked away. He too was in her voice, sometimes in her eyes, Toby's blood father, the missing father, the restless and all-styles guitar player we'd seldom talked about, who was always on the road. "I still have the letter he sent," she told me once, "with a Nashville postmark and a five-hundred-dollar check, saying he'd be coming back to Berkeley sooner or later but couldn't say quite when. I was working part-time then and Toby was one, and wide-eyed, innocent me, I thought sooner or later meant a month or two."

As her loaded voice came toward me, an old memory was rising. No. Less than a memory. Or the parts of one that had slipped away. The thinnest kind of signal, something from so far back it was emerging like the dream finally recalled in your waking hours. It was another woman wearing another hat with a wide, floppy brim. Sun makes the brim a bright lemony ring, with light sifting through so her face is both shad-owed and faintly lit. It is my mother, hurrying across a sidewalk, her sun hat a distant hold on the Southern belle she always secretly wanted to be. I see her eyes, her feet, the scuffed brown walking shoes she wore around the yard. I watch and I'm also running down our stairs in the Richmond, looking back, and the panic I feel is in her voice as she calls, "Danny! Danny, don't cross the street!"

It is the day Hank comes home early to stand in the kitchen in his coat and tie while Verlene, in from the yard where she'd been weeding her flower beds, her hands and knees smeared with dirt, listens to his low, insistent voice telling her she has to get rid of all the letters and photos, every vestige of the brown-skinned fellow who fathered me, and I find myself still as a statue in the doorway—perhaps I've been napping or have come from the far end of the yard where I'd fashioned a dirt track for a couple of my toy cars—looking up and hearing what I am not supposed to hear. Then she sees me and grasps my hand, leads me out onto the front porch, a kind of glassed-in solarium where she keeps marigolds in pots and, on this day, filled with a lemony, lunar light. On the bench she pulls me close to explain how my first father was a wonderful man who died in the war and is never coming back. I bolt then, tear myself from her embrace, go stumbling down the brick stairs and begin to run. To my five-year-old ears the words themselves do not convey bad news. It is in her voice, her smile, the grim and twisted pleading of her smile, an anguish there I have not seen or heard before and cannot bear.

I scamper out into the boulevard called Fulton, while brakes squeal and drivers swerve. Then Hank catches me from behind, lifting with both arms. His jacket smells of cigarette smoke and inside the jacket his shirt is sticky.

"Hey, Danny Boy, it's okay! It's okay now!"

I don't want him to be holding me. I try to squirm loose. I yearn to run, not from him but from Verlene, her face, her voice.

Hearing it again, thirty years later, I knew more about it. Something precious and irretrievable had been wrenched from my mother's grasp. I heard her moan, her muted cry. And in that same moment I knew where my own reluctance had been hiding, my reluctance to become the man in Julie's life, and in Toby's. From Hank I'd inherited the notion that to have her I must somehow take sole possession of her son. And yet I did not want to be the one who could force Julie to choose between a blood father and a second father. I dreaded seeing that crooked smile, hearing again the anguish of that muffled cry.

Mine was an old and useless and unexamined fear, and as soon as I saw it I was able to let it go, just like that. A screen had been surrounding my heart. Between one breath and the next, it fell away, allowing me to be one of Toby's fathers. I don't think it's going too far to say that as I sat there by the phone I fell in love with Toby, or let myself admit I already loved him. He was not mine, yet he was me, the kid with the missing father who bore his father's name, the kid with bloodlines from three directions, with a look on his face that tells you he is none of these, he is all of these, he is who he is.

The voices from the past had faded, the filtered light, the runaway boy in Hank's arms, Verlene at the street corner with one hand on her yellow hat, and now the voice was Julie's.

"You still there, Danny? You haven't said anything. Are you angry? You know I want to work this out."

PART FIVE

Kawika's Voice

San Francisco, 1891

Ragged edges tell us that after Kalakaua passed away the rest of January was torn from Nani's journal, eight or ten pages gone, and after that, no more entries for several weeks. Were they lost somewhere in transit? Or was this a form of mourning? Had his death stifled her desire to keep a record of her days? I suspect it did, but again I'm guessing. And I can only guess at why she didn't return to the rancheria. She still had relatives there, but with her mother's sister gone, and the school closed, and the long-suffering face of the General's Wife to contend with, maybe she preferred some solitude. In among the General's copious papers (and this is where these searches take you, ploughing through the decades of a land baron's correspondence, hoping for any kind of tip or signpost), I came across a letter mailed from San Francisco, full of apology, promising she'd be home within the week. A month later a second letter, more effusive, made the same promise. In fact, years would pass before she kept it.

As far as I can tell she stayed where she was and went to work for Makua, who'd parted ways with Peabody Trade and Maritime. He was thirty then, well connected in the city, and in Honolulu too. He found some vacant office space at a good address a few blocks away and found a partner, a fellow graduate of Hastings Law School who knew a bit about the Pacific and who also shared his politics. Nani was their second assistant, errand runner and filing clerk. Late in life Makua would donate his firm's records to what is now the Maritime Library at Fort Mason Center and there I would find some early payroll sheets from M. Flynn Associates noting Miss Nancy Callahan was paid fifteen dollars for the week of March 22, 1891 (the king then being two months gone).

When at last she took up her pen again, her writing had begun to change. Surely Kawika's passing had changed her. It reads now like the opening of a second phase, and I still wonder if she intended it that way. From her girlhood days at the mission school, these entries had been accumulating, volume by volume, for just about ten years.

May 2, 1891

Where to start? Outside my window the street below is full of noise. Busy busy busy. It is always full of noise and maybe this city is too much for me. How long can I stay here? I am wishing for a time that used to be. I am like everybody else, wishing I could have my childhood days again. In the village where I was born we had a creek for water. We had fire for light. Now I live alone in this apartment on Geary Street. I open my book and look at the many pages I have written. The generals wife told me to write down every word and in those days it was hard to write. Now while my hand moves across the page I ask myself why? Why do I come back to these pages? What will I do with them?

May 15

Kawika was not supposed to die. Not yet. Not here. I was not prepared for it. No one was prepared. After all the confusion people came to watch the horses pull his coffin down Market Street. So many you could not count them. The whole city came to watch. In the long parade I walked beside him to carry the kahili and I knew this was the last time I would carry it. They asked me to come on the ship and stay beside the coffin. I said no. I did not tell them why. I cannot go back to Honolulu. Without him it will be empty there. I watched him from the wharf. I watched the ship get smaller and I chanted the farewell chant. My tears came down. I would not see him any more. I would not see Hawaii.

When the ship was gone around the point I remembered another chant. I remembered how Kawika spoke into the roll of wax. Moana used to tell us how a chant has power. It is our tie to the older time she said. From voice to voice we pass it on. In my mind I heard his voice. I knew when people in Honolulu heard his words they would miss him more. They would wail with sorrow. But I knew they would one day weep with gladness because some part of him was still alive.

June 9

My mother came to me last night. She was a young woman walking all alone yet surrounded by her people. She was on a journey, carrying a burden basket. Her dress was shining in the bright sun of summer. I was watching from a long distance but also I was right beside her. Maybe I was still a little girl walking with her. Or maybe I was not born yet and from inside her belly I could hear her talking. She said you must tell the story Nani, it is not a secret. In my dream I said which story mama? She knew so many stories. She was walking from the place where she always lived to another place far away across the valley and over the mountains to the west. She walked in the sun while the soldiers rode their horses. I woke up from this dream sweating as if I too had walked in hot sun across the valley.

Makua lent her money, found her some lodging, took her under his wing in a brotherly way, as he'd done when they found themselves on the same ship out of Honolulu and bound for the West Coast. This time he needed to ease his conscience, with the shadow of his former boss now looming between them. He felt badly used, and he worried that Giles had misused his cousin, though exactly how he could not say. Nani never spoke of what had happened in the company's suite, and Makua could not bring himself to ask.

Rushing back to his office that day he'd found a message from the Board of Trade but nothing about delivering a report. It was another false emergency, which Giles had tried to blame on a telephone connection. "Damn contraptions are more trouble than they're worth," Giles told him with a wink and a comradely laugh. "Person to person, eye to eye, that's the only thing you can count on."

Makua did not laugh with him. Betrayed, disillusioned, he'd seen a side of Giles he didn't like at all, proclaiming this and doing that, carrying on like a lunatic. It had undermined his faith in the man. And this had nothing to do, by the way, with the king's untimely death. Despite his falling-out with Giles, Makua's view of the future had not changed. Kalakaua's end meant the monarchy had run its course, a final obstacle to annexation had been removed. It was only a matter of time until Hawai'i joined the United States, and what better place to be than the coast of California? Two walls of his spacious new office were covered with shelves of lawbooks. A third displayed a map of the Pacific with thin black lines to mark the shipping routes that linked San Francisco Bay to Chile, Hawai'i, Guam, Japan, the Philippines.

Every other Friday night he and Nani met with a social group who gathered at the small hotel. Hui Hawaii O Kapalakiko (Hawaiian Club of San Francisco) convened for an hour or two in an upper room furnished with couches and upholstered chairs to share news from the islands and welcome visitors who might be passing through. Sometimes a dozen people would show up, sometimes twenty—a law student, an Episcopal minister of mixed blood, an Italian music teacher with a Hawaiian wife. If someone brought a guitar they sang a few songs. If something had appeared in the *Examiner,* the story would be read aloud and discussed. They traded gossip, rumor, family stories, always drawn to the haunting and mysterious. One night in July they were held rapt by a man recently arrived from Honolulu who recounted the day the dead king's voice was heard again in Iolani Palace.

It was a long story, beginning with the docking of the ship that delivered his remains, when the entire city was draped in black, all public life at a standstill, all flags lowered, black crepe above every doorway and arch, around every arm and the crown of every hat. Communal lament had only sharpened the wonder of a radiant emblem that filled the sky. As the procession followed his casket from the blue harbor to the royal palace, a rare triple rainbow arched above the route, a vivid gateway hanging in the air, a heavenly sign. Like the noonday sun that had burst through cloud cover just as he placed the crown upon his head, that triple rainbow was seen as another miraculous blessing from nature itself, a welcome home.

For two weeks—the visitor continued—his body lay in state in the Throne Room, his casket covered by a golden feather cloak, the royal mantle that had passed from king to king, while his subjects wailed the piercing death wail and chanted many songs to celebrate his deeds. Another procession followed his remains to the royal burial grounds behind the town, where a military escort fired off three rounds that echoed from the valley walls. Their thunder should have marked an end to the season of mourning, but on that very day a man had arrived on another ship, claiming to have the king's last words preserved. He had instructions to present them to the royal chamberlain on behalf of a man who once promised to give the king a talking machine, but since the king was gone he sent instead a short, round box and his condolences. Inside this box was a roll of wax, and somewhere inside the wax, he said, the king's voice resided. In all of Hawai'i there was only one machine that could make the wax release the words, and this machine was soon brought into Iolani Palace, to be set upon a table in the reception hall, where the chamberlain listened first, through tubes placed into his ears. He recognized the message, "*Aloha kaua . . . ,*" and he repeated it aloud.

Those present were amazed, listening with awe, some with fear, as if the king's spirit had found its way into this strange machine. The king's wife, Kapi'olani, was not there. She would not listen. The chamberlain passed the earphones to the new queen, Lili'uokalani. The sound of her dead brother's voice seemed to be some final weight she could not support. She bowed her head and wept, while all those around her wept. Some began to wail, some fled the room, while others stepped forward as if approaching the edge of a cliff, as if risking their lives to receive the earphones and listen to these distant words somehow carried across the water in a turning roll of brown wax.

As his story ended, as the Hui Hawaii O Kapalakiko sat in reverent silence, Nani saw the grieving sister standing in the reception hall. She knew that room, knew its chairs and draperies, koa paneling and polished floors. She saw the queen surrounded by all the finery of her new office, yet consumed with loss, and Nani's heart was with her, wishing she'd gone back to Honolulu when she had the chance, so she could find a way to befriend Lili'uokalani, thinking of her not as queen but as cousin, as a sister of Kawika. Her picture had once appeared in the *Examiner,* her low-cut gown, the full-fleshed smoothness of her neck and shoulders, dark hair piled high, her eyes filled with sorrow and yet with purpose too, and Nani remembered someone saying that with a name like Lili'uo-kalani she would one day show surprising strength. She would find a way to stand up to the missionary boys. *Lani* means "sky" or "heaven" or a "highborn person, a chief," or all three at once. *Lili'u* means "a burning in the eyes." A burning in the eyes that comes down from heaven. Maybe she sees things others do not see.

In the silent room Nani was the first to speak.

"What happened when the queen heard his chant? Did it lift her spirits?"

The man who told the story looked at her. "What chant?"

" 'The California Sailor.' There was a second roll of wax. The king spoke twice."

A dignified older man with a trimmed white beard, he almost suppressed a smile, as if embarrassed for her. "There was no chant, my dear."

"No chant?"

"Everyone wished for more, of course. But there was only the king's brief greeting to his people. I saw it with my own eyes, the roll inside a round carton, and this was presented in a fine box lined with velvet."

Others in the room regarded her with curiosity, and Nani filled with shame. When she turned to Makua, her eyes pleading for support, he glanced away. He would not look at her.

Afterward as they stood on the sidewalk waiting for a hackney she said, "Why did you not speak? That man thought I was crazy."

Still he would not look at her. He scanned the street, studying the traffic. "You should have kept quiet like the rest of them."

"His story was not finished."

"There is no second recording."

"Someone in Honolulu has it, but they are keeping it from the queen."

Like an impatient older brother he shook his head.

She said, "I heard them. The Edison man made two."

"I know the Edison man."

"Go ask him then."

Now he turned to her, with the same face she'd seen when she opened the door to find him standing in the hotel corridor, the face of a fugitive treed by a pack of hunting dogs.

"It is gone, Nani."

"It can't be gone."

"The Edison man did not send it to Honolulu."

"I don't believe you. He promised Kawika."

"Suit yourself. Here is our cab. Let me help you up."

"You are deceiving me again!"

They hadn't talked much at all about the day he came looking for her, and he didn't want to talk about it now. He wanted to drop her off, escape her gaze and get home to his pregnant wife. But as the driver flicked his reins and they set out with hooves clopping and wheels rattling across the cobblestones, Nani was the lawyer now, the prosecuting attorney, and he was a defendant in the witness chair. Stung by her accusation, still burdened with guilt for luring her to the company suite, he felt coerced by her insistent silence to tell her what was said in the office of Louis Glass. It tumbled forth like a confession—how Glass would secure the cylinder and eventually dispose of it—and he was much relieved to have this off his chest. Yet Nani's gaze still held him.

"And what did *you* say, Makua? Did you try to stop them? The words of the king . . . if they are lost . . . how could you sit there with those two white men and let them plan to melt away the king's last words? I cannot believe this. You are here with your big office in the big city, but your mother on Maui is still Hawaiian. Can you tell this story to your mother?"

Oh, how he yearned to be away from her, to leap from the cab and send her on alone, this nosy pest of a kinswoman. Why did he ever give her a job? Why did she have to speak of his mother, whose voice was in his ear again, as close and as urgent as Nani's, his mother whose voice reminded him of things almost forgotten, reminding him that if a king's words were truly inside a roll of wax, then they would be like a thigh bone or arm bone, which carries a chief's mana long after he is dead. And you do not defile the bones of a chief. It is kapu, it is forbidden, it brings a curse upon you and your family. Nani was like his mother, the black eyes, the scolding voice, here beside him in the hackney and he would have to tell the rest of his story, the part he thought he would never tell.

"I could not sit there, Nani. You are right. After that crazy day with Giles I knew I could no longer trust him. I did not trust Mr. Glass to keep the chant locked up forever in his drawer, and so . . ."

"And so?"

"You are the only one I can tell this to. And we must never speak of it again, because I am a lawyer, and I have broken the law. But I had no choice. I hired a man, a very small and limber Chinese man, to break in late one night and take the roll out of his drawer. Next to his office Mr. Glass has a toilet room, and above the toilet a small window opens onto an alley. My man climbed in and climbed out again and brought the roll of wax to me, in its cardboard carton."

She had been leaning toward him. Now her shoulders relaxed, as she laughed a quiet, happy laugh. "Makua, you surprise me. Is this really true?"

"Yes. I have it. In a very safe place."

"But what about the Edison man? Will he report it to the police?"

"He already has."

"And?"

"And I was briefly interviewed by a rather heavyset and impatient sergeant who had never heard of a talking machine. A stolen roll of wax was not a crime he cared to think about for long."

They had reached her building, and he was glad to see it. Purged and unburdened, he was ready to step off the witness stand. But Nani was still not satisfied.

"You cannot keep it hidden. It belongs to the queen. It is her brother's voice."

As he moved to step down from the hackney, she grabbed his hand, squeezing, to hold him in his seat.

"She should hear it as soon as possible. The people of Hawai'i should know what was in Kawika's mind."

How could Makua tell her that in this he still agreed with Giles Peabody, that it was too great a risk to stir up false hopes? How could he tell her that while part of him was compelled to preserve this recording like a sacred relic, another part was compelled to bury it, conceal it forever from public eye and ear?

When he didn't respond, she said, "I have money saved. Give me the wax. I will carry it to Honolulu and deliver it myself. I promise you, I will guard it with my life."

Her eyes were on him again, and he tried to match her gaze.

"That will not be necessary. I have reason to return very soon to the islands. In fact, I have already booked my passage. I have been wanting to meet Her Majesty, and this will give me an occasion to call. So I thank you, Nani. You have persuaded me to see what is right."

His broad smile seemed to seal this commitment. With a brisk and youthful hop he stepped down to the sidewalk, then helped Nani down. They embraced in the Hawaiian way, forehead to forehead, nose to nose, said aloha, and he was gone. Much later she would write:

He told me he would take Kawika's chant back to Honolulu where it belonged. He promised me. Yet still I saw fear in his eyes. I knew he did not tell all that was in his heart. Now I know why. I know he did not know how to tell it. Makua did not know his own heart. He was pulled two ways. It is hard to be half and half. Sometimes he heard his mother talking. Sometimes he heard his father, the sailing captain from New England. His Hawaiian side sent the Chinese man to save Kawika's chant. But what would his white side do? I did not know. He did not know. How could I be angry with Makua? I knew the confusion in his face. I too was pulled two ways. I could not go back to Hawaii. I could not go back to the rancheria. So I stayed in the city. I could not choose.

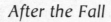

After the Fall

In a holding pattern, working long hours at M. Flynn Associates, she waited and she watched. For months she wondered what Makua would do. Twice he took the steamship to Honolulu—business trips, family trips, keeping tight all the lines that linked his offices with ports and shores and sea-lanes farther west—and each time she asked about the queen. Was she surprised to know of the second recording? Was she moved by the verses her brother had added to "Kaholokai Kaleponi"?

The first time, he turned toward the window to contemplate a trolley passing down below and said yes, she'd thanked him for this gift and would soon send someone to find the man who owned the talking machine so she could play it back and listen. The second time he looked up from his desk only long enough to say that his visit to the palace had been brief, that Her Majesty was much occupied with affairs of state, his dismissive smile implying that he too had larger matters on his mind.

January 5, 1892

Maybe what he says is true. Maybe not. I have searched through all his drawers and cabinets. Once when he opened up the safe I looked inside. Kawika's voice was not there. I will not mention it again. I will not pester him. Makua is a large man, large and fat, with the face of a boy who did something he does not want his mother to know. I cannot be his mother.

He is good to me. Without Makua how could I live here? But sometimes it is hard to look at him now. How can I find another job?

These half-and-half cousins first met at her Kinsman's house when she was seventeen, when Makua, just finishing law school, was an amiable and studious companion, when they'd all gathered at the railroad

...ng to welcome Kalakaua, all enamored of the king, the exotic glamour of their world-encircling leader. Now these same two cousins found themselves on opposite sides of the struggle for power that had outlived his reign. Makua's allegiance was to the unimpeded flow of trade. With Kawika gone, Nani's grieving affection was bestowed upon the sister she scarcely knew.

As bits of news trickled toward the coast to be reported in the papers and dissected by members of the Hui, she prayed that Lili'uokalani would prevail. The queen's success would be Kawika's too. And maybe his voice would reach her some other way, in a dream, or in a spirit form as it sometimes came to Nani, late at night, when she undressed and placed around her neck the strands of purple shells and danced again as she had danced for him, danced until she heard the rhythmic comfort of his chanting, until she saw her mother stepping through the trees, pushing leaves aside, to speak to her and join her.

When Nani read about the fall of Iolani Palace, her mother appeared to her, standing alone in the bright sun of a valley summer, with no trees anywhere. Then she was walking in the sun while soldiers rode their horses with rifles at the ready. This time Nani strained to hear her voice. What did Mama want? Why had she come again like this? She saw the pensive, melancholy eyes. Maybe it was not her mother. Maybe it was the queen. As if there'd been another death in the family, she stared at the headlines:

REVOLT IN HAWAII
A QUEEN FORCED TO STEP DOWN
A PROVISIONAL GOVERNMENT ESTABLISHED
A REVOLUTION ACCOMPLISHED
WITHOUT BLOODSHED

There had been a rising up, an insurrection, backed by American marines with rifles. She read the story several times, word by word, phrase by phrase:

> Obstinate and unreasonable, she has stood in the way of this nation's own best interests. Hence it is fitting that she be replaced by an interim body of responsible business leaders and prominent missionary descendants . . .

"They took Kawika," she thought. "Now they are taking her."

That night she carried the newspaper to a meeting of the Hui Hawaii O Kapalakiko, where twenty-five were gathered in the upper room of the small hotel, all carrying the day's paper, drawn together by this unprecedented news and by the reputation of a man who'd come from Honolulu on the same ship that brought the correspondent's oilskin-wrapped report. He was a splendid fellow, half Hawaiian, wearing a high-waisted jacket and close-fit trousers that gave him a military look.

January 28, 1893

He must be the same age as Makua, his skin the same color, like brown sugar, and the same gentle lips. But the face is thin, not round, with a scar along his chin and jaw, maybe from a knife or from a hard fall. His eyes are not half closed and ready to look away. They are full of fire. He looks straight at me the way Edward used to do. They could make me afraid of him the way Edward made me afraid. But he has much aloha for the queen. Everything he says sounds true to me.

This man, Richard Aikona, stood tall in front of the Hawaiian club and told them that the newspaper report, though columns long, gave only half the story. In the islands there were still many who would always support Lili'uokalani. There were plans to form a new militia, make a stand against this unlawful takeover, and he was raising money, traveling up and down the coast.

With a handsome grin he said, "Let me tell you what I think. I think they thought a lady would be easy to push around because that is the kind of ladies those haole boys are married to."

His eyes had fixed on Nani's—one of three women in the room— and a glint of mischief compelled her to join the general laughter, though not everyone laughed. Makua was not amused. He did not like the sound of this. As if praying for a higher power to intervene, he clasped his hands in front of his chest.

"In the old days when she was a princess you would hear people say she was spoiled, wanting everyone to wait on her, take care of every little thing. Maybe the missionary boys thought that is the kind of ruler she would be. Make her feel important, then other folks could run the show. But Lili'u, she took them by surprise. She laid down the law. She set out to finish up some things started by her brother, Kalakaua. She was going to bring out a new constitution, like the old one used to be, give the rul- ing power back to the queen, with more say for the Hawaiians. She said

Hawai'i was run by Hawaiians for more than a thousand years. Other folks can come and live there and work there and make some money if they can figure out how. But Hawaiians were there first. It is their place, and that is the way it should be.

"So the missionary boys don't like this. They had to get her out of there. And she didn't go easy, you know. They had to get permission from the U.S. minister to bring in marines from American ships waiting in the harbor. They surrounded the palace. We're here to protect the city, they said, in case things get out of hand. And what did Hawai'i do to the United States of America—this is what I want to know—that they have to invade our city with a hundred and sixty marines carrying rifles and bayonets? The queen had to leave her own palace and march down the steps alone, then the haole men came like bandits and stole everything, stole the furniture, tore down all the Hawaiian flags and cut one into little pieces and passed the pieces around like souvenirs of their great victory! But I don't think they know this battle is only getting started. . . ."

Halfway through this speech, the murmuring began, the listeners sharing surprise and consternation. Now everyone was speaking at once, voices lifting to be heard, a law student shouting that it was wrong to disgrace the queen when Hawaiians needed a leader they believed in, a bank clerk shouting that everyone knew she had gone too far, she was a spendthrift just like her brother. With arms thrust high like a preacher at a gospel revival, Richard Aikona said the Hui should take a vote, and before anyone could agree or disagree he called, "How many here stand with the queen?"

Twenty raised their hands, some leaping up as if to testify, among them Nani, tears spilling down her face, tears of pride, tears of aloha for the distant cousin with a burning in her eyes that comes from heaven, tears of relief, tears of wonder that this fellow standing before them could voice her deepest sympathies. She did not notice that Makua had walked out of the room in disgust. Her gaze was fixed on Richard Aikona, she was taken with the passion of his message, with his grace and sense of command.

A week later when he traveled to Sacramento for a meeting with supporters, Nani was his companion. When he returned to meet again with the Hui, she was the one collecting money. For a while they may have been lovers. I would like to think so. I would like to think they had a fling, Nani and her soldier of fortune. I would like to think these years in San Francisco were not celibate and solitary, though it's hard to know

for sure, given her habit of selective reporting. You have to read betwee
the lines.

When he invited her to travel with him to Santa Barbara and points south she almost let herself climb aboard another train, as if she were seventeen again, setting forth on another glamorous journey into territory exciting and unknown:

> He says come with him all the way to Honolulu. We need strong women he says. We will join with all the others who want to work for Liliuokalani.
>
> He is the first one who ever told me I am strong. I wanted to go with him then. I told him yes and he put his arms around me. Later when I told him no he swore at me. You are like all the others he said. I told him so are you. He looked like I had stabbed him. I did not mean to hurt him. I spoke too fast.

Nani trusted Richard's words about Hawai'i, but not his promises to her. She'd seen him through the eyes of other women, brown and white, seen him standing too close to a young recruit who longed to volunteer her services. He was too attractive, perhaps too familiar, with Edward's broad-shouldered warrior looks and Kawika's roaming eye.

And so she stuck it out a while longer in the city, her small office desk now separated from Makua's by an ever-widening gulf neither one could cross. It was not a gulf of silence. They were cordial. He thanked her for tasks well done. It was a gulf made of all that could not be mentioned, Peabody's suite at the Palace Hotel, the elusive roll of wax, her time spent with Richard Aikona, and now this new man in the White House saying America should let Hawaiians make up their own minds about how they would be ruled. If some say they should be annexed, said Grover Cleveland, let them put it to a vote, that's the democratic way. For Nani and others at the Hui this was welcome news, rekindling their hopes for a reinstated queen. As for Makua, he worried about putting annexation to a vote. He knew it was the right thing to do, but feared it would never pass. Unable to speak of the president without losing his temper, he stopped coming to the meetings.

The Oldest Calling

Nani stuck it out until Kawika returned to San Francisco and spoke to her one more time. His clothes came back, his uniforms, his trousers and his shoes, the morning coat he'd worn when he stepped from the railroad car to greet the crowd in Sacramento, the cloak of golden feathers that covered him when he lay in state—all this and more came back across the water to tell Nani what she did not want to hear.

Beyond the city's farther edge a fair had risen from the sand dunes, a sprawling fantasia of domes and pavilions and exhibits from all parts of the world. Years later she would say she had felt his presence there long before she caught the trolley that carried her past the last houses in the built-up districts, toward what were called the Outside Lands.

She had joined half a dozen others from the Hui, all drawn to "the Hawaiian Village," where island food was for sale, or so they'd heard, poi and grilled fish and coffee from Kona. They'd heard of grass houses and palm trees and a band with dancers and a volcano where you could watch lava boil up in a lake of fire. Some said it would be good for the spirit to be around such things; it would be just like home. Some in the Hui had told them it was shameful, all for money, bits and pieces shipped over here by men in the provisional government who wanted to turn Hawai'i into a show.

They were bound for Golden Gate Park, which had only started to be the urban forest it is today. Young groves and flower beds and meadows made a long corridor of green stretching from the fairgrounds three miles out to the ocean, bounded on either side by empty plains. Near the park's eastern end a wide swath had been scraped clean of newly planted trees and shrubs. An oval the size of a racetrack was scooped out of the dirt to become a central promenade called the Court of Honor, with high-spouting fountains on either side of an electric tower made of steel, modeled after the Eiffel Tower, lined with thousands of incandescent bulbs. The searchlight on top of this tower was billed as the largest light on earth. At night its powerful beam, unobstructed by trees or buildings, swept across the dunes to the north and lit ships passing through the Golden Gate.

I confess that until I came across a mention of this fair in Nani's journal I'd never heard of it, though I'd grown up right across the street from where its Byzantine palaces once stood. To see some of what she saw, I made another trip to the downtown library and soon discovered I was not alone. An extravaganza that had pulled two million people through its gates had somehow slipped under the radar of public memory. Like a traveling circus, it went up in a hurry and came down in a hurry. By my day it was long out of sight, yet not entirely forgotten. As the Special Collections clerk set a pile of folders in front of me—photos, maps, magazine pieces, guidebooks and souvenir programs—he said, "Nobody has looked at this stuff in years."

The Midwinter International Fair and Exposition was hatched by city fathers to promote California and stir up interest in the miles of uninhabited acreage north and south of the park. The Court of Honor was surrounded with cathedral-like halls celebrating produce and industry and art, gaudy and glittering with Moorish domes of gold and glass, where banners fluttered from every spire. There were Gothic columns, Spanish balustrades, doorways that conjured a pharaoh's tomb. The pavilions and rides were farther back, a Ferris wheel, the Tamale Garden, a village of igloos, an Oriental village (when "Oriental" meant Arabs, Turks, and Berbers), with a carefully cluttered street of stalls and storefronts named Little Cairo. In the Arizona Village stood an enormous saguaro cactus. In the Hall of Agriculture, Santa Clara Valley had erected a life-size knight on horseback made entirely of prunes. Counties from farther south had built a pyramid of oranges and an elephant made of walnuts. Inside the Hawaiian compound hung a sign saying

THE GRANDEST COLLECTION
OF RARE AND CURIOUS OBJECTS
EVER BROUGHT TO AMERICA

I have imagined Nani on that day, as she stepped off the trolley, paid her quarter at the gate and joined the weekend multitude, the families, the strollers, the visitors from near and far, for a while becoming a girl again, delighted as anyone would be to enter the Disneyland of 1894, amazed by the soaring tower of lights, by the hot-air balloon lifting off to carry passengers even higher, growing small above the park. She would gaze at the lone saguaro cactus, and at the dragon whose gaping mouth, lined with sharklike pointed teeth, admitted you to the thrill ride called Dante's Inferno. And sometime later in the afternoon she would arrive at the fencing made of upright fronds where a painted sign over the entrance said ALOHA.

She was alone, planning to meet her companions there at such and such a time. Paying another quarter, she stepped into the village, which at first glance was indeed a comforting sight. A half circle of grass houses formed a kind of plaza. There were coco palms and outrigger canoes parked at the edge of a small lagoon, and under a lean-to roofed with fronds three Hawaiian women sat stringing beads and flowers, weaving long lauhala leaves into hats. Nearby, three fellows in white shirts were playing an old hula tune, 'ukulele, fiddle and guitar.

At the indoor-outdoor restaurant, also roofed with fronds, she found a table. Her cup of coffee was delivered by a hefty island woman with silver hair swept up and bunched. Did Nani know her from the old days on O'ahu? Their eyes met and the woman's face opened with a generous smile.

"Hey, I remember you!"

"Mrs. Ah Fong?"

"You used to dance with the halau at Moana's."

"And you used to come to parties in the yard. One time you came leading a pig on a rope."

"And we cooked him too!"

They laughed and embraced and she sat down, eager to talk. Nani watched her plucked and curving eyebrows rise and fall as the two of them traded names of old acquaintances, as she told Nani that Moana had disbanded her halau.

"She is getting up there, you know. Just two or three special students now. Keeping things quiet. Keeping an eye on her grandkids, laying low."

In Nani's mind her island auntie had not aged, still the fierce-eyed master in her grove. She could not imagine Moana keeping quiet.

"Is there some kind of trouble?"

Mrs. Ah Fong wagged her silver head. "Lots of folks laying low these days. Waiting to see what happens next. It's a big mess. Even the preachers cracking down again on hula. It's a relief to come here for a while."

She was not a waitress. She had managed a restaurant in Honolulu.

Now she was managing day-to-day operations at the village, and wondered if Nani might be looking for a job.

"Getting so busy I need somebody else out front, taking tickets, greeting folks. You would fit right in, speaking English, and Hawaiian too. You're some kind of *hapa,* right?"

"My mother was Indian."

"Yeah, look at me." With a lusty giggle she said, "I'm Chinese, Hawaiian and Irish." Tilting sideways in her chair she patted her ample hip. "The rest of my Irish part stayed on the boat till I find a bigger place to stay."

They laughed again and Nani said, "This job, how long does it last?"

"Six months, maybe seven. Who knows?" Mrs. Ah Fong's lifted eyebrow implied that something else was sure to come along, implied that she had other enterprises as yet unnamed.

Could this be what Nani had been looking for? A way out of Makua's office? It was feeling like an inescapable trap, with so few other jobs to choose from, that is, jobs available to her—housekeeping in the small hotel, a kitchen helper in Chinatown, waitressing in a Barbary Coast saloon. Maybe she had met her rescuing angel.

"If I am interested, what must I do?"

"Just say yes, and I write to the boss over in Honolulu. But no need to wait. You could start pretty soon, anytime you want. Mr. Peabody gives me lots of room."

"Mr. Peabody?"

"He's the director for the whole thing." She spread wide her chubby arms. "All this was his idea."

"And you know him?"

She shrugged, flashing an apologetic grin. "I know his secretary. She's my nephew's sister-in-law. Look here . . ."

She took a printed card from a small stack across the table. It showed a steamship cruising through placid seas:

Peabody Trade and Maritime
Now Offers Luxury Accommodations
Round Trip Tours to Hawaii
Paradise of the Pacific

Nani studied the card, noticed then the small stack on every table. She'd last seen Giles curled up on the hotel bed in his shirt and vest. She hoped she'd never have to see him again, though in Makua's office his e was heard from time to time, and whenever she heard it or read it e would picture him there, his eyes shut, refusing to look at her, as if ~ying to fall asleep, like a child who'd forgotten to take off his shoes, waiting for someone to cover him.

"I wonder," she said, "it must feel strange to work for such a man."

"Hey, I get a free trip to the mainland, all expenses paid. I never been over here before."

"But he . . ." She didn't want to offend Mrs. Ah Fong. "He used to say such hurtful things."

Her soft hand fell on Nani's arm, a friendly, motherly, cautionary hand. "Look, honey. We are all in a hard place now. The king is dead a long time. Just between you and me, the queen is finished too."

Nani pulled her arm away. "No. No. That is not true! Many are still behind the queen!"

Mrs. Ah Fong's shrewd eyes turned wistful. "How about what the missionary boys told President Cleveland? You heard about that?"

Nani nodded. She had heard, had tried to follow the story in the *Examiner*. At the Hui they'd talked of nothing else for weeks, how the president sent a man all the way to Honolulu to find out why the queen had been removed. It was said that years ago he'd met her, still considered her a friend, and when the man came back with his report, the president sent a letter to the missionary boys telling them they had no right to take over, no right to bring in marines, and she should be restored to power. But they wrote back and told him it was their government now, their country, and it was too late for President Cleveland to do anything about it.

Mrs. Ah Fong leaned in close and dropped her voice. "They say the president got mad and wrote another letter telling them the same thing again. You think they are going to listen? They have guns, and bullets too. And what is the queen going to do? She is writing letters to the president. But from what I see, Nani, the royal family is over. It's *pau*. Just Lili'uokalani sitting in her house writing letters. You don't believe me, go look over there in the exhibit. If she was still in charge, you think she would send her own throne all the way to San Francisco for people to see for twenty-five cents? You think she would send all her silverware and her dishes and her brother's overcoat and the tall kahili from the palace that is supposed to honor her wherever she goes? You take a look and come back here and tell me what you think . . . and then you tell me when you can start."

Mrs. Ah Fong was blinking now, blinking back wetness. Her [...] fell to a husky whisper. "It's a hard time, Nani. You come to work for [...] we could be good friends." Then she mustered half a smile. "One thi[...] we know for sure"—giving herself another pat—"you gotta protec[...] your own behind."

Above the doorway to the exhibit hall, brown coconuts hung in clusters. Inside, one long room was set up as a display of curiosities. Again I see Nani, this time at the threshold looking in and not wanting to look.

Months would pass before she could write of what she saw:

Richard told us they looted the palace. Here was the proof, all those things I saw before. The drapes from the windows. The knives and forks and koa bowls. Kawika's clothes hanging on the wall, his coat, his trousers, his writing desk. The big kahili right next to the throne all made of velvet and the small kahili I used to carry, leaning against the wall. I know those feathers, I know how they smell. And the long cloak of yellow feathers passed down from Kamehameha's time. A sacred cloak, Kawika said, a cloak to honor and protect because it carries all the mana of all the ones who wore it. All these things I knew they should not be in California. She said Mr. Peabody is in charge, and I knew what he was thinking. One more time he was laughing, and he was telling Kawika now we can do anything we want.

From across the compound a barker with a megaphone was announcing the main event, every hour on the hour, the fiery spectacle of a genuine Hawaiian volcano. It was almost dark as Nani joined the crowd, passing under a sign that said KILAUEA ERUPTION. They entered a cave lined with something rough resembling lava. They climbed three flights of wooden steps, then spread out along wooden planking that curved around the top of a small mountain made of plaster painted black. From a ring of jagged, lavalike cliffs, they looked down onto a bubbling lake. It was a round metal tank filled with orange fluid and edged with flames. Smoke rising toward them smelled like sulfur.

She had never visited the Big Island, where the real Kilauea still burned, but she'd heard Kawika's stories of the fire goddess who dwells there, spoken of with reverence, the goddess who'd stopped on every island from north to south looking for a home, each time driven out by the goddess of the sea, until finally she found a place where the water could not reach her and had settled there, at Kilauea. Nani knew this n her body. While Moana chanted, she had danced the dance that it, her arms then were Pele's arms, her hands were the fire. Now, she looked into this little crater made of plaster, a Hawaiian man appeared beside the bubbling orange lake, wearing the white robe of a priest. He raised his arms, and his guttural words cut through the sulfur smell. She knew it was a Pele chant, though hard to hear because the volcano, which was open to the sky, stood close by the Ferris wheel, where girls screamed their screams of terrified glee.

From where she stood Nani could see the great wheel turning. Near it she could see the stretched mouth of the dragon who watched over Dante's Inferno. She trembled with grief. Here at the fair they were all the same, the dragon, the Ferris wheel, the feather cape, the home of Pele. She knew Mrs. Ah Fong was right, the missionary boys would win, and she understood what she'd seen in the exhibit hall. She felt the insult, felt it burning in her eyes, in her hands, in her arms, in her chest.

When the chant subsided, the Hawaiian man ducked through a door. As the fiery bubbles in the lake subsided, other visitors around the crater rim started down the stairs. But Nani lingered. From this vantage point she could also look out upon the Court of Honor, where families strolled in the evening, the fantastical display becoming a nighttime fairyland. In its center stood the electric tower, whose struts and risers were lined with gleaming bulbs and whose high searchlight slowly turned, to illuminate not only the spectacle below but, from time to time, what lay beyond the young groves of pine and cedar and eucalyptus, the miles of dunes and, pointing farther north, the straits, the distant Golden Gate, to shed dim light upon the headlands of Marin. The beam was like a great moon drawn down to earth, with blunt slopes rising ghostly into its lunar glow.

Nani knew then that she would go that way, head north again, to the land between the mountain ranges, answering the oldest calling in the world. It was in the look of the slopes across the water, in the swell of the coastal hills, in the scent of briny air off the bay, which you can sometimes get a whiff of far up the Sacramento River, when tides push through the delta and keep pushing upstream.

As I see her peering through the night sky toward those hills, I think of Hank, the man who raised me, and of Hank's granddad who came west right around the time this fair opened. For all we know he was there on the grounds somewhere that very night, checking out Little Cairo or taking the elevator to the top of the tower, young guy from the

Midwest wandering astonished by all the modern wonders, by this tribute to California, which the program called "Cornucopia to the World,"
the place that had beckoned to him like a woman in a dream. I think of
his sense of destiny, having arrived at last on this farther shore where he
would soon claim some piece of it as his own, that sense of destiny inherited by Hank and by osmosis passed on to me, the idea that ours is a place
of expanding possibility, a land of every promise.

That was something Nani did not possess, a sense of destiny. She
did not see America as a land of promise or California as the world's
cornucopia. Her loyalty to the terrain ran deeper than that, deeper than
ownership, deeper than boosterism or patriotism. At age thirty my great-
grandmother did not know the meaning of patriotism or the power of a
flag to bring tears to your eyes. In the land of her birth she was not yet
considered a citizen. She could not vote. Hers was an ancestral bond
rooted in bedrock not made of documents. Her tears that night were for
her mother and her father, buried in the red dirt of the north country,
whose dancing feet had laid claim to the rocks and dirt of the foothills
and the long valley, as had all the generations of mothers and fathers
before them. That consecrated habitat was calling her back.

Women Walking

Mrs. Ah Fong has a deep laugh. When I hear it I cannot help laughing too. But when she talks about the queen her voice almost goes away as if she does not want to hear the words. She says in Honolulu people still talk about the day she left the palace and what the men did. They made her sign a paper then they told her go. She tried to wrap some old Hawaiian treasures to keep them safe but they said no, there is no time. So she walked out. I can see her walking down the palace steps on the day they took her islands. She walked alone back to her house. It was across the street, away from the palace. I know that house. I passed it many times. It is white with a stone fence and tall hibiscus bushes by the gate. It was her husband's house. Mrs. Ah Fong says he was ill for many months. After she became queen she still cared for him through his final days.

She told her soldiers do not fight. She said they have too many rifles and all the cannons on their ships. She did not want to see her soldiers blood. She did not want to see them die in a battle they could not win. I think she already saw too much death, her husband dead, her sister dead, two brothers dead. She was a woman alone, a small brown woman walking slow in the sun. I see her straight back and her dress with long sleeves and the sun on her skin. She still had the soft skin of a young woman. Then I see mama the way she used to walk by the stream with her burden basket full of acorns. She too was the daughter of a chief, and her body knew that. You could tell by the way she walked. In my dream mama walks toward me. And now I walk toward her.

A Bright Stillness

Nani left San Francisco in the spring of 1894, catching a ferry that took her out across the bay, toward the delta islands once again, toward the broad, ever-flowing Sacramento. She had much more to carry than she'd brought with her when she figured she'd be staying three or four days, a week at most. Makua hired a hackney, helping her to move out and get to the wharf. Just before she boarded he touched her arm. "Nani, please. One more thing . . ." He looked like he was waiting to be shot.

"You should have this," he said, handing her a small package wrapped in plain but expensive paper, tied with red twine. It was about the size of a music box.

She backed away.

"Oh no. I cannot."

"You are the only one I can trust to do what needs to be done."

"And what is that?"

"For you to decide. You knew the king. You knew him well."

"It is not too late for you to deliver this."

"I fear it is much too late. I have waited too long. In Honolulu it is very risky now. The queen has too many enemies. If one got hold of this, it could be used to put a curse on her, a *kapu*."

Nani believed he spoke the truth. In the old days Moana had saved her hair from the comb so no one else could get the strands and use them against her. She knew Kawika's voice should be protected. She looked at Makua and saw a man still ashamed of his own confusion, his eyes begging her to relieve him of a burden he could no longer bear.

He had the eyes of a man asking me to forgive him all his sins. And so I did. I forgave him.

From that point onward I was reading her journal like a mystery novel, looking for the next clue, any kind of detail that might point to the fate of the second cylinder. I was running out of leads. Two trips to the Maritime Library to study the papers of M. Flynn Associates had yielded nothing new, nor had my letter to the Edison Historic Site:

> Dear Mr. Brody,
> In response to your inquiry, I have consulted our curator of sound recordings about the possible location of the cylinder in question. Neither of us has any knowledge. I can assure you, however, that a number of prominent individuals in the late 1880s and early '90s, among them kings and queens, took a keen interest in the phonograph . . .

Nani's diary, from the outset, had been my main source, and so far, just about every name and date and reference had checked out. The West Coast Edison manager really was named Louis Glass. His office really was in the same building as Peabody Trade. Mike "Makua" Flynn, who would one day own several blocks of the downtown district, had in fact opened his own firm in the months after Kalakaua passed away. And yet, as I sped through the pages, as years and years went by, years full of the life she lived—her return to the rancheria, to the women's dance society, her second husband, her children, her long memories, her dreams and tribal stories—there was nothing at all that might offer the shred of a hint, until one of the very last entries, which took me an hour to transcribe, word by word, letter by letter.

In later years Nani's writing grew ever more crabbed and cramped, as arthritis crept into her hands. The last several pages, in pencil, were the hardest to decipher, like breaking a code. Once I had it and could read it, a shiver passed through me, one of those riveting and galvanic moments when the body knows something before the mind fully grasps it:

> *February* 17, 1938
> Sheridan Keala is six today. Each morning I teach him six words, three Indian words and three Hawaiian words. I tell Rosa he is the one who will travel. His mind is so quick. He already has the eyes of an elder. He has such strong arms and strong legs. When Kawika's voice is ready to travel Sheridan will be the one to cross the water.

"When Kawika's voice is ready to travel . . ." What did this mean? A premonition, a prophecy? Would it also have been an instruction, a kind of commission, passed on to her daughter in the months before Nani died? I had to talk to Rosa again, my good pal, my guru.

It was early morning when I called. She tended to pick up on the first ring, unless she was puttering around her tiny yard, or out for a walk. She had a regular route through the trailer court, down the road about a hundred yards and back. This time five rings went by, six, seven. She didn't have an answering machine. "I can't stand it," she told me once, "when I call somebody and this automatic voice comes on. I sure don't want my phone doing that to anybody else."

After the ninth ring her breathless voice whispered, "Sheridan?"

"How do you know it's me?"

"I been expecting you."

"Why? What's up?"

"Give me a minute."

Her phone was on a Formica table right by the easy chair. I could hear her wheezing.

"You all right?"

"One of my dogs ran off. But he didn't go far. I just got back."

As I waited, I realized she was waiting.

"Can I read you something, Rosa?"

"You know I like to hear you read."

"It's one of the last things your mother wrote."

I took my time, so she could absorb each word. In the long ensuing silence I broke my rule and asked her a direct question.

"You want to talk about this? You want to tell me something I need to know?"

Another silence. Then, "We should get together, son."

"Anytime."

"Maybe we should go to Shorty's."

We set it for eleven-thirty the next day. "I'm going to hang up now," she said. "I don't much like talking this way. You can't see anybody. You're never sure the phone is getting it right."

On Interstate 80, as it crossed the great valley, there was no downtime. Heading east toward Reno or west toward the bay, it was three lanes going seventy, morning, noon and night. The big transcontinental semis loomed behind you, grilles taller than your car, demanding right-of-way. Every day it was a hectic, thrumming, rubber-scented speed test and time trial, not for NASCAR drivers but for the common traveler hoping to survive and make it one more time from point A to point B.

With the whir of that manic corridor still humming in my bones, it was all the more remarkable to enter the bright stillness of the Riverside Trailer Court. Driving in I saw no one about. At the Airstream I cut my engine and listened to an uncanny quiet. No radios. No dogs. Usually she was sitting on her patio, dressed up for my visit. I remembered her wheezing and imagined her inside the trailer crumpled on the floor or slumped over in her easy chair. At eighty-six anything can happen.

Outside the door I called her name. I must have stood there for a couple of minutes listening, nose to the screen, squinting into the shadowy interior. I didn't want to go in but felt I had to. Oddly, the door was unlatched. I stepped into a musty, sage-tinted coolness and again said, "Rosa?"

Her chair was empty. So was the kitchen and her cluttered bedroom and tiny bathroom. She wasn't there.

As if searching for some sign of where she'd gone, a note, a scrawled number on her pad, I began to prowl like an interloper, felt the illicit thrill of being alone with someone else's stuff, her unmade bed, her beads and bracelets, her medicine bottles, her dresses in the narrow closet, her shoes and slippers and sandals scattered below, her toaster oven, her mini-fridge with its hodgepodge of eggs and juices, the pitcher of iced tea, the open bottle of low-budget Chardonnay.

I sat down in her padded chair, which usually faced the TV set but now happened to face her family shrine, and found myself looking again at the poster-board mandala of souvenirs, her lifetime of snapshots and clippings and keepsakes, the part-time sleuth I'd become looking for anything I might have missed on previous visits, but also seeing it anew.

Here was the shelf of votive candles and clumps of sage and savory herbs whose heady aroma, at close range, was intoxicating. Here was Nani at a luau in Honolulu with the king and his room full of bright-eyed guests on mats, the food and drink abundant. She did not sit next to him but between two other men, at twenty or twenty-one, secret consort to His Majesty. And here she was in traveling coat soon after she returned from the islands, her look almost imperious, the seasoned voyager.

And here was daughter Rosa, her face hopeful, her smile already wise, after she married Tom Wadell, who looked a bit like a young Jim Thorpe, the great Cherokee athlete, Olympic decathlon medalist and early pro football star. Like Rosa, this long-gone granddad was part Indian, part Hawaiian, part white. In his early twenties he already had wind in his face, already a ranch hand for half his life, bucking hay, mending fence, driving truck, his eyes lined with constant squeezing against the wind that had ruffled the wide valley's yellowing fields for countless thousands of years. And here was Sheridan, my blood father, yet ever the son, his image fixed in the early 1950s, the lean and focused pass receiver made more muscular, more heroic, by the swell of shoulder pads beneath the jersey as he leaped and reached high for the midair catch. And tacked to that old yearbook page, the black-and-white snapshot of Sheridan with Verlene. I yearned to stand beside them, to be the age I was as I sat in the trailer and also be with them then, to hang out with my namesake, talk about his boyhood, his dreams, his games, the music he loved. It was their only surviving photo, and I saw that I would have to make two copies, one for me and one for her, to give back at least a piece of all she had to throw away—sleek-haired Sheridan in his white T-shirt with one sleeve folded to hold a pack of cigarettes, and next to him Verlene in coed sweater, her burnished hair. She was the renegade back then and he was danger, arm in arm in those innocent days before he joined the marines and left for Korea, to be survived by a Purple Heart and a senator's condolences.

"He is the one who will travel," Nani wrote, "Sheridan will be the one to cross the water. . . ." And yes, her prediction had come true, in the fall of 1951, on the troopship from San Diego to Pearl Harbor to Japan. Did this also mean he could have been Nani's messenger? After all those years, had Kawika's voice somehow been passed on to him? No. That part just didn't add up. Even had she managed to keep it in the family, where would young Sheridan have taken it? And who would have believed him, an eighteen-year-old recruit with a three-day pass, bearing Kalakaua's last words on a brown wax cylinder no one knew existed? It was too far-fetched. . . .

A smell broke my reverie, Rosa's smell, soap and lavender and an elder's musty breath. I turned and saw her standing close behind me, looking over my shoulder at her shrine. How long had she been there? I didn't hear her screen door creak. Like a guy in the wrong seat at the theatre, I moved to relinquish her chair.

"Forgive me, Rosa. I couldn't find you. . . ."

With a hand on my shoulder she held me there. "This fellow down the way lost all his energy. . . ."

"I guess I came in to see if you were okay."

"Who knows what it is. I have days like that. You just can't budge. I took him some broth. I thought I'd hear your car."

Her voice was chatty, but her eyes were fixed on mine, lit by the votive candles, her irises rings of obsidian gauging me, as if measuring my readiness for an unannounced task.

"This is a good chair," she said. "Things come to me here. Things I forgot a long time ago come back to me when I'm in this chair."

Her gaze seemed to require something. Lamely I said, "You probably want to sit down for a while."

"Did I ever tell you how your voice is like Sheridan's voice? Talking to you, sometimes I think I'm talking to him."

"I was just looking again at these pictures."

"Isn't it funny? The years go by, your whole life goes by, and after a while all you have are pictures. Later on I'll give these to you, son. But not now. Not today. I want you to help me find something before I forget where I think it is. When you were reading over the phone, it came to me. It was almost like a movie on TV."

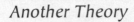

Another Theory

Though it was high noon and sunny outside, she grabbed a flashlight. She told her dogs they could come along too, and we followed her down a short alley lined with half a dozen trailers and mobile homes on blocks, out to the back of the property, through a weedy thicket scattered with rusting car parts and fifty-gallon drums and bales of rolled fencing.

"I don't know why I didn't think of this before," she said, as we stood in front of a tilting metal door, missing a hinge, held to the frame by a loop of chain and padlock. A portable unit set down by a forklift in decades past, the storage shed was surrounded by tall cottonwoods that shaded the roof and welded siding, so it was cool inside, like stepping into a wine cellar.

"After Tom passed away I had a whole house full of this that and the other. I don't know what all I put out here. I haven't even been down this little alley in years. When I take my walk, seems like I always go the other way."

A low-watt bulb hung from a cord, casting thin light across a disheveled sprawl of overflow belongings from generations of tenants, kitchen radios and TV monitors, lampshades and end tables, duffel bags, flowerpots, a refrigerator, a birdcage, balding truck tires, cardboard filing drawers, square black batteries frosted with acid foam, a steamer trunk, a Pontiac hood propped against one wall, next to a set of oars and a fading life preserver hung from a nail.

"My stuff is back behind that washing machine." She waved her flashlight beam toward some stacks of cardboard boxes. "At least it was. Ought to be a suitcase down under there, if you can get at it. I never seen so much clutter."

I pushed my way past a baby's high chair, a roll of wrinkled tar paper, toward a cobwebbed corner of the shed. I dug down through boxes labeled "Christmas Ornaments," "Bible Class," "Dad's Fishing Gear," shoved aside a mound of cartons and finally drew forth a scuffed and scratched leather suitcase held shut with a rusted buckle and one of three ragged leather straps.

"That's it!" she exclaimed. "Mama used to take that on trips, till the straps wore out."

I grabbed a torn T-shirt from an open box, dusted off the leather and set it on top of the washing machine, feeling a bit like the bagman in a Mafia movie who has the suitcase full of wrapped packets of unmarked hundred-dollar bills. I had to break the buckle with a claw hammer.

Inside we found a pair of heavy denim trousers folded to cover two cookbooks, some early issues of *Life* magazine, an empty photo album, half a dozen pulp cowboy novels from the 1930s. Under these, two layers of deerskin were wrapped to make a package as wide as the suitcase. Unwrapping the skins we found first a small woven bag and inside the bag the long necklace, the strands of purple shells from Ni'ihau that she'd worn the night she danced for him—as Nani wrote, "each shell like a tiny ear." Each shell had the soft patina of a dainty sea creature still alive. In a separate deerskin wrapping was the heavy volume called *Legends and Myths of Hawai'i,* a first edition, published in New York in 1888. Under Rosa's beam the cover's gilt lettering sent up a muted glow like the illuminated letters of a medieval manuscript. It was a well-made book, the binding intact, the pages still sturdy, easy to turn, and there on the title page, in Kalakaua's flourishing hand, was the inscription to his rare and singular bird, to Nani. Near it, like a pressed flower, lay the round-trip ticket he'd given her when she left Honolulu.

I glanced at Rosa, whose brown face in this weird half-light almost looked painted, velvet smooth on the dark side, on the lit side webbed and creased with age, and in her eyes something far removed from the freeway-severed realm you passed through to reach her trailer, an ancient blackness tunneling back in time. These eyes were watching me, as if testing me.

I said, "This is better than buried treasure."

"I wonder if I ever told you about my father. He could be a very jealous man. I guess Mama didn't want to have to explain all these things. I guess she made it look like another old suitcase full of magazines and clothes."

"How do you know that?"

"Just from the look, from the way she packed it. You can pretty much tell. He was an honest man and good to Mama most of the time but suspicious too. He knew she married once before and was always afraid Edward would come back."

There was one more package—inside the deerskin wrapping, a rectangular metal box, its lid held tight by a thin latch. Inside this was a stubby cream-colored cardboard tube with black-edged silver letters saying EDISON BLANK. On the back, three words had been scrawled: "Voice of Kalakaua." In the milky beam from Rosa's flashlight these words, the boldly printed silver words, the fading scrawl, had the aura of scripture. As we stood side by side in the dusty reek of the storage shed, I gingerly unscrewed the cardboard lid and withdrew from its protective tube a hollow cylinder of brown wax spotted here and there with little blemishes of grayish mold.

Again I looked at Rosa, as her hand reached out, its skin also mottled with the blemishes of age. Her fingertips grazed the wax, tentative and reverent, as if reading something there by touch.

"It's the king's recording," I said.

"She never told Papa anything about the king. She never told much to me. But I guess she always held him in her heart."

Her eyes were fixed on the cylinder, and I studied her face, the pursing and twitching lips, hoping she'd continue. With Rosa my rule had been to listen, to be guided by whatever she chose to say or not say. But now she fell silent and I couldn't hold my tongue. Once again I broke my rule.

"How long has this been out here?"

"This old suitcase? Seems like forever."

In her eyes I thought I saw a crafty glint. Was she teasing me? I was almost angry with her then, almost ready to shout, "Why in hell did you wait so long?"

As it was, my words were harsher than I meant. "My God, Rosa! You could have told me about this months ago!"

I must have sounded like an interrogator. She looked up at me with a sweet, pensive sage's smile. "You know how it is, son. Sometimes your mind is filled up like a river in wintertime. Sometimes it all goes blank and you sit there wondering where the day went and where the years went."

My phone call, she'd said, had caused this tattered suitcase to pop into her mind, as vivid as a picture on the screen. Was it one more instance of an old woman's fragile memory? Or had she been biding her time, waiting for the moment to spring this on me? I wasn't sure. I'm still not sure. But this much is clear. If she'd taken me out to that storage shed on the day we met, I couldn't have known what I was looking at. First I had to see her altar, the lives and faces pictured there, I had to hear the bits and pieces of Rosa's recollections, read Nani's diary from start to finish and let it lead me—a sequence too well orchestrated to be coincidence. Yet Rosa wanted it to seem that way.

So there it was, fifty yards from the patio where our conversations began, a recording of Kalakaua's voice that Nani had held on to for the rest of her life. It was more than a lover's keepsake. This is my theory, at any rate. She'd watched over it like a self-appointed guardian. The Hawaiian word is *kahu,* the keeper, the caretaker. The way another *kahu* might watch over a hallowed site or a cache of family treasures, Nani watched over the chanted record of his final words. It was akin to receiving her father's "ha," the deathbed transmission of sound and breath from his mouth to hers. It was akin to the reeds and grasses woven into the basket she would later pass on to Rosa, the spirit of those reeds and grasses alive in the basket, where the spirit of Nani the weaver would live on too.

The wax held Kawika's "ha." It held his mana. She'd heard it and felt it. She was lying right next to him with her hands on his rib cage as the vibrant words rolled forth. Something of her father was also lodged inside the chant "The California Sailor" and the journey to Kaleponi that had become a famous legend. Here was a kind of magic she would honor and guard for over forty years, since there was no longer anywhere to send it, no one to send Kawika's voice to, for fear Giles Peabody would get his hands on it and destroy it, or worse, add it to his sideshow. In San Francisco she'd seen what the missionary boys could do. She'd seen their low regard for anything belonging to Kawika and his sister.

As a self-appointed caretaker she kept the cylinder, waiting until the time was right . . . but right to do what? So much had changed. A few years after she returned to the rancheria, word reached her that the use of Hawaiian had been banned in public offices and in all the schools. Just like in the Indian schools, English was the new official language. Did that mean chanting too was banned? Better to wait a while longer, better to lie low.

Until her death Nani held his chanting voice where it would not be disturbed, where her husband would not notice. She kept it first in the cool dryness of the General's cellar, built for storing wine and lined with stone, though never again used for wine after his wife (a lifetime member of the Temperance Society) arrived, used instead for apples and potatoes and canned preserves. Later she hid it in the leather suitcase Rosa would inherit with the hodgepodge of bags and boxes Nani left behind, some marked, some unmarked, to be hauled by Rosa and husband Tom from house to house as their kids grew up, their belongings and Nani's merging into one unwieldy family jumble. That might explain why Rosa never found the time (or so she claimed) to open up the suitcase, just as she'd never found the time (or so she claimed) to read her mother's diaries. But I still have to wonder how she could store it for half a lifetime and not once look inside. Maybe she didn't have to look. Maybe she remembered something her mother told her when they all lived together, when Rosa was nursing, and Nani, a widow near seventy, had held my infant father in her arms.

Rosa knew nothing of the first cylinder, the one with a brief greeting by Kalakaua that ended up in the Bishop Museum, the one that had passed, like a racer's baton, from the emissary of Louis Glass to the queen's chamberlain to the man who possessed the only talking machine in Honolulu and who then kept the roll on a shelf somewhere in his library for almost thirty years. She knew nothing about the early days of the phonograph and how a human voice could find itself contained inside a roll of wax. But she knew what her mother felt for the king. She had to know that this second roll existed and that it held some kind of power. Whatever commission Nani had passed on to her would be honored. And maybe, from that time forward, Rosa knew her task would be to wait. When her boy came of age and set out across the water and then did not return, she knew she'd have to wait some more. As I think back, I realize she said to me three times at least—and these were not the moments of arrival at her trailer door, but hours later, as I prepared to leave—"I have been waiting for you, son."

On the night she first called my show, wary and ready to hang up if things went wrong, was it mere curiosity about my name? Or was she already testing my suitability as the one who would carry out this family duty and along the way somehow decipher her mother's life?

Or am I overreaching here, giving Rosa credit for more than she could possibly have intended? It may well be that I am the one who did the choosing, created for myself a trickster grandma to serve the need for a fated family calling, a way to elevate my own persistent quest.

Read it as you will. By chance or by design, I had in my hands at last what appeared to be the wax roll missing since 1891. But now what? In that tumbledown storage shed, lit by a fading flashlight beam, I almost said, "Don't do this to me, Rosa." I wanted to slide it into its cardboard tube, put it back into the metal box, wrap it again in the layers of deer-skin, close the lid on the ancient suitcase and rebury it under the tilting pyramid of boxes. But of course it was now too late for that.

A Kind of Prophecy

Back in the Airstream I sat again in Rosa's chair and let my eyes roam her poster-board mandala, seeking guidance. On the other side of her kitchenette Formica table Rosa sat looking at the wax roll, which seemed to have a life of its own, like an electric eel lying dormant and untouchable on an underwater ledge. Whose was it now? Who had the rightful claim? Not Rosa. She didn't want it. Her days of stewardship were over. Wherever it went next was up to me.

I reached for the phone and dialed. It was 10 a.m. in Honolulu. At the Bishop Museum Frank the Specialist was into his second cup of coffee, probably hunched over a light table labeling slides, priceless engravings from some nineteenth-century treatise on the fauna and flora of the Big Island. Since my last call a couple of weeks had passed. "Keep me posted," Frank had said. "That would be a bombshell over here, that would be like finding the bones of Captain Cook."

I knew he wanted to believe me. But he wouldn't let himself. Not at first. When I told him what I had he laughed a low and brutal kind of laugh, as if I'd insulted his professional integrity.

"Your great-grandmother knew Kalakaua."

"That's right."

"And her suitcase is just parked somewhere in California for forty or fifty years."

"Probably longer."

"I hope this isn't some kind of gag. It's too early . . ."

"You think I'm making this up, Frank? Why in hell would I call you long distance . . . ?"

"There is just no way."

"What if I tell you his name is on the box?"

"Whose name?"

"Kalakaua's."

That slowed him down.

"Written by hand," I said.

"You sure?"

"In black ink. Like a note."

"What else is on the box?"

"The label says, 'Edison Blank.' Large silver letters."

Now he started asking questions few people in the world would know to ask. What's inside the cylinder core? How thick is the outer coating of wax? And what color is it? Which specific shade of brown? Such details, from the pioneering days when trial and error changed materials from year to year, sometimes month to month, told Frank whether I had a product from 1891 or 1895 or 1899. An "Edison Blank," he later explained, would come from the very early period and would also be the type of carton an employee might have pulled off the shelf for a private session. Cartons done up for sale to the public had fancier labeling.

I could hear him shove his chair back, rearrange his desk. I could see him straighten his double-wide aloha shirt, as he muttered, "I'll be a sonofabitch."

"Help me think about this, Frank. What should I do?"

"I need to see it."

"I want you to see it. I want you to compare it with the one you have in storage."

"My guess is they'll make a pretty close match."

"What if I fly over there?"

"Can you get away?"

"I'd like to, I really would. But I'm not sure. I mean, I have this show."

"Show?"

"Give me a day or two to figure it out."

"Who else have you talked to?"

"Just my grandmother."

"Nobody here in the islands?"

"Not yet."

"Do me a favor, Dan. Don't call anyone else until we get the sound checked out. That has to be the first step. From what you're saying, there probably isn't much to retrieve. But every cylinder is different, and the best people are over on your side of the water. An outfit down in Santa

Clara does first-rate work. They know me there. Why don't I give them a call? I won't tell them what we have. I'll just say it looks like a very rare item that showed up in somebody's attic—which of course will happen from time to time. . . ."

His clipped and efficient tone now turned intimate, almost eager.

"I was thinking about this the other day, how there must be thousands of old wax rolls moldering away in basements and attics all across the land. On every roll there's a voice or a song waiting to be heard again."

I knew then that when he'd laughed at me he was trying to laugh down his own susceptibility to stories like mine. I said, "Frank, do you have a minute, a bit of time to talk?"

I felt compelled to fill him in on the family ties, on Nani's recollections from the Palace Hotel, and my own theory for why she'd kept the cylinder concealed (though not my theory for how the king died. Not yet. That was still between me and Nani). I was glad for the chance to talk it through, and Frank was listening to every word. The more he heard, the more he liked. There were still holes showing, or rather, questions still needing final answers—"Are you sure this guy Makua actually gave your great-grandmother the same cylinder he stole? Could the real one still be lurking in a safe-deposit box in a San Francisco bank?"—but Frank didn't mind. He was like me. He wanted these things to be true. He was part Hawaiian, with degrees in history and anthropology from Michigan and UCLA. He once described himself as a scientist, a man guided by empirical evidence. But his systematic mind was leavened by a lifetime spent in the islands, where the dead often speak to the living, where it is widely agreed upon that rocks and bones have lives that must be honored and attended to. He liked the idea that Kalakaua's last message could have come in the form of a coded and inspiring poem at a time when his beleaguered kingdom hungered for renewal.

At this late date, he said again, there might be nothing left to retrieve. But if a chant *were* still audible, a good technician could transfer it onto high-sensitivity tape and from that, we might get lucky. With patience we might be able to extract a word-for-word transcription. "Translate that into English, and we could end up with something readable in both languages."

High animation had replaced his managerial cool. His voice sped up. I could see the rapid-fire blinking behind his rimless specs. "Think of it, Dan! Something like this, it could still light a fire. I know people over here who would read it as a kind of prophecy!"

The king had made a comeback, Frank said. In recent years, his palace had been restored, as a show of pride in the time when Hawai'i was still run by Hawaiians. His writings were being reissued, his songs recorded and sung. Every spring a big festival in Hilo honored his faith in the power of chant and dance. Hula itself was alive and well again, the old-style hula, the kind preachers once condemned. Double-hulled canoes with Polynesian crews were once again sailing the Pacific. Documents were rising to the surface, letters, speeches, newspaper editorials from the 1880s and 1890s, written in Hawaiian, shedding fresh light on certain writers of the past who'd defended the missionary boys and what they'd wrought. "Here in the islands," Frank said, "it's like everywhere else. It takes a hundred years to find out what really happened. Who killed JFK? We're still not sure."

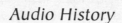

Audio History

An hour's drive down the Peninsula brought me to the Lee De Forest Audio History Center. Endowed by a couple of high-tech entrepreneurs, it was named for "the Father of Radio," sometimes called the godfather of Silicon Valley. Back in 1912, while he was living in Palo Alto, De Forest had figured out how to use a vacuum tube to amplify sound and opened the way to public broadcasting. From the front steps you could see a low-rise industrial park with broad lawns and freshly planted trees well spaced and manicured. The building that housed the center had survived from an older time, an elegantly restored Victorian with stained glass and a wraparound verandah.

You walked into a foyer and a high-ceiling front room that had the look of a small museum, where glass cases displayed tinfoil cylinders and piano rolls and rare shellac discs twenty inches wide and bulbous ancestors of the vacuum tube. There was a mounted sepia-tone photo of some turn-of-the-century orchestra crowded around a primitive studio microphone, and a row of morning-glory sound horns sprouting from polished gramophones, all bathed in light strangely filtered by the leaded panes to feel well aged, like vintage wine. The place called for an Edison-like fellow in rumpled jacket with distracted gaze. But he wasn't there. Frank's friend Louise awaited me at a receiving counter in a stylish lab coat. She looked to be in her mid-thirties, attractive in a wholesome, undecorated way, no makeup, her blond hair drawn back in a ponytail, with a smile both welcoming and strained, doing a favor for Frank though she wasn't sure quite why, until she heard my name or perhaps paid attention to it for the first time. Then her neutral eyes were bright, sparkling like a fan's in the presence of a celebrity.

She knew the show, listened all the time, had seen the rally coverage and in the week since then, whenever they updated the story, she'd seen me on the nightly news doing my tumble from the flatbed. In her view it was both an acrobatic feat and a sign of admirable commitment. And she still recalled the night, some ten shows back, when I'd asked my listeners for help, summed up what I'd learned about the king's final days, sent out my pleas for leads large and small, wise or foolish. She'd almost called in then, out of curiosity, she said, an audio buff intrigued by the thought of a mystery cylinder from the previous century. When I showed her the carton with Kalakaua's name inscribed, color rose into her pale cheeks, as if she were flattered to be chosen for this task by a fellow who'd vaulted from a Berkeley parking lot directly into the Lee De Forest Center. After that, she couldn't do enough.

In a smaller room, at one time perhaps the library or den, she got right down to business. Their inner sanctum, this could have been the set for an underground nerve center in a Pentagon movie, banked with consoles, tape decks, speakers square and circular, gleaming amplifiers with monitor lights blinking, everything up to the minute, climate controlled, pollutant controlled, moisture controlled, a room with no echo, where each syllable hung alone in the sanitized air.

She wouldn't let me touch anything. At a wide worktable of stainless steel I sat on a stool while she assessed the carton with a practiced eye, the cardboard lid, the label, murmuring, "You don't see many of these." She unscrewed the lid and lifted out the wax roll, holding it in both hands like a fragile scroll that might crumble if disturbed, turning it under the light, examining each spot of mold. She couldn't promise much, she said, given the wear and the exposure. But she'd do what she could. After wiping it lightly with a soft dry cloth, she slid it onto a restored Edison machine with an electric pickup and transferred the sound to a high-fidelity tape reel.

I'm not going to dwell on all the tests she ran that day, since I still don't quite understand how they worked. Suffice it to say, Louise was thorough, a real pro. Though I was much immersed in the realm of sound, equipment had never been my strong suit, the electronics and acoustics and so forth. I pretty much left all that to Julie, and as I watched and listened I was wishing she could have come along to be there and talk shop with Louise. They would have hit it off. Too bad she had a class to teach that afternoon. I confess it had been hard to leave her behind on this little expedition, much harder than it would have been a week earlier, before that long, late-night phone call. We were spending all of our free moments together now, eating, drinking, a lot of talking, making love again. Whenever I could, I was helping out with Toby. I think we both realized how close we'd come to losing something neither of us wanted to lose. One night during the show the pane of soundproof glass was like a living-room window, and I was watching like a greedy voyeur standing outside in the yard as she worked her dials and switches, screening calls, totally in her element. I was talking with a caller from Redwood City when our eyes met, a flash of recognition and awareness of those moment-to-moment rituals that had bound and bonded us, all the studio details that kept our show in motion. It was a delicious glance, followed by the fleeting afterthought, the question I didn't want to ask because I had no answer yet. If we ever lost the show, what would replace this dance and dialogue we did five nights a week? All the more reason to stand by Sandy, to keep Argonaut at bay, now that we knew things would get worse before they got better, now that we were lodged between Roy's ambition and protest-for-its-own-sake, now that we knew who'd hired a guy to upend the flatbed and sabotage the rally— not the quirky CEO but Larry the Organizer, setting up his own escalation factor, Larry in search of another martyr or two. Yes, stand with Sandy, I told myself, though I couldn't have said what mattered more, keeping the station intact or keeping Julie in my life. After the show, out in the corridor, I asked her to marry me and watched her eyes go wide with alarm.

"Whoa," she said, stepping back, looking me up and down like a chiropractor checking my alignment. "Where is *this* coming from?" Which I took to mean yes.

We went out for margaritas and finally I told her what had come to me, what I remembered hearing in my mother's voice, seeing in my mother's face, my old boyhood fear of seeing that same look again.

Julie sipped, holding me with her tender, wistful smile. "It's not out of the question, you know."

"What isn't?"

"Toby's father will show up again one of these days. He has to. But he has no claim on me, Danny, not at all. He never will."

"But Toby will want to know him."

"Yes."

"Sooner or later he will need to know him."

"Yes."

"So we'll have to figure out a way to handle that."

"Yes, we will. When the time comes."

. . .

In the Lee De Forest Audio History Center, with its banks of dials and winking red and orange spots, I tried to appear at ease and patient, but my anticipation was extreme. I'd heard old Folkways 78s, unfiltered voices from Louisiana when Alan Lomax was down there gathering field hollers and blues guitars. I'd heard Verlene at age seven, home-recorded on someone's front-room Webcor just before World War II, singing "You Are My Sunshine." I guess that's what I expected. Out from under the hisses and crackles and scratchy hums where mold had eaten into the grooves, a tinny version would be preserved, squeezing through the tunnel of years between then and now.

Yet all we heard during an hour and a half were two possible words, coming to us as if bouncing off a distant canyon wall. One sounded like *ana* or *ama* or *ala* or *eye-nah* (*aina?* land?). One sounded like *poppy* or *copy* or *collie* (*Kale-* as in *Kaleponi?*).

When Louise removed her headphones and placed them on the table, I saw finality there. I heard it in the way she told me that for now those two words were all we'd get. I tried to hear "for now" as "for today," "for the time being," as a way of saying she was merely out of time but had another test or two to run. But she wasn't talking days. Louise had done all she could. "For now" meant years.

"How many years?" I asked.

She shrugged. "Five."

Or maybe ten, she said, before they'd have the tools, before the computer and laser engineers she talked to—she called them "sonic archaeologists"—would learn how to locate and release all the words and notes still lingering in these earliest rolls of wax.

"But that day is coming," she said with another shrug of willing surrender, buoyed up by the promise of techniques that did not yet exist. Her smile was generous, almost complicit, as if we shared a secret kind of hope, like evangelicals who'd been promised a larger reward in the next life.

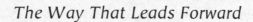

The Way That Leads Forward

Some mornings I wake to a fog so thick the bay below me is invisible and I sit here gazing into a misty swirl the way you gaze at fire or the repetitive roll of breaking surf, as if it holds a key to the riddle of creation. Before dawn the fog will come spilling past the Golden Gate to surround the islands and cover the water. Sometimes it will wander all the way north to the upper bay and through the Straits of Carquinez, spreading inward across the delta to befuddle and stall the pleasure boats just as it befuddled and stalled Captain Crazy Eyes a hundred and fifty years ago when he led his sailors on that foray into Indian country, into the maze of featureless sloughs and channels from which there seemed no exit. But with the rising of the August sun the fog receded, the route revealed itself, and Sutter pushed upriver toward the site he'd imagined months and years before he saw it, where my great-great-grandfather and his mates built two grass houses in the Hawaiian style.

And so it was as I set out for Honolulu on the Hawaiian Air flight from San Francisco International. The very lift of the plane as we cleared the runway seemed to clear the air and clear my head. It was like the morning on Bali when all my scattered graduate school researches came together in a crystallizing click and I embarked upon the hopscotch journey that would eventually become my first book, which led me to Julie and the radio show, which in turn would move Rosa to give a call one night, opening the way to all that followed, to Nani's twelve volumes and the roll of wax I carried with me in a leather bag like a courier for the State Department with classified secrets chained to his wrist.

On the plane, as the glittering and ever seductive Pacific opened out below us, I saw that carrying Kalakaua's voice back to the islands where it belonged would be the final leg. I now knew I would deliver it to Frank at the Bishop, to be housed beside the first recording. They were twins, a pair of relics, those two cylinders that had turned under the same stylus on the same machine in the same hotel room so many years ago.

"I have to be honest with you," Frank said by phone a couple of days before I left. "What you're holding there could be worth something. Maybe a lot. We have a small acquisitions budget, nothing like what we ought to have, of course. . . ." His voice was both apologetic and cagey, feeling me out, ready to bargain.

I told him to relax. Nobody owned this cylinder. It wasn't ours to sell. At Frank's request (his librarian mind insisting on a paper trail), I'd drawn up a document, which Rosa signed, describing a family donation, entrusting it to the museum "until such time as the sound, if any, can be retrieved, a decision then to be made as to a permanent location that will be in the best interests of the Hawaiian people. . . ."

Sometime soon he would do up a press release, though not right away. "Something like this," he said, "the very *possibility* that the king had more to say . . . the interest will be huge. We have to proceed with caution. People are bound to ask what I asked. 'How could it be that *your* great-grandmother knew him?' Somehow her story needs to be heard, or shared, her diaries too, or parts of them. And the inscribed copy of *Legends and Myths,* if his handwriting is on the title page, that's very persuasive, in a way undeniable. . . ."

I began to imagine it then, a volume devoted to Nani's writing, with commentary by me and maybe an afterword by someone like Frank, a sympathetic expert. This was what came to me on the plane. I don't know why I hadn't thought of it before. In my head I was already drafting the proposal to my editor, billing it as a natural follow-up to *Sit Still and Listen,* still in print and doing fairly well in trade paperback, with some course adoptions here and there. "A remarkable woman for her day and age," I would write. "Speaking three languages, she passed back and forth across the borders of culture with a rare mobility."

I unzipped my bag and withdrew Volume One, opened its worn cardboard cover, looking again at the first page, at the carefully printed blue letters spelling out "My Book of Days." I read her opening lines:

March 2, 1881

She says my writing is getting good now. She wants me to keep a diary. I can write anything. She says it is not for school. Nobody can look at it unless I want them to.

The title struck me then as a kind of unwitting prediction for what her entries would become, as the secret gathering of a schoolgirl's thoughts gradually blossomed through the years, as Nani herself began to see it as more than a private record, though the idea of a published book was as remote for her as the farther shore of North America.

As I read again her earliest entries I heard them as they might sound over the radio, and in that same moment, while imagining a book and a proposal, I heard the theme for my next show, the one to start with as soon as I got back to Berkeley. We did not have Kalakaua's voice. Not yet. But we had Nani's, and why couldn't I test it on my ever-willing listeners? They were still writing in about Grandma Rosa. ("I hope it was okay to tape that whole show, Sheridan, she was just such a breath of fresh air!") Why not bring in Great-Grandma too? Call it "Another Adventure in Ancestral Radio." That would startle the programming wizards. No slot for great-grandmas in the marketing survey.

I was still thinking about the Audio History Center, where frontline acoustics met a passion for things antique, where the Edison gramophone stood side by side with the laser beam. I was thinking how lucky for Nani to be a young woman when recorded sound was so new that the reproduction of a voice could still amaze you. These days we're spoiled. With songs and voices coming at us from all directions, from AM and FM and TV, in malls and markets and clubs and elevators, from the amped-up speakers of passing cars, you can easily forget what a miracle it is to hold in one small pocket-size cassette an hour of Vivaldi or *Ray Charles's Greatest Hits* or the breath of Ben Webster, the great tenor man whose breathy endnote was his musical signature. When they come whispering from the bell of his saxophone in a ballad like "Summertime," those exhaling brushstrokes tell us his interior is right there, his lungs, his life, inside each non-noted note. Call it the "ha" of jazz. Yes. That would be Julie's bridging tune for the night, some breath-filled solo from Ben Webster's soulful tenor. I could see her high sign as she dialed it down, and then I would be up close to the mike, the host who never knows who is listening, or how many, or for how long, yet each night prays that they are out there, each show its own act of faith.

"Good evening, folks. Sheridan Brody here, and this is *Sit Still and Listen,* where nothing changes and nothing stays the same. Tonight and every night we ask you to pay especially close attention because who knows which show will be our last. You find us here at the barricades, and what the future holds is anybody's guess. Yet we are not subdued by the spectre of a buyout, whether hostile or benign. Once again we bring you the kind of radio you can only find here, at KRUX, taking our theme from the Chinese sage Lao Tzu, who said, 'The way that leads forward seems to lead backward.' Once again we're going to let the past speak to the present. So sit still for a while and listen to Nani Keala, a.k.a. Nancy Callahan, a mixed-blood woman of the nineteenth century who found her voice right here by the shores of San Francisco Bay. As usual, folks, I have no secrets, nothing to hide. This is my own great-grandmother, living in the upper Sacramento Valley when she began to keep a journal at the age of seventeen. And you are the first to hear this, by the way, the first listeners anywhere. So think of it as a world premiere."

I would read some of her opening entry, and from there jump ahead to give them an idea of what was on her mind thirteen years later, just before she left the city behind. It would be a long reading, but I had plenty of time. "Stay with me on this one," I would tell them, "and then I'll take your calls."

San Francisco, February 15, 1894

Once again mama came to me, walking from where she lived to the place they said she had to go. It is always the same dream.

From faraway I see her walking in the hot sun and her dress is shining. I am there but I am not born yet and I see her raise her hand high. It does not mean farewell. It means begin.

Begin.

When I woke up I was hearing all the stories of my people as if for the first time. They are all made of words but not in writing. When old folks die the stories die with them. I thank the general's wife who taught me how to make things with words.

February 16

I will start with the story of the walk. Growing up I heard it a hundred times. Mama, auntie, all the people told it. Now I know she wants me to tell it too, how white soldiers came and they had to leave the villages.

In Honolulu the missionary boys want her kingdom. They want to rule it and own it. They bring in the American marines with their rifles. I think mama and Liliuokalani are the same woman walking the same path. The marines say to Hawaiians we are here to protect the rights of the people. The soldiers say to indians we are here to protect you from the white settlers who want to kill you. We want to save you from their anger so we are going to take you over the mountain to the reservation where you will be safe.

They were living in the village when a warning came. All the indians had to gather down by the general's ranch. Two white children were kidnapped and killed and the white settlers said they had enough, it was time to get rid of the indians, either kill them all or move them a hundred miles over the mountain. White people tell it one way. The army tells it one way. Indians tell it the indian way. What I know is how I heard it from mama, who made the trip.

What whites forget is that the indians who killed the children were angry because some whites killed four indians. They blamed the indians for stealing horses, so they shot them. But those four indians didn't steal the horses. Some other white men stole the horses. Nobody ever said to the white men who stole the horses you are too dangerous to live here anymore, you are going to have to leave this place and move a hundred miles away or we will kill you.

February 17

Papa was still a citizen of Hawaii, even after he married mama. So he did not have to go anywhere. One of the ranchers told him he could stay and work. They all knew him as Kanaka John. But he would not leave mama and her mother and father, who were old by then. He said he would go with the tribe. They set fire to their huts and the roundhouse where food was stored. Mama said they filled their baskets with as much as they could carry, dried fish and pine nuts and dried grasshoppers and acorn meal. It lasted until they reached the general's ranch and one day more.

Old people and children rode in wagons the soldiers borrowed from white ranchers or on horses the soldiers brought, but not enough for all who needed them. So most of the people walked, almost five hundred indians, mama said, while the soldiers rode along beside the wagons with rifles to protect them, they said, from hostile whites who might try to shoot at them. They walked down Shasta Road to the Sacramento River where they all crossed on ferries. Then they started across the great valley in the hottest part of summer. When the indian food ran out they had to eat white food from the army wagon and it made some people sick. By the third day a dozen of our elders died from foreign food and from bad water from streams that were drying up. There was no time to bury them in the proper way wrapped in skins and with the feather belts and beads to carry them to the next life. The soldiers buried them by the trail and the caravan kept moving.

At the western mountains the wagons went back. So from there they all had to climb the trail on foot. The sickest ones were strapped to mules. Twenty more died and were buried by the trail. At the top of the crossing a hundred and fifty were so sick they fell down by the trail and camped for days. It was two weeks later when half the people who started out made it down to the Round Valley reservation. By that time some young men had run away under cover of night. In the mountains more people died. A hundred of the sickest were carried out on mules. A woman my mother knew died while she was strapped over the back of an army mule.

This is the story mama told about the march to Round Valley. To this day I have relatives there descended from those who survived the march. Maybe I would be living there myself but when papa saw how things were he said we will not stay. As a Hawaiian man he did not have to stay if he did not want to. The men who ran the reservation were not ready for so many newcomers all at once and so many of them sick. The log cabins were falling down. Three thousand bushels of grain stored for the winter were set on fire and burned. Everyone said men from Alabama did it because they did not like anything the government did and did not like indians. All this happened at the time of the Civil War.

February 23

It was a dangerous time to travel. Papa waited a whole year. By then he had a mule. One night he put grandma and grandpa on top of the mule and started back through the mountains. Pretty soon others heard he was leaving and snuck away and joined him, maybe twenty in all. They traveled by night, sleeping in the day, taking game for food. When they got down the other side and into the great valley again they split up and said to meet in the sierras.

It was a low time for the Sacramento. Papa found a place where he could swim it. He swam all of them across, one by one, mama, grandpa, grandma. When they got to where their village used to be, everything was empty and quiet. No one had been there since they left. Charred logs from their huts were on the ground. The roundhouse only burned half way. The roof fell down and buried everything and some of their stored food was still under there, pine nuts and acorn meal, a lot of it, wrapped inside baskets and covered with dirt.

When the others came who started out from the reservation they had a spirit feast to give thanks and bless the place where they would start their life again. Today I give thanks to papa that I could be born in the same mountains where my mother was born and her mother and all those who came before.

I give thanks for Kawika too. When he told stories I remember how his face would shine. He would tell them and we both would laugh together or sometimes cry. It was easy for him to cry. He did not hide it. He did not wipe his eyes. He let his tears come down. Each time he told a story I would tell one. He would shake his head and gaze into my eyes and say Nani when will you write this down for me? I touch Kawika's book. I see his face. I see his eyes. I hear his voice say all our stories must be told.

THE END

ACKNOWLEDGMENTS

The author wishes to thank all those who provided support, counsel, insight and research assistance while this book was being written, among them Judith Puna Flanders, for sharing the blessed space at Pa Lehua, O'ahu; Laurel Douglass, of Kula, Maui, for sharing her many historical pursuits; the late James Bartels, longtime curator of Iolani Palace; the Hawai'i State Archive, the Bishop Museum staff and the San Francisco Public Library's California History Room; Carey Caldwell of the Oakland Museum; Malcolm Margolin and the Clapperstick Institute; Jan Goggans and the late Charlie Soderquist, for leading me to the Sacramento River; and Karen Quick for her manuscript expertise; with a special word of gratitude to B. J. Robbins for believing in this book, and to my editor, Ann Close, for inspiring guidance all along the way.